ENGLAND
1940

INVASION

To Gwen and Don
who were and are real people
but in another world
And to Adolf
who might have been

INVASION

Derek Slade

ORIFLAMME PUBLISHING
London

First published in Great Britain, 1990
by Oriflamme Publishing Ltd.,
60, Charteris Rd., London N4 3AB

ISBN 0 948093 08 0

Phototypeset in 10 on 11 point Linotron Plantin by
Input Typesetting Ltd., London.
Printed and bound in Great Britain by
The Guernsey Press Co. Ltd

CONTENTS

MAPS

Better to have gone down then in our glory
Than lived till now to see our shame

Prologue

ÜBER ALLES

The German invasion of Britain in the Autumn of 1940 followed inexorably from the events of the preceding six years. For Adolf Hitler it was no more than the end of the beginning.

One after another the injustices of defeat had been righted. One after another the enemies of the Reich had gone down. At first it had been careful and tentative: the recovery of the Saar by popular vote, the re-militarization of the Rhineland, the crushing of opposition at home. Then the pace quickened. The union with Austria, the demands on Czechoslovakia. Demands the western democracies had failed to resist. At Munich Hitler learnt the measure of his foe. Learnt to despise the weak and foolish men who ruled in France and Britain.

And so he had taken the border regions from the Czechs; and then swallowed up the whole country. The democracies protested, and finally began to re-arm, to prepare too late for the war they had permitted. When Hitler demanded territory from Poland, Britain and France hastened to give guarantees. The Germans invaded anyway. They had a better guarantee: the Nazi-Soviet Pact. Poland lasted a month or so.

Britain and France declared war in September 1939. In the east they could do nothing; in the west they did nothing. Nor did the Germans. There was no bombing, no terror raids on cities, no assaults on the fortified frontiers. Only at sea was the war real. Neville Chamberlain said that Hitler "had missed the bus." Everyone called it the "Phoney War".

Then the Germans overran Norway and Denmark. The operation was swift and efficient. Both countries fell into the Nazi net. The British put up a token resistance. They even won, at Narvik, the only victory for allied arms over Germany in the war. Then they evacuated. It had cost the Germans dear in lost ships. Ships that might be needed if ever the Führer wanted to conquer an island. But in exchange for Norway and Denmark perhaps it was worth it.

Even before the campaign was finished the stroke had fallen on two more small neutrals. The *Stroke of the Sickle*, as the plan was called. Holland and Belgium crumbled before the advance of the Panzers and the devastation of their cities by the Luftwaffe. But this time help was at hand. The armies of Britain and France wheeled forward into Belgium from their prepared positions on the French border. On their flank was the densely forested Ardennes: impassable to tanks. But no-one had told the German tank commanders that.

The Panzers broke through the forest and out into the open country of northern France. They raced for the sea, reached it — and the allied armies in Belgium were cut off. They had advanced into a trap. It all worked so well that Hitler restrained his captains in the field from shutting the trap tight. He gave the British just enough time to evacuate their troops, though not their equipment, from Dunkirk. It was his first lesson in the exercise of British sea power.

At home in England, amidst the carnage of defeat and disaster, a new mood came over the country. Now Winston Churchill was Prime Minister. And he was committed to war, all-out war, war to the end. His was the driving force behind the miracle of Dunkirk. But there was nothing he could do to save France. The greatest army in Europe had melted away before Hitler's planes and tanks. Paris fell. The French gave in.

Hitler was confident that Britain too would now come to terms.

Chapter 1

EAGLE DAY

The Allied positions in France crumbled before the Panzers. But the attrition of the precious British airforce threatened a worse catastrophe. In the first ten days after the Germans began their onslaught, Britain had lost two hundred and fifty Hurricanes. In the midst of the carnage, Reynaud, Prime Minister of France, demanded a further ten British squadrons for the defence of France. Air Chief Marshal Sir Hugh Dowding appeared before the War Cabinet. He told them:

"If the present rate of wastage continues for another fortnight, we shall not have a single Hurricane left in France or this country."

The Cabinet decided that Dowding was right. In effect they decided that France was already lost. The planes must be preserved for the impending Battle of Britain. For no-one in England doubted that the battle for Britain was soon to begin, and that its opening scenes would inevitably be fought in the skies. The Joint Chiefs of Staff presented their summary of the military realities to the Prime Minister in a series of terrifyingly direct formulations:-

"While our Air Force is in being, our Navy and Air Force together should be able to prevent Germany carrying out a serious sea-borne invasion.

Supposing Germany gained complete air superiority, the Navy could hold up an invasion for a time, but not for an indefinite period.

In these circumstances our land forces would be insufficient to deal with a serious invasion.

The crux of the matter is air superiority. Once Germany has attained this, she might attempt to subjugate this country by air alone."

In Germany the need for invasion seemed less pressing. Hitler twice discussed the possibility with the German naval C.-in-C., Grand Admiral Raeder. The Navy drew up a critical appraisal of the prospects — highly critical. The German army and air force were not even looking into the possibilities. The weeks passed. Britain saved her army from Dunkirk. The Panzers disgorged across France, and the Battle of France was won. On 22nd June, General Halder, Chief of the Army General Staff, was considering preparations against England. But Halder saw these manoeuvres as no more than a *threat* to Britain — a warning to make the stubborn islanders come to their senses. On the 25th of June the old railway carriage where the Kaiser's Germany had been humiliated in 1918 was brought out of retirement for the signing of a new armistice. This time Germany played the part of conqueror and France that of helpless victim. The German radio played *Wir fähren gegen Engelland*. — But Hitler went off on holiday for ten days in the Black Forest!

Hitler did not want the war with Britain to continue. He did not want the British Empire destroyed. He did not want it to become so many rich pickings for the jackals. He harboured a sneaking admiration for the English. They were after all Anglo-Saxons, a Germanic people, right at the top of the Aryan heap. He told von Rundstedt,

"I will make peace with England, and offer her an alliance. Germany will dominate Europe, and England the rest of the world."

The Führer could see no earthly reason for the British to carry on the fight. They had been bundled out of Europe,

5

bag and baggage. Their one real ally, supposedly the strongest military power in the West, had been obliterated in a matter of six weeks. Poland, which they were ostensibly fighting for, had long been swallowed up in the maw of the Greater German Empire. A negotiated peace made a great deal of sense . . . except to the British.

A strange mood had come over the British. Their army had been defeated. It had only just been rescued from utter disaster in a scrambled and disorderly evacuation. All of its equipment had been abandoned. The airforce had suffered appalling losses in the defence of France. The British had not been able to raise a finger to help Poland. They had lost Norway and Denmark. Belgium and the Netherlands had fallen. France was gone. But their reaction was:

"Very well, alone!"

It was almost as if they preferred it that way, unencumbered by allies, unhampered by continental strategies. Just their islands, embattled but unbowed, against the might of the conqueror of Europe.

"What General Weygand called the Battle of France is over," Churchill told his people. "I expect the Battle of Britain is about to begin. Upon this battle depends the survival of Christian civilization. Upon it depends our own British life, and the long continuity of our institutions and our Empire. The whole fury and might of the enemy must very soon be turned on us. Hitler knows that he will have to break us in this island or lose the war. If we can stand up to him all Europe may be free, and the life of the world may move forward into broad sunlit uplands. But if we fail, then the whole world, including the United States, including all that we have known and cared for, will sink into the abyss of a new Dark Age made more sinister, and perhaps more protracted, by the lights of perverted science. Let us therefore brace ourselves to our duties, and so bear ourselves that, if the British Empire and its Commonwealth last for a thousand years, men will still say, 'This was their finest hour'."

"We are fighting by ourselves alone," he said on another occasion, "but we are not fighting for ourselves alone. Here in this strong City of Refuge which enshrines the title deeds of human progress and is of deep consequence to Christian civilization; here, girt about by the seas and oceans where the Navy reigns; shielded from above by the prowess and devotion of our airmen — we await undismayed the impending assault."

Over a month separated these two speeches, a month in which the impending assault had not come, though to be sure the people of Britain still awaited it. But these words gave expression to the new mood of Great Britain. In a dark hour the island race had found a leader, and in that leader their will to fight had hardened into an unshakeable resolve. They were no longer the sort of people who would surrender to anyone, let alone the half comic, half rabid dictator of Europe. But it was hard for that dictator to realise that the British really would fight on the beaches and on the landing grounds, and that they would never surrender. And more time slipped by.

That month between Winston Churchill's two speeches seemed to lessen the darkness of a very dark hour. After Dunkirk there had been something over three hundred Hurricanes and Spitfires, with another forty odd replacements, available to Britain. It was a tiny force to oppose the Luftwaffe. But the Germans let that opportunity slip. There were some attacks immediately after the completion of the evacuation. Then there were ten days without any raids. Then there were renewed pinpricks. The Luftwaffe was active over England, but it was doing little to serve Germany's war effort. These small scale raids were probably as much of an inconvenience to the Germans mounting them as to the English. The confidence of the R.A.F. began to grow. So did the R.A.F.'s strength. By 13th August — a day to assume a fearful significance for the people of England — there were over six hundred Hurricanes and Spitfires in the squadrons of the Royal Air Force, and nearly three hundred immediate replacements.

Meanwhile, German preparations for the assault had ground on slowly under the shadow of the Führer's hope that Britain would give up. On 2nd July Field Marshal Keitel, head of Oberkommando der Wehrmacht — the High Command of the Armed Forces — issued a general order setting out intentions. First, air superiority must be achieved over England. Then, the army would be landed — between twenty five and forty divisions, on a broad front all along the south coast. On 16th July Hitler finalized the policy. England was to be invaded.

As envisaged by Keitel, there was to be a surprise assault upon the South Coast of England. Forces would land from Ramsgate in the East to Lyme Bay in the West. The R.A.F. would be swept from the skies, and the Luftwaffe would provide total protection over the invasion beaches. British mines would be cleared from the Channel, and the flanks of the assault protected by vast new German minefields. Heavy artillery would be installed in the Pas de Calais to protect the beach-heads in Kent. The British Navy would be kept well away by the Luftwaffe, with its free range of the skies. To the Luftwaffe also fell the role of mobile artillery for the advancing forces. To facilitate co-ordination of operations the Supreme Command Headquarters of the three forces were to be moved to a unified H.Q. at Giessen. Hitler's own headquarters were to be established at the nearby chateau of Ziegenberg.

The tempo of the Luftwaffe's action over England had already begun to increase as the plans were being formulated. After 10th July they were already beginning to present a real challenge to the R.A.F. Nevertheless, throughout this period Germany was consistently losing two aircraft to every one British plane shot down.

Even now, the mirage of a negotiated peace still wafted before Hitler's eyes. On 19th July he delivered a major speech in which he offered just such a peace.

"I can see no reason why this war must go on," he said. "I am grieved to think of the sacrifices it will claim." And once again he expressed, genuinely, his desire not to destroy Britain.

"Mr Churchill ought for once to believe me when I say that a great Empire will be destroyed, an Empire which it has never been my intention to destroy or even to harm."

The peace offer received only mockery in Britain, and was formally rejected in a broadcast speech by Lord Halifax. The German papers announced:- "The Die is Cast". Even so Hitler had copies of his speech dropped over Britain. They were headed:- "A Last Appeal to Reason". Dislike it as he might, the Führer found that the British were still not amenable to reason.

So, in the seaways and great rivers of the continent long files of barges began to move steadily towards the shores of the Channel and the invasion ports. The heavy artillery on its giant gun carriages was brought up and emplaced on Cap Gris Nez. The German airfleets were brought up to strength, and their new forward bases in France, Belgium and the Netherlands were repaired and refurbished. At sea, the Royal Navy's light forces were increasingly concentrated in the threatened areas of the south east. So the U-boats had a field day in the Channel, the North Sea and the Western Approaches. British shipping losses rose alarmingly. Both shipping and exposed coastal targets came in for more and more pressure from the Luftwaffe, and in these areas German successes mounted. The great air fleets expanded their operations further, applying the next turn of the screw to the hapless British.

The Luftwaffe had three Luftflotten, or Air Fleets, arrayed against Britain. The most important of these were Luftflotte III under Sperrle in north western France, and Luftflotte II under Kesselring in north eastern France and the Low Countries. These two Air Fleets together mustered about nine hundred fighter aircraft, nearly nine hundred bombers, and three hundred dive bombers. There were over a hundred more bombers and thirty fighters with Luftflotte V under Stumpff in Norway and Denmark. It was an impressive force, but it had flaws. The operational time available over England for the excellent Me109 fighters was very limited. The Me110 two-seater fighters had the extra fuel capacity, but were too slow and lacked manoeuvr-

9

ability, to the extent that the Luftwaffe was soon to consider providing them with their own escorts! The much-feared Stuka dive bombers were also rather slow and vulnerable to a determined fighter attack — something they had not experienced much of in their terrorization of Europe. Furthermore, at the summit of Luftwaffe command, Hermann Goering was a less than adequate leader.

On 30th July Hitler ordered Goering to start the final preparations for the all-out air attack, *Operation Eagle*. On 2nd August Goering issued his final directions for *Eagle*. In a sense the first phase had already been underway for some time. In it the Luftwaffe's task was to probe R.A.F. defences, identify targets, and as far as possible draw the R.A.F. into all-fighter clashes — 'dogfights'. The second phase would develop from these tactics. Attacks were to move inland, with more skirmishing and coat trailing. The aim was to bring on all-out battles with the R.A.F. in which Germany's greater numbers would ensure victory. Then, finally, Britain was to be softened up for the invasion itself. The South-East would be made untenable for British forces. The war economy would be increasingly damaged. The cities, especially London, would be attacked.

Bad weather intervened to delay *Eagle Day*. But there came an ominous prelude. Britain had an efficient radar system. Its high level radar stations provided intelligence about what was happening deep over France and Belgium. Its low level radar gave additional detailed cover of the English coasts. The British could obtain advance warning and accurate bearings of German attacks. The squadrons of Spitfires and Hurricanes could be scrambled to meet the bombers at their point of arrival over Britain. It was an invaluable aid to British tactics. On 12th August the Germans hit the radar stations all along the south-east coast. They were exposed and vulnerable targets — great arrays of poles and masts, hundreds of feet high. Five of the stations were damaged. The high level station at Ventnor on the Isle of Wight was destroyed.

August 13th was *Adlertag* — *Eagle Day*. The day the battle for Britain began in earnest. Airfleets II and III attacked in force. Ten R.A.F. airfields were raided, and seven of them damaged. The Germans ranged far and wide in the skies over southern England. However, Fighter Command proved an effective match for them. In retrospect it seemed no worse to the British than some of the big dog-fights at the end of July and in early August. Forty five German planes were shot down. The R.A.F. lost only thirteen.

The Luftwaffe returned to the attack in an even bigger way on 15th August. For the first time all three Luftflotten attacked at once (for Goering believed that the pressures of defending southern England would force Fighter Command to denude the North). As the Germans struck at the most exposed of the R.A.F.'s forward fields, hitting Hawkinge, and putting Lympne out of action, Luftflotte V appeared off the north-east coast of England. Fighter Command's 12 Group under Leigh-Mallory had not been stripped of its planes to reinforce 11 Group. In fact seven extra squadrons being "rested" from the southern battle were available to counter the new threat. The hundred or so Heinkels and their forty escorting Me110's were so badly mauled that Luftflotte V was withdrawn from the battle for nearly a month.

To the south, the attacks on Park's Number 11 Group — the most vital of the fighter groups — continued all day. Aircraft factories and Coastal Command fields and bases were hit. Attacks on airfields met with varying degrees of success. It was all very far from decisive; and for Luftflotte V it was a straightforward defeat. Germany lost 75 aircraft that day, Britain only 34. The Germans increased the proportion of fighters to bombers. Nevertheless, the concentration on airfields was a development with serious implications for the British.

Attacks continued throughout the next week. The forward airfields in Kent were becoming increasingly battered. If attacks continued at the same rate over any period, Fighter Command might be forced to abandon Hawkinge and Lympne, both only a few miles from the coast, and possibly also Manston. The operations room at Biggin Hill had received a direct hit and the raids on the other sector stations continued. The extent of the destruction steadily increased, and the resources of Fighter Command were stretched ever further. On the 18th August, a Sunday, Churchill was present with Park at 11 Group's Headquarters at Uxbridge to watch the Group's resources reach the very limit, the brink of disaster, before the Germans broke off the attack.

The only consolation to Fighter Command in those days was the withdrawal of the Stuka dive-bombers from the enemy order of battle. Their vulnerability to the R.A.F.'s fighters had resulted in unacceptable losses; the Germans would now save them for later, better days. It was small consolation for the flash of insight which had finally dawned on Luftwaffe High Command. For the attacks of the 18th were the prelude to an all-out assault on the sector stations. The scale of radio traffic and the nature of the signals being sent betrayed the vital role of these bases to German Intelligence. They were the nerve centres of Fighter Command's defence, and the link between Group Headquarters and the front line airfields. Group H.Q. ordered the squadrons up, but the sector stations directed their movements, provided the vital combat intelligence and directed them into battle. If these nerve centres could be snuffed out, Fighter Command would lose its tactical direction. The chain of command from Group to the individual squadrons would be broken.

On 24th August, as the dogfights raged over southern England again, the sector stations were once more among the prime targets. While children watched the vapour trails in the sky, and the young British pilots were scrambled again and again, the battle hung in the balance. By chance that night German bombs fell for the first time on London. The Germans had mistaken their target, and the raid was not intentional, but Churchill was not to know that. He authorised a reprisal attack on Berlin.

Hitler was unaware that his bombers had assailed central London. He regarded the Berlin raid that followed as unprovoked, a deliberate taunt at him personally. He told the world that two could play at that game. As his Airfleets continued to pound at the sector stations, he ordered a massive revenge raid on London to be prepared. Goering was only too keen to oblige. He was finding little entertainment or glory in hammering away at obscure R.A.F. bases, and for Goering such considerations took precedence over the requirements of good strategy. By 6th September the key sector stations at Kenley and Biggin Hill were both near the end. Their runways were cratered and largely unusable. Their operations rooms had both been devastated. That of Biggin Hill was now run from a makeshift substitute in a shop in the village. Though the staffs struggled on against the odds, the usefulness of the stations had already been eaten away.

In those two weeks from 24th August to 6th September, the odds had begun to tilt towards the Luftwaffe. For every five R.A.F. planes shot down the Luftwaffe lost seven. It was a statistic which seemed to show the R.A.F. was winning. In fact it showed the opposite. Each plane lost to the R.A.F. was twice as serious as the corresponding plane lost to the Luftwaffe. The R.A.F. could not survive attrition on this scale. The aircraft factories were just about coping. But it was the supply of pilots that was the crucial matter. There were now not enough to go round. There were planes on the ground because there was no-one to fly them. That, and the wrecking of the sector stations, caused Churchill to tell his Cabinet:- "The scales have tilted against Fighter Command".

The great raid on London on 7th September came as something of a respite for the R.A.F. Park's squadrons were deployed to meet another attack on the sector stations and airfields to the south of London. The actual German attack against the capital — three hundred bombers with a fighter escort six hundred strong — met little opposition. Three hundred tons of bombs rained down onto London. The attack was not entirely indiscriminate. It concentrated on the dockland area. In the process it wiped out whole neighbourhoods among the mean and crowded streets of the East End. The incendiaries fell by the thousand. That night London was on fire, and the glow guided the night raiders in. The raids were a serious matter. The inhabitants of London took them well, and morale was not seriously damaged. Anger was more paramount in their minds than fear. Damage, however, was widespread. Stores and shipping were lost in the docks, and the port facilities themselves disrupted. Two main line railway termini were hit. Communications in and through the capital were badly affected. The homeless placed a further strain on the city's authorities and the public services.

The following day the Commanders-in-Chief of the three armed services were summoned by the Führer to Schloss Ziegenberg for a conference. Goering arrived with some annoyance. No conference was scheduled, and it had interrupted other plans. Nevertheless, he expected to be congratulated. Instead, he and his fellow commanders were subjected to two hours of tirade from Hitler. Though the Führer had himself ordered the attack, his mind was now on other matters. Yes, the operation against London had been a great success and had taught the British a lesson they would not soon forget. But what of the other operations? Had the army and navy co-ordinated their forces for the launch of the proposed invasion? Had control of the Narrow Seas been assured? Were the mines being laid? Was the artillery in place? Above all, why was the Royal Air Force still in existence? Goering bore the brunt of the vitriolic attack, though it extended to all branches of the High Command. He left with Hitler's message ringing in his ears:-

"As I have told you repeatedly, Herr Reichsmarschall, the destruction of the enemy air forces is the first essential. I require you to obey my orders. You are to attack the command bases and the airfields. You are to destroy their radio location posts. You are to strike at aircraft factories. And you are to do it now. Now, Reichsmarschall, now, now, now!"

Hitler's apparent percipience owed more to irritation than to a real grasp of grand strategy. He was happy enough for the obstinate islanders to be given a foretaste of what was to come, and had no objections whatsoever to terror raids on civilian targets. After all, they had served him very well so far. His irritation sprang from the undeniable continuing resistance of the R.A.F., despite a series of boasts from the Luftwaffe commander that the R.A.F. had been destroyed. So he had spelled out to Goering again the primary objective, and the path by which it should be achieved. Before the conference he had told his lackey, Keitel, the nominal head of O.K.W.,

"Goering is too interested in cities. In war it is the enemy's army that counts. And in this war it is his air-force."

Irritation had led him to the right conclusion. The raids on London stopped. Honour had been satisfied, and the British capital dealt a heavy blow. The sector stations and Fighter Command as a whole had been given a momentary breathing space, but that was all. On 10th September the Germans assailed the radar stations for the first time since the battle had begun in ernest. Weather conditions were less than satisfactory, but the targets were not difficult ones. The three high level stations in Kent and Sussex were destroyed, and two low level stations badly damaged. It was the most serious direct blow to Fighter Command for weeks. On the following day, without the accustomed advance warning, the R.A.F. was subjected to concentrated raids. The attempts which had been made in the lull to repair damage to the sector stations were wiped out at a stroke. The control room at Tangmere was destroyed, and all its staff killed. For the first time one of the sector stations had been knocked out completely. The Luftwaffe also hit Group Headquarters at Uxbridge and continued the series of raids on aircraft factories. The Vickers plant at Weybridge, already badly damaged, was burnt out. Destroyers were sunk in a raid on Portsmouth Harbour.

The 12th and 13th of September saw operations restricted by poor flying conditions. On the 14th further raids on airfields reduced the plight of Fighter Command to very desperate straits. Eleven Group was now starting to show signs of cracking, and on Number 11 Group depended the defence of England. The pattern was as usual. One after another the fighter airfields were smashed by German bombs. The R.A.F. lost 46 machines that day, and no less than thirty-five of their pilots. Pushed beyond the limits of their endurance though never of their courage, these young men were falling victim to the unremitting strain and weariness. The R.A.F. could not afford to lose them. There was no-one to replace them.

The following day, Sunday September 15th, was described by Churchill to a secret session of both Houses as,

"A black day. The blackest day this island Race and Empire have seen for many a long and troubled year. The enemy is at our throat, and the hour of decision is come upon us. Gentlemen, we are losing the Battle in the air. We must gird ourselves for the Battle on the land."

On that day Luftflotten II and III mounted a series of attacks involving over eight hundred fighters and four hundred heavy bombers. The attacks went on and on. No longer did it take four fighters to guard one German bomber. The pilots of the Luftwaffe had suddenly scented victory. As Goering sulked at Giessen, and complained to his fellow commanders that if he had been allowed to continue with the bombing of London there would be no need for invasion, his pilots were making that invasion possible.

The day began badly for the R.A.F. This time it was no piecemeal attack. The first German wave was five hundred planes. They began with the radar stations (for though Goering might grumble in private, he would of course obey every word that dropped from the lips of his Führer). As the day wore on only one station remained in operation along the entire invasion coast. Now the R.A.F really was blind.

Before Fighter Command could recover, the second attack was on its way. Croydon, which was serving as some sort of substitute for the wrecked Biggin Hill, was put out of action. Kenley was all but destroyed. Northolt, North Weald and Hornchurch were attacked and disrupted. At noon there was, for a while, not a single sector station operational in 11 Group. Park had no choice but to call on the neighbouring Groups for assistance. Squadrons from Leigh-Mallory's 12 Group were flown in. The still operational sector station of 10 Group at Middle Wallop took over Tangmere's duties — permanently in the event.

In the afternoon the dogfights in the sky reached a new pitch of urgency and ferocity. The stock of pilots was dwindling almost visibly. Their tiredness had become such that they flew almost in a trance. As Park scrambled squadron after squadron, until they were all in the air, and more were still needed, he realised that for his Group the fight was lost. Leaving his Headquarters at Uxbridge he drove over to Fighter Command H.Q. at Stanmore. There Sir Hugh Dowding awaited him. Park told the head of Fighter Command the situation, and offered his own resignation. It was summarily rejected by Dowding. The two men discussed the matter for ten minutes. Then Dowding phoned Churchill. He asked the Prime Minister to strip the rest of the country. Every fighter squadron available anywhere, every pilot who could be spared, must be brought forward for the defence of the airfields in the South-East. Dowding knew that all available resources had to be used now, and had the determination to get his way. Churchill agreed, and the necessary orders were rushed out.

But by now there were few places for the new squadrons to fly from. Eastchurch, Detling, West Malling, Redhill, Rochford and Martlesham — the list of airfields attacked in the course of that endless afternoon itself seemed endless. There were almost no fighter aircraft available to oppose the final wave of the attack by Luftflotte III on Portsmouth, Southampton and Portland. Eight Royal Naval vessels were sunk, including three destroyers and a light cruiser. As darkness fell the Supermarine Spitfire factory at Southampton was blazing out of control.

That night no R.A.F. base in Kent or Surrey or Sussex was operational. By the next morning this was no longer true. But it no longer mattered. For the first time the odds had turned against the R.A.F. The Germans lost forty-nine aircraft. The R.A.F. lost fifty-four. The Germans too readily believed the claimed "kills" of their fighter pilots. They thought they had shot down nearly two hundred R.A.F. machines. They celebrated a great victory. Their figures were wrong, but their interpretation was right.

Over the next three days a terrible inability to influence events gripped the commanders of the R.A.F. and even the Prime Minister. Churchill, the great war leader, had come to power in time to oversee a series of unparalleled catastrophes to British arms. Now there seemed to be no answer. The damage had already been done, much of it done years before by the appeasers and the disarmers. The fighter squadrons went up and contested the air space over southern Britain. They wrought great destruction upon the Luftwaffe, but now their losses were always to exceed the losses of their opponents. They were outnumbered, as they had always been, but the disparity between them and their enemies grew slowly but surely, day by day. They had the incomparable Spitfire, which the Germans could never match, but replacements were already starting to fall below losses. However much Beaverbrook, the Minister of Aircraft Production, might try to provide the replacement machines from his battered factories, no-one could produce replacement pilots. The men now flying the sorties were virtually untrained. Their life expectancy in combat was becoming a matter of days. It was the classic war of attrition.

The Luftwaffe and Adolf Hitler had hit upon their enemy's weak spots — the R.A.F. sector stations and the radiolocation net. In south-eastern England they had effectively destroyed both. And in doing so they had fatally undermined the capacity of Fighter Command to resist. Those three days after 15th September did not bring any new disasters for the British. The same targets were strafed. The Luftwaffe ranged farther afield. The dogfights went on without ending. To the people of Britain watching the tiny specks in the skies, nothing seemed to have changed. The same tense excitement still tingled through the embattled island. The same dread of the enemy, coupled with an unreal conviction that England would come through alright. After all, England always had come through . . .

On the morning of September 19th Air Chief Marshal Dowding, and the four ranking Air Vice-Marshals who commanded the four Fighter Groups were ordered to attend on the War Cabinet. They were kept outside the doors of the cabinet room for three hours. Inside they could hear voices raised in anger and, it seemed, sometimes in despair. The arbiters of Great Britain's destiny were debating a report submitted to them two days before by Dowding. It was an appraisal of the situation in the air war, and its measured paragraphs spelt out the end of all Fighter Command's resources within twenty days. It also offered remedies. But they were not the sort of remedies that would appeal either to politicians or to patriots. At 12.15 the airmen were summoned in. They all knew the contents of Dowding's plan and they had all agreed to it in advance. If it was not accepted they would of course fight on; but they, like their chief, believed that the plan was the only, slim hope left.

"We have talked round and about it all morning, gentlemen," growled Churchill when the officers were seated. "We have talked it up and down until we are blue in the face." He suddenly swung round on Dowding. "Is this the best you can offer us for England, Air Chief Marshal? Is this all you have?"

"Prime Minister, the alternative is for us to go on fighting as we are now and where we are now. The resources of the other Groups of Fighter Command have been made available in 11 Group area, as you know. With them, we could contine — for a while."

"And if we did?" asked Beaverbrook irritably.

"The airmen would go on dying until there were none left, sir," came Dowding's answer, spoken slowly and clearly — and very loud. Beaverbrook subsided.

"We've been round in enough circles," said Churchill. "Restate your proposition, Dowding. Make it simple and make it short. Because this really is the moment of decision. Right here and now!"

"Gentlemen, our forward positions — and by this I mean all our stations in Number 11 Group south of the Thames — have been rendered untenable by enemy action. We can no longer deny the Luftwaffe the skies over Kent, Sussex and Surrey. To continue with the attempt to do so is to expose our remaining forces to complete annihilation. I therefore propose to abandon the Tangmere, Kenley, Biggin Hill and Hornchurch Sectors. The more northerly sector stations are still usable. Our remaining men and aircraft in 11 Group will be withdrawn to these. Fighter Command Eleven Group will be disbanded. Its three remaining Sectors will be attached to Twelve Group. Trafford Leigh-Mallory has offered to stand down in favour of Park as commander of the new Twelve Group."

"Will you be able to defend London?" Churchill snapped out the question almost before the Air Chief Marshal had resumed his seat.

"We will still be able to dispute control of the skies over the capital, Prime Minister."

"Then that must satisfy," came the growled answer. Teeth clenched on his cigar, Churchill now sat silent, staring at the great table and the scattered plans and papers of grand strategy.

"Will you be able to deny the Channel crossings to an invasion fleet?" The next question came from Viscount Halifax, the Foreign Secretary.

"No, sir. We will be able to carry out harrying raids and spoiling attacks, but that is all."

"And what if you stayed where you are?" Lord Halifax asked again.

"Then we would not even have the aircraft and the pilots to do that much."

"So the immediate advantage of withdrawal is that it would enable us to conserve what little remains of our airforce, possibly even create some sort of reserve." This time it was Clement Attlee, the Labour Leader, who spoke. "As I understand it a further advantage would come when — and if — the invasion in fact occurred."

"I would not recommend anyone to build any hopes on

the creation of a reserve," Dowding replied. "But, yes, we would be able to contest the air space over the battle ground, and to provide our ground troops with some fighter cover."

"So my England is become 'the battle ground'," said Churchill. "Thank you, Air Chief Marshall. Thank you all for coming. I think we are now agreed. There is no more talking to be done." He looked round the circle of grim-faced men at the cabinet table. There was no dissenting voice. "Carry out the plan in full as you have presented it to us."

The airmen filed out. As Dowding closed the door he heard Churchill's voice again.

"Already our frontier is the Thames not the Channel."

Chapter 2

HOME GUARD

"Morning, Don!"

Don Gibbard looked round, grinned at the tin-hatted head staring out of the signal box window, then paused to ease the stiff khaki collar of his Home Guard uniform. The uniforms were new issue, and the unit was still one of the favoured ones to have them. They had rifles too. The reason for this abundance of equipment compared with the earlier shortage was simple. They were on the south coast, and the massed might of Hitler's armies was not far away. That morning it seemed a world away.

Don was nineteen, going on twenty. It was gone five o'clock now, and the early dawn of a bright summer day had brought him down to his rather odd duties.

"What? — You have to get up at four o'clock in the morning to guard Netley Station against Hitler?"

The new girl up the street had looked at him, at first incredulously, and then (at least so he thought) mockingly; but she had a nice smile. And her people had already been bombed out twice. It was bad luck on them really, as the air raids so far had not been as bad as everyone had expected at first. Of course, Southampton had copped it fairly badly compared with some places. They said it was part of the German invasion plans. According to Don's dad it was more to do with scaring the British into giving in; and everyone knew there was a fat chance of that.

So that really was what he was doing, getting up at four o'clock in the morning, and biking through the coldest part of the night down to a country station in the middle of nowhere — unless you were going to Portsmouth. That's what made it 'strategic' — or so the members of the platoon had decided when they were debating the matter. There must be some point to it because the officer — a senior clerk of the Southern Railway, no less — reckoned they stood a chance of getting a machine gun. In the Home Guard a machine gun really did mean that you mattered. There were some blokes down at Gosport with two machine guns. One of them was an apprentice with Don at Harland and Wolff. He never let anyone hear the last of his flaming gun either. Still, they were right next to an R.A.F. station, not on an obscure railway platform.

"'Lo there, Bill," Don called back, "What you got your hat on for then?"

"We had a warning about half an hour ago, you know."

Don was sceptical.

"Well I never saw or heard a thing. There won't be any over now. And it was a good night for us too."

A good night meant a cloudy night of course. There had been no air raid warning, so it had not been a night of discomfort in the shelter. They'd had a couple of good nights lately. The Nazis had gone for the town a few times. There had been hits on the High Street too — women and children killed. Civilian targets, just what you expected from the bloody Nazis. Like everyone in England he hated them. They couldn't care less what they hit or who they killed. On the other hand, they might have been going for the docks, in which case they were ruddy bad shots. They hadn't come near — well only once. There'd been quite a big blaze the other night — one of the cold stores, full to the brim with butter and lard, everyone reckoned. Anyway, it had burnt like a torch. You would have expected every German plane for a hundred miles around to use it as a beacon. Made the blackout look a bit daft. Or made the Jerries look dafter. After they'd hit it, they went home.

Don's own firm — the one he worked for — hadn't

been hit at all. Just the same, he knew it had to be an important target. They were shipbuilders, not like the big yards in Belfast or Scotland and up North, but building ships for the Navy. Minesweepers was what they were making, not that Don did much of the making. He'd been an apprentice for over four years now. Seven years was the course. 'Doing your time' it was called — a bit like being in jail in some ways. Then again, it wasn't too bad, and he'd made some good mates there.

The Home Guard thing was a bit of a joke too, like being back in the Boy Scouts half the time — but never quite just good fun. In the back of his mind there was always the thought: what if the bloody Jerries really did come over? There was no-one he knew who would admit to believing it, not in a crowd anyway. But sometimes, if it was just talking to one of your pals — well, then you found out that he was wondering too. But even then it always seemed so unreal. Out there over the water there was this little man with a daft moustache and the biggest army in the world who was going to invade England. It didn't stand to reason somehow.

His dad was in the Merchant Navy, which meant that he ran the real risks, like everyone at sea. That was where the real war was happening. Those R.A.F. types in the Spitfires and Hurricanes, theirs was a sort of fun war, knights in armour, *Yoiks*, *Tallyho!* and all that stuff. Not a war at all, a game in the clouds; and if you copped one, then you baled out, and it was all a jolly good show. Yet he still had a sneaking admiration for them. So did everyone who watched the vapour trails snaking across the sky up there. They were the only ones you could actually see fighting, and for all their silly talk and bravado, everyone knew that they were being killed. You used to listen whenever there was the sound of a plane. By now everyone could tell at once. Ours sounded friendly, theirs snarled through the sky.

The war at sea was nastier though, because everything at sea always is. His father was on the Cape run — big black ships with red and black funnels they had been. They were grey now. Everything was grey now. Their cargoes were food. Don's house managed to supply half the street from what his dad contrived to import in his own way. They had things other people only dreamed of now:- peaches and apricots it had been from the last run. Four days at home, and then back out again. He knew it was getting to his father, and his mother seemed thinner and unhappy. Still, perhaps he'd try that new girl who'd been bombed out with a few of those apricots. If that didn't get her down to the pictures with him then nothing would.

He climbed up into the signal box.

"Just brewed up, Don. Want a cuppa?" asked Fred Williams, another member of the platoon, but one with a sight more justification for being in the signal box. He was the signalman there. Don took the tea.

"Line's out down Cosham, you know," said Bill. Fred nodded.

"They reckon there was a couple of raiders over by themselves," he said. "Derrick Smith down the line phoned me and said that he reckoned he'd seen two Stukas."

"Get away!"

Don looked superciliously at the other two. He leaned against the lever frame grinning at the two older men. He was a tall, almost gangling, youth — keen on sport, had been all his life, and good at it too. He'd play anything, a bit of local soccer, tennis, cricket especially. He'd had a trial for Hampshire — might be a chance there too if the war didn't go on too long. Sport had seen him through school — that and drawing.

He could draw anything. His mother had wanted him to take it up — at least she'd said so at one time. At school they'd said about being a commercial artist. But that sort of thing was too risky. No security in it, his dad had told him, and you couldn't really deny that. No point in taking up a career where the jobs were few and far between — and you had to be damned good too. He probably wasn't that good, he thought.

Engineering though — now that was safe. There was work in engineering alright, loads of it, and it looked as if there always would be. Especially in shipbuilding. Things had never been that bad here in the south of course — but even Southampton had seen something of unemployment and the dole queues, and everyone knew what it had been like up north. That was one thing the war had ended anyway. And engineering wasn't so bad. Lots of people had worse jobs. Some war work was bloody awful. Not the shipyard, though, not for an apprentice anyway, and one well on into his time at that.

To the other two in the signal box he appeared a confident young man. In fact he was an only child, and had been inclined to shyness. Being good at games had helped that. He'd always been a popular boy as far as the other lads were concerned, but never a leader, not quite one of the brash and pushy crowd. Though he had all the apparent know-it-all confidence of any nineteen year-old, he was readier to learn his trade than most, and better liked by the foremen; better liked by the older blokes in the Home Guard too. There were a couple of others his age in the patrol, shiftless youths with too much of an eye to their own importance, both cordially disliked by Don from the moment of his first conversation with them. The only thing he had in common with them was the desire for an answer to the question: when would any of them do any real fighting?

Unlike them he didn't know for certain whether he did want to be called up. They imagined that fighting the Nazis was some sort of fun, damned fools that they were. No doubt they'd get their fill of it in time. Probably before the war was over their particular brand of war-work would have been taken over by women. Don knew his factory was half full of them already. Then there wouldn't be all these restricted occupations. As for himself, when his apprenticeship was finished — perhaps an engineer in the Navy. It had to be the Navy, not some oily ground crew in the *Raf*, not even the dubious delights of driving a tank. No, the Navy was the thing; not down in the bowels of some battleship or aircraft carrier though. It was torpedo boats he fancied. There the engineer really did matter — and of course he would be an officer. That would please his mother and father — though for his own part he found it rather difficult to imagine.

He smiled and sipped at his scalding tea.

"I don't think they were Stukas at all. No-one's seen a Stuka for ages. — I daresay they were just a couple of stray bombers on a hit and run."

"Well, Don my boy, I know you've got your personal line to the Air Ministry, but this time you've got it wrong," said Bill. "There *are* Stukas back. I've seen one myself. Yesterday, across Southampton. Saw it diving and screaming, like they do. Oh, it was one of them Stukas alright, you mark my words. Nothing else it could have been."

"All right, Bill, if you saw it. In that case, I hope we do get that machine gun, and pretty damn quick too. We could have a go at them then."

"Now that precious machine gun is something *I'm* not believing till I see the bugger," Fred interrupted. They all laughed. The machine gun and its non-arrival was one of the standing jokes.

"The pair of you can sort that out between you. I'll be off now. — Be seeing you both."

Bill went, while Don and Fred took down the remaining blackout and then sat sipping their tea in the sunlight. Above them, on a grassy bank, was the pill box. That in theory was the position from which they were to guard the station, an ugly hexagonal structure with the characteristic slits through its concrete-faced brick walls. It looked more impressive than it was. Brick is not the most resistant material, and commanding positions are not so ideal when the enemy have tanks or planes. Even the officer had told them, in training, that if the enemy came with tanks they were to get well away from the pill box. But perhaps the Germans wouldn't be able to bring their tanks over the Channel. Perhaps they wouldn't come at all. — Probably they wouldn't.

The first train of the morning came up from Southampton, a long goods train with closed wagons. It looked as if it was carrying food. The sleepy country line, where the pre-war traffic had been enlivened only by a few busy weeks of strawberry trains at the height of summer, had become an artery of the country's communications network — Southampton to Portsmouth, a crucial link. The engine still carried the green of the Southern Railway. In better days it had been a passenger engine no doubt. The driver was an Eastleigh man. The railway works there had been hit the other day, he told them. It was hardly news. Information of that kind travelled too fast. Fred had heard about it the same morning it had happened. There were always these pinpricks. They never seemed too bad themselves, but there seemed to be lots of them. Perhaps the Jerries did know what they were doing after all. Vital war industries, and all that. But then, they hadn't even managed to hit the docks! The engine hissed steam, and groaned out with its unnatural load. The local trains carrying the workmen and girls into town came and went. Don put his bike on one of them, and went back up to Woolston Station, and then on to work. It was a long day, and he had another stint of duty tonight.

The day's work was uneventful. The newspapers told the usual story of enemy activity over Britain. "Limited by cloud" they said, but then they were talking about a day ago — two nights ago really. There was also the usual thing about British bombers over Germany. More particularly we'd been hitting the invasion ports. Don was not an avid newspaper reader, but he had noticed that 'invasion ports' were now figuring more prominently in the reports. Still, our ships were obviously still in control of the Channel, and Calais and the rest seemed to be an easy target for the R.A.F. We were even shelling the blighters with big guns from Dover. No news at all in fact, not when you thought about it. But everyone knows what no news is . . . Might just as well read about prosecutions for blackout infringements, Don decided. Or some poor bloke had up for "failing to immobilize a motor vehicle".

"Shouldn't have a motor vehicle," Don's mother told

them when the subject came up over dinner. "Ought to be commandeered for war work."

They had sausages — not on ration but usually quite hard to come by — and plenty of veg., needless to say. The Gibbards owned a large garden, sloping down a steep-ish bank. It had previously been done as a rockery. Bert, Don's father, had always been a keen gardener. Just lately he was a darn sight keener on growing spuds and carrots, when he was home. Don's mother, Win, had to do most of the work now.

There was another thing about the garden. Since the bank sloped steeply down, it was into the bank that Bert and Don had cut the shelter. A passage in first, then a corner to cut off the effects of blast, then a door, and finally a proper little room. It was completely cut out of the earth, and shored up with timbers. "Like a flipping coal mine", Don had described it, but he was justifiably proud of their efforts. There was nothing like it except the big official shelters. Most people in the street just had the Anderson shelters, but most people didn't have a garden like the slopes of Everest, and two blokes prepared to dig for victory in a big way. You couldn't even hear the Jerry planes going over if you were in there — well not very loudly anyway.

"Go up the road and have a word with the Renoufs, will you Don?" his dad asked him. "Before you go out to the Home Guard. Your mother says they haven't enough room in that shelter of theirs."

"They could come round here, well two of them could at least," Win added, clearing away.

"The two girls could, easily."

"Don't you think of anything else? You lads! One track minds, that's what you've got."

His mother hurried out with the crockery. Don half smiled, then started to put his collar back on.

"I don't know why you need that, son — just to deliver a message. Not meeting royalty are you?"

Bert laughed, then began to cough, as he did much of the time. One of the things he 'imported' was enough cigarettes to keep his bronchitis going. What with his mum's arthritis, that had her hobbling about on a stick whenever it rained, and his dad's cough, the place looked and sounded like a doctor's waiting room sometimes, Don thought.

Pulling his jacket on, he went down the road to number three, just two houses from theirs. The Renoufs hadn't long moved in of course. He'd heard that they'd come from down near Weston Shore, and there had certainly been bombs down there. Bombed out twice — that was unlucky alright. They were the only people he knew that it had happened to. He knocked on the front door, but no-one answered. It was half open so he stuck his head round and called out.

"Anyone in?"

He heard the lavatory chain go upstairs. At the same time a girl appeared from the front room:- really a girl, not what Don and his mates usually meant by the word. This was Nancy, he presumed, the younger sister, still at school and supposed to be evacuated to Christchurch or somewhere. She'd come back for the summer holidays, and then stayed at home. She must have been going on sixteen, so that meant she was clever enough to stay on at school. But not many kids of that age would stick with schooling, or stay evacuated. They drifted back, even little ones did that. Better the bombs than a strange bed in some market town full of country bumpkins.

"Oh, are you Gwen's new chap?" Nancy smiled at him, and then started laughing. "Well don't look so shocked by the idea. She's not that bad, you know."

"No, I know . . . I mean, I don't suppose she is."

This earned another burst of laughter.

"Come on in then. Mum's just making tea. Do you want a cup?"

"Oh thanks — love one. I can't stop too long though."

"Everyone always wants a cup of tea, even when they don't," she answered, taking him into the front room. "Why can't you stop too long?"

Now Don laughed.

"You're a bright spark, and no mistake. I've got to go on to the Home Guard."

"Oh, them . . . Dad, this is the chap from up the road."

Mr Renouf had followed them into the room. He was a smallish, balding man, still wearing his waistcoat and tie, one hand holding the Daily Herald, the other scratching his head. Like Don's officer in the Home Guard, Mr Renouf was also a clerk, though not such an exalted variety. He was also with the railway, but he worked in the docks. Southampton Docks, with its great sprawling complex of installations was still the property of the Southern Railway. The railway and the harbour it built had made Southampton what it was: Gateway to The Empire, just like the brochures said — and gateway to America of course.

Mr Renoulf presented a very different picture to the Home Guard Officer. He had that ordinary man's look — a decent bloke, but not 'officer material'. Don's summing up was close to the mark. Mr Renouf was more than good at his job, but the bosses weren't quite sure. He had a brother who was always speaking at rallies, a town councillor, but not for the right party. Even to be the brother of a fiery left-winger was to be suspect, and Ralph was known to support George's views. So he was a man to be watched, and he didn't get the promotions when worse men did. He didn't complain about it much, and unlike many clerks the work he was doing actually had some use. What went on in the docks now mattered to everyone.

"Evening, Don. — It is Don, isn't it? My Missus went up to meet your mum the other day. Nice of you to drop round. I'm Ralph, by the way, and this is my daughter, Nancy. You've already met her, I see."

"I introduced myself, dad."

"Ah, and here's my other daughter, Gwen, with the tea."

The girl came in. She was fresh-faced, with mid-brown hair, quite long, and worn in waves, in the fashion. She had a white blouse, with a lace collar, and a tartan skirt, but with dark colours. She gave Don a quick look — a bit serious, he thought. She was rather pretty, and he decided he did like her — quite a lot in fact.

"I heard you come in, so I've put an extra cup out. — Mum's across the road visiting, or borrowing something or other. Are *you* just visiting?"

"Oh, no. My mum and dad, well — we wondered if you'd like to share the shelter. I mean if there's a raid. You see we've got this deep one, dug into . . . "

"Then it'll be a sight better than what we've got," Ralph interrupted him. "Ours sticks up half a mile out of the ground. I've covered it with earth, but I don't reckon it would be much protection. — Will you tell your people it's a very kind offer, Don. We may well take you up on it . . . A very kind offer."

Ralph nodded his approval again.

"We can take another two easily," said Don, glancing up at Gwen as she poured the tea.

"That would be the two off the bunks," she said, " — mum and Nance. Dad and me usually go on the mattresses on the floor."

"Oh!" He obviously looked disappointed, as both Ralph and Nancy laughed. Gwen almost smiled, but not quite.

"Do any of you ever play tennis?" he asked for want of anything better to say, and cursing himself for sounding like a fool.

"Yes, me, " Nancy answered at once. "And my older sister could have a go too. She needs the exercise."

"Don't be cheeky", said Gwen. "Anyway, I wouldn't mind having a go. I know I'm not much good at it though — and I get hay fever from the grass."

"I think we're out of the hay fever season," replied Don persuasively. "And there won't be much of a chance soon. It'll be too cold. How about tomorrow? It's Saturday, and I could get a court in the morning, I think."

"All right then."

It was a great success — apart from the tennis.

"You look like a crab," Nancy told her elder sister, and Don was able to come to her defence, and tell her she'd come on with a bit of practice. And when Nancy cycled home, he and Gwen walked with their bikes, and 'got acquainted'. On the next day, Sunday, he was round having tea with them, and the ice was well and truly broken.

That evening he went to the drill hall in a very cheerful frame of mind. It was not another session of duty, just a lecture. A lot of rubbish about how to recognise enemy paratroops.

"If they were invading, we'd damn well notice them," he thought. For that was the implication of the talk. Not spies for once, but invasion. It was all about invasion now. To Don and to most of them it still had that unreal quality though. Parachutists! He had better things to think about, notably the girl at number three.

As he walked back the sirens were going. He hurried through the evening. Tonight there was not much cloud and the moon was up. It was hardly dark at all. Good bombing weather! He could hear the drone of planes — lots of them too, so it was going to be a big raid. As he turned into Peartree Avenue, he saw the searchlights over Southampton, the town stretched out like a dark muffled creature beyond the faint glow of the river. Now he could hear the planes clearly from that direction. The first flashes came as he turned into his own gate. Then, echoing the thudding of the ack-ack, the louder crump of the first bombs. He hurried down the path and into the shelter.

"I'm going up the road to get the Renoufs," he said.

They had been in the shelter for over an hour, and the raid had not stopped.

"Be careful, Don," he heard his mother calling after him.

Outside, he could see the sudden vivid sparkles of the bombs exploding. Down by the river edge it looked like. There were more incendiaries than high explosive. He could see something big ablaze, and there was another fire farther down the river. He wondered if this time they had managed to hit the docks. There was also one fire nearer, and the sound of explosions near enough to make him run the short distance along the street and down to the Renoufs' shelter.

"Do you want to come round to ours?" he yelled — yelled because there had been another crash near by.

"My mother's in a terrible state," came Gwen's voice. "Take her and Nance, please, Don."

Mrs Renouf and her younger daughter were hurried up the steps, and along the avenue. There was a house burning somewhere nearby, and the sky was full of light. Down towards the town, hidden by the trees, whatever it was they had hit was blazing like a torch. Mrs Renouf was weeping and wailing profusely.

"She's always like this. She can't stand the bombing," said Nancy as they rounded the bend in the shelter entrance into safety. "It's a good job we haven't had many nights like . . ."

The whole shelter shook, and earth showered down on them. Their only light, a candle, went out. A bomb had fallen on the street.

"I'm going back," Don shouted.

There wasn't time to think about it, or explain, or argue. One moment he was reeling from the force of the deflected blast that had caught him as he stood just inside the doorway; then he was back out, running up the steep steps of their garden path. There was a great column of flame across the road now — gas main gone. He saw at once that the house opposite the Renoufs' had all but disappeared. The house next to it leaned to one side, and floorboards hung out over a heap of rubble, yellow in the flames. He ran down into number three's garden. The windows of the house were gone, as you'd expect, and the walls pocked with holes. Also part of the wall looked none too safe. He reached the shelter, and the top of it was all smashed in. Then Gwen came out from the ruin, a little shaky on the wooden steps. He caught hold of her for a moment, just a moment.

"My dad's hurt his head, but he's alright. — Give me a hand to get him out, Don."

He wondered if she would faint. Girls in the pictures

always fainted. But she showed no sign of doing anything so daft. So much for the pictures! He helped her get Ralph out.

"It's only a cut, Don," he said. "But if there had been anyone on those bunks, they'd be dead by now. Funny thing too, it was me and Gwen on the bunks this time. Edith was so scared, I'd made her and Nance lie on the floor. Thanks, Don."

There were no more bombs really after that, not even down in the town. The two families passed the night in the Gibbards' shelter. It was the night of Sunday, 15th September.

"Well, you got me here after all," Gwen whispered to him.

Chapter 3

THE BEST LAID SCHEMES

Though the plans for the invasion had long been in train, the actual decision was not made until after the momentous events of 15th September. It was the day that German victory in the air war was won. It had taken almost exactly a month since the operation began on *Adlertag*. Both English and German commanders grasped the fact almost at once. Suddenly, to the surprise of many in Germany, Goering's pompous boasts had the ring of truth about them. *Operation Eagle* had succeeded — just in time for *Operation Sea Lion* to be possible.

For the whole plan of a landing in Southern England had increasingly been called into question, despite the continued and increasing preparations for it since July. At the time of the great London raid, and for much of the time since, Goering had believed that the war could be won in the air alone, without any requirement for a sea-borne landing. Hitler was also addicted to ideas of victory by show of strength, or show of terror. At the conference of the Nazi war leaders on 13th September, the Führer's mood had swung against the operation. He told the High Command that Britain could, as Goering had said, be brought to her knees by a bombing offensive alone. Perhaps, he speculated, the time *had* now come to switch the weight of attack to the British cities. The O.K.W. chiefs went away thinking the whole show was off. They were wrong. Hitler's moods changed.

He knew that *Sea Lion* was a terrible risk. His enemies might call him mad, but he did achieve moments of clear and shrewd strategic insight. He, and not the Army High Command, had been the victor over France. Now, he was sane enough to appreciate the concerns that had been expressed to him about the landing plan, and the great question mark which still hung over the whole sea affair. On 13th September, the Luftwaffe had not yet, not quite, won the air war. Control of the skies over the Channel could not be guaranteed. Furthermore, more even than the difficulties of the army, he had come to understand the massive problems facing the Kriegsmarine. He himself was a landsman, a Middle European, a 'land rat' to his enemies. He was almost afraid of the sea.

Also, he harboured a healthy respect for the embattled islanders, storm-tossed and alone behind the grey seas of the Channel and the 'German Ocean'. He knew that over those hazy horizons lay the ever-watchful eyes of the British fleet. For though Hitler had peremptorily thrust the British land forces out of Europe, and was even now challenging the R.A.F. for supremacy in the skies of England herself, the Royal Navy remained undefeated.

In the back of his mind, and often near the front of it, there also flickered that elusive but ultimately desirable prospect of a British collapse. It was a frequent theme of his own propaganda; perhaps, like so many, he had even come to believe his own propaganda. He hoped that Britain would fall, not by invasion, but by internal dissent, by war-weariness, disillusion and revolution. Why expend men and arms and treasure, when he could have his prize for nothing? So strategy and temperament combined to create doubt and indecision in his mind — but beyond them that glittering prize still waited.

From the 13th to the 14th, his mood had already swung again. *Sea Lion* was not to be abandoned. The planning and preparations were to go ahead. But there was not yet a decision about the date. That decision was pushed back to the next conference, on the 17th. Since there had to be ten days notice to the three services, this postponement in itself pushed the date of the operation further back, towards the winter of the year. Dangerously late for a major military adventure, dangerously late to risk all on the unpredictable waves of the grim, grey Channel. The service chiefs worried and fretted and still, openly or secretly, hoped for ultimate cancellation.

When the new day of decision arrived, all had changed. The key question had been resolved. In the great equation of uncertainties, the balance in the air had swung decisively away from the R.A.F. and towards the Luftwaffe. The air battles of September 15th had changed the course of the war and, unusually in the fog of war, that fact had been perceived by the two great captains who faced each other across the Narrow Seas. Goering had already told his Luftflotten commanders:

"With additional severe destruction, their fighters should be eliminated within four to five days."

That was the message he now brought to Hitler at the conference in Berlin on 17th September.

The commanders who sat round the table with Hitler represented the three services. Each man was concerned with his own sphere of operations. They were organizers and tacticians; only a few could claim to be strategists. Their function in these set-piece conferences with the Führer was to give advice, not to make the decisions. Furthermore, inter-service co-operation was weak, and rivalry was strong. The High Command of all the armed forces, Oberkommando der Wehrmacht, had no direct operational control over the individual services. Everything had to be referred up to the great strategist, Adolf Hitler, the Supreme Commander. Hitler even disliked conferences. He did not like to be confronted by all his commanders together. He preferred them one at a time, so that they could be browbeaten or cajoled. That was the Nazi way: divide and rule.

From O.K.W. came its nominal head, Keitel, and the

Chiefs of Staff, Generals Jodl and Warlimont. The Army was represented by its chief, Field Marshal von Brauchitsch, and Halder, his number two. Also von Rundstedt, the Commander of Army Group A, whose troops would be making the crossing to the beaches of England. The ships that would carry them fell under the jurisdiction of the Navy's representative, the Commander-in-Chief, Grand Admiral Raeder, *Sea Lion's* most bitter opponent. The most powerful and influential of the commanders, however, was Reichsmarschall Herman Goering, C.-in-C. of the Luftwaffe, and Reich Air Minister. His Chief of Staff, Jeschonnek, completed the line up. These were the men who had to put their opinions and argue their case to Adolf Hitler. In the final analysis, none of them mattered except Hitler. The Führer made the decisions.

The plan they were considering had already been much revised. It had become, inevitably, a compromise between the demands of the army and the capabilities of the navy. O.K.H., the Army High Command, had from the start wanted a landing on as broad a front as possible and in great force. Objectives were originally to include not only the coastal towns of Kent and Sussex from Ramsgate to Brighton Bay, but also Selsey Bill, the Isle of Wight; and, far to the west, Lyme Bay and the Portland naval base. The navy had replied to this with an emphatic *No*. Grand Admiral Raeder had promoted his case repeatedly in meetings with the other service chiefs, and had presented it most convincingly in private to the Führer. His case was simple. The navy could not supply the shipping to convey or protect such widely dispersed forces, unless the landing were totally unopposed by both the R.A.F. and the Royal Navy.

In the event of any opposition, shipping losses, particularly of transports and therefore of troops, would be high, and might be unacceptably high. The victorious armies of Germany would drown in the Channel before they had even set foot on British soil. For the Kriegsmarine could not hope to fight off the British Navy along the whole length of the English Channel. Raeder knew the truth of the matter very well. After its disastrous losses in the Norwegian Campaign, the Kriegsmarine could not fight the Royal Navy at all. So the Grand Admiral won the acceptance of a narrower front, and a substantial reduction in the number of troops to be conveyed.

The attack was now to be centred on Kent and eastern Sussex, spearheaded by Sixteenth Army. Ninth Army would also take part in the assault on a front on both sides of Beachy Head. Brighton now represented the far western extremity of the initial landing area. (There were still reserve troops in Normandy, however, ready to sail for Lyme Bay if the opportunity presented itself — the army still wanted that broad front.)

"We must now sum up, gentlemen. — Too much talk! There is always too much talk. I require your final opinions, briefly stated. I require to know the facts."

Hitler paced the room as he spoke. His uneasiness in the face of his assembled military commanders manifested itself in a testy irritability. For all his power, he was nervous of opposition. He hated any contradiction. He feared, in particular, the prospect of a concerted opposition to his own views. For their part, the lesser warlords of the Third Reich had to beware that their advice and their opinions never seemed to contradict their Führer's opinions, or even his current whims. The commanders were understandably more nervous than Hitler. His distrust of *them* was founded in a profound and dangerous paranoia; theirs of *him* was all too real. A word out of place could bring humiliation, dismissal, and worse.

"Herr Reichsmarschall, do you or do you not have command of the skies over England?"

The question was sudden, and snapped out, as if in anger or impatience. So it was Goering who was the first to be put on the spot. Even he sweated under Hitler's gaze. If anything it was the Reichsmarschall who feared his Führer most abjectly — but he was also the most practised sycophant. He would not offend the Führer, and he had a fair idea what the Führer wanted to hear.

"Mein Führer, the battle in the air is won. The events of recent days can have no other interpretation. The strength of the British Air Force is now broken. They can no longer resist our attacks. Their will to continue the war is itself crumbling. My bombers are poised for the assault on London itself."

"No, no, no! Geography again! Cities and towns always! You military men are obsessed with cities and towns. London, I tell you, my dear Reichsmarschall, is a geographical concept only. — You see, you have not studied the campaigns of Frederick the Great, eh? It is the enemy's forces we must destroy, his ability to resist, to continue fighting. London is a place. It is not the object of our strategy. Do I make myself clear to you?"

It was the precise same lecture he had read Goering on 8th September. Of course in the interim he had held, equally fervently, the view that London and the demoralization of its inhabitants was precisely the object of strategy, but that didn't matter. His face was white and his fists clenched. So far he had only been lecturing, in the pedantic style of a professor with notably stupid students. Any minute he might explode. The fat Reichsmarschall sweated some more in his flamboyant white uniform with its prominent gold trimmings. He had misjudged the mood of the Führer and miscalculated the current whim. He must restate his position in different words, responding to Hitler's famous 'intuition'.

"I promise you, mein Führer, that the Luftwaffe will concentrate all its great forces solely on the defeat of our enemies."

"I thought that you had already defeated them," came Hitler's snapped reply. Goering cringed under the whiplash of his voice. "Still, you promise me, Herr Reichsmarschall . . . But can you promise me this? Can you promise me ten days? Ten days over the Channel coasts. Ten days to land an army!"

"You shall have them, Führer! Twenty, fifty, a hundred days. — You shall have them!"

Hitler nodded slowly several times. A half smile crept

over his face. His own uncertainties faded as he was caught up into his dream of conquest again. He knew Goering well enough to recognise the germ of a true assertion amid the bluster. It was Raeder who presumed to interrupt his reverie.

"Führer . . . "

Hitler returned to the defensive mode. Raeder was too persistent, too meticulous, and too persuasive. He knew his case too well, and he believed in it. Of course he would no more dare to contradict his Supreme Commander than would Goering, but he lacked the appropriate cringing subservience of the Reichsmarschall. Also, the Navy was not a National Socialist service in the way the Luftwaffe often seemed to be. Hitler found Raeder most disconcerting in public debate.

"So, Grand Admiral, you wish to tell us yet again that the Kriegsmarine cannot see our army safe across twenty miles of dirty water. What is it to be this time — shortage of barges, or of destroyers? British bombing? Overcrowding in the invasion ports?"

"No, mein Führer, I think I can report that the assembly of the invasion fleet is progressing in accordance with your orders."

"You surprise me, Admiral Raeder. You fill me with surprise!" Hitler glanced around the table for appreciation of his sarcasm. But Raeder had not lost any of his persistence.

"The problems of collecting such a fleet have of course meant massive withdrawals from all classes of shipping, and very severe disruption and dislocation to the maritime economy of the Reich. But one understands that these difficulties can be borne for a short campaign. Then again, though we are confident that the crossing can be made if the weather holds up, we have indeed suffered serious losses through British air raids. The attacks of three nights ago were particularly damaging. We *have* been compelled to take some measures for temporary dispersal. I am much more concerned, however, about the failures in air support over German-held territory. I would point out that this

enemy activity was occurring at much the same period that
the Reichsmarschall reports the R.A.F. to have been largely
eliminated. The dispersals occasioned by enemy air activity
could well endanger the current timetable. This will become
more significant as we approach the day of embarkation."

The directness of the attack on the Luftwaffe, and on
Goering's claims in particular, was all the more successful
for the measured tones in which Raeder delivered it. Goering sprang to his feet, face suffused with rage and heavy
jowls shaking.

"The Luftwaffe has provided maximum possible support for the Kriegsmarine at all times. The Grand Admiral
seems to forget that the Luftwaffe has been engaged on the
destruction of the enemy's fighter aircraft and their bases,
the radio-location stations and aircraft factories. We do not
possess the resources to eliminate their bomber strength at
the same moment. He has no business to question our part
in this operation. It is his own service that creates the
difficulties. If we listened to him there would be no operation. All he is able to do is set up obstacles."

Raeder was also on his feet now.

"My concern, Reichsmarschall Goering, is precisely for
the success of this operation. I am concerned that if the
British can bomb us in Calais, they will also be able to
bomb us in Dover — if we can get there. And I cannot
guarantee safe passage without air cover. This is not creating obstacles, it is stating the facts as ordered by the
Führer."

"Gentlemen, gentlemen!" Hitler was smiling again now
as he raised his hand to quiet the angry service chiefs. This
quarrelling among his advisers suited him, for it left him as
undisputed sole arbiter.

"Grand Admiral," he went on. "You must tell me this:-
Is the invasion fleet ready, and is it sufficient for the task?"

"Yes," answered Raeder, subsiding into his chair. His
voice was as bleak as his expression. His contempt for and
dislike of Goering were no longer even thinly veiled. "So
long as we have the stipulated ten day warning period to

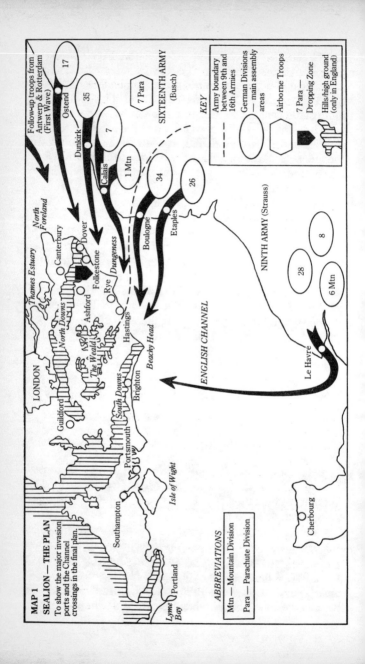

MAP 1
SEALION — THE PLAN
To show the major invasion
ports and the Channel
crossings in the final plan.

KEY

— Army boundary
between 9th and
16th Armies

German Divisions
— main assembly
areas

Airborne Troops

7 Para —
Dropping Zone

Hills/high ground
(only in England)

ABBREVIATIONS

Mtn — Mountain Division
Para — Parachute Division

Follow-up troops from
Antwerp & Rotterdam
(First Wave)

17
35
7
1 Mtn
34
26

7 Para

SIXTEENTH ARMY
(Busch)

Ostend
Dunkirk
Calais
Boulogne
Etaples

NINTH ARMY (Strauss)

28
8
6 Mtn

Le Havre

ENGLISH CHANNEL

Cherbourg

Thames Estuary
North Foreland
Dover
Canterbury
North Downs
Folkestone
Ashford
Rye
Dungeness
The Weald
Hastings
Beachy Head
LONDON
Guildford
South Downs
Brighton
Portsmouth
Southampton
Isle of Wight
Portland
Lyme Bay

complete the assembly. And so long as we have genuine air cover — not just promises."

"You will have proper notice," replied Hitler soothingly. "And you will have air cover over the Channel, and over the beaches. The Reichsmarschall has promised it — to *me*!"

"Von Brauchitsch!" Hitler turned to his army commander. "I take it that the generals are ready?"

"The army is ready, my leader," said Brauchitsch.

"They are a fine force of fighting men," added von Rundstedt.

"I need no advice on the fighting qualities of the German soldier," came the testy reply. "I asked if the *generals* were ready."

Hitler had never forgiven the generals for their blunders of the Great War. He had kept all his front-line-corporal's dislike and distrust of staff officers. His experience in this, his own war, had done nothing to improve his opinion of the generals. They had persistently opposed him. There had been times during the rise to power of the N.S.D.A.P. when they had looked like standing in the way of the Party. But the Führer had thwarted them, and now every soldier in the army had sworn an oath of allegiance to him in person. Nevertheless, *they* had believed Poland was a formidable opponent. *They* had regarded the Maginot Line as a significant obstacle. *They* had failed to perceive the weakness and decadence of France — and of Britain. He had never been wrong, while they had never been right. The generals for their part cordially disliked the Austrian corporal — disliked and feared.

"We are confident that we can defeat the British Army in the field, Führer, even on the reduced and rather unsatisfactory front now envisaged," said Halder.

"No more talk of the width of the front." Hitler waved the issue away with both hands. "There are advantages to a limited front. We may concentrate the mass of our forces for a rapid breakthrough, followed by swift exploitation and advance across the British lines of supply and communication. — This is what we did in France, is it not,

45

gentlemen?" He looked around, but no-one ventured to tell him that the nature of the campaign in England would be different: he had made his disapproval of mere geography too apparent. He nodded. "Good! We cannot repeat every discussion. The decision has been made."

"And is the decision made that we are in fact to launch the planned attack?" came Raeder's voice again. This time it was the Grand Admiral who had misjudged Hitler's mood.

"As I believe I said, gentlemen, we cannot repeat every discussion. We will not engage in endless repetition. Nor can we provide for every possibility. If we had done so these last few years, would we ever have destroyed the Czechs, the Poles, the Dutch and Belgians, the Danes and Norwegians, the oh-so-powerful French? No we would have sat at home and wrung our hands over the difficulties and our own misfortunes. You would probably still not be able to walk in your uniforms through the towns of the Rhineland, let alone the streets of Paris! Admiral, you have your limited front. That is agreed — a limited front. You have your promise of the complete protection of the Luftwaffe. The promise has been made. Now the R.A.F. is effectively out of the way, the promise will be kept. That is also agreed. Yes, gentlemen! Yes! *Sea Lion* will proceed!"

There was a long silence. Hitler looked round the ring of faces, the army chiefs nodding quietly their acceptance of the order, the smirk on the face of Goering and the enthusiasm in the eyes of Jeschonnek, a committed Nazi like so many in the Luftwaffe. Only Raeder sat with his eyes downcast, and it was Raeder who finally spoke again.

"As the Führer orders. But I must have the date. The minesweepers must begin their task as soon as possible, and there are still the majority of our own minefields to be laid. I will naturally need air support over the Channel as soon as these preliminary operations commence. It cannot all be done by night. I will also need the Luftwaffe's presence over the invasion ports. There must be no more dispersals once we are counting down to the day."

Hitler gestured expansively.

"I am well aware of these points. — I am glad to see that you are now prepared to get on with the job, Admiral. For that is what we all must do. The Directive will be drafted by myself and Field Marshal Keitel immediately after this meeting. You will issue the Warning Order to all units today. *Operation Sea Lion* is scheduled for ten days from now. — You have your ten days' notice. On 27th September, 1940, Germany will invade England."

The preparations for *The Day — S-Tag —* were already well advanced. They had been continuing steadily through the weeks of August and September. Along the canals of Holland and Belgium an endless procession of barges moved towards the Channel ports, until there were over two thousand of them assembled in the cramped harbours. Down through the Kiel Canal from the Baltic, from Norway and Denmark, from the North Sea coasts and the Low Countries, from the Rhine and the inland waterways, the steamers and motorboats, the trawlers and tugs collected. The ports of the Reich were stripped of every useful vessel they could spare, and many they could not. Everyone who knew the sea, from old salts of sixty to fisher lads of sixteen, was drafted to the invasion fleet. The commerce of the coasts and rivers of Europe took second place to the assembling of that strange armada.

At the same time, by rail and road, supplies flooded in to the invasion ports and assembly areas. Trainloads of mines — more than five thousand of them — ton upon ton of ammunition of all calibres, shells for the artillery, rifles for the infantry, tanker after tanker of fuel. All these had been rumbling across occupied Europe towards that small area of north-eastern France. And in addition there were all the other, less obvious, needs of a great army. Tents and boots, mobile latrines and soup kitchens. Horses, thousands of horses. The German army, for all its image of the mechanized Panzers sweeping across the countryside, was still very dependent on horse-drawn transport. The areas behind the French Channel coasts had already become a vast supply dump — and a ready target for Bomber Command.

The nine divisions of the First Wave of the assault, the shock troops, had been in position since late July. Their equipment was assembled. The landing craft made out of converted barges, the pontoons, the amphibious tanks. And their training continued apace. They practiced embarkation, and disembarkation under fire. They tried to get temperamental equipment to work properly. They discovered the difficulties of getting horses ashore, even when the enemy was merely a choppy sea. They trained in the storming of beaches and sand dunes, and in fighting their way up hillsides. Some practised the ascent of cliffs. All rehearsed those techniques in which they were already expert, the storming of pill boxes, the infiltration of defended positions held by a well-dug-in enemy, the techniques of house to house and hand to hand fighting. They trained in the arts of breakthrough, and the exploitation of advantage. They studied the handbooks about England produced by the Intelligence Service. Morale was high.

From 18th to 21st September, Major General Warlimont of the Wehrmacht High Command undertook a tour of the invasion area. His fact-finding mission had been set up by Keitel and Jodl before the fateful Berlin Conference. Now his instructions were to report not only to his two immediate superiors but also to Adolf Hitler. The Führer's interest in the invasion had been kindled. He wished to be kept informed. In his perception of events *Sea Lion* was no longer a side show; it was centre stage. The tempo of events changed, as the final countdown began.

Warlimont's report was not clear cut. Everywhere he had certainly found a sense of eager expectancy. The staffs of Ninth and Sixteenth Armies were confident of their prospects. Clearly the training programme was going well. There were, however, evident deficiencies in some areas. Preparations were under way, but Warlimont rapidly acquired doubts as to the time scale. There was no question but that the earlier attentions of British bombers had caused disruption. Barges had been damaged and destroyed. Communications had been interrupted, though only for short periods. There was, as in any army on the eve of battle, a degree of confusion and many petty annoyances. Among these, however, there were clearly some real problems which might even affect the eventual outcome. In particular the quotas of shipping required had not yet been attained. There was also the perennial question of whether the navy really was in a position to cover the assault — though that fell outside the strict confines of Warlimont's brief.

On the other hand, the commanders of the two covering Air Fleets, Luftflotten II and III, had been briefed by Goering to give Warlimont favourable answers. Goering had also made it abundantly clear to his deputies and to all the senior echelons of the Luftwaffe that his promise to Hitler was going to be kept. He would be supervising the air war in person. In fact the commanders, Kesselring and Sperle, had already established a good understanding with their counterparts in the army. Liaison between the two arms was progressing well.

Warlimont's report to Keitel and Jodl stated his worries clearly, though giving a picture which, overall, was not unfavourable. His report to Hitler was more circumspect. On the naval front he only mentioned the failure to lay all the prescribed minefields. On the military front, he reported that though things were now going well earlier delays might make adherence to the timetable difficult. Even faced with these mild conclusions, Hitler's response was a dramatic tantrum. The message went out loud and clear to all involved that the Führer would not tolerate 'failure' on the part of any of his commanders — on pain of summary dismissal. He warned that he might come to 'the front' himself and direct operations in person. There was only one hint that he might consider delay:- the possibility that the weather might not be right on the 27th.

In the event, in those last ten days even the weather began to turn in the Germans' favour. After 20th September there were clear skies over Britain, with little interference in German operations from cloud or rain. This also meant clear skies for Bomber Command over the invasion ports, for there had been no strategic withdrawal of British bomber forces. But the new instructions to Bomber Command to concentrate all its efforts on hampering enemy invasion preparations were nullified almost at once. For the first time, the Luftwaffe hit at British *bomber* bases in strength. These were further inland than the exposed fighter airfields from which the British had retreated, and accordingly still received fighter cover. German losses were severe, but Goering was prepared to accept them. They were balanced by the Spitfires and Hurricanes shot down over southeast England in the defence of other targets. For the R.A.F. had only withdrawn from its exposed positions. It did not, as perhaps it should, withdraw from a commitment to the defence of the counties where those positions lay. The Kriegsmarine was not forced to carry out any more dispersals of invasion craft. The massed strength of the German army behind the ports of embarkation suffered from the R.A.F. hardly at all.

The German order of battle in late September, even under the scaled-down plan which the weakness of the navy had imposed, was still formidable. Von Rundstedt at the head of Army Group A was a determined and experienced soldier. There had been something of a question mark over his National Socialism before the war, but he had returned from enforced retirement to carry his armies to spectacular victory first in Poland then in France. He still held the same command, and Hitler's justified confidence.

His Army Group A comprised two armies: to the east, the Sixteenth under Busch which was intended to carry the brunt of the assault; to the west the Ninth under Strauss.

The eastern forces would sail from Calais, Dunkirk and bases in the Low Countries at Rotterdam, Antwerp and Ostend. Four divisions in two army corps were involved in the first landing wave of Sixteenth Army's sector: XIII Corps comprising 17 and 35 Divisions, and VII Corps made up of 7 Division and 1 Mountain Division (more lightly equipped troops trained for speed of operation). The first echelons of these units which would make the initial landings were to sail from the forward embarkation ports;

second echelons being held at Antwerp and the Dutch bases, to follow up as soon as the beach-heads had been established. The aim was to get the entire four divisions of the first wave over in the shortest time.

Within Sixteenth Army's sector there were two other formations which did not fall directly under Busch's command. Under General Kesselring of Luftflotte II was the 7th Parachute Division. It had been allotted a key role in the initial stages of the action, but was to remain under air force control. Directly responsible to Army Supreme Command (O.K.H.) was another airborne unit, 22nd Air Landing Division. Though it was expected to work closely with the army, its autonomy had been deliberately preserved, and its area of commitment would depend on the circumstances of the fighting. It provided the mobile reserve.

XIII Corps' objectives were on the right flank, in the great curved bay of the East Roads, between Dungeness and Hythe. 17 Division, landing in the northern half, was to seize the town of Hythe and with it the north end of the Royal Military Canal. The badly damaged Fighter Command airfields, at Lympne and Hawkinge were also immediate tactical objectives. Luftwaffe high command was confident that they could make them operational in a matter of days. The ability to operate fighter aircraft from southern England would make a substantial difference, turning the Luftwaffe's general air superiority into total local control over the beach-heads. On the coast beyond Hythe lay yet another desirable prize — the port and harbour facilities of Folkestone. The early capture of a working port would dramatically alter the speed with which reinforcements could be landed. O.K.H. hoped that some at least of the Second and Third Wave troops would enter England via the quaysides of South Coast ports rather than the risky open beaches.

The importance of 17 Division's beach-head was well realised by the army planners, for it was to their sector that the crack 7th Parachute Division was assigned. The paratroops would land in Hythe itself and in a fan-shaped area above the town to provide an extended cover zone behind the sea-borne landings. Once the immediate objectives had been seized, 17 Division, with the airborne troops, was to push northward to capture Canterbury and at the same time cut off the British forces defending Dover. If that great port could be taken, so much the better, but O.K.H. doubted the First Wave troops were sufficient to do so, and its isolation provided a good second best. Farther south 35 Division had been given the task of landing on the exposed beaches leading down from Romney Marsh. Its initial objective was to advance across the marshes and secure the line of the Royal Military Canal. If circumstances permitted, it was to press on into the Weald towards Tenterden.

VII Corps' landing ground lay in Rye Bay. 7 Division was to disembark on Winchelsea Beach and immediately push inland to take Rye and secure the southern end of the Royal Military Canal. 1st Mountain Division, trained to climb the cliffs on its front, would land on their western flank and proceed immediately to the seizure of Hastings. Then both divisions would move speedily forward to the north west.

Just as the two corps of Sixteenth Army landed on two beach-heads separated by Dungeness, so the two corps of Ninth Army were separated by the promontory of Beachy Head. XXXVIII Corps would sail from its bases in Picardy via the ports of Boulogne and Etaples to make landing in Pevensey Bay. It also had a north-westerly axis of advance up along the flank of the Weald towards Uckfield. The three remaining divisions of Ninth Army which made up VIII Corps were based around the Lower Seine, ready to sail from Le Havre for landfall west of Beachy Head in Brighton Bay. The landings in Brighton itself were to be carried out in the first instance from motor boats, and the whole scale of build up in this sector was to be slower than elsewhere. On the extreme left flank, VIII Corps was the hinge on which the advance would swing forward.

As the preparations of the three armed services now moved into top gear, Naval Headquarters in Coblenz and

Rotterdam had already performed a miracle of organization in the collecting and conversion of the invasion barges. These barges, many with newly installed bow ramps, were the vehicles from which the troops would storm up the beaches of England. There were over two thousand of them. They were not, for the most part, self-propelled. To tow them were four hundred tugs and converted trawlers, and an assortment of other vessels. There were also the motor boats for the operations in Brighton Bay, and two hundred larger steamers which would ply the continuing 'ferry service'.

The sweeping of British minefields off the invasion ports had been largely completed by 21st September, and the southern sections of Germany's own minefields laid. Minesweeping and minelaying off Britain's coasts had commenced under cover of darkness. The embarkation ports themselves, despite an appearance of total chaos, were rapidly improving in efficiency and state of readiness. By 24th September there was no doubt of O.K.H.'s ability to fulfil its part of the plan: the question mark remained over the Kriegsmarine.

R.A.F. operations were still causing minor but continuous nuisance in the port areas, but it was evident that the Luftwaffe would have effective control of the skies over the crossing and landings. Command of the sea remained with the British. Kriegsmarine Commander West, Vice-Admiral Lütjens was woefully ill-provided. To protect his right flank he had three flotillas, each of ten Motor Torpedo Boats, fast, useful craft, but hardly a match for a force of British destroyers. To the west he was better provided, with two torpedo boat flotillas at Cherbourg and ten destroyers — virtually the whole of Germany's destroyer strength after the Narvik disaster — based on Le Havre. There were also fifteen U-boats available for the west, and ten for the east, with some other boats to operate in the North Sea. In short, to face the battleships of Britain's Home Fleet, the Germans had nothing larger than a destroyer — and precious few of those.

There were heavier ships, but on Hitler's orders these

were allocated to diversionary tactics, notably a feint from Norway with a fleet of ocean liners escorted by Germany's four available cruisers. This operation, *Herbstreise*, was designed to draw British heavy units away from the Channel by a pretended threat to the East Coast. There were also to be diversions by the heavy cruiser, *Admiral Hipper*, and the pocket battleship, *Admiral Scheer* — if the latter was ready. The Germans also entertained some faint hopes of getting *Scharnhorst* and *Gneisenau* (their only real capital ships) back in commission in time to play a role. The German intelligence service, the Abwehr, had made sure the British were aware of these supposed threats to the East Coast (and the British were very willing to believe that the East Coast was the real target). But the diversion of effort was a risk. It meant that the defence of the crossing against Britain's overwhelming naval might lay simply and solely in the hands of the Luftwaffe.

Germany planned to land, in the course of a few days, a total of 125,000 fighting men on a front seventy miles long. 50,000 of these were supposed to be put onto the beaches in the first few hours. They had been given as their primary objective a line stretching from Canterbury to Brighton, to be achieved within three days of the commencement of the assault. Once across the Channel, the Germans were confident that the British ground forces would melt away before them, as they had done in France. But, "once across the Channel" were the operative words.

And the British defending the South Coast were not the same as the B.E.F. which had been thrust so easily out of France. If anything they were less well equipped, but their attitude and their morale were very different.

The defence of the coasts lay with British XII Corps. In Kent, covering Dover and Folkestone, was 1st London Division, with the New Zealand Division immediately behind them. Between Dungeness and Beachy Head, 45 Division was in the front line, and west of them 29th Brigade Group, which had just moved headquarters into Brighton. 1st Motor Machine Gun Brigade covered the Worthing area.

The concentration area of the G.H.Q. Reserve in Surrey lay directly behind. This was not committed to the initial fight on the beaches, but available to contain any breakout, and (as the British generals hoped) to fling the enemy back into the sea once they had been contained in their beach-heads. Behind them further troop concentrations were also available. It was a flexible defence in depth of the sort that the high command had never succeeded in assembling in France. The British had already learnt that much.

They had also learnt something about armour, and the need to concentrate it where it mattered. Over five hundred tanks were available directly for the defence of south-east England, and there were more anti-tank guns available than ever before. When the Germans came, *they* for once would be weak in tanks. In G.H.Q. Reserve Britain deployed the 1st Armoured Division and 1st Army Tank Brigade, with 340 and 175 tanks respectively. With them were the elite infantry of the 1st Canadian Division. Training standards were improving daily (though initially they had been of variable quality). A high degree of efficiency had been reached, both in the forces of the strategic reserve in Sussex and Surrey, and in the units that gazed out from the Downs and the high Channel cliffs towards the grey sea where the Germans would come.

Chapter 4

WEHRMACHT

He had to admit he sometimes found his name embarrassing. There were plenty of Germans of his generation called Adolf, but they were by natural causes. He was one of the first — possibly the first — to be named after the Führer. His father, Otto Mann, had been named, so he claimed, after Otto von Bismarck. For Otto Mann, Hitler had replaced the Iron Chancellor as the central figure in the nationalist pantheon in 1922, even before the Beer Hall Putsch. Otto Man was a Bavarian from Munich, the capital of that independent-minded province. He had heard Hitler speak in those strange early days, when the name Hitler meant nothing much. He was one of the first to be caught up in the spell of the street-corner orator in the shabby greatcoat.

So his son, born in 1922, became Adolf Mann. Young Adolf's life had spanned the entire rise to power of the Nationalsozialistische Deutsche Arbeiterpartei. Otto had lost his job and his savings in 1923 when the value of money fell through the floor, and with it the old security of the middle classes. The family sold their house at the worst time to sell, and moved into a less salubrious suburb. Otto did not take part in the Putsch. He was not one of the chosen few — the *Alte Kaempfer* or *Old Comrades* — at the core of Nazi mythology. His support for the party was more theoretical, and he was not the sort of person to join a mob.

When Hitler went to prison, Otto found he had few good words for the disgraced Führer.

While Hitler wrote Mein Kampf in the fortress of Landsberg, the father of young Adolf Mann toyed with the Bayerische Volkspartei, but finally decided that the wider nationalism of Gustav Stresemann, the Chancellor who had saved the currency, and thereby the middle classes, was the best available alternative to the Nazis. Otto was in work again as a local government clerk, a secure job with a pension. The years 1925 to 1929 were not bad ones for people of his sort of position in Germany. The Mann family prospered in a small way. Little Adolf grew up and went to school. He was seven in 1929 when the Great Depression arrived.

This time the Mann family did not suffer directly. Otto was an official, so he would not join the six million unemployed. Irma Mann, Adolf's mother, helped with the relief effort, and the boy went with her and saw the queues at the soup kitchens. He did not really understand, nor did he understand why there were children at school who begged him for a share of his lunch. He willingly doled out his mother's bread and sausage in return for glass marbles and tin soldiers, and became rich in the treasures of small boys.

Only his friend, Jakob, did better in trade, but then Jakob's father was a professor — a respected man, well thought of, and from a good family. Adolf's mother was delighted when he was asked round to tea at the Rosenbluhms'. For some reason Otto Mann was less pleased. There were arguments about it. Adolf was finally told to give up his friend after the election in September, 1930. There was no further family debate on the subject.

Otto had rejoined the Nazi Party, and Irma had obeyed her husband's instructions to do the same. Previously he had disapproved of a woman having any positive political affiliation, even anything so safe and innocuous as the Catholic Centre Party to which Irma had once belonged. Now it was her duty to follow her husband into the N.S.D.A.P. After all he, Otto, had been a member in the early days —

"since the early days" as he put it when telling friends and colleagues. And the family must be united. Hitler was the man to end the bread lines, the unemployment, the rabid Bolshevism of the corrupt Weimar Republic. Didn't Irma want to put a stop to it all? Bread for the poor was not the way to do it. Oh no — the way to do it was to make Germany great again. To release the strength of the German Volk. Above all to break the power of the eternal Jew — Germany's curse. Adolf heard most of his father's political diatribes to his mother, and absorbed a certain amount.

As for Irma, she no longer answered. She just listened, and nodded, and the lines on her face grew deeper. She went to church more. Even that brought a slight frown to her husband's face, though he never mentioned it in so many words. Adolf went with her sometimes; she seemed to do nothing but light candles in front of the Virgin. When Adolf asked her why he mustn't speak to Jakob any more, she just told him to obey his father. Though Jakob had been his friend, Adolf had no intention of disobeying his father. Otto had become sterner as he became more dogmatic, and Adolf was wary of him. He was always worst after reading the newspaper, *Völkischer Beobachter*. Adolf was a bright lad. He read it too. It delighted his father to see him engrossed in it, and to explain the more abstruse elements of Nazi policy which it presented so plausibly.

In 1931, as the son of two loyal party members, Adolf was duly enrolled as a *Pimpf*, the first rung in the youth hierarchy. In the following year he passed the tests (outdoor pursuits, and the history of Germany, as filtered through the pages of *Mein Kampf*) to become a full member of the *Deutches Jungvolk*. He greatly enjoyed the oath taking ceremony under the 'Banner of Blood'. There were plenty of such ceremonies in the *Jungvolk*. He also found the drill and the military trappings fun. Most of the boys did. Adolf had the advantage of being an active outdoor type, good in school, but not a real scholar like Jakob. The camping and training sessions were more to his liking. But he learnt quickly, and soon learnt to give the answers that the crop-haired Aryan young man who ran the Hitler Youth wanted to hear. He became well thought of by these petty officials of the Party, and that put him very much in his father's good books.

He never questioned whether he believed it all. In one sense, of course he believed it: it was what he was taught by the grown-ups in charge of him. British boys didn't harbour deep-seated doubts about whether the glories of the Empire were real, or mere propaganda, or about whether the Hun was really as black as the comic strips and war stories painted him. Accordingly, it was no strange thing that German boys believed what they were told about the betrayal of 1918, and the evils of the Jews. Especially as they were now hearing such things in school from their teachers as well. By the time of Adolf's first years in secondary school, Hitler was Chancellor, then President, and finally just Führer.

By now Jakob, his old friend, as Adolf still thought of him, had been barred from the school. One or two of the other boys, often the cleverest it seemed, had also gone — or were doing less well under teachers of the New Order. Adolf found himself on the right side of the racial fence.

In 1936 at the age of fourteen, he entered the Hitler Youth proper. He paraded in uniform, and wore his dagger with pride. He got on better with his father, though now it was his mother who always seemed to be criticizing him. Irma's enthusiasm for the Party was always largely a matter of duty. Her work for the party apparatus always turned towards genuine charity and away from politics. Adolf had to be wary that some of the more rowdy affairs of the Hitler Youth in which he was, inevitably, involved did not reach her ears. But at least she did not make him go to church any more. The old man had seen to that.

'36 had been the year of the Rhineland. Now, in 1940, Adolf realised that it was his first real moment of political understanding. He remembered standing there in his brown, crisp uniform, arm upraised with all the other arms, in the midst of that great crowd in Munich, chanting the endless Sieg Heils in celebration of the return of German self-respect. He recalled the pride of that day, when it felt good to be a German, and Adolf Hitler really had become the Leader of the People. It was then that he had decided he wanted to be a soldier. Not just to do his time in the forces, but to be one of those true warriors of the new army who had risked the wrath and power of France and Britain to re-occupy for Germany a part of Germany's homeland. He remembered with a smile how he had debated hotly with his friends the iniquities of the Treaty of Versailles. Strong stuff for boys of fourteen. Those days seemed a thousand years ago now.

Now the Treaty of Versailles and Germany's humiliation were as remote as the Middle Ages. And in the real army, as a real soldier, politics actually figured much less. His smile broadened. Even his old dad had doubted when the wireless, and then the papers, announced the Rhineland affair. Young Adolf had dared to argue properly with his father for the first time. He still wondered how he *had* dared. — But the old man had not produced the expected reaction to his son's fervour in contradiction. He had shaken his head and muttered,

"I hope you are right, young man. I hope it doesn't all lead to disaster again, like it did before. I hope so."

"It is the Führer's own work. The Führer could not be wrong," he had told Otto. "Surely you cannot doubt him, father?" For just a moment it seemed that something like a flicker of fear entered his father's eyes.

"Of course not!" He had snapped back at Adolf. "Don't even suggest such a thing." Then he had stamped off.

Four years ago, that had been. And now Adolf was eighteen. He was a soldier, a brand new soldier in the new victorious army. It was 1940, and he was sitting on a cliff top in France looking at the English Channel. The last four years had been good to him.

He had been a model member of the *Jugend* in many ways, smart and well turned out; always ready to have a go on manoeuvres and exercises; a good athlete, but one who also had a decent brain. And his loyalty was beyond question. They teased him sometimes, the other young men. "Adolf II" one particular youth, Erich Pfeffer, had called him, suggesting he was Hitler's by-blow. Pfeffer was given to such crudities, and he was a foolish boy. Foolish, because of course the comment would be heard and reported. The oafish Pfeffer was suitably chastised, to Adolf's satisfaction — and for the future would be a marked man. Respect for the Führer — a virtue young Adolf did not lack — was prerequisite for success in the New Germany. And Adolf genuinely did admire Hitler. He had been given every reason to do so, and none not to.

There had been some talk of a possible career for him in the S.S.; there still was some talk of it. But the army remained his ambition. He still had his boyhood collection of flat lead soldiers, all carefully painted by him, the regiments of Friedrich der Grosse. He had saved every newspaper cutting on military matters since that momentous day in 1936 when he had chosen his future career. Since then, one by one Germany's enemies had gone down before her armies. Poles and Czechs, France herself — until finally only England was left.

He was conscious of a sense of privilege in being granted his place in the great enterprise now being launched against England. He was a relatively new recruit in the ranks of Grenadierregiment Number 100 of 1st Mountain Division. He had joined earlier in the year at the divisional depot in Garmisch, appropriately enough a town high in the Bavarian Alps, not far from the border, the former border, with Austria. He could have chosen another Bavarian regiment of course. But he liked the idea of the speed and manoeuvre in surmounting obstacles, both physical and military. And that was what mountain divisions did.

He could have gone for a commission. His father had urged him strongly to do so, and heated words had been exchanged. But the Führer had served in the ranks. Young Adolf would follow in his footsteps. He had told the selection board as much when he volunteered. He remembered the old colonel who had snorted, and the man in S.S. black who had smiled his approval. Adolf reckoned he would be an officer alright by the time England had been defeated:- just as long as it wasn't too short a war.

"What are you grinning all over your face about, Mann? Been up to no good again?"

Adolf gave a start and swung round.

"I can't see anything much to grin about, and that's for certain."

Rudi Meier sat down on the edge of the low cliffs overlooking the sea, next to his friend, and loosened the collar of his uniform.

"Don't you like the look of the sea, then, Rudi? I thought you were supposed to be a Bremen man. You don't look too salty to me."

"Ah, but I was born in Augsburg, don't forget. — Of course only a true Bavarian sausage like you, matured at home, will contain enough salt really — eh, my little Führer?"

Adolf frowned.

"Cut it out, Meier, it's an old joke — and there's only one Führer. You should watch your tongue."

"All right, my friendly bierwurst, calm yourself. I'm as good a party member as you any day, my lad, and I don't suppose the Führer would be that upset at me teasing you. — But I can tell you for a fact, I *don't* like the look of those mists out there. If you were a seafaring type, and did know a bit about boats, you'd be a darn sight less gleeful about making yonder crossing."

Adolf frowned. Though the sun played on his back, there was that first tinge of winter in the air, and the mist out to the north west where England lay was not encouraging.

"I had a letter from Anna," said Rudi.

"Well that should dispel any amount of mist." Adolf smiled again. Anna Hafner was Rudi's girlfriend, from Bremerhaven. She wrote to him twice a week.

"She says they have bombed Bremen, Hamburg and Bremerhaven. Here, she has sent a cutting from *Der Stürmer*." He handed the creased piece of paper to Adolf. "It says they hit a school, you see. That's only two streets away from the Hafners' house. Anna was in when it happened too. She says the blast shook the house. — Bastards, hitting a school!"

Adolf's frown had returned. He stood up.

"I don't know. — War must be against the whole population. Civilians are involved. They are targets, just the same as soldiers are." He couldn't remember which handbook he was quoting — and wasn't at all sure that he believed it.

"That's all very well unless it's your girlfriend that gets near-missed. And I don't suppose you'd be too happy if you had a kid brother who went to the school they'd just smashed up."

"I didn't mean it like that," Adolf replied, his face reddening. "I just meant — well, if they offered not to bomb us in return for our not bombing them, we wouldn't accept, would we? We're all prepared to put ourselves in the firing line in this war. And if you asked your Anna, or even the kids in that school, they'd all agree too."

"Except the ones that are dead," Rudi replied hotly.

Adolf found himself going redder still.

"I don't know why the hell you're trying to make me feel guilty about it," he snapped.

"Because you're so damned philosophical when it's not your girl who nearly got killed."

"Yes, you're right. I should have thought about that before I opened my fat mouth. I am sorry, Rudi."

"All right, don't take it too seriously, my lad," Rudi answered. His annoyance vanished at once. He always called Adolf "my lad" in virtue of his two years of seniority in age. Two years that meant he had fought the French and the Poles, and knew something about war. "I would only have clouted you in the mouth if you hadn't shut up, so you can be sorry you missed that," he went on. They both laughed aloud, and Adolf slapped Rudi on the shoulders.

"Come on, I'll buy you a beer."

"Since you're a philosopher, you can buy me a schnapps!"

There were quite a few of the lads of 100 Infantry

Regiment in the café. Outside the town boundary of Calais on the coast road to Boulogne, it was handy for the regimental depôt, and the *patron* was amiable and helpful. Quite a few of the French had been behaving reasonably in fact, and there had been a lecture the other day from Captain Wolff about the desirability of fraternization — up to a point, as far as the demoiselles were concerned. Rudi had already made contacts in that area, despite his Anna back in Bremerhaven. There were also the sullen, sulky French. Adolf could understand it, but they needed to realize that they had lost. Things were not the same for them, and would never be the same again. Most of the people, in fact, still seemed stunned by the totality of their defeat. They did not give the conquerors much trouble. And, of course, the conquerors were busy.

"Hallo then, you two! — Time for a quick one before we're due back behind the wire? — Waiter, Garçon, deux vins! And make it snappy!"

Max Bauer had obviously been there for some time, and sampled a good deal of the house's wine.

"They have no beer," he told Rudi and Adolf as they sat down. "Not that we're missing much, with what passes for beer here. What I would give for a glass of real German beer!" he announced in a voice loud enough to provoke surly glances from the scattering of other customers.

"Shut up, Max, we don't want a scene," ordered Adolf.

"They don't speak German. You can say what you bloody like," answered Max, but at least he spoke more quietly.

"What do you think about the exercise tomorrow?" Rudi asked him, changing the subject.

"About bloody time, that's what I think about it? How many days till we go? — And we haven't seen the inside of one of those damned barges yet."

"Shut up, Bauer," interrupted Adolf. "You'll be in real trouble if you aren't careful. Some of these Frenchmen may just speak German, you know. — And I don't want to end up shot by some British Tommy because you've got a mouth like the Kiel Canal, and about as full of trash."

This last was a favourite saying of Rudi's, and Adolf borrowed it as appropriate to the occasion. It had its effect on Max Bauer, who put his glass down with a bang. Fists clenched, he half rose, eyes fixed angrily on Adolf. For a moment they stared at each other. Adolf had no wish to be involved in a brawl in a bar, but he did not intend to be overawed by this drunken oaf. Max Bauer was bigger than him, but clumsy. To his surprise, Adolf found himself almost eager to lay the great ox out on the floor. In the event, Max subsided onto his chair, picked up his glass again and drained the last of his wine. Then he looked back at Adolf.

"Your trouble, matey, is that you think you're a bloody officer already, or the bloody Führer. Too fond of giving orders, you are. — Come on, let's get out of here. It stinks of the French."

Rudi and Adolf swallowed their wine, and followed him out. The *patron* ostentatiously picked up the three wine glasses and dropped them into the waste bin. Those Germans who saw him merely looked away, embarrassed. They were young soldiers, but not louts, and none of them, unlike Max, was drunk.

Max was not there for the exercise next day. He had spent the night in the guardhouse. The duty sergeant had also found his 'state of health' objectionable.

"If you ask me, he's the luckiest bastard of the lot of us," muttered Adolf, even his placid disposition upset by the chaos of the boarding arrangements. The exercise had started long before dawn — and now it was mid-morning, and he and Rudi had only just climbed down into the bowels of a foul-smelling concrete barge that had obviously seen much better days.

"Move up you blokes," called Rudi.

"Silence there! I'll have the next man making a row straight on a charge!" came the irritable snarl of the corporal, whose temper had also steadily degenerated through the morning.

"It's like a bloody slave ship," muttered Rudi under his breath.

"More like sardines in oil," replied Adolf, also *sotto voce*. He pointed at the greasy water slopping round their feet. "I hope we get something a bit better on invasion day."

"Right, get sat down," came the order, echoing in the cave-like inside of the barge. There were primitive benches running the length of the vessel, and with much cursing and swearing the mass of men lowered themselves onto these. They could not take their cumbersome packs off because of the water on the 'deck', so sitting was not much better than standing. Their young captain, Heinrich Stein — always simply 'Heini' to all of them, when he was out of earshot — stood under a swaying electric light bulb. For all his youth, like many of them, he was already a veteran of two campaigns. It showed in the handling of his disgruntled soldiers.

"The purpose of this exercise is to see how well our embarkation plans work. Well, now we know the answer. Bloody badly!"

A ripple of laughter went round. 'Heini' was a popular officer. In the new Wehrmacht there was not the same class divide between officers and men. They also knew that their captain had stood in the same endless queue with them all morning, and would be crossing with them in the same crumbling, filthy barge.

"I don't want any moaning and groaning about this. It's our first try. Now we know the problems, they will be ironed out. And the job will be done quickly. That doesn't mean, by the way, that the plush seats will be installed. And I regret to say that the film screen will not be quite ready for the crossing."

The men grinned appreciatively at each other, their annoyance already evaporating. Soldiers are used to discomfort, and expect to moan and to have something to moan about.

"Nor can I do anything about the provision of running water." He kicked up a spray, and smiled wrily. "It is inevitable that an old tub like this will leak when you fit a tin ramp on the front. We're not that likely to sink though!

I can't show you the marvellous operation of the ramp today. That will have to wait till we're on the other side. We've practised the business of what we do on the beach, and how we get up the cliffs enough times already. That's not today's problem. We all know what our job is. Well, now you've seen the old scow. It's dirty, wet and crowded — but we aren't planning to stay on board for long, thank God. Right, lads, any questions?"

"Will this be the actual barge we go over in, sir?" someone on the far side asked.

"The very one. We're lucky; not all of them have the ramp."

"Oh well, that's one hope down the drain," whispered Adolf. Rudi raised his arm.

"Lavatory arrangements, sir?"

Again the laughter and grins.

"You'll have to go up top, son, and piddle over the side. — If you think you're going to want anything else, well, you'd better take a cork."

When the laughter had subsided a gangling youth who didn't fit his webbing very well, Willi, another of Adolf's friends, also put up his hand.

"Any news of the day, Captain?" he asked.

"Not for the likes of you. — We're in an occupied country, and there are plenty of ears to hear a chance remark. You've all already heard more than enough for your own good. You know as well as I do that we're not going to be sitting around here all that much longer. It's 21st September now. We'll be in England before the end of October!"

As the officer went up the steel ladder amid a chorus of approval, Adolf turned to Rudi.

"I'll offer you odds we'll be there before the end of September," he said.

Chapter 5

HIGH COMMAND

The Führer Conference of Monday 23rd September at Giessen met to consider the progress of the *Sea Lion* preparations, and to consider Warlimont's report. Hitler was somewhat reluctant to give his commanders the opportunity to debate matters again. Even *he* had seen from the watered-down version of the report presented to him that there were still real problems. His unwillingness to risk facing concerted opposition struggled with his own unease and uncertainty — and a need to be reassured. Despite his vaunted intuition, he still had a nagging doubt. A doubt that somehow a narrow stretch of dirty water might yet make Britain different from all those other victims which had succumbed so readily.

In fact the Führer had nothing to fear from his service chiefs. The issue of postponement was discussed again. Raeder saw to that. But his isolation among the commanders was now more marked. He could no longer maintain that the Luftwaffe was not winning the air war. Goering's list of victories was too substantial, and for once too well documented, for even that notorious braggart to have invented. Furthermore, the activities of the British air force over the invasion areas had definitely diminished. Part of the reason, though the Germans did not know it, was the transfer of bomber crews to Fighter Command, the latest desperate expedient to which the British had resorted. The expedient was made more possible by mounting bomber losses.

Also, despite his opposition, Raeder had come to realise that what he regarded as an insane operation was now going to proceed. He had accordingly put his considerable energies into limiting the damage it was likely to do, not only to his beloved navy, but also to the army he was supposed to see safe across the Channel. He had recalled all available U-boats from more distant patrols into the North Sea and the Western Approaches, and now reckoned on an available submarine strength in invasion areas considerably in excess of the twenty boats envisaged in the plans. He refrained from reporting this fact to the Führer or the Conference:- he did not want some whim undoing his work. He had also moved heaven and earth to get the minefields laid, and some of the British minefields swept. In both activities his vessels had been accorded the rare privilege of Luftwaffe protection, and even the assistance of a fliegerdivision of minelaying aircraft based in Holland. Goering was being expansive towards the admiralty, having got his way, and Kesselring and Speidl had made specific allocations of fighter cover from the forces of Lufflotte II.

The Grand Admiral had also made another couple of undercover modifications. The heavy cruiser *Admiral Hipper* should according to the plan have sailed into the Atlantic, to draw off the British fleet. If the *Scheer* could be got ready in time, she was to make a similar sortie. Raeder reasoned that in the lead up to an invasion the British would not be fooled or distracted by any such diversion. He might well need these heavy ships, the *only* two likely to be available, on the invasion route. Therefore he had modified the *Hipper's* orders. She was currently engaged on a feint towards the Faeroe Islands, as planned, but by tomorrow she would be on her way back. He did not inform the Conference of this fact: it could be regarded as an operational matter, purely internal to the Admiralty. He had exerted all his influence in getting the repairs on the *Scheer* rushed forward. She might have to sail with dockyard workers still aboard, but he now knew that she would be able to sail on the 27th or 28th. He told the Führer she would *not* be ready.

The immediate purpose of Raeder's subterfuges was a relatively simple one. He wanted back the cruisers *Emden*, *Nürnberg* and *Köln* from *Operation Herbstreise* — the deception plan by which a fleet of liners and warships would simulate a threat to Britain's north east coasts. Raeder seized the opportunity to argue against the whole concept. Once again he did not think the British were going to be fooled. Once again he had not taken Hitler's moods into account. The Führer let him get half way through his reasoned criticism before he volubly interrupted.

"You are quite wrong, Admiral. You do not have the necessary insight into the English mind. Our enemy thinks in terms of ships. Their aircraft will see four great ships sailing towards their coasts. They will see an escort of large warships. And they must be allowed to see, Herr Reichsmarschall." He glanced at Goering and smiled expansively. "I do not want the Luftwaffe to shoot down those particular British planes. When they have seen, the British will draw the natural conclusion. That our real invasion is to come on their east coast."

He looked around for approval.

"The deception is too good an opportunity to be missed," agreed Goering. "It is a master stroke of strategy." Raeder sighed audibly. He lacked tolerance for Goering's fawning. "It occurs to me that we might make it even more of a threat by moving in the direction of this part of the coast — East Anglia." Goering had risen, and was pointing to the map, as he outlined his idea to the Conference. "I would also propose that the operation be launched on the 25th not the 26th, to give the British time to respond. We could then repeat the feint on *S-Tag* itself."

Raeder took more notice of this, overcoming his initial reaction of annoyance at Goering's interference in purely naval matters. For once the Reichsmarschall was proposing something that might be useful to the Kriegsmarine. Firstly, it would certainly look more like a real threat to the British. Secondly, it would bring his few available cruisers closer to where they were really needed. He would be able to detach them for other operations if he needed to. He did not speak; the Führer was more likely to accept Goering's suggestion if he did *not* support it. Hitler was happy to agree to the proposed 'minor' modifications. He was the grand strategist, not the detailed tactician. He waved his hands generously.

"Of course, Reichsmarschall, if you think so. The order can be amended appropriately. — Perhaps Grand Admiral Raeder will see to that."

The discussions then moved to details of Luftwaffe actions over south-east England. The emphasis had switched to the immediate landing area itself. The use of aircraft for mining operations, especially in the Thames Estuary and around the vital British destroyer base at Harwich was stepped up, another matter of satisfaction to Raeder. Goering was also able to report considerable success in rendering both Dover and Folkestone harbours untenable to British warships. The army chiefs expressed their renewed confidence now that the British fleet had been forced to withdraw to Portsmouth. Raeder reflected that Portsmouth was all of fifty miles from the heart of the invasion coast, and that his own intelligence reports indicated at least one destroyer in Dover only the previous evening. However, any withdrawal of the British fleet was important, and for the first time Goering, the generals, and even Hitler himself seemed to appreciate just how crucial to the whole operation the question of British sea power really was. Perhaps Warlimont's report had done the trick; he couldn't believe it was his own persistent efforts.

Nevertheless, the Admiral followed up the advantage by putting in a request for further bombing of Portsmouth, Chatham and Harwich. Goering was happy to oblige. "What about torpedos?" Raeder tried next. The navy had put that question to the Luftwaffe before. This time it was anticipated. Jeschonnek announced that there were now Heinkel He 111's and Junkers Ju 88's equipped for torpedo attacks against British ships in addition to the existing provision of He 115 twin-engined floatplanes. There was also the new Condor Squadron, flying converted Focke-Wulf FW 200 airliners as medium bombers specifically for use against naval targets. Even allowing for exaggerations as to state of readiness, that news was excellent. The Admiral sat back. Wonders would never cease. Perhaps the whole damn-fool scheme was going to work after all.

By not-so-strange a chance, that evening, the day of the Führer Conference, also saw a crucial meeting of the British War Cabinet. Though the British were unaware of the fact, to the Germans the 23rd September was *S Minus Four*, so close was England to her hour of trial. The British were sure, however, that the moment would not long be delayed. The War Cabinet, attended as it always was now by the Chiefs of Staff, met in the fortified bunker beneath 10 Downing Street.

"So we are satisfied that a sea-borne invasion *will* happen, and that it will happen no later than the third week of October."

Churchill sat back in his chair, his heavy face lined with the cares of the last few months. Since he had taken over the premiership, the disasters to British arms which had begun under Chamberlain had continued unabated, and the ultimate crisis of the British Empire drew ever nearer.

"The Joint Chiefs of Staff accept that it cannot be any later than the third week in October, Prime Minister, and we regard the 12th as the most likely date." Sir Cyril Newall, Chief of the Air Staff spoke carefully in an unhurried voice. "I would like you to hear the details from Air Chief Marshal Dowding."

Sir Hugh Dowding, as head of Fighter Command, had also become de facto a regular member of that small group of men who were to guide Britain's destiny in the darkest hour. There were now as many military men as civilians, and the balance of decision had tilted towards their requirements.

"M.I.14 reports continue to confirm the build-up in the Channel ports" Dowding told them. "Indications from the enemy's mining and minesweeping activities also point in the same direction. I have the file of reconnaisance photographs here, if you would like to inspect them, gentlemen." The photos of the invasion harbours and German naval activity were passed round, as the Air Chief Marshal continued. "There can now be little doubt that the assault will fall entirely on the Kent and Sussex coasts, with some possibility of a subsidiary attack further west. We have a hint of something in Lyme Bay, but rather vague. You will have seen mention of it in the Air Ministry report that has been circulated. I am sure that you will also have seen that our back-room boys regard the October date as dangerously late from the enemy's point of view. On the other hand, there are doubts that he will be ready to do anything before then. There is, I suppose, a possibility on the basis of moon and tide etcetera that he *might* try for the 26th or 27th of September."

"That is in three days' time," observed Halifax drily. "If it were correct, there would be little we could do about it at this stage."

"Except what we are already doing," Churchill interrupted with some testiness. The relationship between him and Halifax had always been one of mutual suspicion verging on dislike. "Sir Hugh, we all have a fair idea of how the Nazis stand, or how we think they stand. What of our own position?"

"German attacks on airfields in the territory of the former Eleven Group have lessened, but not by any means ceased. A majority of fields are still unusable, and most are in practical terms untenable. There have also been enemy forays further north and west. Park's enlarged Twelve Group still has single Hurricane Squadrons at some forward bases . Our position has been eased a little by the transfer of bomber crews, though there is the re-training problem there of course. However, we gave the Luftwaffe a nasty shock over the East End yesterday. Really, that's all I have to say on Fighter Command's current position. I feel the strategic withdrawal has started to have its effect in restoring our ability to fight this battle — but it will take another two to three weeks for us to have enough men and machines to return to the assault."

"I hope and pray you will have them," said Churchill. "Still, perhaps there is some comfort in what you have told us." He looked up from lighting another of his famous cigars. "Is there better news from the Royal Navy, Sir Dudley?" He glanced across the smoke-filled room at Sir Dudley Pound, First Sea Lord and Admiral of the Fleet. It was also currently Pound's delicate job to chair the Committee of the Joint Chiefs of Staff of the three forces. The admiral stood up.

"Prime Minister, gentlemen. As you know the abolition of Fighter Command's Eleven Group and the withdrawal of air cover has necessitated some modification to our disposition of naval forces in the Channel. We have lost seven destroyers and one light cruiser since the last of these meetings. Such losses, in a single restricted area, would become serious if allowed to continue. Four of the ships concerned were sunk in harbour. We have therefore withdrawn operational forces from all ports in the Dover Command — except as occasional visitors. I am maintaining a token force at Newhaven, but the majority of our strength and *all* heavy ships have been withdrawn to Portsmouth, the Nore or Harwich. I might add that I am unhappy with using the Medway for anything except light forces, partly due to the enemy's air force, but also in view of their recent mining activity in the area."

Churchill made a note on the pad in front of him.

"Pray continue, Admiral, — tell us what news of the Home Fleet."

"The Battlefleet is now brought forward from Scapa Flow to Rosyth, sir. I have the *Hood*, *Nelson* and *Rodney*, with their escorts, available to sail at a few hours' notice. My only other capital ships in home waters are the *Repulse* and the *Revenge*. I have already ordered *Repulse* to leave her present duties and sail for Plymouth. *Revenge* is already at Portsmouth, and has again bombarded the coasts of Normandy. I anticipate that the maximum naval forces the enemy can muster are the two *Scharnhorst* class battle-cruisers, one or two pocket battleships, and half a dozen cruisers, or even fewer. They are very short on destroyers. We have five battleships or battle-cruisers, eight heavy cruisers, over twenty light cruisers, and over seventy destroyers."

"So, given a little good fortune, you feel you may have an even chance of defeating them at sea?" It was a rare glimpse those days of Churchill's old humour.

"We will beat them at sea, sir. It's over the sea I'm worried about. — I wonder if Fighter Command can give me more information on the likely availability of the mobile air reserve to cover seaborne operations. I would also request the permission of the War Cabinet to withdraw *Barham, Resolution* and *Ark Royal* from Dakar at once — and provisional orders to be given to *Renown* to be ready to sail from Gibraltar."

"No!" The Prime Minister snapped it out immediately. "*Operation Menace* may yet be crucial. We cannot risk the remaining French battleships and cruisers falling into Axis hands. Also, Admiral, *Renown* is the *only* capital ship left at Gibraltar — which is today under enemy air attack."

"Sir, Gibraltar is under Vichy French air attack precisely because of *Operation Menace* at Dakar. We run the risk of losing important operational ships of our own at a crucial moment because of the potential risk from one, non-operational enemy battleship."

"All right, Dudley," Churchill replied in a deceptively smooth voice. "I accept the point. I agree to our reviewing *Menace* — tomorrow. We will in fact keep it under daily review — and respond to circumstances. We may still have it both ways, you know. *Renown* stays at Gib. But you may instruct her captain and the authorities on the Rock to have her ready to sail at all times without notice. Agreed?"

All nodded, though not all agreed in fact. In some ways it was as with Hitler. Churchill got his way. The difference was that the British service chiefs would speak their mind, and could change things. The politicians present also preserved their own freedom of action and debate. Churchill might well have intuitions, but unlike his opposite number in Germany he did not believe they were infallible. In this instance at least, Pound could sit down with some degree of satisfaction. Dowding took his place:

"On the subject of the new reserve. It is now officially designated Strategic Air Reserve. It is in existence, under direct operational control of Fighter Command H.Q. I have five squadrons available at the moment, four Hurricane, one Spitfire. Since Park now has Twelve Group, I am requesting, gentlemen, that Leigh Mallory assume command of this force — under my general direction. By the way, I have told Park that, as a matter of policy, he may not request assistance from the reserve, nor may reserve squadrons be offered to him. They are available only in the event of an invasion warning, and only for the defence of the beaches, harbours and seaways of the invasion coast."

"Quite right, Dowding. — I hope that will do for now, Admiral. Given time, given time, the air cover may yet be there," was Churchill's reply.

Leigh Mallory's new appointment was duly agreed. Then, once again, it was the Prime Minister who spoke.

"That leaves us with the military measures. But before we move to consideration of our army's dispositions, I have a few words to say. I have been asking these military intelligence fellows a few questions of my own. And I have also been listening carefully to some of the comments here today. I am told that Germany's heavy ships continue to be based in Norway or in German waters. I am told that major transports — and I do not mean barges — are in the same waters. I hear now that German minelaying and mine counter-measures are taking place in the Thames Estuary and off the coasts of Essex. Like the Admiral of the Fleet, I want to take out some extra insurance. I still think that these Nazis have their eye on East Anglia. No doubt *as well as* the Channel . . . But I don't trust 'em — and I want to be prepared, like the Boy Scouts, eh?" He looked round again, belligerently. He found an unexpected ally.

"There is a great deal in what the Prime Minister says," came Attlee's quiet voice. "We should be wary of putting too much faith in *our* interpretations of intelligence reports.

The fact is, we still do not *know* what the enemy plans are. I would not like to think all our eggs were to be put in one basket." The unemotional voice of the leader of the Labour Party sounded eminently sensible, except to the military men.

"Gentlemen, I hope you are not proposing any transfer of troops from the South Coast to East Anglia, or from G.H.Q. Reserve." Sir Alan Brooke, Commander-in-Chief, Home Forces, spoke with some vehemence. Although he had originally shared the view, with Churchill and most of the British military leaders, that the East Coast was the most probable enemy objective, he had been fully converted.

"Sir, I fully support and agree with General Brooke." Sir John Dill, Chief of the Imperial General Staff, stood up next to Brooke. These were the two ranking army commanders. If Churchill had considered any south to east transfer he did not press on with it.

"No, I am not making any such proposal. Have no fears on that score," he answered. "What I think we might consider is a strengthening of your reserve." He rose and went over to the wall map of Britain, marked by the flags that represented divisions of men, squadrons of aircraft, and ships of the Navy. His proposals were drastic. Brooke also came over to the map.

"Prime Minister, that means utterly stripping the whole of the North West and Wales. Two divisions left from Cardiff to Carlisle, Sir!"

"Neither Cardiff nor Carlisle are likely targets," Churchill replied at once.

The debate was long, and at times almost acrimonious. Brooke and Dill opposed any disruptive movements of troops. The C.-in-C. Home Forces felt in his bones that divesting the west of its forces was unwise. He had no objection to regarding Western Command's divisions as part of a larger reserve, but he did not want them committed, even potentially, at the outset. In the event he got most of his own way. Only a single independent brigade was brought forward.

The discussion moved on to states of readiness and

levels of equipment. There was continuing report of steady progress. The disastrous losses after Dunkirk *were* being made up, and the lessons of the campaign on the continent learnt. There was also a tale of increasing practical difficulties in the South-East. For the previous three days all three railway lines into Dover had been out of action. The main line to Brighton had twice been cut for periods of more than twelve hours in the preceding week. The key cross-country line from Kent to Guildford and Reading had been repeatedly interrupted. Every one of the Southern Railway's great termini in London had been hit by the Luftwaffe. On occasions, each of them had been put out of action for varying periods of time.

All this mattered. To a large extent troop movements depended on trains. Roads had also been hit, though, with serious disruption in the Ashford and Rye areas, and in the sprawling mass of south London. Further diversion of resources was ordered by the War Cabinet. More manpower was to be obtained for necessary repairs:- Ernest Bevin at the Ministry of Labour could be relied on to organize that. The Railway Executive Committee was to be ordered to transfer repair trains and additional locomotives from the L.M.S. and the Great Western to the Southern. Plans for evacuation of key personnel from threatened areas were also considered, and shelved. Brooke used the opportunity provided by the discussions as a whole to point out that it was *not* East Anglia which had come in for such Luftwaffe interest.

Finally they turned their attention to the Home Guard. There had been very significant progress in training, and even to some extent in equipping, the volunteer units. Further orders were now drawn up for absolute priority to be given to units in the South-East and London — and East Anglia. There was a brief but heated discussion as to whether Home Guard units might, at military need, be moved out of their own localities. The military men believed that in an emergency every last man must be made to count. Churchill doubted that units would be effective outside their home towns and villages for which they would

fight, and die if necessary. They compromised. Home
Guard units could be called upon by local commanders to
plug urgent gaps in the defence, but only for short periods.

The whole meeting, imperceptibly and unintentionally,
had slipped into a mode of thought in which the invasion
was no longer remote and academic, no longer even a mere
probability. In the course of that evening the leaders of
Britain came to believe, in their hearts as well as their
minds, that the Germans would invade, and that they would
do it soon. From now on the combined War Cabinet and
Chiefs of Staff would meet every day, until the 27th.

That night, the 23rd and 24th, brought more random
bombing of London, sideswipes at R.A.F. targets — largely
missed in night-time attacks — and a crescendo of raids
on Portsmouth, Dover, Folkestone, and finally Brighton.
Three warships were lost, one of them a cruiser. Bomber
Command continued with its attempts to respond in kind.
Attacks were made on Calais, Boulogne, Dunkirk and Cherbourg. Everywhere the bombers met stiff opposition.
German flak had reached a hitherto unequalled pitch. The
only notable success scored was a direct hit on the Headquarters of Luftflotte II in Brussels.

When the bombers returned home it was to a day of
unprecedented attacks on their airfields. Throughout the
following day the Luftwaffe ranged unchecked over the
South-East, while engaging in selective penetrations beyond
to strike at Bomber Command and fighter airfields they
knew to be still operational. In Kent and Sussex the targets
were harbours and communications — there were hardly
any airfields left to hit. All day reports flooded in to the
three service headquarters of increasing dislocation of the
war effort. There were also worrying reports of civilian
panic. There had been fighting outside a shelter in south
London, and a woman had been trampled to death in a
fleeing crowd in Brighton. This was the legacy of the
decision to withhold the R.A.F. from the skies. Though
Leigh Mallory now commanded a small but useful fighter
reserve, to the ordinary people it merely seemed as if the

Spitfires and Hurricanes had been suddenly withdrawn. It seemed like a failure of nerve by the hitherto indomitable R.A.F. And that was unthinkable. When the people thought it, *their* nerve began to falter.

Farther afield, the British were learning that strategy by committee and compromise, and worse still strategy by the hunches of the supreme commander, is not the best way to run a war. *Renown*, the last capital ship at Gibraltar, had sailed from the harbour, every gun blazing defiance at the Vichy bombers. During the night, responding to London's directive but against his own better judgment, Admiral Somerville had brought the battle-cruiser back from Mediterranean patrol into the shelter of the Rock. Admiral Pound had wanted the ship brought home. Churchill had wanted her loose in the Mediterranean. The compromise was that she should wait, 'at the ready' in harbour. The bombers returned in strength on 24th, and when they left the great ship lay out of action, her armament intact, but one boiler room badly damaged and the propeller shaft smashed. *Renown* would not be sailing for England in the near future.

Nor would the battleship, *Resolution*. On 25th September two torpedos from a French submarine, had crippled the old ship. Seriously damaged, and in danger of sinking, she was taken in tow by her fellow battleship, *Barham*. *Barham* herself was also slightly damaged by the gunfire of the unfinished French battleship *Richelieu*. The 8-inch gunned cruiser, *Australia*, was put out of action. *Operation Menace* had proved menacing only to Britain's naval plans. With Churchill's permission, Pound now ordered *Barham* to return to England as soon as she had delivered *Resolution* safe to Freetown. The *Ark Royal* was to sail for home immediately.

Meanwhile, at home, through the night of the 24th the Luftwaffe had for the first time launched an all-out attack against London. With Fighter Command evidently broken and the invasion due in a few days, Hitler's earlier opposition to the tactic was removed. Goering authorised indiscriminate attacks, aimed in great measure at demoralizing the civilian population. The bombers were mostly armed with incendiaries. The raids were infinitely more destructive than the previous London attack. As the fire bombs tumbled in endless succession onto the close-packed houses of the East End, London experienced a new and more terrible version of the Blitz.

No longer was it merely an endless succession of blazing streets. The fires became so fierce that they began to generate their own wind. Great tunnels of fire, growing out of their own ferocity, turned streets, neighbourhoods, whole boroughs, into charnel-house infernos. No fire service could fight those fires. The flames of the dying city lit up the skies of the Home Counties like some livid sunset, and their eerie glow formed a monstrous backdrop as far away as the South Coast. The Germans in Calais watched London burning. This was firestorm.

Dowding rang Churchill direct just before four o'clock in the morning. The Prime Minister had been awake most of the night, and knew of the horror engulfing the capital. His permission was asked for the new Strategic Air Reserve to be used. He did not argue. The flames from the burning city made it possible for the fighters to operate just as if it were daylight. The Germans had already sent their fighters over. The Me 109's were engaging the Spitfires and Hurricanes of 12 Group's depleted squadrons, while wave followed wave of bombers.

There are angry skirmishes, the gleaming planes reflecting the fires below, like fierce sparklers darting through the sky. By 4 a.m. the Luftwaffe was finally withdrawing. The R.A.F.'s reserve was committed too late to make any difference, and was recalled with the dawn. It was a dawn like no other for London. The fires continued unabated, turning the sky an unnatural lurid purple, cutting off the sun with the vast pall of smoke which now, like the fires by night, was visible from afar to tell all what had occurred. Corpses lay in the streets, often charred and unrecognisable. Many people in the heart of the storm vanished without trace, utterly consumed. Buildings were reduced not just to rubble but to ash, and where the firestorm had passed what was once a city had become a great grey field, broken only by jagged stumps of walls and twisted skeletons of buildings.

The Germans opened their daylight operations with a creeping barrage of raids — Dover first, then the other South Coast ports, then the road and rail links inland, and the nodes of communication, the bridges and junctions, the power lines and public utilities, finally striking at south London in the late afternoon. Only there did they encounter determined R.A.F. resistance. North of the River was still ablaze from the edge of the ancient City to the docks at Silvertown.

Reports already placed the death toll in London at 30,000, an unimaginable figure. This was no longer the Blitz that Churchill had deftly and defiantly mocked in his speeches. Against this no rhetoric would prevail. London's population was too numbed to panic now. A mood of despairing resignation had descended over the broken capital like the grey rain that fell during the day, full of the dust and ashes of the city's destruction. Yet all the leaders of Britain knew that this was not the real crisis. It was merely the prelude. The gloomy apprehension with which they heard the full tale of the horror of the night before, and the grim story of the day as it unfolded, grew sharper in the afternoon.

News reached Downing Street that a major force of German heavy ships had been sighted by naval reconnaissance over the North Sea, on course for the English coast in the region of the Wash. First reports suggested that at least one battle-cruiser was present, and this error was never corrected. But soon it was clear that there were several cruisers, and major passenger ships — liners. This last could only mean troop transports. Invasion transports! Admiral Forbes sailed from Rosyth with *Nelson*, *Rodney* and *Hood*, the core of the Home Fleet, to intercept.

Meanwhile, in mid-afternoon, as a prelude to their return to the stricken capital, the Luftwaffe were bombing Harwich, forcing the destroyer flotillas to put to sea where they were safer. To coincide with the daylight attacks on

London which followed there was also a series of hit and run raids on the surviving, more northerly sector stations in East Anglia. The Luftwaffe suffered severe casualties in these raids. They had relied on the London attacks to draw off Fighter Command. They encountered Strategic Air Reserve, and were worsted. But that was no comfort to the haggard-faced men in the bunker under London.

Air raids in East Anglia, and the German *Herbstreise* deception plan had achieved the aims of that deception. The War Cabinet now believed that there would be an attack on East Anglia, at least as important as the cross-Channel effort, and very probably preceding it. In fact Goering's Luftwaffe had become over-confident. The mauling his bombers received over the more northerly RAF bases came as a shock to the Reichsmarschall, and earned him a scathing phone call from Hitler who was insisting on hourly reports of events, much to his service chiefs' annoyance. The Führer had now taken up permanent residence in the château near operational headquarters at Giessen. There would be no more need for his commanders to come to Berlin. Their Warlord would be there with them, to run the war.

That night, the 25th/26th of September, the Luftwaffe resumed its raids on the South Coast and left the hotels on the fronts at Worthing and Brighton ablaze, sunk cargo ships in the docks at Southampton, and found time and resources to blitz Merseyside as well. And the Codeword *Cromwell* went out in southern England — 'invasion imminent'. None came. Admiral Forbes's battleships had found nothing in the North Sea, and were already heading back to Rosyth. *Herbstreise* had returned home. It would sail again the following morning. The morning of the 26th September. England's last day before invasion.

Chapter 6

THE WAITING IS THE WORST

"Well, I'd like to know where the fly boys have got to."
The youth who spoke was a short, sour-faced creature of
nineteen, with close-cut ginger hair; Ernie Prescott. He had
been to school with Don, and Don had disliked him then.
Now he worked for his father in their garage, and being
the 'boss's son' had plenty of opportunities to be a know-
all. His remarks had been addressed to no-one in particular
but were heard by the Corporal, Mr Archer, an ex-soldier.

"Get that fag out of your mouth, and get off that wall,
you young layabout!"

Ernie scrambled to stand up straight and stub out the
offending cigarette, as the bristling moustache was thrust
into his face. Archer was a large man, and Ernie's ado-
lescent swagger melted away before him, but then Ernie
had always been a spineless individual. Don grinned to
himself. He had enjoyed seeing that lad taken down a peg
or two.

In the drill hall the rest of the platoon sat talking idly
during the ten minute break after drill, and before the
lecture. It was the usual Home Guard routine, except that
this was an extra session, in addition to the regular twice a
week and the equally regular duties guarding scattered and
unlikely targets. Don still found it difficult to relate their
activities to the ever-present talk of the blitz, and the
invasion. It seemed to be all 'invasion' now, though stran-

gely enough the prospect of the grey-clad soldiers of the Germany arm wading ashore had fewer terrors than the air-raids. The air-raids were all too real, and to talk about them was to talk of neighbours, sometimes friends and relations, injured and killed, of homes or workplaces smashed and destroyed. The idea of invasion still held that unreality of something wholly beyond anyone's experience. People said they expected invasion, but no-one really acted as if they expected invasion.

"What are you grinning about then, young fellow-me-lad?" Bill lowered his large frame into one of the chairs they had just put out for the lecture. He was a middle-aged man, tall and heavily built, much what you'd expect of a dockyard worker, but quietly spoken, not given to shouting and making a fuss about things.

"Oh, nothing much," Don answered.

"Now it's not very nice to be laughing at another's troubles," Bill told him, and then they both laughed. Bill's opinion of young Ernie was similar to Don's.

"What do you think *has* happened to the Raf, though, Bill?" Don asked him. For the obnoxious Ernie had only voiced the question which many were thinking, and increasingly asking. The sudden absence of the Spitfires and the Hurricanes was inexplicable. It had made people afraid, where they had not been before.

"I wish I knew, Don. Maybe there aren't enough to go round — planes I mean. So all we can do is put up with it, while what we *have* got is busy defending somewhere else."

"That's all very well for the somewhere else," replied Don. "What about us?"

"Don't you know there's a war on? Sometimes you just have to put up with things." The Corporal had finished sorting out Prescott, and come over to join the conversation.

"Oh, I wasn't moaning about it." Don was quick to defend himself. He didn't want to be put in the same category as Prescott. "It's just that . . . well, it seems as if something's gone wrong."

"Well, if you want my opinion, I'd say it's a strategic

withdrawal. — Regrouping, something of that sort." Mr Archer nodded sagely at his own opinion — which by chance was not far from the realities of the situation.

"Do you think it's to do with the Supermarine, Corp.?" Bill asked. 'The Supermarine' was the factory down by the River Itchen where Spitfires were made, or had been made. It had been gutted by fire bombs on the night of the fifteenth, the same night Don had brought the Renoufs round to their shelter. Now it stood, a blackened shell, overlooking the River Itchen. They said that the work would be moved away, to an inland site, less vulnerable to enemy attack. The factory would not be rebuilt in Southampton.

"Oh, it might be partly. — Serious loss to aircraft production, I should think." Archer was enjoying his role as an authority on strategy and tactics.

"Do you think there's going to be an invasion, Mr Archer?" Don asked, providing the expert with more opportunity.

"I think they'll give it a try, but they won't get many across. — I can tell you something about that too, though I don't know as I should." He looked doubtfully at Don and Bill, then the desire to pass on his snippet of information proved too much. "A pal of mine who works at Portsmouth says they've caught a German ship. Right in near our coast it was too. The Admiralty authorities" — he paused to let his listeners show they were suitably impressed at the nature of his information — "believe it's a minesweeper or a minelayer. — Probably come in too close to check out our defences, my mate says."

"On the other hand, it might have got lost in the fog, Corporal. Not very good sailors, those Jerries. Probably mistook Spithead for the River Rhine."

The cheerful voice of Tom Wilson served to break the spell of Archer's important war news. Tom was another of the regulars with Don on the Netley Station guard, not that many years older than Don, always joking about something or other — which was no bad thing on a deserted railway

The Waiting is the Worst

station in the early hours of the morning. The corporal was not amused by the interruption.

"Very funny. You can see I'm laughing so much my head's going to fall off." He got up and addressed the platoon at large. "Right you lot, get yourselves sat down. Lecture about to start."

It was about parachutists and enemy agents. — What to do if the enemy landed from the skies in strength. ("Run like hell," Tom had whispered to him). And what to do about people you suspected of being saboteurs and infiltrators. It was quite interesting in itself, though they had already had the same talk once before. Now the captain was telling them it was time to be particularly on their guard. This was no longer some theoretical situation; they must be ready to deal with it any moment, any day now. When the invasion came. Don found himself wondering idly about that German ship they'd captured. Perhaps the enemy really were spying out the coasts ready for the great attack. Or perhaps it was another one of old Archer's tall stories.

The next night, Monday, he had arranged to take Gwen Renouf to the pictures. There was some romantic comedy on at the Odeon. She'd said she wanted to see it. It wasn't exactly his cup of tea, but it was in a good cause.

"I don't think it's a very good idea. What if there's a raid. — You'd be better off staying here," Gwen's mother had announced with a sniff when he came round. Don thought she might as well have added: "where I can keep an eye on you". He wondered if she disapproved of him. During the last week, since the shelter business, he'd been a regular visitor.

'Don't be so daft," Ralph had interrupted. "She couldn't be in safer hands. — Go on you two, have a good time."

"There you are, you're safe in my hands," Don told her as they caught the bus.

"You can keep your hands to yourself — for the moment. I hope there isn't a raid tonight."

"Portsmouth's copping it tonight, love," the bus con-

87

ductor told them. "So maybe you will see the film to the end, not that you'll be too interested in it."

"Cheeky devil," said Gwen. "Men have one track minds."

The picture was less than half way through when the siren went. The bus conductor had been right; it was Portsmouth's turn that night. The bombs falling on Southampton were from half a dozen planes that had mistaken their target. Everyone stood up in the usual way. There were people putting their coats on, one or two hurrying more than necessary to get down the rows of seats to the aisles. The cinema wasn't all that crowded. Don and Gwen were near the back — not exactly the back row, but near enough.

Then came the sound of the explosions, one quite nearby, loud enough to be heard clearly in the relative quiet that came with the film stopping. The second was far closer, a sickening thud, extending into a long roar. The picture house shook, a thin sprinkling of plaster falling from above, the ornate chandeliers swaying. The house lights flickered, then went out. A woman screamed, then another, Don felt himself shoved violently from behind. He put his arm round Gwen and shoved back. They were still in their own row. Everyone was shouting now, and there was a woman, no several women, screaming. As his eyes started to become accustomed to the sudden darkness again, he realised that the crowds in the aisles were pushing and struggling to get out.

"What's going on, Don? We haven't been hit?" Gwen's voice was frightened, but also angry.

"No, we haven't. They've gone mad." He reached into his raincoat pocket and took out his torch. In the beam he made out flailing arms, punches being thrown. He saw one man go down under the feet of the frightened mob. He shone the light down towards the front. Most of the rows were empty. All the people were crushed round the doors at the back.

"Come on. We'd better play tiptoe through the tulips." With the help of the torchlight, they scrambled over the backs of a dozen rows of seats or more, before finally getting into a relatively clear aisle. They got out with no difficulty through the emergency exit in the gents' toilet. The only obstacle was an old bloke, ignoring the riot elsewhere in the cinema, who objected to Gwen's presence. Outside they both found themelves laughing at his indignation. It took a moment to realize there was no sound of planes overhead, no more bombs.

"I've never seen people go like that before," Gwen told him on the bus back home. "Why did they do it?"

"I suppose they were just afraid, and it caught on. I wonder if anyone got hurt — badly hurt I mean. If any of them had thought, they must have known there were the other exits."

"They weren't thinking . . . You'd better not tell my mum about what happened, Don. She'd have fifty fits. I could imagine her being like that lot, you know."

"I can imagine lots of people being like it, once the fear takes over."

Gwen forgot to tease him for his seriousness. They had both themselves been more scared than they cared to admit — not of the bombs, but of their first sight of panic, and the mob. The mob that fear created out of ordinary people.

Next day seemed to bring nothing but alerts, constant interruptions at work, constant trooping down the shelter, and then trooping out again. Nothing came of any of them. It was just a waste of time. People were irritable, and tempers were lost easily. Don found himself arguing with the foreman for no reason over a window he'd shut. You could see the foreman was tired, tired out by the look of his eyes. And that was how everyone seemed to look now. He felt thoroughly fed up when he went home, the only consolation being that there was no Home Guard duty today. He went to bed early, but couldn't sleep, and got up to make himself a cup of tea in the night after tossing and turning for seeming hours.

At the bottom of the stairs he noticed a light through the doorway of the front room. At first he couldn't make it out. He didn't know what time it was, but surely it couldn't be dawn. And the light was the wrong colour. He went in. His father had pulled back the blackout curtains before going to bed. The windows were squares of sullen red. So somewhere outside was burning. There must have been a raid, though it couldn't have been nearby, for there had been no warning, and he had heard no planes go over. Still, sometimes the light of fires from incendiary attacks could be seen a long way away. He went to the windows. The whole northern sky seemed to be aglow with that same reddish sheen, overlaying the clear dark sky of the night. He made his tea, then, taking the cup, quietly let himself out of the back door.

He stood in the street, gazing at the phenomenon for some time, dressing gown wrapped round him, sipping his hot tea. He could see someone standing at the gate over at the Bests' house too, also gazing at the sky. There was absolutely no sound, just the unnatural colour in the sky. He jumped and nearly spilt his tea as he felt a hand on his shoulder.

"Oh, hello, dad. I didn't wake you up did I?"

Bert Gibbard shook his head.

"I heard you come down, but I was already awake. — Well, what do you make of it?" He gestured upwards.

"It must be a raid somewhere, but it's a good way off, I reckon."

"There aren't any big towns up that way. — Its over to the north-east that it's brightest."

"Could be Winchester, I suppose — or Basingstoke."

"Who'd want to bomb them? — Besides, it seems farther away to me. I'll tell you what I think that is, son. I think it's London, London on fire. — Anyway, come on in now, you'll catch your death and so will I. You've got a job to go to tomorrow. And so have I."

He had forgotten that it was tomorrow that his father sailed again for the Cape. He felt guilty about disturbing his last night at home. But the distant fire in the sky haunted his thoughts. Next day, after he'd said goodbye to his dad, off on another twelve thousand miles of round trip, he called in at the Renoufs. Mr Renouf had seen it too, but Gwen hadn't and for some reason he was glad of that. At work, it was the day's topic of conversation. As usual the wireless was kept on all the time, partly for the music, partly for the frequent news bulletins. The funny thing was, there was no news of any big raid. It all seemed to be minor news in fact. None of the listeners knew that for now the enormity of the disaster was being suppressed. For the light in the sky they had witnessed as far away as Southampton was the light of the firestorm that had enveloped London through that dreadful night of the 24th and 25th of September.

The news blackout was broken in the evening, when most of the worst fires had been got under control in the devastated capital. Don heard it at the drill hall; they always listened to the nine o'clock news. The Captain liked to include things from it in his pep-talks and lectures. Alvar Liddell's voice came over as cool and dispassionate as ever.

"In the course of last night London was subjected to the most severe air-raid of the War, resulting in serious damage and loss of life. Numerous fires were started and the emergency services have been stretched to the limit of their endurance. Casualty figures are not yet known, but are reported by the Home Office as very high. Many people have been made homeless, and emergency steps for their rehousing in other parts of the country will be announced tomorrow."

"His Majesty the King, Mr Winston Churchill and Mr Clement Attlee have spent the day in the devastated areas, where Mr Churchill spoke of the unshakeable resolve of the common people not to be broken by Nazi frightfulness. Her Majesty the Queen has visited many of the victims of the bombing in London hospitals."

"The fire service reports that all the serious incidents have now been dealt with, and that the fires which raged in parts of London throughout today are now all under control. The authorities stress that there is no need for panic among the civil population. Please do not leave your homes, either in London or other major centres, unless you are told to do so by an official of your local council or the central government."

"Despite the size of the enemy forces attacking London, fighter aircraft of the Royal Air Force engaged the enemy throughout the night, and heavy losses were inflicted upon them. Raids on airfields further inland were driven off with additional severe enemy losses."

The bulletin went on to other matters, as the captain called his sergeant and two corporals into the little office at the back of the hall. The Bitterne Platoon were left to discuss the report among themselves. Though the full extent of the truth had not been revealed, by now most Britons were expert at reading between the lines, and piecing together their own picture of events.

"It's like they did in Poland, and that Dutch place," said Tom. "Terror attacks, then you send the army in. It's the lead-up to the invasion, I tell you."

It was a conclusion widely reached among the British people. It had already been reached by their leaders. For the detachments of the Home Guard and the regular army along the South and East Coasts, there was one more alarm to come that evening.

The soldier burst in through the doors of the drill hall at a run. It was the man on telephone duty. The drill hall, by a masterpiece of bad organization, was not on the phone. One of the men was therefore kept on duty at a house three doors up the road to relay calls received. The family concerned were not entirely happy about this contribution they were making to the war effort, particularly when it involved outgoing calls too. But this time it was clearly something important. Something was up.

"Where's the captain? Where's the sergeant?" He looked round at them in considerable agitation.

"In there, Joe. — But we'd like to hear too." Bill's calm voice had a far from calming effect on the agitated Joe.

"Oh, you'll hear soon enough, don't worry. It's code-word *Cromwell*, that's what it is."

He rushed into the office to deliver his news. It took

the officer two seconds flat to emerge. They were soon all fallen in in their ranks. The officer inspected. He told them — officially — that *Cromwell* had been received, and what it meant. Everyone knew, or thought they knew, that already. It meant the enemy were on the way. The invasion was coming — or had already started. The nervous excitement was like a current in the hall. No-one needed, or listened to, the captain's pep-talk. They stood to attention, hands tight round their rifles — and waited.

The sergeant was sent to phone someone. They were stood at ease. Time went by in nervous conversation. It was already obvious that no-one knew what was happening, and no-one knew what to do. The sergeant returned, and after a whispered conversation, it was the captain's turn to go off to the phone. The sergeant even gave them permission to smoke.

"We ought to go to our posts," Don told Bill, Tom and Fred, as they sat quietly in one corner.

"You're flipping eager to go and sit up all night in the cold," said Tom. "Anyway, we might be wanted somewhere else. We don't know where it's happened yet do we?"

"Well I'm on duty in an hour and a half's time," said Fred, the signalman. "And mine's war work. So I'm going then, Oliver Cromwell or not."

"You'll be shot as a deserter, mate," said Tom, but without the usual response. No-one was in the mood for any sort of repartee that evening. The news about the London raid had sounded bad enough, and now it seemed that everyone's worst fear was about to be realised, and the unthinkable really was about to happen. Had even happened already. The nervousness increased, as a whole hour dragged by. Finally the captain returned.

"Men, I'm sorry to tell you that there has been an error."

The groan was loud and angry. They had all expected something different, infinitely worse. The tension released in anger. Sensibly, the captain gave it a full minute to subside.

"I'm as annoyed about it was you are," he told them. "But we all know there's very little we can do about this sort of thing. So the best thing for all of us now is to get off home now and go to bed."

"Well the next time there's an alert, I'll be taking it with a pinch of salt, I can tell you," Don announced to Tom as they went out. "A mistake — after all that. — They don't know what they're doing half the time, those high-ups."

"I tell you what, mate," Tom answered. "I'm bloody glad it was a mistake. — 'Cause next time it might not be. Cheerio, now."

Don went home full of righteous indignation, fully agreed with by his mother.

"I'm not going to believe any more invasion talk until I see a German soldier with my own eyes," he told her.

Chapter 7

SEA LION

After the alarms and excursions of the day before, the British Admiralty was more than jumpy on 26th September. Coastal Command anti-invasion patrols had been doubled, and the great ships of the Home Fleet had no sooner arrived back in Rosyth than they were prepared for a second search. By mid-morning there were confirmed reports of a major German force in the Heligoland Bight. By noon the two battleships were at sea and making their best speed towards the distant German coast. But they were old, and comparatively slow. As soon as reports confirmed the enemy ships as cruisers and very large transports, the fast battle-cruiser *Hood* and her destroyers had left the *Nelson* and *Rodney* to race ahead towards the reported German position. *Hood's* 15-inch guns should be enough to deal with mere cruisers.

British plans were shaken almost at once. There had been another sighting — this time of a solitary heavy cruiser, identified as almost certainly the *Admiral Hipper*. She was east of the Shetland Islands and steaming south at full speed. Orders went out to *Hood* to intercept her. The ships of *Herbstreise* thus became the responsibility of *Nelson* and *Rodney*. The Admiralty had no reason to expect they would present two massive battleships with any problems, even without the additional support of the *Hood*. At the same time Bomber Command was alerted to be prepared to launch attacks on either the *Hipper* or the cruisers and transports; Thirteen Group of Fighter Command was ordered to be prepared to escort the bombers, at least for some of their trip out over the North Sea. The R.A.F. and the Royal Navy were both now implicitly assuming that they were dealing with a genuine invasion fleet. One flight of bombers did take off, from Wick in the North of Scotland, but failed to find the *Hipper* in the mists.

Farther south, Coastal Command's patrols were revealing even more alarming news as the day progressed. There was no doubt that massive troop movements were taking place on the Channel Coast, in the invasion ports themselves, and in the hinterland. There was now a constant forward movement as units came up into their positions ready for embarkation, while the advance troops were already filing in endless rows along the docksides into awaiting barges for a long and uncomfortable delay before they set sail for England. The bombers of the Luftwaffe were present over the Kent and Sussex Coasts, with Stukas to the fore in all the attacks. One raid penetrated as far as London, but otherwise enemy bomber activity was less than of late. The German fighters, though, were up in force. The skies over the Channel buzzed with Messerschmitts looking for someone to fight. They found them.

Churchill had ordered Bomber Command to make an all-out effort against the invasion ports. He realised that he was risking a great deal on such a throw, but he had to have precision daylight attacks on the enemy build-up, and that meant fighter escorts for the bomber wings. If he could disrupt the build-up, if he could buy a week or two of time, that might be enough. So Twelve Group was ordered to provide the fighter cover, precious little, but more than it could spare. — Nearly half of its operational strength. So the Whitleys, Halifaxes and Wellingtons took off from Bomber Command's fields in the heart of England to be met over the Home Counties by their inadequate escort of Hurricanes. Churchill had specifically ordered that *no* Spitfires could be spared.

The Luftwaffe encountered them before they had got across the English coast. Once again there was the snarl and crackle of dogfights over Kent and Sussex, and the people in the battered towns of the South Coast were heartened by the sight and sound, the spirals of smoke as planes went down, the brief sparkling flames of destruction. They cheered the British bombers lumbering southwards, to give the Nazis some of their own medicine, as they thought. — But it was the British fighters (outnumbered three to one) that bore the brunt of the losses in the air battle. The bombers for the most part managed to get across the Channel, but even before the bombs began to fall on the inviting targets below, the Me109s and 110s were diving out of the sky onto *their* prey. Some disruption was caused in the invasion ports, but it cost the British 41 bombers — that in addition to the 32 fighters lost. And many of the ports and assembly areas were not even hit.

The day wore on. The Home Fleet had not encountered *Herbstreise*, nor had *Hood* found *Hipper*. A day of frustration and failure at sea as well as in the air. In the afternoon the Admiralty ordered the battle-cruiser *Repulse* and the old "R" Class battleship *Revenge* to the Normandy coast. As night closed in, the darkness was broken by the flames of their 15-inch salvoes crashing down on the docks of Cherbourg. Farther north, *Nelson* and *Rodney* were steaming back across the North Sea, zigzagging partly to continue their search for the elusive German ships, partly to avoid submarines. They did not know that the liners had once again turned back into the safety of German waters, the deception played out with total success. Even the Führer did not know that their escorting cruisers had not returned to Germany, but on Raeder's personal orders were already making south for the Dutch coast. From there they would go on into the real invasion area, the English Channel. Farther north still, the *Hood* and the *Admiral Hipper* were both steaming south on parallel courses, each unaware of the other.

As the depleted forces of Bomber Command took off on their night-time sorties against invasion targets, and the expanded reconnaissance patrols of Royal Navy destroyers surged through the waters off the dark coastline of France, the news began to filter back to London. German transports and barges were putting out to sea. There were tugs hauling ungainly loads through the harbour mouths. Unlikely steamers and diverse motor vessels were congregating together, ready to form convoy and sail northward. S-boats were buzzing up and down along the coast at the eastern end of the Narrow Seas, while in the western passages German destroyers were visible en masse for the first time since the Norwegian campaign. Shots were exchanged at long range between British and German flotillas. Around midnight a British destroyer was torpedoed and sunk by a U-boat off the North Foreland. By the small hours of the morning of the 27th the warning signals were being heard loud and clear in London. It was already apparent that it was no drill being practised by the enemy. The signals were made all the louder by the uncanny silence of the skies over the capital. No German bomber came near that night. But far away to the south, the rumble of distant thunders told of the fate of the coastal towns as ton upon ton of high explosive rained down on them.

By two o'clock a vast expanse of the Channel was alive with the tiny shapes of the immense armada, dwarfed only by the sea itself, as the little ships crept forward under the moonlight towards the embattled shores of Britain. In the myriad transports, the cramped, tight-packed ranks of German soldiers sat silent, or joked, or prayed, each according to his temperament. The lucky ones could gaze out over the shimmering waters at the great fleet. The vast majority could only look at the tin walls of barges, dragged along behind their clanking tugs, with all hatches battened down.

The Prime Minister had been awakened, and he in turn had summoned the War Cabinet and the Chiefs of Staff to meet in the night. His hope that it was no more than an exercise faded by the second. Strategic Air Reserve and all squadrons in Twelve Group were put on full alert. Bomber Command was told to prepare for dawn attacks, aimed at targets in England. The destroyer force from Harwich, beefed up by cruisers, was ordered to sea. So were the remaining units in the Nore. *Repulse* and *Revenge* had already been active in mid-Channel, and would now be held ready at Portsmouth for deployment against the invasion force itself. *Nelson*, *Rodney* and *Hood* were also told to make all speed for the Naze, ready for deployment either in the Channel or the southern North Sea. For even now the mirage of invasion in East Anglia had still not wholly faded.

Out across the dark waters, the flotilla crept onwards. Over them, waves of bombers crossed in regular procession, as airborne bombardment of the invasion targets took the place of the conventional softening-up by artillery. The flak burst among the Dornier 17's and 215's, the Heinkel 111's and the Junkers 88's with little effect. The situation in Dover, Folkestone and Lewes was already beyond the control of local fire-fighting and civil defence forces. This would soon also be true in the great resort of Brighton. At 3.30 a.m. Churchill personally ordered the issue of the code word *Cromwell* in Kent, Sussex, Essex and Hampshire. This brought the Home Guard and all the regular forces of the Crown to the highest degree of alert. But its effect was greatly blunted by the false alarm of the day before.

The moon was still up and it was well before dawn. The planes of Bomber Command passed over the beacon fires of blazing towns that marked the coast, then descended rapidly towards the great scatter of tiny, insubstantial targets scattered over the wide sea. Theirs was a very different mission to that of their Luftwaffe counterparts whose targets were sprawling ill-defended towns. The British bomb aimers had to hit moving targets, widely spread out, grey against the grey sea. And they had to do it by moonlight. The decision to send the bombers out at once, rather than wait (as originally intended) for dawn, was based more on the overpowering need of Britain's warlords to 'do something' than strict strategic requirements.

Nevertheless, for all the difficulties, there were hits. The invasion fleet suffered its first casualties, as bombs ripped through the decks of transport steamers, scattering torn steel through the tight-packed press of helpless soldiers. Already one old river steamer from the Rhine was heeled over sinking slowly. Frantic, insignificant figures scrambled down her sloping decks, while others writhed and bled below as the waters rose to claim them. A second transport settled by the head, tugs and launches clustered around, lifeboats lurching into the water from tilted davits.

Even near misses could sink the thin-skinned barges, opening their rusty seams and prying loose their creaking rivets. More men in field grey struggled in the sudden chill of the waters, or watched their friends and companions, face-down and silent, moving up and down with the rising and falling swell. Where the barges suffered direct hits there were few to struggle and shout, and many to float with the tide towards the shores of England. The men in the bombers saw none of this, any more than the Luftwaffe aircrew knew of the neat houses and pleasant streets that their bombs were tearing apart, or heard the screams of the dying, or saw the staring faces of the dead. But the Luftwaffe could fly back to the airfields of conquered Europe conscious of purpose achieved. Bomber Command had done little more than take a passing slap at its target. As statistics, the casualties held no horrors for the German High Command.

Bombers were not the best weapon for that battle. As the planes returned, and the winking lights of German gunfire faded behind them, the British prepared a blow far more deadly to Nazi plans. For now, in the hour before dawn, the Germans were to come up against the often and hopefully ignored fact of British sea power. In the mouth of the Straits three lines of destroyers, each led by a cruiser, bore down on the invasion fleet.

Amidst the spreading mist, as the cloud covered the moon, out of Calais and the Belgian and Dutch ports, three flotillas of Germany's motor torpedo boats, the *Schnellboot*, came to meet the British ships. The engagement in the darkness was confused and bloody. The guns of the destroyers made what practice they could as the little boats rushed at them out of the night and fog. A hit meant destruction. One, then a second and a third blew up, and still they came on. In British despatches the Commodore commanding described the attack as "pressed home with the utmost courage, coolness and audacity".

The little ships came on. On, between the wreckage of their fellows, the blazing oil and the flowery trees of exploding ammunition. On, until at last they were near enough to fire their torpedos — those that were left. The fan of torpedos cut silent through the waves, as all eyes on the decks of the destroyers strained to catch sight of the tell-tale wakes. Searchlights flecked the waters with confusing trails of light as the destroyers turned to comb the wakes.

Some turned too late. Two hits and two destroyers crippled. One already down by the stern and burning. Two more hits, both on the flotilla leader. The cruiser shuddered to a stop in the water, and lay still as her six-inch guns continued to blaze in fury at the small craft which had crippled her. Then, for a moment or two, the night sky was dyed red, and the sea shone like a sheet of blood. From the manoeuvring destroyers and the turning, fleeing M.T.B.'s, men watched in awe. A second or two of silence for the stricken ship. Then the wave of sound hit them. *H.M.S. Sheffield*, nine thousand tons of warship, nearly six hundred feet long, had already capsized into the awaiting tomb of the waves. There were seven survivors.

Among the other squadrons the damage was almost as serious. The heroism of the German seamen had now cost them half of their own force, but it had inflicted a grave reverse on a much superior British force, and for the time being dispersed its attack. As the destroyers re-formed, their losses were two sunk and three crippled — and a cruiser sunk. The M.T.B.'s sped home to refuel. The destroyers plunged on towards the invasion fleet. It was still dark when they engaged.

Almost at once, another ship was put out of action, again by torpedo attack, but this time to an unseen assailant. The invasion fleet's U-boat screen had at least found one of its enemies. Not so the Luftwaffe. In the darkness and mist the Stukas and the larger Messerschmitts, the Me 110's, were not very effective. Dive-bombing itself was an immensely chancy business in those conditions. There was also the constant risk of bombing or strafing their own vessels, a risk not always avoided. For a while, the fight tipped in favour of the British.

The Royal Navy began to sink the invasion fleet, the guns of destroyers and cruisers cutting swathes through the fragile barges. Men, tanks, guns — all went to the bottom. The German High Command had anticipated a hideous attrition of the invading army. In the brief minutes before dawn, their expectations were thoroughly fulfilled.

Then dawn brought the Stukas and their fighter cover back in full force. Visibility was still poor, but the Luftwaffe were making an all-out effort, regardless of risk and losses. Three more destroyers were hit, one of them forced out of the action. Another of the cruisers, a smaller ship, *H.M.S. Cardiff*, had a bomb go off just forward of the bridge, her captain and officers killed. Only the most northerly of the three British lines of ships had been relatively unscathed, but the destroyer force had punched right through the heart of the invasion fleet. New orders now reached them — to continue westward to Portsmouth, and there join the forces under the command of Vice-Admiral Whitworth, the victor of Narvik. During the night Whitworth's two battleships, *Repulse* and *Revenge* had been active off the Normandy Coast, their mere presence sufficient to frighten a German destroyer flotilla back into Cherbourg. Now Whitworth's flag was strengthened by the cruisers and destroyers that had punched so effectively through the Straits, and another cruiser from Plymouth. It was a formidable force.

Already the intervention of the Royal Navy had wrought havoc in the first wave of the invasion. But the damage was selective. The British had missed altogether the vessels conveying 17 and 35 Divisions towards Dungeness and Hythe, though some of their transports were to be attacked by the R.A.F. later in the day. 7th Division and 1st Mountain Division were punished far worse. Nearly half their transports had been damaged, and very many of them sunk. The command structure had gone, and so had much of the available armour and artillery, particularly that of 1st Mountain. Generalleutnant Ludwig Kubler, its divisional commander, crossing with the first wave contrary to orders, was dead, and with him the entire divisional staff. A large number of the transports had been driven many miles off course in their attempt to escape the British ships. Some had crossed into the Ninth Army sector. Some even found themselves beyond Beachy Head.

The Generals were still in the dark when dawn came on *S-Tag*. Busch, Commander of Sixteenth Army, already knew that something approaching a disaster had befallen two of his divisions, and that a potentially catastrophic gap might now exist in the very centre of the invasion front. He had passed the news to C.-in-C. Army Group A, von Rundstedt. Rundstedt told him that there was no way to abort now. It was unthinkable. Busch urged him to telephone Hitler at Giessen. Busch wasn't to know that von Rundstedt had just been listening to half an hour of Hitler ranting over the phone.

Raeder had called on the Führer in person — he was also at Giessen — as soon reports reached *him* that things were going ill. Hitler was not interested in the heroism of the torpedo boats, or the reported sinking of a 'battleship'. He reacted only to the destruction — worse in fact than he was told — wrought on the invasion fleet. In his rage he sacked Raeder (only to re-instate him later in the day). He summoned Goering from his bed and ordered him to get the whole of the Luftwaffe airborne over the Channel. Finally he vented his wrath over the phone to von Rundstedt. In Hitler's fury the general detected a note of rising panic. The events of the night had sounded like the prophecies of "that cowardly know-all" Raeder; and had not Raeder asked at once for cancellation? The Führer paused, and then, in a quieter tone asked von Rundstedt,

"Can it be called off?"

The General answered,

"It cannot, my Führer. The first troops have already landed."

Chapter 8

THE GREAT SALT SEA

Adolf was almost physically sick with the excitement. It was not just fear, or even apprehension — though they were both part of it as he knew well enough. He had felt afraid before, but he could cope with it. It was not even the cold logical truth (sat irrevocably at the back of his mind — and often pushing itself nearer to the front) that by tomorrow there was an even chance he would be dead. There might have been some ancestral Teutonic battle-lust, which combined with arrogance of race, confidence of superiority and pride of youth to fill his heart and lungs to bursting, and to choke the back of his throat. For he, Adolf Friedrich Mann, was one of that happy chosen few. He was now, at this moment, marching to conquer England.

Well, not marching. He grinned at his own thoughts, deflating their pomposity, but not abating their hold on him. In fact he was sitting in the gloom of a decrepit barge of tin-plate and crumbling concrete, swaying alarmingly to the thunderous chugging of the tug-boat's labouring engine; also grinding against another barge; also full of nervous, sweating, exhilarated men. Metal grated again, and rust crumbled from a bulkhead.

"At this rate we'll be sunk before we've even started", said the blond, ever-grinning Willi who sat next to him. He shifted his awkward frame in the cramped space. Adolf grinned back at him, hoping the tension wasn't showing in his eyes the way it was in Willi's.

"This is nothing." Ernst Hartmann leaned over towards them. He was not one of their group. Too much of a moaner, and unlike the rest of them he meant his moaning. "You wait till we're out in the Channel. Then there'll be a few bumps and grinds." He sniggered. "You know that the tug is pulling three barges, all in a row. Talk about incompetence."

"When we want your expert opinion, we'll ask for it," interrupted Rudi, sat on Adolf's other side. " — Hallo, here's 'Heini'. We'll hear something now."

Captain Stein was smiling between his pulled-down cap and turned-up collar. His greatcoat was drenched. Only the officers had the doubtful privilege of going onto the flat, low deck, over which the merest ripples sent a constant spray. The barges were not sea-going craft, and now they were experiencing the first of the Channel swells.

"Right, men, I want you to listen carefully." He was almost shouting above the myriad noises of the groaning barge. "We are now clear of Calais harbour, and making good headway into the English Channel. — It is therefore time to reveal to you your part in this great operation, called by the codename *Seelowe*. As you know, the Hundredth Grenadierregiment and First Mountain Division are part of VII Corps. I can now tell you that we have the honour to hold a key position in the centre of the assault. Furthermore, we are among the troops of the First Wave. We will be among the first German soldiers to set foot on the soil of England."

"Divisional objective is the area of coastline from Rye Bay, west of the great promontory of Dungeness to the town called St. Leonard's. You have all studied the maps of the English coast. All N.C.O.'s will now be issued with detailed maps of our own objective. Hundredth Infantry will land at the western end of the sector in the town of Hastings, and beneath the nearby cliffs. Our company has drawn the short straw, as you would expect. We have the cliffs, not the town. Our immediate objective, once we have got to the top, is to swing round behind the town and assist our comrades making the frontal assault. You will find the countryside hilly, with many small areas of woodland. But the hills do not compare with what's in our practice area. Once the coastal positions have been secured, the whole division will be advancing on a north-westerly axis into the hill country known as the Weald. I want you all to study the maps carefully when they are given out."

He paused and looked around at the attentive faces.

"All troops of the Wehrmacht are being given a clear picture of our intentions, as a sign of the confidence which the High Command of the Army places in every single German soldier. Do not think for a moment that this will be an easy fight. It is not the Poles or the French we are fighting. It is a Germanic nation defending its own soil. These people came originally from Germany. They are no untermenschen. They are the first real test of our mettle. Fighting will be hard and bitter. I know that you will conduct yourselves in that fighting like soldiers of the Wehrmacht and men of the German Reich."

There was no applause, only a low rumble of approval, only the glint in the eyes of men, sparked off by the images their young officer evoked. One of them began to sing, and one after another they were all joining in, the captain, the grizzled old sergeant at his side, the lieutenants, everyone:

> "Our flag floats above as we march on our way,
> The badge of our Fatherland's might,
> No longer we Germans shall suffer the day
> When the Englishman laughs at its sight;
> So give me your hand, your lovely white hand,
> 'Ere we sail to the conquest of Eng-el-land!"

Then they cheered, as the barge rolled and bucked in the choppy waves, and the labouring tug turned westward up the Channel. In the distance came the first clatter of gunfire. Time passed. The men studied the maps obediently. There had been little shooting. The whole journey began to take on an unreal quality. Though the captain had not spoken of the dangers of the crossing, no-one had forgotten them. "Where are the British?" The thought flickered in Adolf's mind. "Where is their navy?" Sergeant Schmidt clattered heavily down from the deck.

"It's going well up there lads, damned well," he yelled. "Lots of planes over — all ours though. For once those lazy swines of airmen are up there doing their stuff." Everyone laughed. Sgt. Schmidt's dislike of the pampered Luftwaffe was a standing joke.

"There's no British airforce left, Sarge, not even to give us a firework display to welcome us over," someone called out. It wasn't even a joke, but it got more anxious laughter from the tense, eager young men.

"You can keep your trap shut, soldier. You'll see there are enough fireworks to welcome you when we get there. And you lot won't think it's so funny then, I'll tell you that for certain. Oh yes, the first taste of action'll soon sort out the men from the boys."

"Are any of our blokes ashore yet?" Rudi called out.

"Now how would I know that, you blockhead?" Schmidt answered. "Do I have telescopes on my eyes, eh? I can tell you this though, we've run through a big bank of mist up above, and it's my opinion that that's the reason we haven't seen the British navy yet. There's some shooting up north of us, so we may still get our share, though. — Don't be too eager for it, my lucky lads. We'll have more than our fair share of it, if you ask me. We've come out of the mist now, and there's a moon up. The last quarter, thank God, so not too bright. But you can see our fleet by its light, boys, like a lot of little black beetles crawling about on a sheet of steel."

"You're a poet, Sarge," came a catcall.

"You'll get my boot up your backside, soldier, if you aren't careful," growled the Sergeant. "I've never yet heard of a poet that wasn't a queer. And there's no poetry to me like the sound of a machine gun."

He clattered off up the ladder again. Adolf glanced at his watch. It was nearly three o'clock. They had been at sea for over four hours. Obviously they would not be making any great speed. How far away was the English coast? Were they half way across yet? Were they almost there? He knew that the crossing before the war hadn't taken long, but that had been Calais to Dover. They were going farther west. How much farther he wasn't sure.

He had a fair idea which of the English towns was Hastings, their objective. He knew Dungeness was one of the bits of the coast that stuck out, but he wasn't sure which of them. The map given to their corporal had just shewn the operational objectives. It was all very well O.K.H. coming clean to the poor bloody infantry now, but why hadn't the men been allowed to know more, been shewn proper maps — trusted more? They were none of them fools. Germany's excellent educational system had seen to that. And they were all true Germans, every one a member of the Herrenvolk. Still, there had to be proper military security. He dismissed his momentary annoyance, recognising its origins in his own apprehension.

He still wished he knew more about their opponents. Some of the men said that the British had been no better than the French as fighting soldiers. They had been pushed out of Norway and France easily enough. Then, there were also stories about their powers of resistance. And there were more than stories about the British navy. Like everyone on that barge, and like everyone in that great poorly armed and weakly defended armada, the thought of the battlefleet of Britain was ever present. But they had been told the Luftwaffe would handle the British fleet.

There came a sudden burst of automatic fire, far nearer than before. All of them ducked, instinctively. The rattle that followed was their own deck-mounted machine gun, the barge's only protection. The sergeant came down the steps at a slide this time, stumbling and shouting as he came.

"Get those helmets on, you men! Now! Off the seats, and crouched down. All of you! Get a move on! You'd rather get your backsides wet than have them shot off, wouldn't you?"

"Well, this is it," muttered Rudi, as they crouched into the cramped spaces awash with dirty water.

"It's the enemy airforce, if you ask me," said Hans Stumpf, another of Adolf's group of associates. "Can't you get that rifle butt out of my ribs, Mann?"

More machine gun fire — and then the deeper, slower crump and crash. The shaking of the barge as shock waves through the water caught it. Again the thud and roar, already nearer than a moment before. Not the guns of the famous and feared Spitfires, not even the explosions of bombs. This was the sound of naval guns, big guns. And it sounded like a number of them — several ships firing salvoes. Adolf looked into the face of Hans next to him, and saw how frightened he was. The other faces, half hidden in the erratic light, were the same. Suddenly the fear had gripped him too, tighter than a hand on his throat. He couldn't breathe. He wanted to be sick. He wished to God he could only *see* what was happening.

The roar and crash that followed was deafening. The barge seemed to be lifted out of the water, and then flung back again. The men inside bounced against the walls and bulkheads, were flung against the benches. Adolf cracked his arm on a seat, and felt momentarily dizzy with the pain. He saw another man with blood on his face.

"Get out quick!"

"We've been hit!"

" . . . taking water!"

The shouts and bits of shouts echoed amid the chaos, and outside the crump and thud of those guns was repeating itself, again and again. Endless thunder crashing overhead, and sparks of light in the darkness. Darkness, for the feeble light bulbs inside the barge had gone out. Flashes of light, for there was a great rent in the fragile crumbling concrete that made up most of the hull. Adolf saw it above his head, reached up and felt the edges of the yawning hole, warm from the impact, a yard wide, and yards long. Through it the sounds of battle came more clearly, but none of them yet knew what was happening. They were close to genuine panic, when the torch light flickered from the hatchway.

The beam played round, over them. They quietened down at once. For a moment the beam was carefully shone onto the face of the man holding the torch, Captain Stein — 'Heini'. The men waited.

"Stay down on the deck for the time being, men. If there is anyone badly hurt near you, bring him aft to me. All of you check first to see if anyone is unconscious . . . "

A silence, while they looked. It seemed a miracle, but there was nothing more than cuts and bruises. They began to talk again. The captain went back up, and after a while one of the corporals came down.

"What happened, Corp.?" As usual it was Rudi asking the questions, with all the cheek of a twenty-two year-old veteran.

"It's not us that's hit. The barge on the end of the line was." The man's voice shook. Anger not fear. "Most of the lads on it are gone. Those British bastards have got about fifty destroyers out, if you ask me. The water's full of our men. It's shrapnel from the other barge that got us. Two of the lieutenants are dead up top. Schmidt's dead. And our navy and our airforce is nowhere . . . "

"That'll do, Corporal Brandt!"

It was the captain again. The corporal stood, fists clenched, minus cap, his great-coat smeared with oil and dirt, blood on his hands and soaking into the sleeve. Then he sat down abruptly on one of the benches. He was a steady man, normally, never given to shouting and ranting.

"I've served with the sergeant for twelve years, sir," they all heard him say.

Captain Stein reached the bottom of the ladder, and looked around at the men. His face was drawn too, the lines in it clearer, stubble on his chin and suddenly a grey rim round his eyes. The image of the Master Race trembled in the balance in all their hearts.

"You've heard the news. If you're surprised, then you're fools. This is war, not a game. You all know the British have the largest navy in the world, and our navy didn't exist ten years ago. There will be heavy losses, and this is just the start of them. So stop snivelling like half grown kids! The British ships have withdrawn — and the reason is *our* airforce. Two of their ships are on the bottom. But the rest will be back, and some will get through, however good our air cover. So some of our men will be killed. They're soldiers. It's their job. You are soldiers too. It's your job. So shape up! Keep low — and if we're hit, be ready to get on deck quickly. That's all!"

He didn't give them a second look. He didn't need to. His words had done the trick. Training, and the mode of thought in which they had all been brought up, reasserted itself. Adolf saw the shamefaced glances towards poor Corporal Brandt, half sorry for him, half angry at his outburst — because it had shaken them all so deeply. He realised that it had shaken him too. He realised that what the captain had said was true, and it was no game. The first light touch of the realities of war had left him disturbed and uncertain. At the first return of gunfire he jumped inches off the deck. So did most of the others. They were nervous and jumpy, all now wearing their steel helmets. Fingering their rifles which they knew were less than useless against the steel warships out there in the darkness.

The distant reverberations of naval guns began to draw nearer again. The captain had come down once more to tell them that they had altered course to try to avoid the worst of the attack. The return of the gunfire dashed their hopes. Again the barge shook in the surging sea. There was also the drone of planes, and then the whistle of bombs falling. It couldn't be far away. Were they German bombs perhaps, hitting British ships? But the crash of the shell bursts was ever nearer. Once, amid them, an explosion. A blaze of light through the rent in the barge's thin, torn skin. Now they could all recognise the unmistakable scream of the Stuka. The whispers went round once more.

"We're fighting back now."

"The Luftwaffe will give those swines hell!"

"Wait till they get a bloody Stuka down their funnels!"

And finally the crash so loud that it couldn't really be heard at all, only felt with the whole body. Again the sensation of the barge being lifted up from the water, but as it fell back it seemed that it was falling apart. The screech of metal sheering as the stanchions broke, and the grinding of collapsed concrete. Jagged edges in the air, and the screaming of men. Blinding light followed by utter darkness, with water pouring in where half of the landing ramp had been ripped away.

"Out! Out! Everyone, get out!"

At first the shouting didn't register on Adolf's consciousness. He heard it, and the blowing of a whistle, repeated and irritating, as if from a distance. It didn't seem to mean anything. Then he felt Rudi's hand on his shoulder, fingers digging in.

"Move, Adolf, move! We've got to get out!"

'We're sinking."

He said it more to himself than to Rudi, trying to give meaning to the fact by uttering the words. But he followed Rudi in the press of men, stepping over other men. He saw one lad crying, another with blood on his tunic, pale-faced but with his lips tight closed. He saw the staring-eyed face of Ernst Hartmann, looking up into emptiness, dead and already forgotten. His comrades, those who had liked him, those who had hated him, those who had despised him, all stepped over him, and his wide eyes watched them pass.

Adolf stared back at the blank face he had so disliked earlier, and remembered the whining voice of the man who was no longer a man. He felt no pity or regret. It wasn't really that lousy, moaning swine, Hartmann, who lay there. It was something else. And Hartmann was still alive in a past more immediate and real than the shadowy present in which he, Adolf, and the others moved in a state of shock. He felt his hands on the greasy metal of the rail, realised that the hatchway was twisted out of shape, squeezed through it, pushing his rifle before him and almost fell forward onto the deck. Rudi again jerked him upright. He thought:

"Rudi can cope. He is taking it better than me. — But I am still calm. Perhaps I *am* in shock. Why didn't I realise this is how it would be?"

"Get those life jackets inflated!"

He obeyed the order automatically, noticing for the first time that his legs were braced against the slant of the deck. More men pushed against him. The deck was crowded with men, shuffling forward away from the hatch. They were trying to drag out the wounded now, and the dead. He looked away. He did not want to see Hartmann again. One side of the deck had water lapping at it. Yes, they were sinking. He felt fear again, and the paralysis of will left him.

"Down this way, Rudi!"

He pulled his friend. Rudi grinned at him. Adolf realised he could see his face — and there was Hans too, behind him. The sky was rapidly lightening. It was dawn, the morning of Friday 27th September, the day he should have set foot in England.

The three of them edged down towards the water that spilled out onto the flat deck. He looked up. There were no planes except far away. He could see other barges, but they were moving away from them. The towline between their own barge and the tug was gone, the tug itself nowhere to be seen. They were abandoned on the great salt sea. And dark to the north was the long humped shape of the land, enemy soil, the grim grey cliffs of bloody England.

"Those nearest the starboard — the right side — don't hang about. Into the water with you, lively now!" One of the few sailors aboard the barge was yelling.

"That's us mates," said Hans.

The three of them clasped hands, and stepped off into the sea.

Adolf forgot to shut his mouth, and the mouthful of water he swallowed was saltier than he could ever have imagined. He came up spitting and choking and coughing. As he came up, he realised how bitterly cold it was. His whole body was shivering already from the shock of it. He could feel his toes going numb. He could feel the weight of his boots, then the sodden weight of his uniform. He must get those boots off. Then he realised that in his left hand was a waterlogged and useless rifle, weighing a seeming ton. He laughed aloud as he threw it away from him.

113

"Adolf, you're a raving bloody lunatic," came Rudi's voice.

They both laughed, and more sour water slopped into their mouths.

There were men everywhere in the water. He felt a swirl and suction below him, and for a moment the panic returned. — But the old battered barge had already gone, slipping softly into the deeps. He looked back over the oily waves where the barge had been. He saw other dark, hunched shapes, long and low, like the land away to the north, but flickering with intermittent fires, sudden bursts of orange followed later by the thunder of the guns and the distant scream of the shells. These must be the British ships, the implacable enemy that had swept their ancient tub full of landlubbers away like a toy in a boating pond, and were now showing the rest of the Wehrmacht a different blitzkrieg. These were Britain's panzers.

"Cruiser!" yelled Rudi. He spat and spluttered as drifting oil clung to his face. "That's not just a destroyer there, boys. The smaller one might be, but that's a damned great cruiser!"

Adolf twisted himself round in the water to where Rudi was trying to point. Both ships looked huge to him, and they were nearing fast, the massive bulk of the cruiser, with its three fuming funnels, cutting the water so that great churning white bow waves were thrown up along her tall dark hull. Yet another destroyer came into sight behind the cruiser.

"Oh my God!" yelled Adolf. "They'll ride right over us!"

For a moment he thought of the myriad little shapes the sergeant had described to them, the tugs and barges and lighters of Germany's tin-pot armada. He remembered that the sergeant was already dead. The dream of the panzer armies and their blitzkrieg seemed a long way away on the plains of Poland and France. Many others as well as Adolf realised it then. For out there, on the endless plain of the bitter, salt sea it was those dark ships that counted for everything. Beside them the landsman's efforts were a puny shaking of the fist.

He and Hans and Rudi swam, desperately fighting to make their way through the slimy, numbing waves, struggling to get their heavy army boots off. Even when they had succeeded they were still pulled down by the weight of their greatcoats. Adolf felt icy cold, and more and more weary every minute that they spent in the water. The British ships swept past — a few hundred yards away. Hans and Rudi began to wave and shout. Then came the rattle of machine guns and the flashes from the deck of one of the destroyers.

'They're shooting our men, Rudi! They're shooting them in the water!"

Adolf's voice, hoarse with the salt water and the struggle to stay alive was almost a scream. The horror of it filled him. Helpless in the water he watched while others, as helpless, as defeated, as entitled to rescue and succour, were murdered by a ruthless and monstrous enemy.

The ships drew farther away. The sky was completely light now, but from the sea Adolf could make out little. The rising and falling waves were strewn with debris. There were men shouting, but the voices drifted away or died. The only constant was the dismal line of the English coast along which the current was drawing them as if in mockery. Though Adolf had not been close enough to see the men in the sea die, the imagined images of their death remained before his eyes.

Planes went by, a long way to the east, very many of them. They were flying towards England, so they were German planes. The weight of water seemed to be dragging him down now. He was sure he was floating lower in the water. Fears that the life jacket was deflating, that it would not hold him afloat, preyed on his mind. None of the three young men spoke any more, each concentrating on his own battle for survival. There came more planes, directly overhead. Stukas this time, thirty or more, with no sign of fighter cover. Though they knew these were their own side, they did not dare to wave, and the pilots gave no sign that they had seen them.

There were more boats too as the sun came up, bright through the flags of mist, and then a squadron of large motor boats, rushing from behind, near to them — very near. It was Adolf who dared to wave and shout. If they were not German, it was only a question of bringing inevitable death an hour or two sooner, and in his numbed weariness he did not mind that. One of the boats swung nearer, until it was so close that they could see the faces of the men aboard, grey uniforms crowding the deck. They saw the dark blue of the Kriegsmarine on the bridge, and the officer point to them. The helm went over, and the boat veered in, slowing to a crawl.

The three found their strength again now from somewhere, clutching at the boathooks as many hands dragged them aboard. The moments of the rescue remained unclear in Adolf's mind. He remembered hugging Rudi and Hans, someone yanking off the life jackets and uniforms, a flask of schnapps pressed to his lips, choking on the burning liquid. He remembered stammering out the story to a general — half-recognized as such by the red flashes on his collar — telling him his unit and the regiment — and what had happened to it. He remembered wondering,

"What is a general doing here? Why are there so many officers — high ranking officers?"

"Well, sonny, you've landed on your feet," one of the matelots told him, as he and Rudi and Hans were wrapped in blankets, while the boat sped on its way again. "This here is forward H.Q. of 28 Division. We're on our way to Brighton Bay — a bit late in the year for swimming parties though." He laughed at his own joke.

"What about our regiment, the Hundredth?" Adolf asked.

"From what I've heard, your lot — the Mountain Division isn't it? — was badly chopped up last night. The bloody Luftwaffe were in the wrong bloody place. We picked up another one of yours, but he died as soon as he got on board — no more than five minutes before we found you." He gestured at the wrapped shape on the floor of the cabin. None of them had asked about it before. Now Hans went over and lifted back the edge of the blanket. Adolf heard his own voice say,

"His name is Willi Müller. We knew him. He was in our platoon. He must have drifted down with the current like us . . . He was one of us you see." He covered Willi's face again. "Thank you for pulling him out of the sea."

"I'm sorry," said the sailor, and there was nothing more to say.

"What will happen to us now?"Adolf asked, pushing the latest image of horror out of his mind.

"You're with the General Staff now, friend." The sailor let the bitterness in his voice express what the three soldiers could not. "You might as well be on the General Staff and running the show, for all the bleeding mess they've made of this shambles."

Chapter 9

FIGHT ON THE BEACHES

In the darkness before dawn, out of the sky billowed the opening white shapes of hundred upon hundred of parachutes. The men and equipment of Seven Parachute Division drifted down upon the silent countryside of Kent. The airmen high above peered through squinting eyes, trying to pierce the darkness and the mists in the hollows, searching out their landmarks. They were looking for the Folkestone to Ashford railway, and south of it the Royal Military Canal. Then as the ground rose to form the North Downs they should see the north–south line, running dead straight, of the ancient Roman road of Stone Street. At the southern apex of the triangle formed by road and railway, on the coast itself, lay the little, blacked-out town of Hythe. This was where the dropping zone began. To the east fires leapt skywards, marking the site of the wrecked port and town of Folkestone, pounded continuously for days by the Luftwaffe. But Hythe itself was wreathed in the spreading sea mists. The planes over-shot, and the drop began some miles farther inland.

The first German soldiers to set foot in Great Britain landed in and around the village of Lyminge, nestling in its little valley amidst the Downs. The paratroops were fired on from the ground as they came down. One or two were even shot. There was momentary panic and dismay, for a German paratrooper drops separately from virtually all his equipment. However, it became apparent almost at once that these were not regular troops, nor were they in any force. There was a brisk and conclusive engagement, as more and more Germans descended from the skies. Soon most of the men of the Home Guard of the little village lay dead or wounded, tended by the paratroops' field medics.

In their homes, some slept through the invasion of England. Others huddled in their air-raid shelters, staring up, pale-faced in fear of terrors to come, at the young, tall men of the Wehrmacht, who gazed in on them — and then went away again. Within an hour of the first soldier landing the Southern Railway branch line and the two B roads that ran north to Canterbury had been cut. Units were already pushing tentatively down the railway towards Folkestone. There was some fighting in the streets of other half-awakened Downland villages, but not much. It all seemed very strange to the Germans.

Similar experiences were met with by the paratroops who managed to land farther south from the second flight of aircraft. British regular troops of the 1st Battalion, London Rifle Brigade were encountered on the Royal Military Canal, but not in sufficient strength to prevent both banks being seized at several points. — By a strange chance up till a week before these very troops had been stationed at Lyminge, until divisional command decided to use them to beef up the coastal forces at Hythe. Again localized resistance from Home Guard units was fierce but limited.

One group of Germans, landing by accident too far to the west, had the good fortune to find themselves astraddle the important lateral railway link from Hastings to Ashford at an obscure but useful road junction called Ham Street — and the ill fortune to find that it was held by 18th Batallion, Royal Fusiliers. There was fierce fighting, slowly swinging in favour of the Germans as more men landed in the vicinity. Captured almost at once, on the other hand, was the former Fighter Command airfield at Lympne. The runway was still cratered by the bombs of the Luftwaffe, and all facilities destroyed — but far from adding to the wreckage with suitable mining and demolition charges, the British had been engaged on repairing the landing strip.

Excited messages were relayed from platoons and companies, and 7 Para's Divisional H.Q. formed a picture of a successful initial assault. But the fact was that the paratroops had fallen in a very dispersed area, over nearly *fifty* square miles. They had failed altogether to land in Hythe, their prime objective. Their command structure was in some confusion, and they would be in no position to hold onto any of their gains without speedy and continuing reinforcement.

Directly south of 7 Para's dropping zone, the first troops were wading ashore in the pale light of an early dawn up the long, curved beaches that stretched from Hythe down to Dungeness. Machine gun fire from British positions began as soon as the barges first loomed out of the mist. The coastal batteries of the Royal Artillery which should have ripped apart the fragile craft before they neared the beaches were fatally hampered by the fog, and German losses from their heavy guns were slight. Nevertheless, barges were hit, and Germans were left struggling in the water. Some of the tugs stopped engines too far out, wary of the artillery. These units had had only the merest of brushes with the Royal Navy and the R.A.F. in the night, but everyone was jumpy. Radio messages for Luftwaffe support jammed the air waves. The messsage that returned from unit H.Q.'s on the Continent was unequivocal: "Get in close and land at whatever cost. Air cover to follow."

The tugs began to drag their unwieldy charges in under the crackling machine guns, exposing themselves more clearly to the greater menace of the artillery. Then a great mass of field grey, steel-helmeted men was swaying and stumbling, sometimes swimming, through the gentle breakers onto the beaches of England. Many had still been landed too far out. They did not make it. Unloading any sort of equipment in those first minutes was a nightmare. There were more hits from the artillery emplacements concealed in the low sandhills. The cries of the wounded rose above the interminable small arms fire. One of the tugs blew up in a spectacular explosion, the ammunition loaded on her deck hit by a British shell. And on the beaches, the machine guns in their pill boxes and martello towers, in their concealed dugouts and prepared positions, cut through the struggling German infantry like swaths through standing corn.

But once they were on the move, once they were out of the cramped, blind holds of the barges, once they had breasted the waves and reached the shore, the discipline and training of the German army re-asserted itself. Chaos or not, there were grey-clad figures making it through the murderous rain of automatic fire. Racing from cover to cover, what little there was on the open beaches, stumbling over the bloodstained bodies of their comrades. The Germans also began to return fire from the barges, and even from the beaches themselves. The first of the specially adapted amphibian tanks began to swim or crawl ashore — those that did not sink at once. Even a few tanks made a great deal of difference, not least to morale.

Fierce little hand-to-hand combats developed in the scrubland and the dunes which shaded imperceptibly into the marshland beyond. The *Pilot Inn*, near Dungeness, was defended for an hour by thirty men against nearly a thousand. The sea wall north of the little village of Dymchurch was approached by the Germans over a mound of bodies, and then crowned by other dead, this time clad in khaki. The infantrymen and machine gunners of the Somerset Light Infantry had made their enemy pay dearly for the position. In Dymchurch itself the fighting raged down the burning street. At New Romney the Somersets were able to fall back on an armoured train — almost a piece of British whimsy, for it ran on a narrow-gauge seaside line. Yet, steaming back and forth from the village station, its machine-guns and AA cannon at maximum depression pinned down substantial forces, until it too succumbed to the Stukas.

The Luftwaffe's promise of early support was not fulfilled until well after 6 a.m. When it came, the force was considerable, in view of the limited strength of the British opposition. By eight o'clock, the tide had turned for the

invaders and was running fast in their favour. 35 Division
had established its H.Q. in the battered British military
camp at Lydd. A giant swastika had been raised on the
coastguard station at Dungeness, above the captured R.A.
battery — a victory signal to later waves of invaders. The
three British battalions defending that part of the coastline
had been wiped out.

On the outskirts of Hythe, at the other end of the sector,
the situation was rather different. Another British battalion
had been overwhelmed by the strength of the attack — this
time the Buffs. The Royal Military Canal and its
accompanying road were already in the hands of the Paratroops, and by eight o'clock German 17 Division was
already funnelling troops across to strengthen the vast but
weakly-held salient taken in the pre-dawn airborne landings. All direct westward communications out of Folkestone
and Hythe were cut, but the towns themselves had not
fallen. Hythe itself was rapidly developing into the centre
of a bloody and sustained conflict.

The British held the town in force from a secure perimeter stretching from the martello towers on the beaches
up through the village of Saltwood onto the Downs. Initial
German attempts to drive up from the beaches directly had
been repulsed with heavy losses to the invaders. Surviving
barges and other transports were diverted farther west to
already secure positions, as the Germans attempted to build
up sufficient strength to push into the town from the landward. Inside the perimeter, the defenders began to suffer
a systematic hammering from the Luftwaffe. 1st London
Division, under Major General Liardet, was entrusted with
the very forefront of the British defence. Its troops stood
along the coast, facing the occupied continent. The beleag-
ured garrison of Hythe constituted its right flank.

By breakfast time on the morning of the 27th, General
Liardet was already facing a dilemma. He knew that landings had occurred all along the coast on his right, and that
the thinly spread troops along the beaches to Dungeness
had been swept away, as the Germans established a substantial bridgehead, perhaps ten miles long and already five or

six miles deep in places. He also knew that there had been a substantial air drop north of him, that it was continuing, and that the Germans were in some measure at least in command of the heights behind his own coastal positions. Finally, he knew that the enemy paratroops and the sea-borne forces had made contact. He was *not* aware that the airborne troops were very widely scattered, and did not yet constitute a coherent force.

The question facing him was should he move west in force, relieve the pressure on his right flank, and attempt to clear the important A20 road and the main line railway to Ashford. This would drive a wedge between the paratroops and the rest of the invading army and open a route for reinforcement to reach him. However, if he did so, he ran the risk of leaving the vital objectives of Folkestone and Dover fatally denuded of troops in the face of possible further landings from the sea or air. He was not of course to know that no such landings were envisaged by the enemy. He chose the path of caution. He reinforced his right flank, but only with the minimum necessary to hold the perimeter, and sent an urgent request for full support to the New Zealand Division, lying directly behind his position.

East of Dungeness forces of the Wehrmacht in the sector from Rye Bay to Hastings had encountered the full wrath of the Royal Navy. Up to a quarter of 7 Division's transports had been sunk, forced to turn back, or so thoroughly dispersed as to be unavailable in the first wave's assault. Over a half of 1st Mountain Division's first wave troops had suffered the same fate, a scale of attrition far in excess of even the gloomiest of O.K.H. prognostications. Furthermore, 1st Mountain had lost virtually all its command structure. Even as the first troops plunged into the icy sea and waded or swam for the shore, Sixteenth Army Commander Busch was issuing orders for the combination of the two divisions under the intact command structure of 7 Division. A corps had been reduced to a division before a single one of its soldiers had set foot in England.

The disorganized landing was met in strength by British 45 Division. 7 Division found itself fighting every inch of the way across the low ground on either side of the River Rother towards Rye and Winchelsea. The two ancient Cinque Ports were defended as fiercely as ever they had been against the French in forgotten wars of earlier centuries. The immediate beach defences were in German hands by sun-up. Progress beyond was limited, despite the appearance, with the rising sun, of the full force of the Luftwaffe. Twice the invaders were repulsed from Rye by the Royal Irish Fusiliers.

In Hastings and St. Leonard's an even more bloody struggle developed. Major General Schreiber, bearer of a German name but commander of British 45th Infantry Division, had set himself the task of holding onto Hastings come what may. His resolve was strengthened by a telegram from the Prime Minister direct. Churchill was keenly aware of the significance of the events of 1066 in British folklore. He was determined that no new conqueror should gain his victory at Hastings. The rocks and pebbles, interspersed with wooden groynes, of the narrow beaches provided little cover for the remnants of 1st Mountain Division that swarmed up them. They wilted under the disciplined fire of the Devonshire Regiment, and the heavier assaults of the artillery of the coastal battery. Those few invaders that got into the town found every rat-run of a street enfiladed by snipers high in windows and on rooftops. There were three hours of mounting losses in troops, equipment, and, most serious of all, invasion barges. Then the battered men of 1st Mountain were withdrawn from the beaches and the sea-wall. The Battle of Hastings, such as it was, had gone to the British.

The units of 1st Mountain which scaled the cliffs to the east of the town had better fortune at first. They had been well trained for their task, and the British resistance was less concentrated and less determined. A small but significant beach-head was established and consolidated. Contact was made with 7 Division. But their day of disasters was not yet over. Out of nowhere, and largely unhoped for by

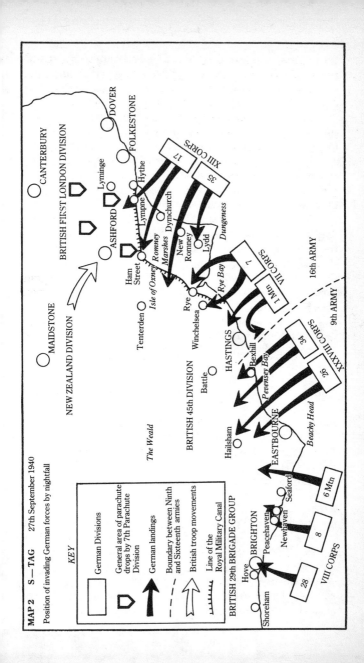

MAP 2   S—TAG   27th September 1940

Position of invading German forces by nightfall

KEY

German Divisions

General area of parachute drops by 7th Parachute Division

German landings

German troop movements

Boundary between Ninth and Sixteenth armies

British troop movements

Line of the Royal Military Canal

CANTERBURY

DOVER

FOLKESTONE

BRITISH FIRST LONDON DIVISION

Lyminge

Hythe

Lympne

XIII CORPS

17

35

Dymchurch

Romney Marshes

New Romney

Lydd

Dungeness

ASHFORD

Ham Street

Isle of Oxney

MAIDSTONE

NEW ZEALAND DIVISION

Tenterden

Rye

Rye Bay

Winchelsea

VII CORPS

7

1 Mtn

16th ARMY

9th ARMY

Battle

The Weald

BRITISH 45th DIVISION

HASTINGS

Bexhill

Pevensey Bay

XXXX

34

26

Hailsham

EASTBOURNE

Beachy Head

6 Mtn

Seaford

Newhaven

Peacehaven

8

VIII CORPS

BRIGHTON

Hove

Shoreham

28

BRITISH 29th BRIGADE GROUP

the British, came the R.A.F. Three bomber squadrons, two of Wellingtons and one of Halifaxes, with Hurricanes to escort them. This was the Strategic Air Reserve's contribution.

The bombers hit the troop transports off Hastings as they were trying to take off the men they had so recently landed. Tug-boat and steamer captains attempted to flee, and in the confusion the last remains of cohesion in the German units broke down. Bombs also fell on German positions on the neighbouring cliffs. There the fighters too, finding no Luftwaffe to fight, made good practice against the scurrying figures on the ground. To the Germans it began to seem unpleasantly like Dunkirk in reverse. The reports which filtered back sent new waves of dismay through Germany's higher echelons. Von Rundstedt did not delay in complaining to the Führer, and Hitler was not prepared for a second shock to his system so soon after the events of the night.

This time he did not lose his temper. He sent for Goering, reiterated his instructions of earlier that same morning, and informed the Reichsmarschall that he held him personally responsible for the success or failure of the Luftwaffe. Goering was ordered — along with the other service chiefs — to attend a conference that afternoon. He was to ensure that there was a continuous Luftwaffe presence by day over the invasion areas, and to subordinate all other tasks to that one over-riding objective. Neither the British navy nor the British air force must ever again be permitted the freedom they had apparently enjoyed on the night and morning of 27th September. Goering did not attempt to argue his — in fact wholly reasonable — case that the Luftwaffe already was doing its job, and some enemy sea and air forces were bound to penetrate any degree of cover. He had never seen his Führer so icily calm and decisive before. It frightened him more than the rages.

Meanwhile, as the assault of Sixteenth Army on the English coast wavered, Ninth Army, regarded by O.K.H. as less significant to the overall plan, was encountering fewer difficulties. The long curve of the coastline down to Pevensey Bay was the objective of the leading elements of 34 and 26 Divisions. They were not landing in such strength as the formations of Sixteenth Army, but they found the opposing forces were also weaker. British interference with the landings themselves from the martello towers and the Royal Artillery's coastal batteries was, as with the attacks farther east, hampered by sea mists and poor visibility.

The Germans did not suffer too severely on the beaches, but stiff fighting soon developed in the village of Pevensey and the town of Bexhill. In the centre of Bexhill another battalion of the Devons was eventually cut to pieces, and the town taken. British troops in Pevensey were able to retire in good order westward down the coast into Eastbourne. By mid-morning a general German move away from the beaches had begun across the low-lying ground of the Pevensey Levels towards the market town of Hailsham. This movement presented a real threat to the British coastal positions in Eastbourne and around Beachy Head, not themselves the subject of seaborne attack. However, it also exposed the relatively weak and widely extended German troops in the developing salient to British counter-attack.

In the forward Corps H.Q. newly established at Bexhill, the mood was highly uncertain. Requests for instructions flashed back across the Channel to the commanding officers. The two divisional commanders were both eager to come across themselves and take charge of the situation. Their immediate subordinates on the ground wanted to call a temporary halt to the steady advance. But the difficulties encountered in communicating with their own forward troops prevented them. In the event the Army Commander, Strauss himself, authorized the divisional commanders to go over and sort things out. He had just received a most disturbing call from General von Schobert in Busch's Army. It appeared that a desperate situation was developing in the general area of Hastings on the immediate right of his own army. There was a real possibility that a deadly gap had already opened between the two armies.

As Strauss worriedly studied his maps, he took some

consolation from the events unfolding beyond Beachy Head. There the open waters of Brighton Bay had led the High Command to provide a different organization. The first echelon of each of the three divisions involved was itself divided into three subsidiary waves:- an advance force to cross direct from Le Havre by fast motor-vessels; then units also sailing direct from the mouth of the Seine, but in larger and slower steamers; and a final wave, also in large steamers, but despatched via the more northerly embarkation ports. The switch in point of departure was in deference to the Royal Navy's probable ability to interfere with the longer crossing.

At dawn on the 27th no such caution seemed necessary as the motor-boats and launches sped into Brighton Bay. The men in them had seen evidence of Britain's naval might in wreckage encountered and survivors picked up from engagements far to the eastward; they themselves were unscathed. The most westerly units, from 28 Division, missed their mark and landed on the beaches of Brighton itself. The Palace Pier was taken undamaged, an immensely useful adjunct to any landings. The British order to set off demolition charges had been inexplicably delayed. Furthermore, only half of the charges on West Pier, which *was* blown up, went off. Though damaged, the remaining structure was sufficient to provide a second valuable landing stage. The coastal battery and emplacements of 88th Field Regiment R.A. were overwhelmed before they could offer serious resistance. Oberstleutnant von Grolmann, directing the landing, realised he had somehow taken the British by surprise.

In fact the crossings from Le Havre had not been successfully monitored by British reconnaissance, and the (normally excellent) intelligence reports had failed to remedy the situation. General Hans von Obstfelder himself, crossing with his divisional staff very little behind the spearhead, radioed instructions to press home the advantage as soon as he was told of the initial success. As his speedboat turned towards Brighton, those instructions were about to be fulfilled beyond his wildest hopes.

In a hotel, near the promenade, a platoon of young German soldiers and their younger lieutenant found that they had captured a whole gaggle of apparently senior British officers. Naturally pleased, they herded their prisoners down towards the beach. Around them the fighting had intensified as 49 Grenadierregiment pushed towards their immediate objective of the railway station against the resistance of 50 Battalion, the Queen's Regiment. It was only about an hour later that anyone of importance in the German army realised that they had captured the commander of 29th Independent Brigade Group, Brigadier Sir O.W.H. Leese, Bart., together with his entire brigade staff.

Brigade Group H.Q. had only recently been moved onto the coast itself, in response to directives originating from the very summit. Churchill felt that such a move for the forward units, and particularly for their senior officers, would serve to foster a clearer understanding of the situation in the field, and a more offensive spirit — the latter not in fact being a quality they were lacking. Though individual units of the Brigade Group fought on with great courage and tenacity, both in Brighton and later north of the Downs as well, the loss of their entire command structure rendered most of their actions futile. It also resulted in the complete destruction in the course of the 27th of two entire battalions of the Lancashire Rifles, and the effective loss of the whole of Brighton. The elimination at a stroke of the local command structure also meant that the British High Command did not fully grasp the gravity of the démarche on their right flank for over a day.

The rest of the German Corps was less favoured by fortune, but still remarkably successful elsewhere on its front. 6th Mountain Division was forced to fight a series of stiff engagements on the beaches at Cuckmere Haven and under the nearby cliffs. Notable feats of valour were performed in the scaling of the Seven Sisters under fire, and the silencing of the artillery piece emplaced at Birling Gap. The fiercest fighting, however, was at Seaford, where the Sussex Regiment was defending some at least of its own county soil. Here for the first time the Germans were able to use their amphibian tanks with some measure of success. More of these strange vehicles were landed at the mouth of the sleepy stream that comprised the River Cuckmere, and they spearheaded a speedy advance up its pleasant valley — a valley which cut straight through the South Downs to the open country beyond.

German 8 Division also practiced its rock climbing on the cliffs under the sprawling 'unofficial' settlement of Peacehaven. These troops were the first to land and were able, after local skirmishes, to move speedily on Newhaven from the heights overlooking the harbour on the east. By coup de main they seized Fort Newhaven, an impressive position set into a hill, from behind, and silenced the main coastal batteries as the first German units entered the harbour. Bereft of direction from above, and at risk of being surrounded, the British withdrew in good order up the line of the Ouse to cover the county town of Lewes. The port installations were not destroyed. Though Newhaven was only a little harbour, it was the Germans' first harbour, and it had been taken largely intact.

By the mid-afternoon of *S-Tag*, at least as far as the Germans were concerned, the fog of war was beginning to lift a little. The eastern sector was largely a success story. The hastily established British perimeter at Hythe had just been breached, and 17 Division was pushing towards Folkestone, though resistance was still fierce. The paratroops were already in occupation of a very large area behind Folkestone and reinforcements and supplies were being fed into their salient. The Romney Marsh area, up to and in places beyond the Royal Military Canal, was largely secure in the hands of 35 Division.

By contrast, the left flank of Sixteenth Army's two-pronged assault, was in a precarious position. 7 Division was still fighting for the possession of Rye (though Winchelsea had fallen just after one o'clock). The survivors of 1st Mountain had been withdrawn altogether from the beaches of Hastings. The sole fruit of their efforts was a foothold in the hills above the town.

In Ninth Army's area, the picture was once again favourable. XXXVIII Corps was rapidly expanding and consolidating its substantial beach-head at Pevensey Bay. To the west beyond Beachy Head, VIII Corps, though numerically the weakest of the four army corps that made up the first wave, had achieved a considerable and unlooked-for success in the capture of the centre of Brighton. It had also secured intact the harbour at Newhaven. Between the two wings of Ninth Army the British position at Eastbourne, held by a battalion of the Devonshires, looked increasingly precarious.

On the British side, things were far less clear. 1st London Division was holding on in Folkestone and Dover, but direct communications from divisional H.Q. in Ashford to the coast had been cut by German parachutists, and on the coast itself the attempt to hold Hythe had failed. However, the New Zealand Division, despite heavy enemy air attack in the course of the day, had moved its own H.Q. forward to Ashford and was beginning to advance down the A20 towards Folkestone, pushing the enemy paratroops aside.

In the centre it was apparent that 45 Division had won a significant victory at Hastings, and was continuing to put up a spirited resistance around Rye, though its right flank was threatened by enemy landings in Pevensey Bay. The extent of British naval successes in the pre-dawn raids was not appreciated by the War Cabinet or the Chiefs of Staff. Though it was known that elements of the invasion fleet had been severely disrupted and losses inflicted, the countervailing losses of British ships was given too much weight by British commanders. The opportunity to follow up using naval forces available at Portsmouth was let slip. The successes of Bomber Command and the fighters of the Strategic Air Reserve at Hastings were more apparent to the British leaders, and the achievement of even local air superiority over an invasion beach together with an almost immediate German withdrawal seemed to open a door to repeated exploits of the same sort.

On the western flank of their line, however, the British were operating almost entirely in the dark. The High Command was unaware that Newhaven had been taken. It knew that there was heavy fighting in Brighton, and that things were not going well. Communications with 29 Brigade Group had been lost. The British remained unaware that the brigade group had effectively ceased to exist. Acting on the assumption that it was still in place, and fearing further assaults at other points on the coast, G.H.Q. failed to send reinforcements into the town.

At the end of the 27th September, *S-Tag*, the invasion hung in the balance. Both sides had reasons to hope for success and to fear disaster. The course of the battle to come would now depend on the two warlords, Hitler and Churchill. The time for lesser captains, whatever their skills and experience, was over.

Chapter 10

THEY'RE COMING

"Don, Don! Wake up!" His mother's voice was full of alarm, as she shook his arm and pulled at him. He could recognise that even while he was still befuddled with sleep.

"What is it? What's happened?" He tried to rub the sleep from his eyes, still disorientated. The curtains were half open, but it was pitch dark outside, and it was very cold. He sat up in bed.

"What time is it? What the heck's going on?" he demanded again.

"It's five o'clock — no twenty to. And don't ask *me* what's going on. Do you know I've been shaking you for five minutes. — There's that Bill Lawley downstairs, and he's acting very strange if you ask me. He says you've got to get up. The Home Guard want you. And if this is some sort of game, or exercises, or whatever you call it, I'll give that Bill of yours what for. I don't know what your father would say if he was home. Waking decent people up in the middle of the night . . . "

"All right, mum, it's not Bill's fault. He's just a private like me." Her nagging had at least served the purpose of waking him up. "There is a war on, you know," he called after her — the excuse for everything and anything, that was. He struggled into his shirt and trousers, still shivering.

"It had better not be some bloody exercise though," he muttered to himself as he stumbled downstairs. Bill's face

133

told him that whatever it was, it was no exercise. Bill never looked worried. He was the calmest bloke Don knew. Tonight, though, his face was drawn and lined. For the first time Don realised he was a middle-aged man, almost an old man.

"What the hell's happened, Bill?" he asked.

"None of that language in this house," said his mother, but without conviction, her self-assurance suddenly dropping like the mask it was.

"You took your time, Don." At least Bill's voice was level and sensible, as it always was, but even then his eyes betrayed him. "Well, you're to come with me — and I can't tell you yet what's happened. Not in front of civilians." He glanced at Mrs Gibbard, who folded her arms and bit her lip, glaring at him.

"He's not going out till I've given him some breakfast."

"Come on, mum — I have to. Look, don't worry. It's just another flap on. We had one the other night, you know — I told you about it."

"Don — be careful, son," she said suddenly, catching his arm, as he flung on his great-coat and collected the usual gear. The clutter of gas mask and tin hat, rifle and pouches did not seem so comical for once. He and his mother were both aware that something had happened to change things, something real, and serious. And in her eyes was that dread which had lurked at the back of everyone's mind for so many weeks and months now. Not the fear of death, though that was there, of course. Rather, the fear that nothing would ever be the same again — that the old, familiar, homely world was dying around them.

The two men climbed onto their bikes and cycled through the earliest light of a misty dawn. It was very cold still, and their breath trailed in plumes behind them. The suburbs were silent, no inkling of war disturbing the sleep of all those other houses. Don drew alongside Bill.

"I'm just the messenger boy, old son," said Bill. "You're the last one of my batch to collect. The others will all be down at the hall by now. Pity you weren't on the phone. Would have saved me a tidy ride."

Don waited for him to take his own time to pass on the news. He realised that there was a sound now, muffled through the mist. It had been nagging at the back of his mind for some moments, because he hadn't heard it for ages . . . His bike slewed round and he wobbled from side to side. He knew why he hadn't heard it, not since a year ago.

"My God, Bill! It's the church bells. They're ringing the church bells."

"Silly sods," Bill grunted. "There'll be a ruddy panic now."

"But the church bells means invasion, Bill. They're coming!"

"They're not coming, son. They've come. Invasion's happened. Now, tonight. Here, in England!"

For a moment Bill was shouting the words, as they rode together into the grey yard outside the drill hall. Then he half grinned, lopsidedly.

"Never mind me, Don! It's not you I'm shouting at. You needn't worry too much . . . It's not right here that I meant. Up the coast a bit." Bill seemed completely calm again.

"They'll be here soon enough though," said Don. "I'll bet they won't hang about." The catch in his voice betrayed that this was not just bravado in the face of disaster, it was the bleak truth. Bill looked at him squarely for a long moment.

"I'm not much of a betting man, but I hope to Christ you've backed a wrong 'un there."

"Sorry, Bill," he muttered.

Their homes, their lives, their everything were there in the pleasant ordinary suburbs, the neat brick houses, the city terraces. The thought of grey-clad parachutists descending on those sleeping streets, of panzer turrets above the well-trimmed privet, had seemed laughable once. Just as the idea of English towns being bombed had seemed unreal. Now invasion was to become as hideously real as the bombing.

There was a murmur of voices from inside the hall, a quick crack of yellow light, pale in the dawn, as they opened the door. The room was full of men, all in varying degrees of army uniform. Not only men from their unit, but from others. Don remembered thinking:-

"Perhaps it is an exercise. They shouldn't all be here. Everyone should be at their own station . . . I should be at Netley station . . . " He had smiled to himself at the pun. It still didn't make sense. There hadn't been a raid in the night. Everyone said there would be big raids before they landed. He found his mind drawn back to the hollow, ceaseless ringing high above of the bell. This was what a passing bell for the dead must sound like. A voice dammed the flow of his thoughts.

"Right, you men! Quiet there! Form up in ranks behind your own units' sergeants. Let's be having you quickly now."

A regular with sergeant's stripes up was shouting the orders. Even his voice sounded strained, squeaky almost. There was another regular there too, tall and aristocratic looking — the way you imagined a captain. Straight out of something by Noel Coward. The Home Guard officers clustered around him were all short, running to fat half of them too. The way you imagined *them* to be as well.

"Very well, men, I want you to listen carefully to what I have to say to you. It may be the most important thing you have heard in your lives." The captain looked around, all Eton and Sandhurst. "I have to tell you that the code-word *Cromwell* has been issued — on the authority of the War Office — and you are therefore now on full invasion alert. This does not mean there will be an enemy landing in this area, nor does it mean that such a landing is imminent. But — at any rate — we, er . . . must be prepared for any eventuality."

"He's waffling on," Don thought. "Worse than our own flipping captain and one of his lectures. What's the point? Dragged out of bed at half past four for this . . . "

"Men, I have to tell you that the German army, supported by paratroops, has landed in strength on the coasts of Kent and Sussex. The invasion is on. It's all up to us now."

While he had rambled on they had all let the relief grow in them, daring to hope again. Now the silence ran on and on — a minute or more perhaps. The passing bell tolled overhead.

Don found his mind wandering down inconsequential alleyways. He remembered standing in the school hall in Bitterne School, listening to the headmaster going on about some terrible schoolboy crime, and wondering whether the old buffer knew all along that he, Don, was the guilty party. It was like that now. Wondering what was going to happen. Whether it was going to happen to you or to some other poor blighter. Only now none of them was the guilty party, all just victims.

He awoke from his reverie. The aristocratic captain was talking again, something about units being split, some men being assigned to their usual positions, some to go down to the coast. He still wasn't taking it in properly. Then they were moving out. In the cold, grey light before sunrise, in the yard, the sergeant was calling off names — the lads to go down to the coast.

"Defending Lee-on-Solent," he heard someone whisper, that oaf Prescott. "They can have it as far as I'm concerned."

"No," he thought. "No, they can't have it, or anything else, anything at all. Then he thought that the joker might be dead before the day was out, if the Germans did come here as well.

Don wasn't one of those detailed off to the coast. He was to go to the usual billet, down at Netley station, along with the usual crowd. Not that it was very far from the coast, he reflected. And if the Germans were in Sussex they could be moving up that railway — after they'd captured Pompey. Then again, capturing Portsmouth would take them a while. It was hard to think seriously in those terms, impossible to associate enemy objectives and lines of advance with the real places he knew. They'd sent him home to get his breakfast before going on duty.

"Make sure you take a packed lunch too," the corporal had said.

It was like a Boy Scout hike. And he was to call in at work on the way, and give them a form to say why he wouldn't be in. Give them a form! The Germans had landed in England, and he had to hand in forms. It was worse than a Boy Scout hike. The Boy Scouts knew what they were doing. He found Gwen Renouf and Edith, her mother, at the house when he arrived. Gwen came out to meet him as he leaned the bike against the wall.

"Your mum's in a right state," she told him. "What's the big flap about this time?"

"We've got to listen to the radio. I'm not supposed to say, not till it's given out on the News. They told us there would definitely be something on the News."

Gwen looked suspicious. He wondered if she could tell from his face that something was wrong, badly wrong.

"The kettle's boiled, Don," Gwen's mother announced as they came in. "Nice to see you back. Just sit down and I'll bring you a cup in. — We've pooled our tea and sugar rations for the day."

She fussed and bustled about, but she was worried too. His own mother paced the room. Her complaints about her son being dragged off in the night "when it was only an exercise" alternated with relief that that was all it was. He was glad he was not allowed to tell them the truth.

"There's been nothing at all on the wireless," said Gwen. "Just music. Classical music as well!" She handed him the plate. "Is it really serious, Don?"

He nodded, munching the toast, thinly smeared with precious butter.

"Your mum heard the church bells ringing, so did I. Thank goodness my mum didn't. She's bad enough as it is."

"Yes. Good job they've stopped now. I can't see the point." He was still carefully non-committal. "You'd better put the wireless back on. It's just coming up to eight o'clock."

Everyone knew what ringing church bells was supposed to mean. — So perhaps they had guessed already. He watched the three women, sat round the set. There was no music now, just the crackle of static. For a moment he wondered if the B.B.C. had gone. Perhaps the Jerries were already in London, and it was all over. Then the announcer's voice cut in, precise and level as usual, speaking in the same tones as if he was announcing the Boat Race result.

"This is a special news bulletin from the B.B.C. in London. A communique issued at 7.30 this morning, Friday the 27th of September, makes the following announcement. Units of German land and airborne forces have, in the course of the night, attempted to land in Great Britain at several points on the South–East Coast. The German landings have been met with spirited resistance by the Army, the Royal Navy, the Air Force and the local Home Guard. The invaders have been confined to very limited beach heads against which constant counter-attacks are continuing. You are advised to keep tuned to the Home and Forces Service for further half-hourly bulletins. All citizens should go about their normal business. No-one is to leave his or her home district unless instructed to do so by an authorized person. All members of the Armed Forces and the Home Guard who have not already done so are to report to their units immediately. There is no cause for immediate alarm. That is the end of the communique."

There was nothing else on the news. That was all that was needed. A band came on, playing martial music. Don turned the wireless off.

"I've got to go down to Netley station," he told the women, in as matter-of-fact a voice as he could manage. "Some of the lads have to go to the coast. It's only just in case, though. So far the Jerries have only landed in Kent and Sussex. — Apart from that we don't know any more than you do."

"Oh God, they won't be sending you down there will they, Don?" His mother's voice was shaking. He tried to keep up the façade of re-assurance.

"No, mum, of course not. The Home Guard stay put in their home areas — that's the whole point. There's no more danger to me on Netley Station than there is going to work. The Nazis are miles away. And it sounded like they were having a hard time of it.''

"They'd have to say that, wouldn't they?" she answered doubtfully, but she looked relieved, her first concern at least somewhat lessened. She didn't know he was mainly trying to convince himself. What she'd said was quite right. They could hardly say anything else. Oh, the army would put up a fight, no doubt about that, but everyone knew about the shortage of equipment, and everyone knew about what these Jerries were like. We'd lost in France. For all anyone knew we might be losing, might have already lost, in Sussex. Perhaps he would be one of a handful of defenders, fighting tanks with a rifle from a badly-built pill box. And perhaps it would be soon.

"I've got to go," he announced, getting up in a hurry to get out of that way of thinking.

"Whatever are we going to do?" Mrs Renouf remained seated, moaning aloud.

"Oh don't start, mum. — Don's got to go now."

"There's nothing happened to us yet, dear," said Don's mother. She sounded cheerful enough. Probably just what she needed, someone else to cheer up. They weren't taking it too bad at all, considering. Probably better than he was!

"Be careful, son!" His mother called as he wheeled his bike up to the gate. Gwen had come out with him.

"Be careful, Don!" She briefly held onto his arm. She knew the truth of it all right.

"I'll try." He half smiled. "Keep an eye on my mum for me too, love."

Cycling down to Netley was just like a thousand other times. There were people about in Woolston and Sholing, the occasional little group on a corner, but mostly men and women hurrying to work, delayed by listening to the news perhaps. Someone called out to him and gave the Victory sign. He called something back, something cheerful and confident, God knows what. At work the foreman moaned at the news he wouldn't be in.

"There's hardly anyone here. Don't they know that we're doing war work as well?"

"They probably think we'd better beat the Germans first," Don answered, irritated. "It's a pity you're not coming with us."

'Watch your cheek," was the mumbled answer, but the shaft had gone home. Unfair to the old boy, really, Don thought, but even now there still seemed to be so many who didn't realize that everything had changed. He wondered if others shared his own doubts and apprehensions. Even Tom and Fred at the station seemed confident, Fred in a quiet, determined way, Tom bubbling with eagerness. Don found himself pretending to share that confidence, perhaps in some measure even taking on a little of it.

"We'll show the bastards now," Tom announced, as they waited for the next bulletin around the signalman's ancient wireless set — imported into the box contrary to Company regulations, as he had several times informed them.

"Language!" said Fred. "And I doubt they'll get far enough for *you* to be showing them anything, Tom Wilson."

The bulletin told them nothing new, except that there was heavy fighting in the invasion area, and British land, sea and air forces had inflicted very heavy casualties on the first wave of the invading troops.

"I don't like the sound of that 'first wave' bit," muttered Fred. "Sounds like there's more of the blighters coming."

"Of course there's more of them coming," Don interrupted. "The whole bloody German army more of them."

"Come on you two, let's have a bit of quiet." Bill Lawley had come in just as the news came on. "I want to hear the rest."

"The Prime Minister will broadcast to the nation at seven o'clock this evening. His message will be repeated at eight, nine and ten o'clock," the announcer's voice was saying.

"Well, we'll know the worst then," said Tom. "Winston will give it to us straight, if we're all still here then . . . "

Don found it easy to join in the laughter this time. Through the day, inevitably, the tension abated. The apprehension became less oppressive, as the fact of invasion became accepted — and as it proved to impinge very little on them.

At about four thirty in the afternoon, Don left the pill box, where he had been putting in a boring stint, to answer the needs of nature in the gents along the station platform. It had been a long day, and he was looking forward to the arrival of their replacements, due in about an hour's time. Though there had been no 'flap', it was obvious that something was going on. In wartime the line always carried more traffic than usual, but today there had been a never ending procession. It was mostly goods trains: closed wagons or flat cars with vehicles. One train obviously had some tanks, hardly concealed under the tarpaulins. The driver of another, held at the signals, told them he was carrying ammunition. The young soldiers on the trains called out to them too, laughing and joking as they were carried eastward towards the war.

"Now there's a cushy number for you," one of the soldiers had called out to him and Tom from a train full of soldiers.

"I'll change places any day," Tom called back. "Who are you anyway? Where are you going?"

"Surrey Regiment to you, son, moving up to Chichester to fight the Nazis," another man called. "Don't tell anyone will you!"

"I'll send a letter to me uncle Adolf," Tom yelled back as the train pulled out.

Don was about to come out of the toilet when he heard the scream — the wail of a siren. For a moment he thought it must be an air raid siren. Only for a moment though. The screech mounted to a crescendo, falling out of the sky above him — Stuka! Then the crash and roar. He didn't know if he dived onto the floor or was knocked there by the blast. He saw the grey glazed bricks of the wall sway and bend inwards like cardboard, and plaster fell from the ceiling in lumps, bouncing off his body. He thought:

"I'll never get this uniform clean for parade . . . " Then lay there.

The snarl of an aero-engine, an enemy engine, came nearer again. Then the staccato rattle of machine gunning, louder till it almost deafened him. He put his hands over his ears and wished he hadn't left his tin hat in the pill box. Now he was simply trying to cover his head, as he heard the crack and spat of bullets hitting into the brick walls, and saw the walls tremble again, and chips of brick splinter away and fall off on the inside. Twice the German ran the length of the platform, once in each direction. Each time the mad frenetic clatter of the gun; the drumming thud of bullets into the wooden platform farther up, then the screech of ricochets off stone and concrete, and the shatter of glass and tiles as the station buildings were shot up.

He lay there a good five minutes after it had gone, face-down and rigid, hands still clenched over his head. Then the tension in his muscles went, not so much relief as collapse. He wanted to stand up, but couldn't, had to drag himself up, and then lean, swaying like a drunk, against the wall. More minutes went by before he could walk properly. On the platform, the wreckage was the first thing, holding all his attention. The booking hall was burning, lazy flames licking through a shattered roof. All the windows everywhere were gone. He began to walk through the debris of broken glass and smashed wood.

Half way along he found Tom. The khaki of his uniform was ripped open across his back in three jagged holes, the stained cloth stood up from them in crater walls. The holes were black, not red as he had expected. The red lay under Tom like a carpet, not spreading any more, beginning to congeal round the edges, already darker and dirtier than when it had flowed in Tom's veins and made him laugh and joke and sit drinking tea. Don didn't turn him over or look at his face twisted to one side — not beyond one quick meeting of eyes, alive to dead.

He came to where the signal box had been. Fred, the signalman, lay below it across the track, on top of a mound of rubble from the smashed platform face, his body covered with debris. One of the bombs must have gone off right behind the box, blowing it to matchwood. Don cleared the splinters and glass from the old man. His eyes were shut. He looked only asleep, not like the staring corpse-face of poor Tom. Then he stopped clearing, and pulled away his stained hands. Blood dripped from his fingers where he had touched the shattered ruin of Fred's chest, all broken in and bleeding, the blood soaked up in the heavy serge of his greatcoat.

The other bomb had hit the pill box. None of the walls were left. What had been Bill lay half through the shattered doorway. One side of his head seemed sheared through, the pulpy grey of ruined brains mixed with blood and tangled hair. His lips were drawn back in the horror of his own death, and the one eye left stared up into the blue of the sky.

Don didn't remember dialling 999, or swearing at the man on the phone who only wanted to know whether the line was blocked. He didn't remember going back into the station building and helping some people drag out the body of the booking clerk and two passengers, both badly wounded, one obviously dying. The thought that echoed round his mind was that he had been in the only brick building on that station — the lavatory. He wanted to laugh about it, loudly for all to hear. Laugh as if he hadn't seen Tom, Fred and Bill lying there dead.

Chapter 11

BATTLESHIP

The morning of *S-Tag* had been a traumatic time for the Führer of Germany. He had finally been converted to a belief in the importance of sea power. The carnage wrought by British light forces on the crossing had been the agent of his conviction. His initial reaction to sack Raeder had soon changed. Even Hitler could not fail to recognize that Raeder had been the very man who had warned of just such an outcome. Hitler had been the one who had ignored him. But it was unthinkable that he himself could be wrong. There must be someone else to blame.

His growing conviction that the fault lay with the unfortunate Goering was fixed once and for all when news of the R.A.F.'s activities over Hastings arrived. The navy simply did not possess the resources to protect the crossings and the beach heads:- Raeder had made that point often enough. Whose job, therefore, *was* it to protect the troops? Surely it was the job of the man who had promised that he could do it, the Commander of the Luftwaffe. When Hitler interviewed the Reichsmarschall in the course of the morning his earlier fury had also abated. He was icily calm. Goering left him believing firmly that at the afternoon's Führer Conference he would be relieved of his command.

The summit of Goering's humiliation, when the conference met, was the presence of the generals, and above all of his smirking, know-all rival, Grand Admiral Raeder.

They were present to hear Hitler offer Raeder direct operational control of all German air forces operating over the Channel and the invasion beaches. Goering protested, promised, and wept. Raeder politely declined the Führer's offer. He had no wish for that poisoned cup. There would be little enough credit if the Luftwaffe did succeed in protecting the invasion forces. If it did not (and Raeder's doubts had not diminished) then someone's career would be at an end. The admiral had been walking a tightrope too long to undertake a new balancing act. If anyone was going to be ruined, the admiral intended it should be Goering.

"My Führer, I have every confidence in the Reichsmarschall," he told the gathering. "I could not begin to equal his abilities in the sphere of air warfare. Also, my own responsibilities in dealing with the Kriegsmarine are such that I simply could not devote the necessary time to that great task. The Reichsmarschall is the man for the job. I implore you, my Führer, to maintain your confidence in him. I do not doubt that if you make your instructions very clear, then Reichsmarschall Goering will not fail to carry them out."

Hitler turned to Goering.

"You see! You have quarrelled endlessly with the Admiral, and now he is your loyal friend. He at least is confident of your abilities! Well, Admiral Raeder, you must tell Reichsmarschall Goering and myself exactly what the naval situation is, so that action can be taken. For I will not have any more of my soldiers slaughtered like cattle in those damned rafts."

Goering cringed under the lash of his voice. Raeder ignored it.

"The naval situation is not encouraging, and less so now than yesterday. The damage inflicted last night was essentially the work of light forces. We were able to deny them a real victory by the actions of our own light forces. Inevitably, we suffered grave losses, and I refer to warships, not invasion barges. We have very few reserves to play with. Accordingly, I would like to bring my destroyers and torpedo boats right onto the invasion routes. In effect, rather than employ them as an ineffectual screen, I wish to operate a convoy system covering the shuttling of the troops. I shall also require the four light cruisers now available from *Herbstreise*, and the *Admiral Hipper*."

"By all means, Admiral. But proceed with your proposals."

Raeder smiled inwardly. For this it was worth being sacked at six o'clock in the morning and reinstated at ten.

"This means the flanks must be covered by the Luftwaffe against enemy naval action. We have surface ships to deal with those *few* enemy ships that do get through. I stress *few*, gentlemen. Most of them must *not* get through."

"What about your U-boats?" demanded Goering sullenly.

"They will remain on the flanks of course, Herr Reichsmarschall, and on patrol in the approaches to the invasion area. I do not leave the Luftwaffe entirely alone in its task. Particularly as the guarding of the flanks is only one of its three tasks."

He paused to sip from a glass of water, knowing now that for a day or so, perhaps longer, he *had* effective operational control of the Luftwaffe, without the labour, the responsibility, or the risk.

"The second task is the one already recognized from the outset. Total air superiority over the sea lanes of the invasion convoys, and of course the beach-heads. There must be no more trouble from enemy daylight bombing in this decisive area. We do not want another slip up there . . . " Again he paused. Sweat was rolling down Goering's neck into his collar.

"Thirdly, and this is the most disturbing of all . . . As yet we have only seen the effects of British light naval forces. Last night a battleship and a battle-cruiser were active off the Normandy coast. Latest intelligence now places them in Portsmouth. Somewhere in the North Sea, steaming south with all speed, are the two British battleships, *Nelson* and *Rodney*, and the battle-cruiser *Hood*. I have no doubt that these great ships and their escorts will, in the next forty-eight hours, execute a pincer movement upon our invasion corridor from both ends of the English Channel. The operation is much the same on land as on sea. The classic double envelopement envisaged by Clausewitz. It will leave our troops in England in the net, ripe fruit for the picking. The Luftwaffe *must* stop those battleships, my Führer. They are the cornerstone of British sea power. Without them, the edifice begins to crumble."

Hitler looked sidelong at the admiral, the old astute glitter in his eye.

"Are you certain that planes *can* sink a battleship, Admiral? Or do you have another view on the matter?"

"It is Goering's view," Raeder replied. "Now is the time for him to prove it. He must find those ships, and he must make sure that they do not come up into the Straits."

"My resources are stretched, Führer," interrupted Goering, making a last appeal. "There are too many tasks for the Luftwaffe already. I have the enemy troop concentrations to deal with, the railways and road junctions, ports, airfields, the enemy air force. And now the invasion routes, the beach-heads — and according to Raeder half the ocean as well."

"What do you say to that, eh, Raeder?" For all the utter seriousness of the situation, Hitler still needs must play off his subordinates against each other.

"Consider," Raeder answered — for he *had* considered it — "the disparate nature of these tasks. To cover the convoying of the invasion forces and the protection of the beaches your main requirement is for fighter aircraft. The protection of the flanks depends partly on dive bombers, but above all on aircraft capable of launching torpedo attacks. There are, Herr Reichsmarschall, according to your own Chief of Staff, such planes available. The search for the battleships is in fact over a limited area. I have already pointed out that two of them are in harbour at Portsmouth. It is the battleships that are the main target of the squadrons I have mentioned, perhaps with the aid of your new Condor Squadron and some heavy bombers. Your main heavy bomber force remains available for targets in England, with the emphasis on night attacks."

"An impressive commentary," suggested Hitler. Goering glared bitterly at Raeder.

"It is not so simple. None of it."

Hitler leaned across the table.

"Simple or not, it is to be done. Understand me, Hermann. You have heard that our navy can do very little. So it is up to you and the Luftwaffe. Do not let me down. Do not let any more of our men be drowned in the sea without firing a shot." His voice had become quiet again, almost cajoling and wheedling — but not quite. The steel was still there. Goering's weak will swayed in the breeze of his Führer's voice.

"I will draw up the orders and make all necessary arrangements, my Führer. I will proceed at once to the front, to the H.Q. of Luftflotte II. I will take personal charge."

"Exactly as the admiral outlined it. No doubt he has a copy of his notes he can let you have. And, Hermann, keep me informed regularly, through every day."

Once before in the great battle for Britain, Hitler had exerted his personal influence. Previously he had insisted on Goering's relentless pursuit of the R.A.F. to destruction — ignoring the more tempting civilian targets in favour of the Sector Stations and the radar posts. His insistence had been the key to the war in the air — the defeat of Fighter Command. Now for a second time that influence was brought to bear, this time on the war at sea.

The conference turned to the war on the beach-heads. Raeder sat back, well satisfied. Though Hitler's influence had prevailed, it was Raeder's plan that the Führer had forced upon Goering. Only as he left the conference was he met by a staff captain with a radio message just deciphered from the Admiralty.

"*Admiral Hipper* reported sunk off Jutland by British battle-cruiser *Hood*, 1410 hours, 27 September."

Raeder's euphoria vanished as he remembered that he had been telling the utter awful truth. The sea affair was now in the hands of Goering's Luftwaffe. Could planes sink battleships?

The mighty *Hood* had had a frustrating night and morning. None of her crew, including the captain, knew that England had been invaded — though rumours of imminent invasion had been rife when she set sail. *Hood* had made good speed during the preceding night, and morning found her in the middle of the North Sea. She had changed course at dawn to south-east, to bring her to rendezvous with *Nelson* and *Rodney* (whose orders to look for *Herbstreise* had not been countermanded). In London, the Admiralty was wracked with indecision about its heavy ships. The light forces had been committed at once. But the debate raged on whether also to commit the irreplaceable battleships in the hazardous waters of the Straits. There they would be ready targets to the lurking U-boats, always at risk from mines, possibly even threatened by aerial attack. The rendezvous between the three principal units of the Home Fleet at midday was not therefore changed. Admiral Forbes on the *Nelson* was given advance warning to expect emergency orders at 13.00 hours. That was when the admiralty had to make up its mind.

So it was that Captain Holland in the *Hood* was moving on a converging course towards the battleships. He was also converging faster and more decisively on the heavy cruiser, *Admiral Hipper*. *Hipper's* commander, Captain Meisel, was making due south at good speed, confident that a full scale search for his ship was being conducted far to the north. When the fighting tops of the *Hood* appeared over the horizon on his starboard quarter, she was not at first seen. *Hood's* four escorting destroyers were spread out in echelon on either side behind the great ship. So, it was the lookouts of the British battle-cruiser herself who were the first to sight the enemy.

"Warship on the port bow!" was the message. Men often see what they expect to see. "Battleship, sir — Nelson Class," was what Holland was told. In fact the *Nelson* and *Rodney* were still well to the south and west. None the less, a recognition signal went out to the *Admiral Hipper*. It was Captain Meisel's first warning that he was not alone on the wide sea.

Binoculars were trained on the distant shape, whose upperworks were now visible. There was no mistaking the tripod mast. The pages of the recognition journal were hastily thumbed. In their hearts the officers on *Hipper's* bridge were praying that it might yet be an old "R" Class dreadnought from the last war — something they were fast enough to run away from.

"Go to full speed. Change course three points to port!"

The distant shape of the British warship made no corresponding change of course at first. Minutes slipped by, and the sighs of relief were beginning to squeeze through pursed lips.

"Enemy has changed course, sir!"

"Enemy challenging us, sir!"

At first the officers on the bridge of the *Hood* had merely been surprised by the behaviour of a ship they continued to believe was either *Nelson* or *Rodney*. Binoculars were trained on the retreating vessel. In moments the engine room telegraph had been rung, and the great turbines were pounding away to bring the *Hood* up to her full thirty knots. Bells clattered "Action Stations" and men ran across the steel decks to their positions. The great fifteen-inch gun turrets were shut down, and the guns slowly swung to port as the course was adjusted to allow the forward barrels to bear on target. Only four of the battle-cruiser's big guns could be trained on the fleeing enemy. The two after turrets were masked by the ship's own superstructure. The two twin turrets forward would be enough.

After less than half an hour of stern chase, the first salvoes crashed out, and spouts of water flowered like trees out of the grey sea ahead of the fleeing enemy. *Hood* was already overhauling the German cruiser. Her salvoes moved steadily closer. The *Hipper* was straddled, then hit. One shell ripped through the thin armour to explode on the mess deck, another sliced through the ship's single large funnel. Then another straddle, and another hit on the stern of the ship. Miraculously *Hipper* had still lost nothing in firepower and speed. But *Hood* was gaining by the minute, and *Hipper's* eight-inch guns still remained silent, outranged by the huge guns of the *Hood*.

Then the moment came. One minute the officers on the bridge stood tense and alert, intent on commanding the powerful vessel that throbbed beneath them. Then they were gone. All dead, as the huge high explosive shell erupted in their midst. Steel was shattered like glass as the roof was ripped off. Only smears of blood and rags of flesh marked the place where Captain Meisel and his officers had stood. It was only one of four shells. All of them hit, in a salvo of unprecedented destructive power. Another took out one of the after turrets. Another exploded under the very stern of the ship, wrecking the propellers and shaft. The fourth blew up in a boiler room. *Hipper* wallowed in the rising and falling swell. Flames spread from the shattered turret. Some light ammunition ignited, and streams of fire sprayed outwards. Amidships a petty officer was shouting,

"Abandon ship! Abandon ship!"

He was the most senior officer left. The engine room officers and their men were trapped below behind collapsed bulkheads. Rafts were being pushed over the side, as the scream of shells again whistled above — one scream louder than the others, and another hit scored. Where the petty officer had stood was only a black pit into the ship's vitals. From it came the dull flicker of flames. The doomed ship took on a pronounced list to starboard. Another fifteen-inch salvo crashed out. Two more hits, and the ship momentarily righted, as if resisting the hammer blows to the last. Then she settled deeper, and the list increased. At 13.40 hours, *Nelson*, *Rodney* and their escorts appeared over the western horizon. *Hood* radioed:-

"Are you after my prize money?"

At 13.55 *Hood* ceased fire. The *Hipper's* colours were shot away, and Captain Holland regarded her as incapable of further defence. In fact she had put up *no* defence. She had not fired a shot. The destroyers closed in cautiously, ready to pick up any survivors. There would not be many. *Hipper* settled deeper, her list steadily increasing, till the main deck was under water all along the starboard side. She capsized suddenly at 14.10. Floated for a moment upside down. Then slid, bow first, in a few seconds, beneath the engulfing waves. The destroyers picked up thirty-five men. Her last moments were witnessed by a German reconnaisance aircraft, and the news of her loss reached Berlin almost as soon as it came to London. Sir Dudley Pound telegraphed to Admiral Forbes:-

"Roll on the *Nelson*, the *Rodney*, the *Hood*. Especially the *Hood*!" He did not add the second line of the Navy's scurrilous little rhyme:- "The whole bloody airforce is no bloody good." Instead a long message in code. Within the hour the *Nelson*, *Rodney* and *Hood* were rolling on, screened by fifteen destroyers, two light cruisers and an anti-aircraft cruiser, course south west, destination the Straits of Dover, objective — the German invasion flotillas.

At the same time, in Portsmouth, Admiral Whitworth was opening sealed orders, just delivered to him by despatch rider, in his cabin in the battle-cruiser, *Repulse*. She and the *Revenge* were to sail that evening. Their mission was simple. They and their escorts were to sail into the mass of the enemy's invasion fleet, and endeavour to destroy it. They were to draw all enemy naval and air forces upon themselves. During the hours of darkness, they would be joined in the attack by the capital ships of the Home Fleet. Three battleships and two battle-cruisers — the full panoply of Britain's naval might. Defending the enemy invasion barges were destroyers, torpedo boats, a cruiser or two at best. The British Navy would rip them apart, and the invasion would vanish forever to the bottom of the sea. Both British fleets received a message from Churchill himself — for much of this decisive strategy sprang directly from him.

"Seamen of Britain, the Nazis are even now ashore here in England. They will not stay here. For behind them lies the English Channel. And into the English Channel I am now sending you, in the great ships of the Royal Navy. I am sending you to destroy the enemy's ships. To wipe out his soldiers, while they are still afloat. To cut for good his lifeline. If you achieve these objectives, and achieve them you will, then Germany's hope of ever winning this war is gone for good. We are all depending on you today. I know you will win through."

On the decks of the *Revenge* and the *Repulse* in Portsmouth the ships' companies were assembled to hear Churchill's rousing order of the day. They cheered his words to the echo. In the Home Fleet at sea, the message added to the heady euphoria provoked by *Hood's* effortless destruction of the *Hipper*. Everyone on those ships knew, as surely as Churchill, that they would win through. The *Hood's* victory was an omen:- the beginning of the end for Germany.

It was six o'clock on Friday 27th September, a fine evening now after a dull and misty day. In Portsmouth the two capital ships were starting to get up steam. To the east, the armies of Britain and Germany were locked in combat in the English counties of Kent and Sussex. To the south, high over the Channel, one squadron of Heinkels and one of Ju 88's, unescorted by any fighters, lumbered northwards. Each of the planes had been converted to carry torpedoes. Farther south, behind them, came the second wave of the raid, three squadrons of Stuka dive bombers. The attack was to be on Portsmouth.

British radar picked up the enemy early on, for despite all the efforts of the Luftwaffe the radio-location net had never been entirely destroyed. But the reports from the radar stations only served to warn the anti-aircraft batteries. There would be no immediate R.A.F. response. The fighter reserve was never committed in advance: there were simply too few planes. Also the probable course of the enemy aircraft did not suggest 'invasion targets'.

As the Heinkels and Junkers crossed the Isle of Wight, the wail of sirens rose over Britain's great naval base. Civilians in the sprawling naval complex and the city beyond hurried for the shelters. The ack-ack batteries went onto alert, the ships in the crowded harbour went to action stations. In the two capital ships and their attendant squadron, the engine rooms and boiler rooms pulsed with activity, as steam was desperately got up. If there was to be a raid, then the best place for the ships was at sea. Particularly as their own A.A. defences were still appallingly weak.

The first wave of German planes came in from the west, out of the sun. They had taken the line of Southampton Water as far as Lee-on-Solent, then swung due east, coming in towards the harbour across Gosport. The British were not prepared for this sort of attack. Bombing was the order of the day; this was something new. The enemy came in low, almost at roof height over Gosport, their planes spread out in a great fan. The flak was intense from ship and shore alike. The course the Germans took brought some of them over the A.A. cruiser, *H.M.S. Naiad*, and her 5.25-inch batteries brought down two planes almost at once. Another roared away northward, to crash blazing somewhere in the Downs. A fourth disappeared over the town, flames pouring from her port engine.

In the hectic uproar, only at the last minute did the British realise exactly what was happening. From the surviving planes a wide pattern of sleek grey fish had dropped into the sea. Against the dock lay the two great ships, the vast bulk of the *Repulse* outboard, the *Revenge* inside, completely masked by the much longer hull of the battlecruiser.

Five of the torpedoes plunged into the hull of the *Repulse*. One, near the stern, failed to explode. A second hit amidships, rocking the ship, but not hurting her too badly. That torpedo had been set to run too shallow, and it exploded on the armoured belt, strengthened from its original six to nine inches of steel. But the last three hits were decisive. They ran at the right depth. Two of them were amidships again. They went under the belt, and blew up against the thin plates of the ship's bottom. The last exploded just abaft of the after turret.

Towards the stern of the ship, a great fire leapt up, dangerously near the after barbette and the magazine. The risk of an explosion was great. Fire fighting equipment from the quayside was dragged across the decks of the undamaged *Revenge*, while at the same time desperate attempts were made to get the old battleship out, lest the stricken *Repulse* blow up and take her to the bottom as well. Elsewhere in the harbour, two destroyers had already settled, single hits enough to sink them. The large cruiser, *H.M.S. Manchester*, was on fire forward, but making headway northward in a desperate attempt to beach herself on the mudflats of Porchester.

Slowly the *Revenge* got under way, her cables cast off from the dockside and from the blazing hulk of the *Repulse*, which already seemed to be settling deeper in the water. The firefighters still had good hopes of extinguishing the fire. They did not know (only a few did know then) that the bottom had been ripped out of the ship. Too many compartments had been breached. *Repulse* was an old ship, and though she had been modernized, it would not be enough to save her. Three of the boiler rooms had been flooded instantly. Another had now filled up, and water was pouring into the forward of the two engine rooms. As the *Revenge* came out beyond the bow of the battle-cruiser, the long low form was almost perceptibly sinking.

Steadily she cleared the stricken ship, and set her bows towards the harbour mouth and the sea. It was then that the Stukas fell on her — three squadrons of Germany's deadly dive bombers, armed with thousand-pound bombs designed to pierce armour plate. The thickest armour on the old ship's decks was two inches; most of her decks had less. Even the tops of her turrets — encased in steel on front, sides and back — were relatively lightly armoured. Suddenly the ship was surrounded by mast-high splashes in the sea. More ominous lurid fires indicated hits on the ship herself as they twisted skywards, turning the waterspouts red and yellow. Flak burst around the planes. Three had already gone, then two more, and yet another, unable to pull out of its dive.

Revenge came out of the forest of giant flashes, smoke and flames pouring from her starboard side, but still making good headway towards the narrow entrance between Round Tower Point and the Blockhouse Fort. A ragged cheer went up from the decks of the *Repulse*. But there were three squadrons of Stukas. The second squadron fell out of the sky above the wreck of the *Repulse*. Few of their bombs hit the sinking ship, but the quayside was turned into a mass of fire. And meanwhile, the third squadron, one after another, were plunging steeply, their sirens wailing, into the column of smoke that rose above the *Revenge*. Once more the great spouts of water were torn out of the sea, and there was the ominous grinding crash of high explosive ripping through steel. Once more the *Revenge* came out of the inferno, fires still burning on board, but all the time making better speed.

"I think we're going to make it," said Admiral Whitworth, who had transferred his flag to his surviving capital ship amidst the chaos. He turned back from the observation slit in the conning tower smiling at the captain and the ship's officers.

And then the whole ship stood still, as if gripped in a great fist that held her unmoving a long moment, then raised her bodily from the water, crushing the steel of her body, before dropping her back, riven and ruined. Only then did the sound assault the ears of the officers. None of them even had time to think that their war — and their lives — were over. From the shore, observers said that it was like a pillar of fire rising up between the two rear turrets. In an almost leisurely fashion the roof of one of the turrets spiralled skyward, turning over and over. The other turret was jerked upwards from its mounting, the barrels of the fifteen-inch naval guns snapping like bamboo sticks as the whole turret slipped over the side of the ship. For a moment her stern section was visible, floating free of the wreck, then almost at once it had sunk. The front two thirds of the *Revenge* lay silent amidst the great pall of smoke that shrouded her death throes. She slid backwards into the waiting waters. *Repulse* had settled on the bottom a minute or two earlier.

In half an hour Britain had lost a battleship, a battle-cruiser — and the harbour of Portsmouth. For the wreck of the *Revenge* lay full across the harbour entrance, trapping everything inside.

Raeder heard the news from an ecstatic Goering just as he was writing the draft orders for the Reichsmarschall's next task. He didn't believe Goering. He automatically, and with some justification, distrusted pilots' claims of hits scored. He distrusted the Reichsmarschall's self-glorifying exaggerations even more. Nevertheless, it did seem that some sort of havoc had been wrought at Portsmouth. And that boded well for the mission he was now ordering, with all speed. For the reconnaisance plane that had seen the death of the *Admiral Hipper* had also reported the position of the British battle fleet. The battleships were not free of watching German planes from that moment. At Giessen the calm, collected Raeder and the bubbling, gloating Goering discussed the strike to be made against them.

"Remember, Herr Reichsmarschall Goering," Raeder told him in his most acid lecturing manner, "to damage, or even — if that is what happened — to sink a battleship with bombs or torpedoes in the confines of a harbour is one thing. To sink a battleship at full speed on the high seas is a very different thing."

"Perhaps the Grand Admiral's views on the vulner-ability of battleships will be further modified later today," replied von Waldau, Chief of Luftwaffe Operations Staff. He and Jeschonnek were accompanying their master as moral support, and the inter-service antipathy extended to them. Raeder did not reply. When they had gone he turned to his own Chief of Staff, Admiral Schniewind.

"I doubt it," he said. "And that is why, in addition to Goering's Stukas and his torpedo bombers, we have no less than six U-boats right here, in the entrance to the Narrows. I'll have one of those battleships, Schniewind. And it will be a Kriegsmarine 'kill'. And I'll believe it more than I believe that pompous windbag."

So Goering reported his triumphs in person to a slightly sceptical Führer, and the Führer telephoned Raeder for his view, and the photographs of the colossal victory at Portsmouth were rushed to Berlin. And meanwhile, on the airfields of II Fliegerkorps between Ghent and Lille on the plain of Flanders, the heavy bombers were loaded with their deadly cargoes. Torpedoes were once again being slung beneath the adapted Heinkels and Junkers. The Condor Squadron's FW 200's — converted specifically for attacks on naval targets — were rolling down the runways. While beneath the waves the net of U-boats spread out across the approaches to the Straits of Dover. Their commanders gazed through their periscopes northward in the steadily gathering gloom after sunset. Somewhere out there were the giant battleships they awaited. Behind them lay the Channel and Germany's vital link to the embattled troops fighting desperately to hold and enlarge their beachheads on the implacable shores of England.

The first German bombers found the British ships at half past seven. It was already getting dark, and visibility was poor. The ships were running fast and without lights. The bomb aimers had only darker shapes against the dark of the sea to aim at, as the glow in the westerly sky faded fast. There was enough light to make out the capital ships, the primary targets, from the others. As the bomb doors opened, anti-aircraft fire broke out from the ships below, their searchlights probing upwards. The heavy bombers were too high to suffer much damage. They were also too high to achieve any degree of accuracy against blurred and hazy moving targets. There were several near misses, one of which damaged a destroyer. Only one hit, also on a destroyer and sufficient to cause her to fall out of line. The bombers returned home. The fleet ploughed on. The night was now almost complete.

The torpedo bombers arrived to repeat the process. The fan formation went into action again, but this time against almost totally invisible ships, zig-zagging at full speed on the high seas. Most of the torpedoes were a long way off their mark. The *Nelson* and *Rodney* both reversed course to comb the tracks. *Hood* was missed by a torpedo which passed three hundred yards ahead of her. The second torpedo of that same salvo was the only lucky shot for the Germans. More lucky than they could yet guess. It hit one of the escorting destroyers, stopping her dead and burning in the water.

The bombers were already disappearing. The Condor Squadron had abandoned its mission and turned for home. *Hood* also turned, coming back to rescue survivors from the wrecked and sinking destroyer. She was the only ship near enough to assist in time, and with the abandonment of the air attack there was no apparent danger.

Raeder's screen of U-boats in fact lay far ahead, but U100 did not. One of the boats earlier placed on patrol between the Dutch Coast and the Thames Estuary by Flag Officer U-boats, Karl Doenitz, she was now presented with an incredible opportunity. Despite the darkness, the unmistakable shape of a British battleship was there, unmoving in the water, silhouetted against the flames of a burning destroyer. Captain Schepke's eyes did not leave the periscope as he delivered his orders. His voice calm, but with an underlying tremor. All four bow tubes were to fire a pattern towards the target, then reload immediately in case something went wrong. U-boat commanders knew all about missing sitting targets, and torpedoes that failed to explode; the latter had saved British capital ships before.

Schepke, already a veteran of the U-boat war with many kills to his name, realized that few U-boat commanders had had a chance like this. Steadily U100 closed the range. The Captain knew now that the ship ahead of him was huge. The flickering flames behind its bulk revealed the two funnels, the fighting top and the forward gun turrets. It was too dark to be certain which ship he was looking at, but it could only be one of Britain's battle-cruisers. The *Repulse* or *Renown*, perhaps even the legendary *Hood*, the largest warship in the world. The destroyer was going down now, and more smoke billowed out of the great ship's stacks into the night. She began to move off.

"Fire! Fire now!" Captain Schepke shouted in the tension of the moment. In quick succession the four torpedoes sped across the short space of intervening water. The *Hood* was already moving. She had been stopped for less than fifteen minutes. As long as her Captain dared in those deadly waters. — Too long. All four torpedoes had been set to run low. No-one saw the thin white tracks across the water. In the submarine the officers and men counted the seconds. Also too long! The first torpedo had missed, or failed to explode. In fact it had passed under the hull. The second one hit, beneath the mainmast and behind the funnels. It blew up beneath the armoured belt in the main engine room. As water gushed in through the ship's torn plating, the third of the salvo struck, beneath the two after turrets. The anti-torpedo bulges did not do their job very well. The final torpedo struck in almost exactly the same place as the third. The battle-cruiser was on fire astern, and taking water in the engine room. In the submarine which had remained on station to see the effects of her attack, the men cheered wildly. In her torpedo flat, another three fish were being loaded, the last on board. They were never needed.

At eleven minutes past nine, on the evening on *S-Day*, in the southern North Sea, seventy miles from the Dutch coast, the after magazine exploded aboard *H.M.S. Hood*, the pride of the Royal Navy and symbol of Britain's maritime power. A vast fireball was seen to rise above the stern of the great ship, with a curtain of flame billowing forward from it. Ammunition on the deck ignited in the intensity of the heat. The whole ship had become in moments one long funeral pyre. Like the *Revenge* earlier in the same day, she had lost her stern. Huge fires raged in her surviving forward parts. Both masts had fallen, and a jet of fire was shooting upwards from one of her funnels. Every ship in the fleet saw the holocaust, though at first the *Nelson* and *Rodney* were too far away to see that it was the *Hood* which had been destroyed. Only slowly did the realization dawn. At nine twenty-three, *Hood's* forward magazines also blew up, and the ship capsized and sank immediately. Not a single man of her crew of one thousand five hundred men was saved.

As the destroyers criss-crossed and depth-charged the

place where she had been, U100 slipped away towards the coast of Holland. The two surviving capital ships turned south-westward with the rest of the fleet. Admiral Forbes radioed ahead:-

"*H.M.S. Hood* sunk by enemy submarine 21.23 hours. Am making for Thames Estuary. Provide new orders or confirm existing. Urgent. Forbes."

At first the Admiralty did not — could not — believe the encoded message. There must be an error. It could not be "sunk"; it must be "hit" or "damaged". They radioed for confirmation, and the message was confirmed. In the Admiralty, Sir Dudley Pound sent orders to Admiral Forbes to make for the Medway. There would be no battle-ships in the Channel that night. He had already told Chur-chill about Portsmouth, as much as he could piece together of the disaster. Now he must ring the Prime Minister again. For the unthinkable had happened — worse than the raid on Portsmouth in many ways. The *Hood* had represented the Navy for most people, Britain's flagship, the "Mighty 'Ood". And now she was gone. The weight of the news pressed on him like an intolerable burden. He, better than most, knew the realities of sea power, and suddenly now he felt that power slipping through his fingers like sand. He reached for the phone. It took him few words to tell Churchill. The Prime Minister asked if there was any possi-bility of a mistake.

"There is no mistake, sir. *H.M.S. Hood* has been sunk."

"Thank you, Sir Dudley. Goodbye now."

In his room in the bunker under 10 Downing Street, Winston Churchill put down the phone. He got up and walked over to the map. No-one was with him. All day he had been trying to assess the strength of the invasion, to move troops, to commit his forces, to thrust the enemy back into the sea. The invasion had never unnerved him, for behind those Germans who dared to stand on English soil lay the great grey wastes of England's seas. Knowing that, he had faced the prospect unflinching, and had spoken words of defiance to the listening people. For he knew he wielded the spear of Britain's sea power. And now the spear was broken. Suddenly before his eyes was the vision of defeat. He sat heavily on the edge of his cot, and there were tears in his eyes.

At eleven o'clock, *H.M.S. Nelson*, flagship of the Home Fleet, struck a mine. It was a new field, put down by Commodore Ruge's minelayers in a north easterly line off the North Foreland, specifically to protect the invasion area. With her bows damaged, and taking water, the *Nelson* finally limped into the Medway at dawn on the 28th. Pound did not tell the Prime Minister till the next morning. He himself went to bed convinced, like Churchill, that the naval losses of the day constituted, more surely than any actual or potential German victories on the South Coast, an utter disaster to British arms.

Chapter 12

ACTIVE SERVICE

Don waited by the phone box in a daze. He had dialled
999, told them about the bomb, shouted at them, tried to
make them understand that his friends were there, dead on
the ruined station. Then he had tried to ring the emergency
number for his Home Guard unit, but no-one had answered. The people at the emergency services had just told
him to wait by the phone box: there would be a call back.
He waited, trying not to think. The call came, an officer,
asking for details. Don wasn't asked the details he wanted
to tell, details of the broken bodies, of who and what those
men had been. So he told them the track was blocked, and
the officer said, "Go back and wait on the station." But he
couldn't. He just stood there on the corner by the phone
box, and fought off the thoughts, the memory of those
faces. It must have been an hour or more. A policeman
came on his bike. And the ambulance, at last. It was the
army that had told him to wait at the station. They would
want to talk to him, he supposed.

When they did come it was just a motor-cycle and side-
car, a sergeant on the bike, officer in the side-car. The
officer was a captain. Not one of the very, very young
officers the war had thrown up, but a middle-aged man.
The bike screeched to a stop in the dust.

"Are you the man who reported the incident?" the
sergeant demanded. It was always called "the incident".

Don was still seeing the dead faces, all that mattered or would matter to him of "the incident".

"Stand up, laddie!" The sergeant was brisk, a large bull-headed man. Don did as he was told, too numbed to be angry at the indifference. "I thought you were supposed to go down to the platform and resume guard?"

"All right, sergeant, no harm done. Would you get down there and assess the situation for me." The sergeant saluted, and was gone at a run.

"You've lost some of your friends down there, I know." The voice was sympathetic. Grey eyes in a tired face looked straight at him. There was no indifference there. "It's happening to all of us now, son, now they're here." He didn't even talk much like an officer. The upper-class twang was missing, nothing like that bloke in the drill hall this morning — only this morning, that had been. "I need you to give me a precise report of the events, that's all," he was saying. "The sergeant will tell me what it's like down there."

Don described the attack as best he could, leaving out the real horror of it. It took a few halting sentences. The sergeant was back before he had finished. He added to Don's account a brief description of the extent of the damage. It seemed to be worse than Don had thought.

"Well, the railway crew will be down here as soon as they can — but what that means I don't know." The officer was talking half to the sergeant, half to himself. "Our boys will probably be sooner, but if there's track to be replaced it will have to wait on the platelayers . . . ." It dawned on Don that they were Royal Engineers. "I'll have to leave you here sergeant, for liaison. Come back with our team. And the moment it's clear see that the report goes in. That's the first priority on this one."

"Yessir!" The sergeant had come to attention, presumably because he was being given an order. "Begging your pardon, sir, but. . . . "

"But I can't drive the bike myself. — I wonder if this young shaver can." He turned to Don. "Well, can you?" Don nodded, then remembered who he was talking to.

"Yes, sir," he replied. The officer rolled up his right sleeve to reveal an artificial arm. Don hadn't realized. Only now was the pink unnatural plastic of the hand obvious.

"Oh, try not to be embarrassed by it, I'm not any more," he said, smiling. "But you can see that I can not ride a bike and guarantee to stay on. — What's your job in civilian life?" Don told him.

"Well, that's better than a bank clerk. Considerably better. So you'd be enough of a mechanic to mend this thing if it broke down?"

"I'd have a go, sir," Don replied.

"Excuse me, sir, but this man is Home Guard, sir. Not a regular, sir. Might it not be advisable to phone for a rider, sir?" The sergeant was looking distinctly unhappy.

"No doubt it would — but I *have* to be in a conference at Division at half past seven, and what I have to say to them might, for once, be of some importance to somebody. So, I'll take full responsibility, sergeant. Oh, you'd better give the sergeant your Home Guard unit, the C.O., and their contact number. Phone through and let them know the score, sergeant. Tell them he's not hurt, and should be back late this evening. Get them to tell his people he's all right. The news of the casualties will have gone back via the emergency services. Well then, on you get, private!"

Don straddled the bike and kicked the starter. The engine throbbed into life at once, sweet running and full of power. The captain scrambled into the side-car. Don opened the throttles and felt the surge as they leapt away. It was an exhilarating feeling. He had never ridden a bike as powerful as this before. He realized the captain was yelling at him, his voice almost blown away in the slip-stream.

"Straight up the road till you come to the crossroads at Old Netley, then right into Bursledon. After that turn onto the Portsmouth Road, the A27. We're not going to Portsmouth, though."

"Where are we going, sir?" he managed to shout back.

"Chichester — Divisional H.Q. Number Four Division. Though no doubt I shouldn't have told you, in the course of the evening you can hardly fail to find out, so I've saved you the trouble."

Don was getting the feel of the bike now, and feeling more confident as he squeezed the accelerator harder. Not that he could go too fast. A bike with a side-car was proving a very different proposition to riding solo. Also the captain had admonished him after they took their first corner at speed.

"Not too fast, private. I want to visit Chichester, not the hedgerow! By the way, what's your name?"

"Private Gibbard, sir," he yelled back, after slowing down. Then he remembered to add his number — since he was now apparently serving with the 'real' army for a little while. He was enjoying the experience too.

"I am Captain D.A. Sawyer, R.E. — an engineer, you see, like yourself."

Don smiled to himself at this crazy officer. He felt the wind on his face, and felt the exhilaration. Then the memory came up to hit him, jerking his body physically, so that the bike swayed on the road. He wondered how he could have forgotten so soon, how he could have forgotten even for a moment the sight of those dead men on the station.

They turned onto the main Southampton-Portsmouth road, and crossed Bursledon Bridge over the Hamble. There seemed to be a vast amount of military traffic — more if Don had known that many of the lorries and some of the private cars they passed were now under army control. As they came out of Fareham and into Porchester, the harbour of Portsmouth spread out to their right, with the built-up area of the town beyond. The town was veiled in smoke, blown back across it by the westerly wind. Smoke from the fires that ringed the harbour. Don saw the distant shapes of the navy's ships, and the flames swirling about. Some were on fire, some seemed to be trying to move out into the open waters in the middle of the harbour. A big ship, smoke rolling out from her, was half aground on the mudflats near by.

"Slow down!" ordered Captain Sawyer. "Slow as you

can. It might be none of my business, but I like to keep informed."

The captain's eyes were fixed on the events in the harbour. Riding slowly, Don could look too, until they came to the crossroads, and the turn-off into the city. Don half expected Sawyer to order him to go there. Along the last mile or so there had been people walking by the roadside, or sitting on the grass verges overlooking the harbour in the shadow of the Downs. Don had seen 'trekkers' before — people who came out of the towns into the countryside to avoid the raids, especially the night raids. Now there seemed to be more of them. A steady stream up the road from Portsmouth could be seen from the crossroads. Don turned to the captain as they rode on.

"That looked like a bad one for us, sir. Lots of ships hit."

"Yes, very bad. — I wonder how very bad?" He seemed more subdued, and obviously not in the mood for conversation.

As they rode on through Havant and Emsworth, there were more and more people, a constant trickle, along both sides of the road, all walking, mostly carrying suitcases, mostly women. Some had children with them. There were some handcarts. All were moving westward. Everyone knew that the enemy had landed in Sussex. These were not people avoiding raids. Don realized that for the first time he was looking at refugees. They were not fleeing the fighting itself, not yet. They were running from the endless rumours and the dread of the unknown, from the towns of Sussex where the enemy had not landed yet, but might soon, the towns that might fall if there was an advance. It was not like the scenes they had witnessed on newsreels of the Spanish Civil War. It was nothing like the scale of the fleeing peoples who had trudged south down the roads of France. But it was the beginning of the same — English civilians, fleeing the Blitzkrieg.

On the outskirts of Chichester there were roadblocks, manned by military police. The city was under martial law, like the rest of Kent and Sussex. At one of them there was some difficulty explaining Don's presence. The MP corporal had eyed him frostily, but finally let them pass without "ringing up to check" and all the interminable delay that involved.

"He obviously regards me as more than a little mad," said the captain as they drove into the city. "Gallivanting about the countryside with a stolen apprentice dressed up as a soldier." Don wanted to say that he was old enough to *be* a soldier, but he didn't feel like arguing with an army captain. He also desperately wanted a cup of tea, far more even than he wanted something to eat.

Everywhere in the city centre seemed to be protected with sandbags. There were few people about as it began to get dark. All the people he did see had that wary, apprehensive look. It was the usual expression at night-time when the siren was going. But here it was on every face, the most obvious token of the German presence in England — that and the preponderance of the military. There were soldiers everywhere, laughing, talking, a visible contrast to the civilian population. Though it might not be the front line, it was *like* the front line all right.

He followed his captain, Captain D.A. Sawyer, R.E., into the H.Q. building, formerly the court-house. He thought after he had done so that he probably should have stayed outside. The captain was accosted in the hall by another officer. A major, this time, Don noticed, and a man in an obvious hurry. Don half listened to 'his' captain reporting on the cut railway line, and alternative routing via Eastleigh, and estimated time for completion of repairs. Then his ears pricked up. Invasion talk — the real thing. . . .

"No-one has the faintest idea what's happening in Brighton," the major was saying. "Twenty-nine Brigade Group have been incommunicado all day. Of course everyone knows that Jerry's in the town and there's fighting going on, but it looks as if something's gone wrong for sure. I can tell you Monty at Corps is in a flap about it, old man. Still, not your worry, eh?" This was more like the usual officer. Don could see that Sawyer was nettled by him — didn't like being called "old man" perhaps.

"The point is this, Sawyer," the major was continuing, "1st M.M.G. is due to go up in strength to give aid and assistance at twelve hundred tomorrow. — Well that's the whisper I have anyway. But, this is the problem: — we've lost the bridge on the Adur, here at Shoreham." He held out a folded section of a map, and pointed. Sawyer looked. "Now Major Gould is in the process of lining up some of your chaps to get over there p.d.q., but we shall need you there too. Assessment, you know. No point in trying to put a bridge back up if it won't go, eh?"

"I very much doubt we shall be putting a bridge back up," said Sawyer drily. "I would have thought a Bailey bridge was required."

"Well, there you are, old man, your pigeon now. Time for a quick bite to eat, then on the old bike again."

"Yes, I'll get over there straight away. . . . It sounds as if Division might be going up as well."

The major tapped his nose.

"That'll rather depend on your Johnies getting a bridge up for us, won't it?" he replied — then suddenly exclaimed, "My God, what's that?"

Don realized that the major was looking straight at him. Not quite sure what to do, he stood to attention and saluted.

"'That' is the man who drove me here," replied Captain Sawyer in a calm voice.

"It's a bloody Home Guard! Christ Almighty, Sawyer, what the hell do you think you're playing at? There are regulations you know. You can't just commandeer civilians. There'll be the devil to pay for this, I can tell you."

Sawyer looked at him as if deciding whether to answer or not. Don knew what *he* wanted to say. This bloke obviously didn't know there was a war on.

"I'm supposed to be attending a conference," was all Captain Sawyer said.

"Oh that — cancelled."

"Thank you for telling me." He turned to Don. "Well then, we'd better get you something to eat, my lad, and then see about getting someone to give you a lift back home. — You've done a good job today. — Then I'll be off to see about building a bridge somewhere in twelve hours flat. Wouldn't have been able to without you, Private." He looked back towards the major again. "Any further orders for me, Major Howard?"

The major did not have time for a reply. The sudden wail of the air-raid siren cut in above them. Sawyer caught hold of Don's shoulder.

"Come on, Private!"

Don followed the captain, a sudden sick feeling welling up inside him, the sort of dread that had never been there in air raids before — before he had seen his mates killed at the station. There were A.T.S. clerks running down the stairs, and a tall chap with brigadier's tabs on his shoulders. Many other officers too, and the N.C.O.'s attached to the divisional staff. He realized that he was by far the most insignificant person there. The shelter was in the cellars. They were deep and furnished with tables and chairs, maps on the wall, electric light. Not much like a shelter at all, not what Don meant by the word anyway. There was the same feel as any shelter though: the chattering at first, nervous — a sudden laugh. Then a dull crump outside somewhere, stilling the voices. Louder thuds followed, and the shaking of the earth.

"Christ! It is us they're after this time," said a voice, quietly, though everyone heard.

A series of shattering crashes seemed to burst directly overhead, so that the whole cellar swayed. The brick walls bulged inwards on them, the wooden joists above twisting as if in some great vice. Floorboards snapped across in the corner: there the ceiling of the shelter was the floor of a room above. Everywhere else, flaked mortar and brick dust and a thin rain of distemper showered down on their heads. The banisters of the staircase collapsed with a rattle and bang. Lightbulbs swung wildly and flickered momentarily, but stayed alight. A fourth concussion — farther away, but still near enough to shake the still-trembling walls another time. Everyone waited as the sounds receded. There were other bombs, but no more for them. Many other bombs. It was a long while before anyone spoke.

"Well, Grover, this will be something of a nuisance to our communications, I'm afraid."

"Oh, I daresay we'll manage, General Eastwood. Their bomb aiming does seem to have come on a bit lately, though."

The spell broke, and others started talking. Don looked over at the two officers. His first general of the war, chatting away to the brigadier he'd noticed earlier. There was still bombing farther afield, and everyone was aware of it, but you learnt in a war when it was your turn and when someone else's. The whole raid had taken less than half an hour. They waited till the all-clear, then filed up the steps. One corner of the entrance hall above had taken some blast. Two of the large windows had been blown in, as well as the door, despite all the sandbagging. Where one window had been, the brickwork of the wall had come down too, and rubble lay across the floor. It was night outside now.

Everyone started chasing round at once, trying to sort out the mess, finding out how bad things were. Don stood feeling useless and wishing even more for a cup of tea. His mouth was like cotton wool, and he was feeling hungrier than ever now. Also, he didn't know quite what to do. 'His' captain had vanished, and amid the havoc he didn't like to ask anyone else. Everyone obviously had more urgent things to do. And if that major had been anything to go by, he'd probably get himself arrested as a spy. He stood around, while another half hour or so passed. One of his problems was solved almost at once though. Two of the A.T.S. brought in great trays of tea — in cups, not mugs, unfortunately. Don gulped his down, and dared asking for another. He was given one and grinned appreciatively at the girl, getting a wink back for his trouble. She hadn't noticed he was only Home Guard, he thought. Then he thought: "only Home Guard" — for all he knew there were Home Guards bleeding and dying along the beaches and in sleepy villages just at that moment, just like those who had died beside him on the station. Before the thought could get hold of him again, a hand fell on his shoulder.

"Come on, my lad, get that drunk, and then follow me." It was the captain again. Don swallowed the hot tea in one gulp, and followed Sawyer outside into the night. The bombs had fallen across the street — at least those which had done the damage to the Divisional H.Q. The other side of the street was flattened, illuminated by a fire still burning fiercely among the ruins. A gas main, it looked like, a great blue and yellow jet of flame, spearing up, with a lesser fire blazing away around it. He caught a glimpse of another fire, farther away. There were clearly more as well, distant flickers of red light against the darkness marking their presence. The gas main roared as it burnt. There was also that pervasive smell, the smell of dust and burning and cordite, and the bitter taste it left on the lips.

"It seems they *were* after H.Q.," said the captain. "Their intelligence service is improving. Two nasty hits, one of them on a shelter. A lot of our people hurt, a lot of men dead." He was shouting, partly above the sound of the fire, partly, it seemed, in anger. "And now there's no-one to take me down to the coast. Not tonight anyway. — Unless you want to do it."

"Yes, sir!" Don answered immediately, not even thinking about it, and forgetting that he wanted a square meal before he did anything.

"It's highly irregular, you know. I've no business doing it, and you've no business doing it. We'll both be in a great deal of trouble if we get killed."

They both laughed, though it was true, of course: they might be killed. But so might anyone, sitting in their own home or their shelter. And he wanted to *do* something, not to sit at home or in a shelter, or like a sitting duck on some pointless guard duty. Part of it was plain excitement, the strange thrill that comes from real risk. Part was the mood engendered by this weird and wonderful officer, who seemed to be a walking defiance of everything the hidebound, pompous British army was supposed to stand for.

"I'll check the bike over, sir," he offered.

"Yes, do that. Look busy in case anyone enquires what you're up to. I'll go and give a note to one of the desk sergeants. A bit fuller this time, so that your people won't worry. Here, scribble down your address on this, and you'd better put down your unit's details again."

Don wrote on the pad, then busied himself with the motorbike. There was still plenty of fuel. Soon Captain Sawyer had come out and they were off again, eastwards along the coast route. They left behind the fires that marked 4 Division's H.Q. in Chichester, passed through Arundel, where there were more roadblocks, and along the winding stretch above Worthing on towards Brighton. Don wondered idly when he'd finally get back home. This time tomorrow, he wouldn't be surprised. He'd have a story to tell some of them when he did!

They had been stopped at yet another roadblock, on the Brighton Road, when Don first heard the sounds of the invasion — the war on the land. As the engine cut out, the sound of artillery fire came clear through the night. Still distant, but not *that* far away. It was nearly continuous, one or two heavy guns firing at regular intervals, with a fainter background crackle underlying it, like static on the wireless. This was the first audible evidence of the conflict. The visible evidence was plainer to see. All along the roadside, as they approached the battle, the tide of humanity had steadily swollen. People in the night, running away. It made the earlier trickle of refugees seem insignificant.

The authorities had already abandoned the attempt to stop the flow so long as it did not obstruct the roads, though at times the people were halted or cleared back to let priority traffic have a clear road. Don did not know any of that. What he did know was the expressions on the people's faces. Much of it was simple weariness, that and shock. Disbelief at what had happened to them. He had seen something like it before on the faces of people bombed out, but there had been few of those, and these were so many. What had been their world had been taken away, and now they were moving blindly away into a future where nothing was sure, and hope was dying. Women glancing up in sudden apprehension at any sound, old men shuffling, tired out, children grizzling to themselves, ignored — no words to the soldiers on the roadblock, no jokes, no questions. Until then, Don had believed that England would win through in the end. Now that faith was profoundly shaken. For this was only the beginning.

The last roadblock had been at Lancing. It was where they turned off the main A27, down to the coast itself. From here the flashes of the big guns could be seen. They arrived at the bridge which had once carried the A259 across the estuary of the River Adur at Shoreham harbour. They were six miles from the centre of Brighton, perhaps four from the nearest fighting — the front line. The bursts of small arms fire were more insistent now, the regular thud and roar of the artillery plainer. There seemed to be aircraft overhead, and the sound of bombing too. What Don was watching was the mopping up of the remnants of 29th Brigade Group in Brighton by the German 28th Division. The fighting had not abated with the night.

Almost as soon as they pulled to a halt, a lieutenant came running up to the motorbike. Don took off the goggles. It had been a hair-raising journey with only slit headlamps — all the blackout allowed. He helped the captain out of the side-car, using the opportunity to stay close to him, and to listen.

"Glad to see you, sir. Have you been briefed?"

"Briefly!" Sawyer laughed at his own pun. "You'd better tell me what's really happened. All I know is that we've got a main road-bridge down on a crossing needed for tomorrow."

"Worse than that, I'm afraid, sir. The bridge just here is completely out, as you've been told. Metal girder-arch bridge, carrying one of two main roads. Not much question of repairing. The second bridge, farther north, is also damaged. That's the one that carries the A27. Not usable by vehicular traffic, but still open to pedestrians. — Lots of refugees crossing, but nothing else."

"Yes, I've seen the refugees. Not pleasant . . . Why

couldn't they have told me this at Division? — What about repairs on that bridge, Peter?"

"I don't think so, sir, but you may want to go up and look at it tomorrow morning."

"So you reckon on a Bailey bridge down here?"

"If you agree, sir. We've been working at getting the debris cleared out of the way. I think we've got a good location just upstream. Nothing too complicated, so long as the equipment arrives."

"Well, you seem to have things safely under control. Thank God it's you down here. I had a horrible feeling they'd sent Walter Ridley." Both of them laughed. "Any other bridges, by the way?"

"Oh yes, the Southern Railway, double track line on a causeway affair. They missed that altogether. It was a tip and run raid, by the way. Precision stuff though; Stukas."

"Hm — well I'd like a look at the railway bridge. I'll have to go down and see the shambles here of course. And we might get up as far as your pedestrians-only bridge. Look, have your men got any rations spare. My driver here hasn't eaten for goodness knows how long." He had suddenly turned to Don, who felt absurdly gratified that he had been remembered amidst all these important matters.

A platoon of sappers was, as it happened, just in the middle of preparing their evening meal. From the soldiers Don came in for a little easy banter. They seemed more concerned about his well-being than anything else. As for Don, he was merely happy to wolf down the hot stew.

"You shouldn't be here, mate. Bloody daft bringing you here," they told him, as he consumed more than his share of the rations and gulped the tea that was offered. They even had chocolate, a rare luxury available only to troops, in the depths of rationing. He told them he was alright, so long as someone had informed his people at home where he was.

At home, his mother got the message, delivered by the sergeant of Don's Home Guard platoon at about seven o'clock. She had made his supper long before. Now it was in the oven, getting all dried up. She sat in the front room looking at the sergeant. A big man, he stood awkwardly, fingering his tin hat. This was not easy for him, but his last call had been harder. — Bill's wife, his widow now. Bill who had been killed on the station that afternoon. He'd known Bill for years, since they were nippers. Knew his wife, too. Bill had three kids. Sergeant Stevens' round face was strained and unhappy. Mary, the widow, had taken it badly, terribly badly. He'd had to leave her with a neighbour though. He'd go back as soon as he'd finished here. The officer had been to the families of the other two men that had died. He felt an irrational annoyance at this poor woman — because her son wasn't dead. . . .

"I'm sorry, Missus, I can't tell you more than that. Volunteered to take this officer down to Chichester. On a motorbike! That's the message. Should be back this evening, late though. That's all I know."

"Why couldn't this officer drive his own motorbike?" Win Gibbard's voice was fretful and worried. "He's only nineteen, Mr Stevens. It's not right he should be allowed to volunteer for this sort of thing."

Privately the sergeant agreed. It all sounded a bit 'unofficial' to him.

"He's only taking this bloke down on the bike, then coming back," was what he actually said to her.

"Are you sure it was only the others — I mean, he wasn't hurt . . . ?" She realized what she had said, saw the look on Stevens' face. " — Oh, I'm so sorry, Mr Stevens . . . Sit down, now. Have a cup of tea, and a piece of cake. — Were they friends of yours, the ones who got . . . ?"

He saw the understanding in the eyes of the fussing, frightened woman. At least her sudden concern for him, for the others, the dead ones, had lifted some of her own worries for her son. He couldn't blame her really. He sat down, ate some of the proffered cake, tried to chat — about other things. Then he got up to go.

"Don't worry, then, Mrs Gibbard. Not a scratch, he

didn't get. And he'll be back this evening. Just a joy-ride, if you ask me. You give him what-for for volunteering."

She managed a smile as he left, then busied herself clearing away the tea things. There was no point in keeping his dinner hot now. She thought of putting the radio on, but decided she didn't want to hear the news. There was supposed to be a broadcast by the Prime Minister. She would listen to that when they repeated it later on though. After Don had come home.

"He'll be home soon," she thought. "Though Mr Stevens said late — that might mean not till ten or eleven o'clock. . . . "

Don shared the sappers' bivouac. He would not be home that night, however long his mother sat up and waited. She did not get the second message about him till the following morning. He himself woke up feeling dirty, hungry and intolerably stiff. He had camped out a few times in his life, but never on ground so uncomfortable as this. It had been an uneasy night too, with the sound of the sappers working away on clearing the rubble of the wrecked bridge, and then the arrival of lorries in the small hours, carrying pontoon sections and steel girders. And of course, the regular backdrop of the sounds of fighting, only a few miles away in Brighton. He was up well before sunrise, reflecting that it was a Saturday. In normal circumstances he would have had a bit of a lie in. There were no normal circumstances now.

He ate breakfast with the soldiers, joined in the banter, now a recognized member of the little group, if only for a short while. They were no older than he was, some of them. They watched the distant shapes of planes over Brighton. A formation of bombers, from the south as you would expect now. Enemy planes. Just after sunrise there were British planes though, a line of six Hurricanes coming over from the west. Two of them peeled off, and flew low right over them. The Tommies around the wrecked bridge stopped work to wave their hats and cheer them. The planes

178

waggled their wings. Don went to look for his captain, to
see if there was anything useful he could do.

"I'll have to go over to the other bank again, Peter,"
Sawyer was saying to same lieutenant, the officer who commanded the Sappers. They obviously knew each other quite
well. "We had our money's worth out of that rowing boat
last night, didn't we?"

"I hope the owner doesn't mind, sir. Hang on a minute,
and I'll detail a couple of men."

"No, no. Let them get on with it. — Come here, Private
Gibbard!"

He turned and called Don, who had been waiting near
by.

"I can see your ears flapping from here, Private. I suppose you can pull an oar as well as you can ride a motorbike?"

"Yes, sir, of course." Don had lived in a seaport all his
life; his father was a sailor; and apart from anything else,
he liked boats. Of course he could pull an oar!

"I imagined you would. Good! Then I'll not need to
disturb your men, Lieutenant Brooks."

Don and the captain stepped gingerly into the grimy,
black-tarred rowing boat, and Don fitted oars to rowlocks.

"Not long till we get you home now, Private," Sawyer
said, as Don pulled away from the bank. "You've made
yourself very useful to me, and believe it or not to your
country's war effort. What's your first name, by the way.
Just so that I know."

Smiling, pleased with himself, Don told him.

As he spoke, came the sound of cannon, up above,
cannon and aero-engine. They both looked up. Coming in
from the south, low over the flat coastal plain, a trio of
Me109's. The machine guns on each side of the river cut
in, one in a sandbagged emplacement, the other in a pillbox.
There was rifle fire too. For a moment Don could not move
the oars. He felt as if the water had become solid, and in
that frozen moment his mind was observing and noting
every detail. The running scattering figures on the bank,
the wriggling machine gun barrels with their abrupt chatter,

the varnished wood of the oars in his hands. Above all, the plane. The tilt of its wings, the wink of tracer. He saw the spurts in the water, high straight columns.

He could move the oars again. Desperately he pulled. The plane was over and gone, but there were already more waterspouts. The second Messerschmitt was coming straight at them. The line of waterspouts cut into the boat. Wood splinters flew up, one catching Don in the head. For a second he felt the pain, then he was falling. He half saw Captain Sawyer, stood up in the stern of the boat, shooting uselessly with his revolver towards the departing Me109. Out of the corner of his eye he glimpsed the third plane shooting up the lads on the bank. Then they were over. The boat had turned turtle.

He felt the sudden chill of the water. Swallowed water. His feet were caught up in the wreckage of the boat, and for a long hideous moment he hung upside down in the river, under the boat, breathing in water, choking and struggling. Then his feet came free. He turned over, pushing his head up, suffocating, his lungs full of water. His head broke the surface, struck something hard, almost knocking him out. He went down again for a moment, then his mouth found air. He sucked it in, gasping and retching. His hands were holding on to something for support, his head still reeling.

It took a few moments, so intent was he on breathing again, to realize, with a sudden utter shock, that he was in darkness. For a moment he thought he had been blinded, and the horror of his situation overwhelmed him. He was sick again, his hands grasping the wood. Grasping! It dawned on him that he was holding on tight to something — to wood. It must be the boat. At the same time came the realization that the darkness was not utter. There were chinks of light. The water below was murky brown, not black, brown with sunlight diffused in it.

He suddenly understood what had happened. He had come up inside the capsized hull of the boat. It was still floating upside down. And there was air. His eyes rapidly grew accustomed to the dimness. He felt around him. He was holding onto a stretcher, one of the crosswise strengtheners. There was about a foot of clear air space, narrowing off behind him. His head hurt though, and he reached up to touch it. He could just make out the dark stain on his hand. It felt as if that splinter had given him a nasty cut, but that was all. He wasn't shot, or drowned, or blinded. He hung on, breathing deeply, getting his breath back, as the current carried the upturned wreck of the boat downstream.

Captain Sawyer felt the bullets of the Messerschmitt's cannon cut into the wood of the boat. In moments the plane was over and gone. He had stood up firing, stupidly as he knew very well, with his service revolver. In the same instant he knew both that he was unhurt, and that the boat was going as the shells smashed into it. He felt it begin to turn over, and fell sideways. The last thing he saw was that young Home Guardsman, still holding the oars. His face had not shewn fear, just bewilderment. Across the side of his head a bright red patch of blood had been spreading.

The captain hit the water, already struggling to kick off his shoes and shed his battle-dress. His head broke surface, and he saw the upturned boat, already some way off. He went under again. It was proving impossible to get out of his uniform and his clothes were rapidly becoming waterlogged. With only one arm he could not swim well at the best of times. Then he felt an arm round his chest, and the pull of a strong swimmer. Steadily the Tommy who had dived in got him to the bank. He stood up and looked all around. The lieutenant hurried over to him from a burning lorry.

"Where's the boy? Where is he?"

"The young Home Guard in the boat, sir . . . ?" The lieutenant spoke quietly. "He didn't come up, I'm afraid, sir. We think he was hit."

"Oh my God," said the captain, and sat down on the muddy grass.

Chapter 13

SEASIDE HOLIDAY

Adolf appreciatively sipped the mug of cocoa he had been given, then cautiously looked around him, still shivering under his blanket. The motorboat that he, Rudi and Hans were now sat in was quite a large vessel, more motor yacht in fact. Very impressive in appearance, with a swept-up bow, now raised above the scudding waves as they raced along. It was the sort of thing Adolf associated with millionaires and the South of France. Up in the cabin he could see the peaked caps of the officers, the glint of epaulets and silver insignia. So this was the divisional command 28 Division. And he had been addressed by Generalleutnant von Obstfelder himself. (He had only once seen his own divisional commander, and that was on parade with the whole regiment.) He craned his head round to look out over the Channel. There were other motor boats, all travelling in approximate lines, stretching out in both directions. It looked a very different sort of invasion to the slow and vulnerable barges, with their clanking and grinding along behind ancient tugs. On the other hand, it was obvious to anyone that there weren't nearly so many soldiers here. He turned back, realizing with a start that one of the officers had come up and was looking at them quizzically.

"You may remain seated." — Rudi and Hans abandoned their attempts to stand to attention clad in blankets. "I hope you are now recovered, men." The officer spoke in a polite, even voice, without the arrogant undertone of some of them, the old junker class. At least under National Socialism the army wasn't quite so snobbish as it used to be. "I know you have already been spoken to by the General. You will now please give me your names, ranks and numbers, so that in due course your regimental authorities may be notified." That hadn't changed — the red tape. They gave the information.

"I am sorry to say that your division in particular has suffered great loss at the hands of the English navy. There is no question, as you will see, of being returned to your own regiment. Accordingly, you will now regard yourselves as attached to 7 Grenadierregiment, Divisional Staff Unit, first echelon. I am Leutnant Weber, and you will join the men under my command. Our function is to provide a personal guard for the General and the Staff. You are fortunate. It is a much sought-after duty."

"Will we get a chance to have a go at the English, sir? We've lost some of our friends, you see, sir. And we watched those bastards gunning our men down in the sea." It was Rudi who asked, not that he had any business to be doing so.

"We will be landing on an enemy coast, under fire. — You may get your revenge soldier — but you will do it as a soldier of the Wehrmacht. There will be no private scores settled."

"Sorry, sir," muttered Rudi.

"New rifles will be issued to you shortly by Corporal Taubert. Make sure you do what he tells you. He's your corporal. And try not to get in the way."

Adolf sensed the smile in his eyes, though he had kept a straight face. Well, they had landed with a decent officer again, he thought. The officer had been right to tell off Rudi too. The shooting of those men in the sea had been vile, sickening. But he, Adolf, could imagine himself doing it, if it was his country being invaded by an enemy. Perhaps if it had been Frenchmen swimming across the Rhine:- he decided that was the parallel. It didn't fit in with the usual image of the English, though. Playing the game and being fair, and all that. On the other hand, they'd been reminded often enough that the English were a Germanic people really — with the same ruthlessness, perhaps even the same devotion to *land und volk*. But he could never forgive them for the death of Willi — that much he knew. Not after he had seen Willi's face, here on the boat, rescued too late to cheat the sea.

"Right, you three, rifles!" Corporal Taubert had arrived. "I don't know if the lieutenant told you, but your job will be to act as a screen for the officers, along with me and twenty others. The difference is that them and me are trained for it, and you're not. So just remember, my lads, if anyone gets shot it has to be one of us, not one of the officers. 'Cause we don't matter, do we now?"

"Is it right we're landing in the Bay of Brighton, Corp.?" asked Hans.

"My, my, we have found out things quickly. Well, I suppose you should know that much. Yes it is. The town of Brighton, a great holiday place of the English."

"I hope it's a holiday for us too," muttered Hans.

"Oh, it will be, private. We're landing on the pier, captured intact while the English were sleeping. And now you know as much as I do. So get those rifles checked, and as soon as you're ready, get those blankets off and try to look just a bit like German soldiers!"

"All corporals are the same," whispered Rudi, as Taubert went about more important business. "I used to think it was only ours. But this one came out of the same mould."

The sound of artillery had been audible for some time now, and it was starting to be joined by the crack of small arms too. The English coast was plainly to be seen along the whole northern horizon, rapidly taking shape, turning from a grey humped mass into cliffs and hills rising from them, and a town spread out above beaches. Adolf shivered in the cold. His clothes were still wet, and he was still uncomfortable. Also he could feel his stomach tightening in anticipation. They were not far away now. The moment they had all prepared for was coming, late, in a different place, but this time much as he had envisaged it in his daydreams.

"Better than a barge any day," said Hans, putting the thought into words.

Above the town hall, spreading trees of smoke were rising in dozens of places. One bigger fire than the others could be seen off to their right, blazing away near the coastline. Along the beach ahead of them were more motor-boats. Coming in with them, the flotilla of ships was now spread out in one long line. Adolf ducked instinctively as a plane roared down towards them, along the line. Then recognized the friendly growl of the Messerschmitt. There were other planes in the sky, all of them looking like fighters, and all German.

Their boat came under the shadow of the Palace Pier, Brighton, England. Among the girders there were some grey-clad figures working — in fact removing the last of the charges the English had failed to blow. In a moment he found himself scrambling up an iron step-ladder, ahead of the officers he was now, partly, responsible for guarding. He had been expecting to scale cliffs. Tying up at a jetty seemed definitely preferable. They were right on the end of the pier, clambering up onto a catwalk, then again onto the wooden decking. A tall ornate building, the pier theatre, displayed its flaking facade above them.

"Clear a way there. You men, out of the way! — Divisional Staff landing now!" Lieutenant Weber was shouting orders loudly to all and sundry. There were throngs of German soldiers, down the whole length of the pier, the grey mass being hustled along by officers obviously eager to get *off* the pier as soon as possible. For all its convenience, it was a very exposed target, as the Germans were well aware. Adolf looked out along the beach. There were other soldiers landing from other boats in the low breakers, and hastening up the beach. What was missing was the enemy. So much for landing under fire!

They had formed a small cordon round the head of the stairs. As the general and the rest of the staff came up, a lieutenant colonel arrived from the landward end, obviously in a hurry.

"Ah, Oberstleutnant Grolman, good to see you, my dear chap!" The general shook hands warmly with the latest arrival. Since they were stood right behind him, Adolf had the benefit of hearing their conversation in full, much to his satisfaction.

"I am pleased to report that the invasion is progressing well, Herr General," said the lieutenant-colonel, obviously highly pleased with himself. "The beach area between both piers — you can see the other one up there, sir — is entirely safe. We are in possession of the coast to the east as far as the landing area of 8 Division. My patrols have made contact. The city itself has been penetrated in depth, and the fighting is now for the railway terminus and the western suburbs, where there is a useful harbour. All the large buildings you can see are of course in our hands."

He gestured towards the line of sedate hotel façades that made up Brighton front. Adolf let his eyes also glance in the direction indicated. The town seemed a strange sort of 'objective' for the invasion, but then, the landing had to be somewhere.

"What about losses?" the general asked.

"Very slight indeed in the initial stages of the landing. Virtually all of those on the beach were caused by mines. Now the fighting in the streets is stiffer, and casualties begin to mount. I have provisionally established Headquarters in one of these places — the Grand Hotel. It is well appointed. — And there is one other piece of news for you, Herr General." It was obvious that the Colonel had been saving the best till last. "We believe we have captured intact the command structure of one of the units holding this coast. I have already given orders for them to be brought down and held in our new Headquarters."

"Well, I am hardly needed here at all!" The general, a middle-aged man, made no attempt to conceal his gratification. "I look forward to telling Heitz as much as you looked forward to telling me, eh Grolman?"

The group of officers set off, following the general at a

brisk pace down the pier. Weber had made a good job of clearing the way. Adolf looked from side to side, trying to see more of the town. Now it was apparent that several of the large prestigious buildings had been bombed out, especially on the ground rising away from the beach to their right. The only gunfire was coming from well into the town, some of it ahead of them, but mostly away to the left.

He became conscious of the distant sound of aircraft again, behind them. Like many others he looked up. The formation was visible, dots against the sky, getting steadily larger. German bombers. There was a ragged cheer from the soldiers.

"Even the Luftwaffe's on time!" yelled someone, and there was the usual banter. The officers didn't bother to quell the good humoured noise, and the general was obviously very happy with life.

"Has air cover been adequate?" he asked Grolman.

"We had fighter cover at dawn, and there has been a sortie at selected targets by a Stuka squadron. No enemy activity at all yet. I have the battle diary to date at H.Q."

Where were the English? Adolf felt himself caught up in the heady exhilaration that was spreading through the soldiers of the three regiments disembarking on Brighton beach. This was a walk-over. The enemy had run away after all. It was going to be like France, another victory march. They reached one of the large sea-front hotels. Adolf could see why it was called the *Grand*. It was like a palace. Trust the generals to do well for themselves!

The three of them, Adolf, Rudi and Hans were told to guard the main door, along with two other men, from whom Rudi cadged cigarettes.

"Our tobacco was lost at sea," he explained.

"Look out, you three water rats," muttered Konrad, the donor of the cigarettes. "Don't light up yet. Officer approaching."

The five men flanking the steps up to the doors came to attention. A solitary lieutenant was approaching, with some enlisted men as escort, and prisoners.

"They're the first ones we've seen since we arrived —
Englishmen I mean," hissed Hans.

"Except dead ones," Rudi muttered.

They got a very good look at the file of Englishmen,
marched dejectedly in through the doors by their escort.

"Did you see that?" Rudi whistled between his teeth.

"Every one of them an officer," Adolf answered. "One
might have been a general — I'm not sure though."

"They must have surrendered," Rudi agreed, and Hans
added,

"Now that's real proof we're winning."

"They looked too smart to have been captured in fighting," Adolf said after a pause. "You know they might just
have surrendered . . . "

"You mean I got it right for once," Rudi answered.

The British remained in the hotel under guard, and
news of who and what they were leaked out in various
distorted forms, the nearest to the truth being that they
were the divisional staff of a captured British infantry division which had laid down its arms without a fight. It was
a story not contradicted by anyone on the German divisional
staff, and it spread rapidly even on that first day. A product
of and a further catalyst to the high morale which permeated
the first echelons of 28 Division. In fact they were the
officers of 29th Brigade Group, whose early capture had
deprived the British troops still fighting in Brighton of
coherence and direction.

"Well I didn't expect to find myself on sentry duty all
day. It's hardly what we came to England for, is it?" grumbled Rudi.

The day has passed in increasing boredom for the three
survivors of 100 Grenadierregiment's disaster at sea. They
had been relieved in order to eat their field rations, already
being supplemented by local additions. The field kitchen
was the kitchen of the Grand Hotel, and the General had
brought his own cook over — along with the other essential
personnel, as Rudi put it.

"You should be more appreciative. Everyone in the

regiment would be glad of this assignment," they were lectured by Erich, the other man from 7 Regiment who was sharing the sentry go with them. "You sit here, smoking our tobacco, eating the best rations in the army, and all you can do is complain. You young fellows don't know when you're living."

"You are lacking in National Socialist spirit, old fellow," Rudi told him. "We just want a crack at the enemy, you know. Not a quiet life sitting on our backsides opening doors to generals: 'Good morning, General! Nice weather we're having, Herr Oberst! Fancy seeing you, mein Führer.' I'm not very good at that sort of thing, even if you are."

"Rudi, shut up," Adolf interrupted. "You talk too much, you great clown."

"Quite so, Private Mann." All five of them stood to attention. They had failed to notice the arrival of Weber, the lieutenant. "Well, soldier your wish for a more exciting war may soon be fulfilled. You will be the general's escort when he goes to look at the front line fighting. In about ten minutes. Mann, come in and tell me when the transport gets here. The rest of you, get in the Kubelwagen."

"As Adolf said, Rudi, if your mouth got any bigger, the top of your head would fall off," said Hans.

"You earned us this pleasant little job," Erich added. "Next time you decide you want front line action, make sure I'm not included!"

Adolf glanced at the rather abashed Rudi. He knew him well enough to know it wasn't "National Socialist spirit" that made him want to see some real action. Now the relief of their rescue was beginning to fade, the anticlimax of what had been their landing in England was more apparent. Weeks of intensive training keying you up to fight didn't dissolve in a moment. Adolf found himself looking forward to the prospect of action, though it was only a faint prospect. The general would hardly be going where the bullets were actually flying, he decided. He glanced along the road. Two personnel carriers, flanking a staff car, were approaching. One of them already had troops in it. He hurried in to tell the lieutenant, then joined the others in the second Kubelwagen.

"The driver says they're starting to land a fair amount of transport on the pier now," Hans told him. "It's going to be used for that, while the infantry land directly onto the beach."

"Poor bloody infantry as usual," muttered Erich. He was one of those small, middle-aged men who was only happy when he was complaining. Rudi had observed the fact too.

"You made enough fuss when I was moaning just now, mate, so why don't you shut your mouth too for a little while, and give all our ears a rest." He leaned over belligerently. Erich snorted, but shut up.

"Well done, Rudi," Adolf thought to himself.

They drove a short distance along the front, the sea and beaches busy with German craft and troops scrambling ashore, then turned up a street which rapidly ascended northward. There was much more evidence of bomb damage here, with the shops and houses flattened and gutted more often than not. Funny they hadn't hit many of those big places down on the sea front. . . . Adolf's eyes roamed round, partly sheer interest at seeing this captured British city at close quarters, partly his training reasserting itself. They had heard enough about snipers, and this was ideal territory. The little convoy was proceeding very slowly. There was still some rubble on the street. The thought crossed his mind that there might also be mines. . . . Good job they weren't the lead truck!

He noticed that everyone had rifles at the ready, their barrels moving warily, covering the buildings on either side, sometimes steadying in aim, only to drop again as the potential target revealed itself as German. There were obviously patrols working through the area, rooting out any snipers there might have been, making this, the centre of the beach-head, secure. They passed a ruined clock-tower in what looked like an important crossroads. All the buildings that had once faced onto it were ruined, two of the streets completely blocked by their wreckage, smoke still rising from one blackened shell. This was the result of recent bombing, possibly only the day — or night — before. It was the first time Adolf had seen the effects of the bombers' activities, apart from some damage in Calais, where they had embarked. But that had obviously been aimed at military targets — the German army. This seemed more indiscriminate. In fact it seemed obviously to have been aimed at the civilians, the ordinary people, who had once lived and worked and shopped here. He tried to image this in Munich, and the fury and hatred it would provoke in him. He found himself disapproving. And wondering. Would the English also do the same, if they needed to? They had shot those men in the water. Also, in a way more worrying, had any of it really helped their own landing? Or helped the invasion at all? He shook his head to dismiss the thoughts. It was more important to concentrate on what he was supposed to be doing, unless he wanted to get shot.

A shot suddenly did crack across their path, to be followed by a series of short bursts of machine-gun fire. Adolf saw the running men of the German patrol, steel-helmeted heads low as they entered the wrecked shop. There was more firing inside. Presumably it had been an English sniper, and they had got him. Up ahead was much more firing. He could make out an ornate façade of a large building on their right.

"Bahnhof," announced the driver.

The vehicles came to a halt outside the station. For the first time there were British military vehicles there, a burnt-out staff car, the remains of a lorry, and two other trucks, undamaged apparently. There were some civilian cars too, all smashed up quite badly. They got out of their transport and formed a protective screen to cover the general's inspection. Adolf and Rudi didn't get a look inside the station at all. Hans and the others told them after that it was damaged, but not too badly. Part of the roof had come down, and there were burnt-out coaches in the platforms, while the tracks to the north had been mangled by bombing. Then they were on their way again, leaving behind the obvious sounds of continued fighting in the streets that fell away down the hillside to the right of the station, and out along the railway line ahead. Instead they went on up the hill to the left, stopping again at another main junction of several roads.

Again the general got out to have a look around, and they formed their protective cordon. Adolf heard a mud-and-dust-stained officer telling the staff officers that the fighting was heavy a few hundred yards to the north. Maps were produced.

"We are on the line of this road here, Herr General, running west to the town of Shoreham. The English are holding out north of the road."

"What about the London Road?" The general pointed at the map.

"The British troops holding the station have managed to regroup here," the major was telling his commanding officer. "We are hoping to work round to their right here, but it is a rabbit warren of houses and . . . "

Adolf saw the movement in the house, and wrenched his mind off this interesting conversation. — It was bound to be another one of ours of course. A stray from one of the anti-sniper patrols . . . He was sure it was a single figure. He saw the head for a moment. Recognized the flat brim of the helmet. Soup bowl not coal-scuttle. He had fired the first shot before even thinking about it. Was running towards the figure, firing again, conscious now of the terrible risk, but not interested in it, discarding it as unnecessary clutter. A shot went by him from behind, and splintered the stone work of the building. He heard Rudi yell,

"Adolf, get down!"

Then he saw the Englishman, against the light for a moment in the ruined window, standing up, so that he could aim. Saw the Tommy's rifle pointed straight at him. Stood still for a moment, his own rifle brought up to the shoulder. The bullet went past and hit the ground, just behind him. He was sure he felt the wind of it going by. Then the crack and recoil of his gun. The Englishman fell forward out of the window. As he had seen men fall in films, hundreds of times, except this was a real man, really shot.

He ran on to the body, dropping his rifle and kneeling beside the khaki form. The man's neck was twisted back, out of shape, his head at the wrong angle. The wound was in the shoulder, jagged with dripping blood.

"Broken neck! It was the fall that killed him," said a voice behind. Adolf looked round. It was the major he had been listening to, discussing strategy and tactics in the abstract. Perhaps the disbelief on his face shewed.

"Your first one, eh soldier? Mine was in Poland, you know. — Well done! The general will be pleased with you, eh!"

Adolf let himself follow the others back to the transport. He felt Rudi and Hans slap him on the back, tell him what a superb shot he was.

"You're the one we fished out of the sea, aren't you?" the general asked.

"Yes sir," Adolf answered automatically. He was half furious with himself for his own reactions. This was what he had trained for. This was what soldiers were supposed to do, and were doing by the thousand today, at every moment.

"I'm glad we did," the general went on. "Quick thinking, that was. You may have saved my life. Who knows? Hm . . . I'll bear you in mind."

It hadn't been the shot that killed him, Adolf was thinking. He fell and broke his neck. It wasn't really me, not entirely. And he would have shot me. He would have been rejoicing if his bullet had taken me out. Not winding himself up in foolishness like I am.

"I wish it had been me that got him," said Rudi as they bumped back down the streets towards the H.Q.

"So do I," snapped Adolf.

Chapter 14

OUT OF THE BEACH-HEADS

From the late afternoon of 27th September onwards, Britain's resistance to the invasion was in the hands of the 'Committee of Home Defence'. Constitutionally a cabinet committee, and replacing the former Defence Committee of the War Cabinet, this body in effect consisted of Winston Churchill and representatives of the armed forces. Churchill could summon whoever he chose to the committee. In fact he relied almost entirely on Brooke, Commander-in-Chief, Home Forces; First Sea Lord, Admiral Pound; and Air Chief Marshall Dowding. Dowding found himself elevated to further heights of command by the combination of Fighter and Bomber Commands as Flight Command. He became its first (and only) Commander-in-Chief. It was a logical move. Both bombers and fighters now had only one strategic and tactical objective — the air war against the invaders. Portal moved from Bomber Command to chief of the Air Staff.

The Chiefs of Staff Committee and the War Cabinet continued to meet on a weekly basis, often more frequently. But operational control had passed away from them. There was much dissatisfaction in high places at the new arrangements. Only the presence of German soldiers on English soil sufficed to let Churchill force them through on the afternoon of Invasion Day. Some senior officers felt slighted, as did some politicians, notably Beaverbrook, whose friendship for Churchill did not entirely survive the occasion. Dissatisfaction was effectively stilled in the days that followed by two men who let their support for the Prime Minister be known — Clement Attlee, the Labour leader, and the King. For Churchill was right in his actions. At the moment of supreme trial he was gathering into his own hands all the reins of command with which he must direct the defence of England.

The Prime Minister had gone down to Parliament in the course of the afternoon to meet the two Houses in emergency session. He did not speak at length, nor was it one of his memorable orations. He was visibly shaken by the events of the day, and for once looked all of his sixty five years. The mood of Parliament was sombre. Unasked, the Premier was given a vote of confidence in his direction of the war. It was that resolution in fact which gave him the authority to push through the Committee of Home Defence. Parliament had no illusions that it could control the day to day running of a war, least of all a war on English soil. It recognized that everything hinged on the choices and actions of one man. On the evening of Invasion Day, the Prime Minister broadcast to the nation.

"This then is the tale of today's invasion of these shores by the Nazis. Our enemy has unleashed upon us all the panoply and strength of his vast and hideous war machine. The hour of trial has come to us in our island home. We will not be afraid. We know the measure of his power. We have already suffered the fury of his onslaught by air. Now we shall test his mettle by land and sea. We will renew the contest in the skies. We will make the very seas run red with the blood of his invading armies. We will make him buy each inch of English soil with German lives. And it will cost us dear. For he is driven on by arrogance and wicked pride. By greed and envy, by festering hatreds and lust for revenge. But we are fighting for our homeland and our happiness, for all we hold dear and cherish in this world. Nothing now can shake our resolve. We are united in all our hopes and dreams, despising death and strangers to despair. We can never be defeated."

Thus he ended. Earlier he had told the people the full

extent of the invasion, insofar as he knew it. He told them both the successes and failures of British arms, speaking as frankly as he could without helping the enemy. The depth of feeling which he had not found when speaking to Parliament was revealed now directly to the people. Once again he inspired and uplifted them, cutting through the doubts and uncertainties of a bleak day, rekindling the flame of their defiance. Similar, more specific, messages had also been sent by the Prime Minister to the troops in the field, the squadrons of the R.A.F., and the ships of the Navy.

Returning to the first meeting of the new Committee of Home Defence, the first news that came to him was of the navy, and of the heavy blow struck at his plans by the German action at Portsmouth. The decision was taken to proceed with the commitment of the Home Fleet in the Channel, if no other losses were incurred. Pound returned to the Admiralty to keep the movements of the heavy ships under his personal control, and to try and assess the extent of the destruction at Portsmouth. The rest of the Committee turned to the war on the land.

The position on the coast remained unclear, but as intelligence reports and the urgent demands of front line units accumulated, some promontories of fact loomed out of the fog. First London Division was hanging on in east Kent. Dover had not been attacked directly. The New Zealanders had already been committed to re-open the A20 to the coast from Ashford. Churchill now proposed that 1st Canadian Division also be brought into the attack supporting the New Zealanders. The Canadians were part of G.H.Q. Reserve, and Brooke was unhappy about their commitment so soon. He wanted his reserves retained intact for enveloping moves after the Germans had been drawn forward away from their cross-Channel supply lines.

"That is all very well, Alan," Churchill told him. "If I happened to be Mr Stalin, with a thousand miles of steppe to retreat into. But it's no damned good to me at all. We're talking of Kent and Sussex. By the time I've fallen back to draw the enemy into a trap, the Panzers are busily rolling over London Bridge."

"I think you're exaggerating, Prime Minister," Brooke replied with equal vigour. "I do not want to sacrifice our mass of manoeuvre to a linear defence. Because once such a line is broken, there is then nothing left."

"It's not a linear defence, damn it, it's a linear attack. I want those villains thrown back into the sea. *Now*, when they're weak! Every hour they stay here they get stronger. *Now* is the time to deploy your mobile reserves. Now and *here*, on the South Coast."

It was Churchill who carried the day, for Brooke was a good enough general to see that the arguments for either course were evenly balanced. However, Brooke was able to prevent Churchill sending 1st Army Tank Brigade from reserve to the coast at Hastings. Even a casual glance at the map revealed that much. 45 Division might have won the 1940 version of the Battle of Hastings — one of the more popular headlines on the 28th. But their position looked very dangerous should enemy advances on each side continue. It was agreed to move the Brigade's hundred and seventy-five tanks forward as far as Hawkhurst on the Kent-Sussex boundary. From there they would be able to respond to events. Farther westward, it was evident that something had gone badly wrong. Though Churchill remained unaware of the disaster in Brighton, he had now given 1st Motor Machine Gun Brigade orders to support. 4th Infantry Division at Chichester was also preparing to move. There seemed little else to do immediately on the front line. Behind the line, the deployment of the Reserve began. A general movement of troops eastward towards the battle area.

In the air war, Dowding was able to report some degree of success in interfering with enemy landings, particularly in the Hastings area. Elsewhere, a policy of localized concentration had enabled the R.A.F. to contest the skies over the battlefield. It had created some disruption in the eastern sector and against the landings around Rye. However, the Luftwaffe had continued to operate a round the clock shuttle of fighter cover over the invasion forces. In the aerial combats that developed both sides had incurred losses, more serious to the R.A.F. with its chronic shortage of planes and pilots. That night British bombers would again hit German embarkation ports in France. From the 28th September British fighters, and the Strategic Air Reserve in particular, would be given the priority task of defending British troop movements against the wide-ranging hit-and-run raids which had seriously impaired British communications throughout Invasion Day.

Shortly after the meeting broke up, Churchill was informed by Admiral Pound of the loss of the *Hood*. He slept little that night. Morning brought him news of the mining of *HMS Nelson*. He concurred with Pound's decision not to proceed with the commitment of the remaining capital ships in the Straits. The enemy had identified the weapon on which Churchill had relied most heavily to win the battle, and had succeeded in neutralizing it.

Through the night of 27th/28th German reinforcements continued to be shuttled steadily across the sea. Once again cruisers entered the Channel, but they were German, the four ships, *Emden*, *Nürnberg*, *Köln* and *Bremse*, released from *Operation Herbstreise*. The British did not challenge their presence as convoy escorts. Admiral Pound was trying to put together an alternative naval strategy out of the wreckage of Britain's plans. A strategy without four of his capital ships, and without the great harbour of Portsmouth. The Germans reaped the benefits of Raeder's policy to the full. The Führer was pleased with developments.

The two army commanders, Strauss and Busch, and von Rundstedt who commanded the Army Group, had, however, been forced to come to some compromises over transport. Initial losses due to British naval and air action had been serious. The rate of breakdowns was substantially in excess of that planned for. Confusion and disruption of organization had further reduced availability. They decided to divert part of the available transport from Sixteenth to Ninth Army, to enable the unlooked-for successes on the left flank to be exploited.

As reinforcements continued to come in through the night, German strength steadily built up. In the original dawn landings on the 27th some 45,000 men had been put ashore. During the first few hours, reinforcements had not in fact kept pace with losses, as the British fought desperately on the beaches. By mid-morning only about 40,000 German troops were actually fighting in Britain. By mid-afternoon this had increased to 50,000 and by evening to 60,000. The night's efforts, culminating in a dawn landing on the 28th of similar proportions to that of *S-Tag* itself, brought the strength up to something approaching a hundred thousand men.

As the dawn landings progressed, the forward echelons were already carrying out their orders for the day's offensive. Ninth Army renewed its attempts to break out northward towards Lewes and the Vale of Sussex. At the same time 26th and 34th Divisions were ordered to continue their own parallel advance in the general direction of Uckfield on the edge of the Sussex Weald. In Sixteenth Army, 35 Division was to establish contact with 7th in Rye and then press on with the advance towards Tenterden. On the right 17 Division had objective Ashford, while 7 Para was to operate northward towards Canterbury.

Plans never go according to plan. As 17 Division moved down from its woodland positions north of the Royal Military Canal into the open country of the Vale of Kent, it was brought up hard against advancing units of the New Zealand Division south of Ashford. There followed some of the fiercest fighting of the campaign, often at bayonet point. They contested obscure villages house by house. Steadily the Germans were forced back into the hills above the Canal, and the New Zealanders moved down the road and railway towards Folkestone.

The seaward flank of 17 Division's position also began to crumble. 1st London Division mounted a two-pronged attack. They struck along the line of the A20 from Folkestone, brushing aside the thinly-spread paratroopers. They also assailed Hythe, won by the Germans at the cost of much blood the day before. Fighting continued in the little town throughout the day and the following night. The Germans hung on desperately as their position continued

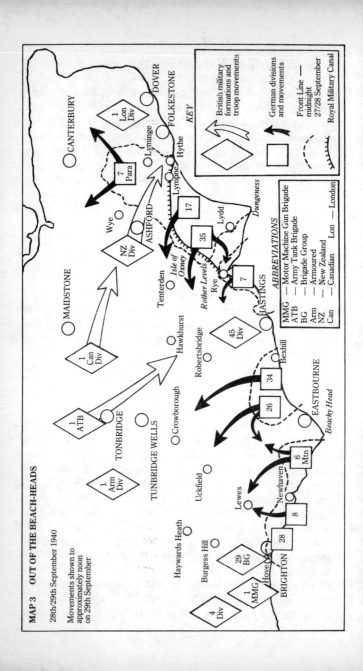

MAP 3   OUT OF THE BEACH-HEADS

28th/29th September 1940

Movements shown to
approximately noon
on 29th September

KEY

British military
formations and troop movements

German divisions
and movements

British military
formations and movements

Front Line —
midnight
27/28 September

Royal Military Canal

ABBREVIATIONS

MMG — Motor Machine Gun Brigade
ATB — Army Tank Brigade
BG — Brigade Group
Arm — Armoured
NZ — New Zealand
Can — Canadian   Lon — London

DOVER
FOLKESTONE
CANTERBURY
1 Lon Div
Lyminge
Hythe
7 Para
Wye
ASHFORD
Lympne
17
NZ Div
Lydd
35
Dungeness
Tenterden
Isle of Oxney
Rother Levels
Rye
7
HASTINGS
MAIDSTONE
Hawkhurst
Robertsbridge
45 Div
Bexhill
34
EASTBOURNE
1 Can Div
Crowborough
26
Beachy Head
1 ATB
TONBRIDGE
6 Mtn
TUNBRIDGE WELLS
1 Arm Div
Uckfield
Lewes
Newhaven
8
Haywards Heath
Burgess Hill
Hove
28
29 BG
1 MMG
BRIGHTON
4 Div

to fray at the edges. By nightfall they were fighting the New Zealanders too, around the ruins of Saltwood Castle, and all along the high ground that ran westward. If they were once pushed back down the escarpment that dominated the Royal Military Canal, they might never regain it. During the night the British restored road and rail communications between Ashford and Folkestone. German 7th Parachute Division was now cut off.

The isolation of 7 Para had in it all the seeds of disaster for the Germans. Their commander, Major-General Putzier, had joined his troops on the afternoon of *S-Tag*, and established his Divisional H.Q. at Lyminge. And he was unwilling to recognize his precarious position. Instead, he proceeded to execute his original orders for a spoiling offensive against British communications. His paratroopers appeared out of the blue to cut the vital A2 road. They pressed on to take the railway as well and sever all direct British communications between Canterbury and Dover. At the same time, fifteen miles to the east, other paratroops swept down into the valley of the Great Stour. They cut Canterbury's road and rail link to Ashford as well. It was not the behaviour of a dangerously isolated force.

On the rest of their front it was a less traumatic day for the Germans. 35 Division speedily established contact with 7 Division, and relieved much of the pressure on Rye. They also continued to advance across the difficult marshlands and secured the Isle of Oxney. By evening their forward troops were in Tenterden. 26 and 34 Divisions pushed steadily forward too. Hailsham was taken and junction made with 6th Mountain Division, thus cutting off the remaining British troops in Eastbourne. The advance continued through the day, curving westward along the relatively easy country of the Vale of Sussex. 26 Division provided the spearhead, with 34th holding the flanks up the streams and valleys cutting into the southerly ridges of the Weald. The only worrying event came in the evening. Probing towards Robertsbridge on the right flank of the advance, the Germans encountered British tanks.

During the late morning British 1st Army Tank Brigade

moving south had become entangled with 1st Canadian Division trying to move east. Nevertheless, by evening Brigadier Watkins had managed to get his forward units from 4th Royal Tank Regiment as far south as the town of Battle. He established his H.Q. in Hawkhurst. When the members of the Devonshire Regiment fell back outnumbered, before the German Corps' advance it was onto a new bulwark of British armour. That armour reinforced 45 Division's continuing hold on the centre of the front line, between the two invading armies.

At the western end of the front, the Germans had secured the Downs on either side of the River Ouse, and the valley up as far as Lewes. The town itself, and the commanding heights to east and west continued to be held by the Duke of Cornwall's Light Infantry and the East Lancashires. Nevertheless, the Germans did not anticipate being long delayed. During the night of the 28th they began to develop flanking manoeuvres. The British in the northern suburbs of Brighton had finally been mopped up but they continued to hold out on the coast. The Divisional Commander, Obstfelder, was increasingly aware of growing British reinforcement on his left, and began to divert his own new arrivals from the continent in that direction.

As night ended another fine day, and Germany's weather luck continued, it was apparent to both of the warlords that the invaders were now out of their beach-heads. Neither of them doubted that the real fight was yet to begin. That evening both Churchill and Hitler were in conference with their service chiefs, and both were absorbed in their maps. At Schloss Ziegenberg the Führer had entertained his High Command to a sumptuous dinner prior to getting down to the evening's work. He had been greatly elated by the destruction of the British battleships, and wanted to celebrate that event, together with the successful landings. Over the meal he chatted with Raeder, seated directly on his right, about the need to obtain a reasonable harbour as a matter of urgency. Afterwards they retired to the map room, and Hitler ordered von Rundstedt to report on the

strategic situation. (The general was an unwilling partici-
pant. He felt, not unreasonably, that he should be supervising the two great armies under his overall command.) So
he spoke concisely and to the point.

"In conclusion, gentlemen, I have two main areas of
concern," he told them at the end. "One is here in Kent.
We have the British breakthrough back to the coast. The
threat to our landing grounds from the counter-attack in
Hythe. 17 Division is strung out in a dangerously exposed
position. It is now forced to turn and fight an enemy to its
east. 7th Parachute Division — completely cut off."

"Most alarming, Herr Generalfeldmarschall. But do you
have a proposal?" demanded Hitler.

"Simply this. To halt any further advance by 17 Division. Turn it entirely eastward. Hold the flank at all costs,
and order the Paratroops to break back to our lines whatever the risks."

"Which will deprive us of any prospect of capturing
Folkestone or Dover for some time — weeks perhaps,"
Hitler replied.

It was fashionable among the professional military to
deride their Führer's intuitions and scorn his strategic
knowledge. But the fact was that Hitler possessed a natural,
if distorted, grasp of strategy. The distortion lay in the
belief that, ultimately, he could not lose. Nevertheless, it
was a conviction that had not yet overmastered his insight
and his inherent cunning. The underlying self-doubt which
had caused so many earlier tantrums also lay behind the
icy determination and single-mindedness he had shewn over
the preceding two days.

"Would it be possible, von Rundstedt, to bring over a
Second Wave Division early?" he now asked.

"Which one, Führer?" Rundstedt looked puzzled.

"A Panzer Division, to smash through the British corridor to Dover. Because that is all it is — a corridor between
two German positions. Ripe for the chop!"

"No, not without a port, my Führer. They could never
be landed on the beaches."

"Is this correct, Jodl, Brauchitsch, Halder. . . . ?" He

looked round at the generals, pausing only long enough to see that they would agree with Rundstedt and disagree with him. Only Field Marshal Keitel had anything to offer, more loyal to his Führer than to any principles of strategy.

"The Führer's plan for a breakthrough could be operated by infantry alone," he suggested. "If we concentrate our reinforcements on 17 and 35 Divisions, and bring both to bear for the attack . . . "

An impatient wave of the hand was all Keitel got for his loyalty. It was not the answer Hitler wanted to hear. They moved on to discussion of the central sector, leaving the matter unresolved. Hitler accepted that the going was slow there, and did not make any irritating suggestions. Not until Rundstedt mentioned that there had been unconfirmed reports of British armour operating in the area north of Hastings.

"And this is why the Hastings front is your second area of concern," announced Hitler.

He immediately returned to his idea of bringing a Panzer Division over early. The presence of British tanks might make it essential to do so. Had not the amphibian tanks (those which made it up the beaches) already proved their worth? Was Eastbourne a port? If it could be taken, would it not be suitable? The generals told him no, it was not suitable. Von Rundstedt agreed that the amphibian tanks were proving useful — and sufficient to present needs. He was worried about the Hastings sector because it represented a British salient in the German front right between the two armies, not because of vague suggestions of enemy tanks. The Führer continued to peer at the map.

"Is this place, Newhaven, not a port?" he demanded.

"It is too small, my Führer. It would take too long to land a whole Panzer Division there. Besides, it is a long way from the Hastings sector, and further still from 17 Division."

Hitler looked around in obvious anger at the ring of generals. His intuition told him he was right, yet he hesitated to rely totally on it and over-rule them all.

"Even a relatively slow disembarkation and assembly would be better than none."

It was all Hitler needed.

"Ah . . . so there we have it." His eyes fell on the dissenting general, towards the back of the group, and not a regular visitor at such gatherings. The new Director of Army Operations, Generalleutnant von Paulus.

"Could you make the arrangements, General?"

"I think so, my Führer."

Hitler was now addressing himself entirely to Paulus, beckoning him forward to the map.

"What is our nearest second-wave Panzer Division?"

"The Seventh, north west of Paris."

"And its nearest port?"

"Le Havre."

"That is outside the zone for which I am providing convoy protection at the moment," interrupted Raeder.

"You will provide a convoy for this, though, Grand Admiral, and you will use the heaviest possible naval units you have available."

Hitler's eyes blazed. Goering saw a chance to wheedle his way back into favour at Raeder's expense.

"I can guarantee air cover for the operation. I will give twenty-four hour support. I have the planes, now that the British navy is no longer the problem we once believed."

"Very well. We have our tactics devised then. A large scale reinforcement of 17 and 35 Divisions to hold their present line until the armoured breakthrough. Further reinforcement of 7th Parachute Division in its present bridgehead. Also, gentlemen, a warning order to 22nd Air Landing Division to be prepared to go in with them if necessary. And 7 Panzer Division to be embarked and transported to Newhaven with all speed. Von Paulus, you will undertake this matter personally. — By the way, who is their commander?"

"Generalmajor Erwin Rommel, my Führer," answered Paulus.

In London, the Committee of Home Defence was not

dissatisfied with the developments of the second day of the invasion. Churchill had recovered something of his spirits, though none of the commanders realized how bitterly the naval disasters had afflicted him. Admiral Pound wanted to put the remaining battleships into the Channel regardless. The *Nelson*, it transpired, had not been too badly damaged by the mine, and temporary repairs could make her seaworthy again in a matter of days. He had already ordered *Warspite* back from the eastern Mediterranean and *Barham* back from Freetown. Though these Queen Elizabeth class ships had fought at Jutland they were modernized, heavily armoured and could still produce a fair turn of speed. The name-ship of the class, the *Queen Elizabeth*, had been under repair in Portsmouth when the harbour was blocked and was now trapped. Efforts were already underway to clear the wreckage from the harbour mouth, but the task was fraught with difficulties. Though he understood the depth of the naval disaster as well as Churchill, Pound tried to put a brave face on it. The one thing Britain could not survive was the demoralization of her great war leader. In the event Churchill would not let the remaining battleships up the Narrow Seas. Instead they were to return northward under cover of darkness as soon as *Nelson* was ready. The light forces, however, were to return to the Channel.

On land, distinct possibilities were unfolding for the British. Brooke, the CIGS, Dill, and Ismay, Churchill's Chief of Staff, were all present at the Committee. They combined to present a plan based on Brooke's preferred strategy of envelopment. Churchill had seen the possibility of destroying the German paratroops in detail, but the generals were interested in a wider plan. They saw the continued German progress out of their beach-heads into the Vale of Sussex on the right and the Weald on the left offering long exposed flanks to the undefeated British in eastern Kent and at Hastings, and to the new troops being brought up towards Brighton in the west.

"To sum up, Prime Minister, gentlemen," Brooke told them. "I want to launch an attack in strength from the line Ashford-Folkestone, employing 1st London, the New

Zealanders and the Canadians, and spearheaded by our armour. That will be the first hammer, and we shall push the enemy back onto the anvil of 45 Division and 1st Army Tank Brigade here in the centre. While our first attack is still in progress, and the enemy is diverting all his efforts to containing it, the second hammer will fall. Here in the west against the German position around Brighton. The infantry for it is already in place. The single brigade of Second Armoured has been ordered up from Western Command, and I shall need it as my spearhead. I have reserves available for commitment as we progress."

"You can employ the Australian Imperial Forces as well," said Churchill thoughtfully. Previously he had withheld the Australian Division due to the political problems of Menzies, the Australian Prime Minister. Now things were somewhat resolved.

"Have you ordered 1st Armoured to move yet?" Ismay asked.

"No. I thought I had better mention our plans to the Prime Minister before we proceeded too far with them," Brooke answered. There was laughter, joined by Churchill.

"I trust you will remember that it was *I* who demanded just such an early commitment of reserves, gentlemen," he replied, pointing at Brooke with his cigar. "Now, how early can your double hammer blow fall?"

"I am not prepared to have the operation go off half-cocked," Brooke answered. "Not before 7th October for the beginning of the attack at the eastern end of the line, and then only if I have 1st Armoured in place."

Brooke had allowed himself only nine days to prepare his offensive. He knew that Churchill would try to hold him to that 7th October date. It would now all depend on two things. How quickly he could deploy his own forces, and what the Germans did.

Chapter 15

BRIGHTON BEACH

Clinging on underneath the upturned rowing boat, Don tried to take stock of his position. He was a strong swimmer, and had few doubts that he could make it to the shore, but he had heard enough in 4 Division's H.Q. at Chichester to know that the Germans were very close. They'd landed all along the Sussex coast, and he knew that he was rapidly floating down to that coast. He was in the River Adur, and it reached the sea somewhere near Brighton. That was about all he knew. He calculated that by now there would probably be Germans at least on the left hand bank. If he swam for it, he stood a good chance of getting shot. He felt his legs and body getting colder, and began to fear that he might get cramp. His arms were already stiff from clinging on. And how long before the wreck of the boat finally sank?

"Must try to change position. Keep moving about," he thought.

He cautiously changed his grip a few times. Began to move his legs up and down in gentle swimming strokes. The water was cold, but not freezing, and there was almost no pain at the moment from the cut in his head. That was something at least. He wondered what his mum was doing. Hoped the messages about him had got through — telling her he was safe. How would she take it now if he got killed? He had never thought about the possibility before, not seriously. It was always other people who were killed. Now it might happen the moment he emerged from his strange shelter.

He remembered vividly the sight of that plane coming for him and Captain Sawyer. Perhaps the captain had made it alright too. He hoped so. Even then he hadn't believed he was going to die. Now, just waiting, drifting along to goodness knew where under a thin shell of wood and caulking, death seemed a more likely proposition, made worse by the imagining of it. He decided he must screw up his courage to get out and make a break for it. It would have to be soon. How long had he already been drifting in the current? Was it hours? It seemed like it.

In the faint light filtering in through the water he could make out some sort of shape, over to his right. He put his face into the water, keeping his eyes open. It was too murky to see much, but the bottom wasn't very far away, and that might be a sand bar of some sort, or even the bank on his right. He tried to make it out more clearly, finally lifting his head to gasp for air. He licked his lips, gave a sudden exclamation, his voice hollow in the upturned shell, and dipped his face in the water again. Salt! Definitely a strong tang in the water. Now he was alert he could perceive the surge, the rise and fall of waves. This was nothing to do with the river current, it was the swell of the sea.

At once new anxieties presented themselves. The shelving bottom on his right couldn't be the beach, unless he was already well out of the river mouth and being carried westward. He had no idea of the way the currents ran along this coast. If he *was* being carried west, then it was back to safety. He tried to make out where the light was strongest. That should be south. But he couldn't make up his mind. And the suggestion of a beach on his right had vanished now. He guessed it must have been a sandbar, probably at the river's mouth. Certainly the tide was running stronger now, the rise and fall of the sea catching the boat and spinning it along, so that he had to hold on tight.

He weighed up the possibilities as carefully as he could. The remains of the boat could sink at any moment. After that the biggest risk was probably being swept out to sea. If he was being carried along the coast, by now he must be back well behind English lines, or definitely in German-held territory. If it was the latter, and he swam to the beach, he'd have to surrender. Better that than be drowned. Whichever way, he had to give it a try. Perhaps he could just hang onto the outside of the boat at first, and at least get his bearings.

Then the decision was taken from him. He felt his feet scraping on sand and the push of the sea behind, sweeping its rollers up onto the beach. The boat was being carried in by the second. Now there were rocks beneath his feet. He scrambled to bring his legs inside the protective wood. The boat jarred against an obstacle, scraping on something metal, and then hit with a grinding crash. The planks splintered just above his head, and he ducked under the water. His upturned vessel was stuck fast.

He waited for a while, then began to work away at the cracked plank where the shell of the rowing boat had struck. Finally he worked a piece loose. As soon as his eyes were used to daylight he looked out. At first it was difficult to get his bearings. There was a long stretch of beach before him, rising up to the usual hump at high water mark. Beyond that he could see buildings, the front of some seaside town. It might be Brighton, of course, or Worthing. He didn't know either. The beach was full of the usual litter of barbed wire and tank traps. But there were bodies hanging in the wire, feet dangling in the rippling waves. Wrecks of vehicles wallowed in the sand, some of them burnt out.

He screwed his body up, shivering for the first time as he leaned against the planks. This was an invasion beach. It had to be Brighton, or one of those other towns near it. And if this was where the Germans had come ashore they would be here now. He cursed his bad luck. He was trapped for certain. If he did try to get out, the chances were they'd shoot him. He stiffened suddenly, pressing tighter against the side of the boat as if it offered some protection. There were voices coming nearer. He was terrified to look, but curiosity overcame even that fear.

A long line of Germans was marching up the beach, grey soldiers in their coal-scuttle helmets, rifles slung on their backs. Beyond them he could see another column, and possibly a third. Perhaps it was another landing, or reinforcements. He watched, fascinated. A tracked vehicle of some sort slithered up the wet sand and overtook the men. It was near enough for him to see the sand fly up from the tracks, and the wheels spinning.

Hours passed, as Don continued to watch part at least of the great invasion unfolding before him. He had realized quite early on that in fact the upturned wreck of a rowing boat amidst all the other debris was not of the slightest interest to the Germans. He could stay there as long as he needed — until he got hungry or thirsty in fact. That thought made him realize how thirsty he already was. He would have to get a drink some time today — or tonight. He had decided as soon as the thought came to him. As soon as it was dark he would make a break up the beach and into the town. There had to be people there who would give him something to eat and drink, perhaps who would hide him. Or perhaps British lines weren't far away . . . He might even try to make it all the way back. To a hero's welcome of course! He let himself daydream idly along those lines, his mind for a while taken off the facts that he was cold and wet and parched.

He had been left high and dry for some time, the tide still going out. The sun was round behind him, a little to the left he thought from its intermittent appearances through the cloud. That meant it was past noon. He guessed it as mid-afternoon, maybe even later, when the tide turned. Definitely late afternoon before there was water under his boat again. Now another dilemma faced him. If the boat was stuck firm, he would have to get out now, or be drowned. He still didn't know what the obstacles were for certain. That on the right was concrete. He had felt its base. Probably an anti-tank obstacle, that meant. On the other side, he had no idea.

211

He tried using his shoulders to heave the boat forward as the water started to come in more strongly. It budged a little, and with more buoyancy from the flow of the tide, he was able to ease it forward. The wood was scraping along some metal surface for a while, and grinding on the tank trap. Then he felt it come free. Shaking from his exertions in the cramped space, he held on tight and let the tide do its work. It was rough and bumpy ride, buffeted back and forth up the beach, worse as the soft sand was replaced by shingle. His shins and knees were soon black and blue, and he had a good few cuts. The process seemed to go on forever, made worse by the fact of renewed German activity. Many more troops were landing this time.

Finally it was obvious he was going no farther up the beach. The waters washed higher around him, diminishing the air pocket all the time, until his face was pushed into the last couple of inches. His body was wracked with impotent fury. If this went on any longer he would be forced to get out now, and he would be captured. Just as darkness was at last closing in. Just before the night became his protection and the boat could be discarded. Then the tide turned. He lay back in the receding water, wracked with numbness, his body a mass of aches. Through his spyhole the blackness was total.

He let himself recover for a good while, then began to try and massage some feeling back into his limbs. Finally he moved back into the splintered after part of the boat. He managed to lift it up with his body as he slid his legs out first. Then held it with his arms, just long enough to wriggle his body through. For a moment he knelt by the boat, then lay flat out beside it, easing his legs with careful movements, massaging the muscles, before he tried to stand up.

He was conscious of the noise on the shingle made by his movements, and wondered how he was going to get up the beach quietly. But then, the Germans would not be listening for stray Englishmen strolling up 'their' beach. He carefully assessed the lie of the land. He could make out several of the tank traps, all of them large enough to hide behind. The barbed wire coils were a problem, but they had obviously never been that extensive, and were now chopped up by the Germans. Farther up the beach there was a large vehicle, but that was plainly abandoned. It was almost directly in line with him. The closer he got to it, the better cover it would provide. He glanced round behind to see what the obstruction was that his wrecked rowing boat had lodged against. It seemed to be some sort of motor launch, from what he could observe in the darkness, still awash to its deck in the receding tide. The moon wasn't up, or was hidden in the cloud, so that was another advantage. There was wispy mist being blown down across the beach from the landward. It was a good dark night, and under German occupation the town was preserving its former blackout rules.

"Well, everything's for me, and it won't get better," he muttered under his breath. "So here goes."

He stood up, and almost at once fell again. His legs were horribly unsteady. He found he could only walk with his knees bent, and the clatter on the shingle was unavoidable. He made his way from one concrete anti-tank trap to the next, crouching behind each to massage his legs again, and look around for any sign he had been sighted. His progress seemed to be agonizingly slow, but he was obviously unseen. He paused for longer when he made it to the truck, some sort of lorry with tracks on its back wheels, now burnt out. He knew that the last part of the journey would be without cover — except the bodies. There appeared to be only English dead on the beach. He had tried to avoid them so far. Now he might be glad of them.

He began to crawl. It was even slower, it had to be to avoid the clatter of those damned pebbles. But he was on the top of the beach now, clearly visible to anyone who might care to look over the sea-wall. Like a great wandering crab he made his zig-zag way between the dead, concentrating on the sea wall above, ignoring the hunched silent shapes around. Once he saw a figure standing there, and heard voices. He lay unmoving. The Germans talked for a while, then moved away. He gave them a long time, counting out five clear minutes before he moved again.

When, finally, breathing in long shuddering gasps, he reached the shelter of the sea-wall a new horror awaited him. In the shadow of the stones lay heaped bodies. He had seen German stretcher parties moving about on the beach, collecting their dead, but leaving the English where they fell. From his position down the beach he had not been able to see the sea wall, where the Germans were pushing their dead enemies over, out of the way. Now he found them, ragged shapes like dolls, twisted in unseemly postures, arms thrown out across each other, or faces staring suddenly at him. He had no choice but to edge his way along beside them, fighting down the nausea, and muttering,

"Damn you, damn you, damn you," a continuous litany under his breath at the creatures who had done this vile thing.

At last he reached the flight of steps. He had spotted it as he hid behind the burnt-out half-track. Hunched against the stonework, he cautiously mounted. Brought his head up to the level of the parapet. Looked across an old-fashioned promenade, with some sort of gardens or green behind it, and the road immediately beyond that. There was no-one in sight. He didn't give himself time to think about it. He darted up the last few steps, and ran, still hobbling, across the open space, scrambling over a low fence onto the garden. He realized the road was slightly raised again, so that was more cover. Once again he cautiously put his head up. Almost at once he had to duck once more, as two troop carriers hurried by towards the west. He could just make out the black crosses on the grey, saw for a second the faces of the men inside, lit by the glow of a match or cigarette.

This time, he realized, he could not risk making a run across. There were some people on the other side, bound to be Germans. A good way off, but they would see him, and be curious. Yet he had to get over, in among the houses and streets where there was cover. He could not return to the beach. The bodies under the wall had removed any idea of working along that way. He felt horribly afraid, for he knew how he would have to do it. The only way was to step out and walk across. There were no lights. He could only just make out the distant figures, so the same would be true of them. They would not be able to tell the colour of his uniform. He would just look like a stray German soldier. So long as there weren't any real stray German soldiers about. So long as no-one challenged him . . .

His heart seemed to be beating loud enough for them to hear. He got up onto the road, stood up, and began to walk. As steady strides as his weak and shaking legs would allow.

"Not too fast, not too fast," he told himself. "Not a straight line . . . " His boots seemed to ring on the asphalt. Already he was nearly there, the shelter of buildings ready to close over him. There was a square, grass with trees around it. He made his way towards it. In a moment he was in the darkness under a tree, and then safe, sitting down, gasping among the ornamental bushes.

For a while he could not stop shaking. He had had no choice but to sit down. His knees had turned to jelly. But no-one had challenged him, no-one had even noticed. He was sure of it. He forced himself to get up again, trembling with relief. While he was still keyed up he had to go on. He made his way round the edge of the square. It was oblong in fact, sloping up into the town, a grassed area, but plenty of cover at the sides. At the top was a narrow street, which led on up the hill.

He made it into the street, sheltering in a porch, then moving on. Always ready to dodge into hiding, as he hurried from house to house, pausing in shop doorways to look all around. The street was deserted. Even though it must be pretty late he had hoped for some people at least. The utter loneliness added to the thrill of fear which kept him going. Then in a shop doorway he collided heavily with someone. He yelled out, biting off the cry at once. There was a flicker of torchlight in his face, a hand clasping his collar.

"Who the hell are you?" said a whispered voice.

"English . . . soldier." Don said the words without thinking, without realizing that "English soldier" was just what he had become, fighting his own strange, individual war.

"Bloody hell!" The man released him, and Don got half a glimpse of the muffled face. "What are you doing here? Don't you know those bastards have got a curfew down? This is enemy territory, mate."

"I'm trying to get back to our lines," Don answered simply. The man replied with various expressions of amazement. Nettled, Don demanded,

"Well what the heck are you up to then?"

"Black market, mate. As they call it. — No harm in telling you here, is there? Business as usual. Life's got to go on you know."

Don shook his head, finding it hard to believe that business could go on.

"There aren't many people left in the town anyway," the man continued. "So your only chance is carrying on by night. Watch out crossing Western Road. That's the big street up ahead. And keep going uphill. That's the way out of town. — Good luck mate!"

Then the shadowy figure was gone. Don leaned against the door lintel, still not really believing it. Here was someone, one of his people, an Englishman, risking his life for a few bob. Carrying on in the midst of the enemy as if nothing had happened, the day after England had been invaded. Admiration for the man's cool nerve combined with disapproval of his motives. Somehow it increased Don's own determination to get back, and then to fight properly, as everyone should be fighting.

Even more cautious, now that he knew there was a curfew, thankful for the cloud and the blackness of the night, he pressed on to the road junction. If anything it was darker than ever, and he found it hard to see his way at all. This must be Western Road, though. It looked like shops along it, and it was obviously a main road. Lorries lumbered by, as he pressed back into the shadows. Military traffic, going westward. There was the sound of artillery fire from that direction too. The fighting was probably on this road itself, somewhere. Not the best way out, not through the middle of the battle.

He decided he would have to make a run for it to get across the road. Then on up, another hill — leading out of town. There was an opportunity straight away, and without pausing to worry about it, he had taken the chance and darted across. He was into another street, and starting to make his same careful way along it. Almost immediately there was another danger, the sound of a voice, and foot-steps — quite a few of them, moving in time. The houses had basements with stairways down to them behind low walls where there had once been railings before the drive for metal to make Spitfires.

He vaulted over the parapet, and quickly descended the steps. Hidden behind dustbins, he listened to the unmistak-able clump of marching feet. There was also a light. Some-one carrying a strong torch. He heard a command called out in a clear loud voice, and someone answering from the distance. It was the first time he had heard German spoken. Then another command, that sounded exactly like, "Halt!" The marching feet stopped, not very far from him. He crouched lower, holding his breath. Had they found some-thing, some trace of him? Then there was a shout, and now the soldiers were running, the whole crowd of them clattering off down the street, the way he had come. He heard a shot, and then others, farther away. The thought of the black marketeer crossed his mind. Perhaps he was their quarry. Perhaps they had found him.

Don let a good while go by, then edged up the steps. There was no-one in sight, and the road was in complete silence. Still dodging in and out of cover he continued an erratic course, mostly north, sometimes following side streets off to the left, if they seemed the best way. He was sure the centre of the city was to his right. There were two more major crossroads, and another German patrol, but somehow his luck held out. He crossed the last main road, the houses already beginning to thin out. It was surburban villas now, with large gardens. The road continued to rise, more steeply. The moon had come up, fitful among the racing clouds, but at least it gave him some light — and increased the risk. By a small workshop of some sort he left the road for an unmetalled road, that degenerated into a track, as the houses finally ran out.

He felt a heady exhilaration. He had made it out into the country. Now there was nothing to stop him making it all the way. The rounded hilltops close above him were the Downs. He paused to rest, as the climb became steeper. He looked back towards the darkness of the city, and the paleness of the sea beyond. Somehow he had come through the heart of an occupied city. Surely the front line couldn't be far now? Or could it? He realized that he had no idea how far the Germans might have advanced. If they could take a whole city in a day or two, they could also be well beyond it. After the excitement of success these cold considerations came like a douche of water. On the other hand, there was no matter of choice involved. He could only press on.

To his annoyance the track rejoined a road, though not a very good one. He came to another crossroads, a strange deserted place up in the hills. He took the road to the left, on upwards. He had not gone far, still turning things over in his mind, when he was shaken from his thoughts by a sound from behind him. There was something coming up the road, and not too far away. He had let his attention wander. Angry with himself, he took the most obvious means of escape. He had been lucky again. On his right was a house, the first for some time, standing alone with a tall hedgerow round it, and a garden gate. No time to undo it. No time to check things. He jumped the gate, landed with a thud that almost winded him, then rolled sideways, close under the hedge.

He lay silent, praying that the dimmed headlights had not caught him. One after another vehicles passed, a whole convoy. He had to look, had to know. He half pulled himself up, glancing obliquely round the hedge. Now there were no clouds hiding the thin crescent of the old moon. In its light he saw the pale, glistening grey of the trucks and the dull black German crosses. The hope that had risen in him unbidden was crushed. He should have known. They were coming up from the town, he thought, so they had to be Jerries.

Despite the danger he continued to watch, hypnotized by the strangeness imparted to the scene by the softness of the moonlight. After the vehicles came a long line of carts, horse-drawn, each of them crowded with soldiers, the moon-light glinting on the steel of their helmets, or catching their pale faces momentarily. It went on for a long while, the neighing and snorting of the big horses, the muffled conversation, guttural voices, sudden bursts of laughter, cut short.

"So many horses," he thought. "Do they really use horses?"

He realized with a jolt the risk he was taking. There was no need to see any more. He knew the worst. Not only was he still in enemy territory, but by the look of that column he was well within it. He crouched down and waited till they finally passed. An immense weariness swept down upon him, after two days of such utter extremes, so far beyond any previous experience, and after the unrelenting physical effort. He had to rest, had to sleep. And he must drink. His mouth was agonizingly dry. It hurt to swallow. He looked round at the house, some way up a neatly kept path. There was no choice but to give it a try.

As he approached he could see that several windows were broken, and the door hung loose. The place was obviously deserted. He reached the door and pushed his way in. Part of the house was clearly ruined, damaged very recently in the fighting by the look of it. The stairs hung precariously, and the ceiling had completely fallen in the first room he entered. He realized that part of one end wall must have come down. There was moonlight trickling inside. He began to explore and found two treasures. A torch on the table beside the stairs, a torch that worked. Shielding its beam carefully with his hands he found his way to the kitchen. Water flowed from the tap as he turned it. He drank noisily from cupped hands. Then took a mug, and drank more deeply. Once his thirst was slaked, he looked for the pantry. There was food as well, and plenty of it.

"I didn't know I was hungry too," he said to himself, whispering aloud in the ghostly light of torch and moon.

He ate ravenously. Bread, only a bit hard, cheese, precious rations of butter and jam. The meal made a real difference to him, giving him a feeling of well-being, almost safety. But if anything it seemed to increase his tiredness. He would have to sleep very soon. Continuing his exploration, still munching at bread and cheese, he discovered the cellar door.

The cellar was spacious, the sort of thing you only found in old houses, and obviously rigged out to act as an air raid shelter. There was a bunk bed, more stores of food, a photo of children in a gilt frame. Idly he had flicked on the light switch, gasping with horror as the room flooded with brilliance. The light was off again in the instant, but it had given him a shock. Now with the torch he checked thoroughly. There was only one small window, and it was blocked off on the outside with some sort of board. There was also blackout material taped over the panes. If he closed the door as well he could have the light on. But that was not what he wanted at the moment. He jammed the door with a baulk of wood. Hardly bothering to undo his jacket he flopped onto the lower bunk, and was asleep almost at once.

Chapter 16

UNDER FIRE

"Well, my lad, that looks like all the excitement we'll be getting in our war." Rudi looked around as he spoke.

"I see you're being more cautious when you express these opinions of yours now," laughed Adolf. "I don't think being shot at will scare the general out of visits to the fighting anyway."

"And no doubt he'll want to take his ace sharpshooter with him?"

Adolf reached over to bang Rudi's helmet, but an officer emerged, and he rapidly turned the action into a salute.

"It's too early to say whether we'll see any more action," Hans joined in once the officer had gone.

It was the second day of their time in England. The three of them were on the door of the Grand Hotel again, performing what looked like becoming their regular duty, that and guarding the English prisoners. Taubert, the corporal, had as good as told them as much.

"You three are unlucky you see," he had said. "Being oddities, you get the jobs left over when I've used everyone else." Then he had promptly taken Konrad and Erich who had shared the guard with them up till then off for other duties. Now Adolf looked reflectively out over the Channel. The wind had got up during the day. It was quite a cold northerly, not that they felt it much in the shadow of the hotel doorway. Really it was fine for the time of year.

"I think we're a darned sight luckier than the other two. You know what they're on, don't you? — Lists! Writing out longhand lists of killed, wounded, enemy captured. Give me chief commissionaire any day. I'll tell you something else, too, our general is pretty confident if he thinks three men are all that's needed on the front door of his H.Q."

"Oh, we're winning all right," Rudi agreed. "What did you expect?"

"I expected to be drowned, and so did you," Adolf answered. "After what happened to us on the crossing, I don't underestimate the enemy."

"Come on, Adolf, you sound like a text book," said Hans. "That was at sea. Now we're on the land, we'll win all right."

That evening they had their first real spell off duty, another sign that things were going well for the Wehrmacht. They went down together and looked at the beach. The German dead there were now being collected, stretcher parties and trucks marked with the Red Cross among the debris and litter of the fighting, not that there had been much on the beaches. The wounded had already been seen to, both German and enemy. The British dead still lay there, among the barbed wire and tank traps, as the stretcher bearers took up the grey from among the khaki. They looked like a narrow tide line of jetsam, thrown up by the sea, the colour of their uniforms and their stiff strange postures blending with the seaweed.

There had been more on the sea-wall itself, but these had been pushed back over onto the beach, to form a second line of broken sea-wrack piled up against the stones they once defended. There was brown-staining blood on the parapet as the three Germans leaned on it. Adolf felt a curious detachment about these English dead. They were people he didn't know, could never know. He had no image of their thoughts and hopes and fears. Their deaths lacked the immediacy of that of the Tommy he himself had shot. Even the German dead seemed not quite real.

The reality was the joking and grumbling and sweating of the living soldiers. Soldiers manhandling a field gun up the steps onto the front. The fat sergeant sat astride what had recently been a British pill box, brewing up his coffee. The men easing their rough collars and grabbing a quick smoke behind the lorries drawn up at the roadside. The confusion of troops and transport still thronged the pier continuously. They helped the men with the artillery piece, then strolled back to 'their hotel'. That was already the standing joke.

"Do you know, we still haven't seen an English civilian," said Hans as they went in, round the back; the doors they guarded were officers only.

"Not even a dead one! Perhaps the British evacuated them," Rudi suggested. "Or they're all still hiding."

So the day passed, and other days. Adolf, Rudi and Hans settled into their role with the resignation and obedience appropriate to German soldiers. In fact their life was not without interest. Being in Divisional H.Q. they picked up much more information about how the war was going than most privates in the infantry. You could never be sure of course, but to Adolf it all sounded very good. There was apparently quite fierce fighting on some of the other Corps' fronts, but the army was safely ashore, and advancing away from the beaches. All except 1st Mountain Division. Despite enquiries, he and the other two could learn little of their former division, and nothing of 100 Grenadierregiment. Any of their comrades that had made it across were now fighting under 7 Division, or on the far right with XIII Corps, and that was the sum of the information available.

In Brighton, they continued to see the sights of invasion whenever they could get off duty. Over the days the whole great strength of an infantry division was being brought across. They saw the cranes rigged on the pier to swing vehicles up from the barges which had now replaced some of the motor boats as ferries. Then there were pontoons towed over and assembled to make a lower deck to the pier and to create an entirely new breakwater and landing jetty. They watched the trucks lumbering ashore, the chains of men formed to pass down the cases of ammunition from pierhead to beach, the heavy guns, landed in their parts then reassembled on the promenade. What had once been the promenade. Adolf couldn't recall a moment, while he was watching, when the activity ceased. And the flow of men seemed never to end.

There were also the air raids. Three of them in the first week, one a daylight attack by bombers escorted by a considerable force of fighters, the other two at night. The daylight attack was terminated by the arrival of the Luftwaffe, the usual Me109's going into action. Adolf saw a certain amount of it as he ran along the front towards H.Q. He had been off duty when it started. Unlike the British civilians he had not grown used to air attack. There had been raids on their embarkation ports, but nothing near his unit. There had been the R.A.F. on the crossing, but it had been the Royal Navy that sunk them. He found air raids his most unnerving experience.

H.Q. — the hotel — had been provided with shelters by the provident British. It was not hit, but the bombs came near. As he told the others, after what he saw of the daylight raid, the British were going for the beach itself, and the pier. Equally, he thought as he sat in the shelter, they might be going for Divisional H.Q., if they knew where it was. Most difficult was simply to sit and wait, while explosions echoed in the distance. Or came closer, shaking the ground. Unable to do anything except wait for the direct hit. He knew he was not a coward. He had often feared that he might be, but those hours in the water waiting to die had taught him otherwise. In action, he knew he would not have time to be afraid, only to react — as he had when he shot the sniper. Yet somehow the ability to sit calm and waiting, down in the ground, utterly powerless to escape the violent death from above that might or might not come. . . That seemed to him now a sterner sort of courage. He wondered about the ordinary people in so many places who seemed to have learnt it.

The British bombers in fact failed to hit the Grand Hotel. In the night attacks there were some hits on the beaches, and several in the town. The shops along Western Road were set ablaze, and the street burnt from end to end.

The Royal Pavilion was badly damaged. Such results had little effect on the German war effort. After one of the raids Adolf saw his first civilians. He had gone up to look at the effects of the bombing. In the distance he saw them, all women or old men, all for some reason in grey or drab browns. They were picking over the smoking ruins. Looking for food, he realized. He went back to the sea-front via a couple of backstreets, even though it was contrary to orders to do so alone. He wanted to see others of this English people. When he did see them, he was struck above all by the haunted glances they gave him. The quick looking down. The fear of offending the conqueror under whose glance their life had become a scurrying furtive existence. It was not how he had imagined being one of the Herrenvolk would be like.

And so a week passed for Adolf on English soil. He had a palatial room, shared with only two others, and the beds were soft. It was an officer's life, he reflected, as he sat in what had been one of the bars of the Grand Hotel, and was now the other ranks' mess room. The food had been good right from the start, and always plenty of it. Apparently large supplies of provisions had been captured. Also, when you are living in the same quarters as the top brass, you tend to acquire some of their perks. Lt. Weber had come in, the usual efficient but worried expression on his face. The men stood up.

"I require a volunteer. One of the staff majors is to be taken to the western sector, and I have no drivers. . . . "

"I can drive, sir. Permission to volunteer." Adolf spoke at once, at the risk of being slapped down for interrupting an officer. The lieutenant didn't even notice. It was not the sort of thing he got concerned about.

"Ah, good. You will go round to the motor park and collect the car. Then be ready to pick up Major Hoffman at the front door in thirty minutes."

They saluted as he hurried away.

"Adolf, you are a thick-head," said Rudi with some emphasis as they sat down again. "I've learnt my lesson about keeping my big mouth shut, but not you."

"Ah, but I didn't get all of us into a fix, just myself," Adolf replied grinning. "Anyway, I happen to want another look at the front line. I'm bored silly here."

"Better be bored than dead," put in Hans.

"Lots of bang-bang at the front you know," said another soldier, an older man, leaning over from the next table. "Some of us have seen it without having to volunteer."

"You obviously haven't heard of Sharpshooter Mann here," said Rudi, waving his hands airily. "Saved the general's life under fire as a matter of fact. Just needs one more exploit for his Iron Cross . . . "

Adolf got up, quickly hit Rudi across the back of the head, and dodged out of the way of a return swipe.

"I've got a car to get ready," he said.

"After last time I bet this officer doesn't want to go near the shooting," Rudi shouted after him.

"Disrespect to an officer. Put you on a charge!" Adolf called back. He had long since given up attempts to make Rudi stop telling the story of "how my mate saved the general's life". Rudi was one of those uncontrollable fellows, always landing himself and his mates in it, never worried about the consequences. Adolf saw himself as a much more careful character. On the other hand, he was the one who had just volunteered. And he was looking forward to it.

He hurried round to the park. There weren't many cars there. The general's car had come over right at the beginning, but apart from that heavier transport obviously had the higher priority. He asked a mechanic which one he was supposed to take, and after the usual exchange of rudery took possession. This car had not required any priority on the crossing, he thought as he got used to the controls. It was British, an unprepossessing vehicle. The log book was still inside. He discovered it was a 'Utility Austin 10'. More a van than a car, with a canvas cover on the back and only the two front seats left. It was still painted the standard British khaki, but with black crosses applied to the sides and bonnet.

"Couldn't you do better than this?" He yelled after the

departing mechanic. "It's an officer I'm supposed to be driving, not a farmers' outing."

He took a last glance at the log book, discovering that the car had till recently been the property of 29th Brigade Group, then settled himself into the seat, and started her up. The car started first time, and he drove cautiously round to the front of the H.Q., trying to get used to the right hand drive. One thing at least, the army had introduced the German rule of the road, so he would not have to get used to driving on the wrong side as well. Though he could drive — taught by the Hitler Youth — he was far from experienced, and had never owned a car.

"I don't suppose Weber would have let me get in a spot of extra practice if he'd known that," he thought, coming to a rather unsteady stop.

His officer, Major Hoffman, was late, and in a bad mood. His appraisal of the car apparently produced the same conclusion as Adolf's had. Which also didn't improve his temper. He handed Adolf a map.

"Your route is marked on this, soldier. Study it carefully. I do not want to end up lost or in the sea. When you know the route, you may set off. You will drive at not more than 40 kilometres per hour. If you are unsure of where you are going or there is an obstruction, you will stop the car and consult me. I can do without initiative."

"Yes sir," replied Adolf, and pored over the map. With this sort of officer, he did not intend to put a foot wrong. "Ready, sir," he said finally, opened the door for the major to get in, then got in himself, and pulled away smoothly. The car ran well, and he was already congratulating himself on his driving as he threaded his way between the lines of trucks on West Street.

The route was not the one due west along the Esplanade and into Hove. Everyone knew that that way the front was still close — near enough to walk it, Adolf thought. The British were hanging on at the edges of Hove itself, and 28 Division had apparently made little progress along the coast that way. Their opponents were the remains of the British formation shattered at the outset, now known by the Germans to have been some sort of independent infantry brigade. That plus a substantial machine gun unit, and major elements of an infantry division. All this was naturally common knowledge among even the lowliest of privates in H.Q. building. Also, Adolf and the others had seen, and talked to, some of the casualties that were brought back. There was a field hospital now, set up in what had been the town's main hospital, though it had been knocked about a bit in the fighting. Many of the wounded were still ferried back to the continent on the return leg of the continuing shuttle of craft bringing in new troops.

He drove steadily up Brighton's hills, out into the suburbs, occasionally glancing down at the map on his knees. Along the Shoreham Road the military activity was more obvious. The road was thronged with transport, demonstrating the disdain for the British air force which the German army had already learnt. As they drove along, a flight of aircraft from the east hardly merited a glance. The familiar growl of Messerschmitt engines. These 109's were flying from an airfield in England too, the new strip constructed by the army on the flat ground near their big base at Lydd — another piece of information that had seeped down from the officers. The familiar backdrop of gunfire hardly intruded at all into Adolf's consciousness now, though it was louder as they neared the scene of the fighting.

"Turn right here, private," snapped the major. Adolf had been going to do so anyway. They swung round towards the line of the Downs, the ground already rising towards the outlying hills. Then began to climb steadily up a winding road. The place was marked on his map as Blatchington. Now the sound of the fighting was unmistakable. There was a sudden crash and column of smoke among the scattered houses to the left, near the road. Near enough to make him jerk the wheel. The car slewed, but he soon straightened her up, glancing sidelong at the officer, expecting an acid rebuke. The major gave no sign.

"That'll teach me to be complacent," he thought, telling himself off, since the officer hadn't. "They can't be more than a couple of miles off now, the British. And that shelling doesn't look as if they're beaten. Not yet anyway."

At the top of a steeper rise they came to a crossroads. He turned left without waiting for instructions, wondering how much nearer they were going. They were high up now, the city spread out behind them, and the sea beyond. The pop of mortars firing was just ahead, and he saw shell bursts, almost level with them. They passed a burnt out Hanomag at the roadside.

"Pull in on the right, a hundred yards past the half-track," the major ordered. Adolf stopped beside a gap in the hedge, as soldiers ran past them.

"You will accompany me. Carry these and bring your rifle. We are under fire here."

"I hardly need telling that," thought Adolf.

He took the papers and maps, collected his rifle and followed. Even the major ran, crouched down and careful, making for what looked like a long mound. He realized it was camouflage netting as the shapes of the vehicles underneath became clearer. Good camouflage too. They ducked in under the nets, strung between two armoured cars, one of them the usual light version, noted among the troops for the thinness of its plating, the other one of the big eight-wheel jobs. There was also one of the standard Opel Blitz trucks. Between the vehicles were desks and chairs, a bank of wireless equipment, a board with maps propped against one of the armoured cars — and a gaggle of officers around the major he had brought. It was obviously some sort of forward command post. He casually moved towards some of the displayed information, and discovered it was the property of the 83rd Infantry Regiment, one of the formations making up 28 Division.

Adolf stiffened as the crack of exploding shells shook the flimsy netting. That was close, and it was followed by others. A machine gun opened up, by the sound of it only yards away. A lieutenant hurried in, saluting perfunctorily.

"Attacking down the road again, with an apparent feint from Round Hill on the right. Heavy artillery already engaging us, and another report of armour."

"Now you see why I need something more than three submersible Panzer IV's." It was a lieutenant-colonel, apparently lecturing Major Hoffman.

Then the first shell burst. It was probably some way outside the position, but ripped the netting apart with flying shrapnel. He saw the radio sets fall. Heard the smashing of glass in one of the trucks. Saw a man fall, blood spreading like liquid paint across the grey uniform. For a few seconds everyone just seemed to stand, then it was all frantic movement.

"Command Post to fall back to rear position A at road junction," he heard the colonel call out. Then Major Hoffman was shouting at him.

"Back to the car immediately. Move, you fool!"

He moved, crouched lower this time and running faster, back down the slope, till a shattering impact behind him, hard as a kick in the shoulders, flung him flat. The sound of it followed, blasting his eardrums. For a moment he lay in the grass, feeling its damp touch on his face, wondering if he was injured. He half stood, feeling the lump on his forehead where he had hit the ground.

"It would have hurt less if I wasn't wearing a helmet." He spoke the thought aloud, reassuring himself with the sound of his own voice.

He fumbled for his rifle, then turned to look for the major. Major Hoffman was crouched, kneeling on the grass, looking back at the command post. It had taken a direct hit. One of the scout cars was ablaze, so was the lorry, the tarpaulin over its back flapping like a red rag, fanning its own flames. The bodies of the officers and men were strewn around. Without thinking he started back, pausing beside Major Hoffman. He glanced down at him.

"Come on, sir, we must help them." Adolf spoke automatically, giving orders to an officer. Before he had finished the sentence his eyes fixed on the jagged splinter of metal stuck like an arrow in the side of the major's neck.

"Take the car. Report back to . . . "

The words came bubbling with blood out of the major's mouth. He toppled slowly forward, face down onto the ground, his cap rolling away. The next second Adolf was knocked over again, a blast of force followed by sudden heat. He knew what had happened as he fell, before even the sound hit him. His mind seemed to be working on an ordinary, everyday level amidst the unreal world about him.

"Lucky I didn't go back. Lucky I stopped to check Major Hoffman." He heard his own thoughts, while his eyes were fixed on the new column of smoke rising above the wrecked command post. "Petrol tank gone up. Better move. The other one will blow too."

The remains of the lorry was now a tangled mass of wreckage, still alight, but torn apart by the explosion. Both the scout cars were burning. He turned and began to run, down the hill, through the gap in the hedge, and on along the road. There were other soldiers running past him, down in the ditch beside the hedgerow. They were running uphill though, faces set and determined, hardly sparing him a glance. He felt, for no good reason, a silent reproach in them. They were going to fight. He was hurrying away — running away.

At the same time the image of the major dying filled his mind like something from a nightmare. How the man had tried to speak with that fearful wound in his neck, and the blood bubbling through the words, choking him. And all he had wanted to say were the next orders, for someone else to get on with the war, while he died by some unlucky chance in a minor skirmish over unimportant fields far from home. That was the reality behind the message they had been told so often — what it meant to be a German soldier. His perception of that reality deepened, as the sea of things he had witnessed washed against the crumbling cliffs of his ideals.

He reached the car, with shaking hands got it started, reversed and managed to turn round, oblivious to the new bursts of machine gun fire which had suddenly erupted behind him. He began to drive down the road, drawing away from the fighting all the time, feeling relief, and feeling ashamed of himself for that feeling.

The shell burst ahead of the car, a little to the side of

the road. It was so unexpected that he swung the wheel violently, crying out despite himself. The car swayed on the road, was past the shell-burst, and then the second landed. It exploded dead ahead, near a wayside house. Not ready for it, he tried to swerve too late, felt the car slide into the new crater, and then only a blinding pain in his head as he passed out.

Chapter 17

WHERE THERE'S A WILL

Through the 29th September, *S plus Two*, the movements of the two great strategists unfolded across the chessboard of south-east England. It was as if the armies had stood back from each other, like wrestlers gaining their second breath. In the east, the British continued to funnel the New Zealand Division down the corridor to the Kent Coast, behind them the Canadians and then 1st Armoured Division also moving up to take their places in the line for Britain's grand double envelopment. The operation was covered by the R.A.F. in strength, with a full commitment of Strategic Air Reserve and the bombers and remaining fighters of the new Flight Command. In fact the planes saw little of the Luftwaffe, which for some reason was leaving the extensive troop movements alone. The British thanked their stars.

Beyond their corridor to the sea, however, things seemed to be going less well for them. The continuous reinforcement of the German 7th Parachute Division went on with glider-borne troops and freight gliders bringing in more heavy equipment. Just as the Luftwaffe did not interfere with British movements, so the R.A.F. was unable to do anything about the German reinforcements. The paratroops continued to edge northwards. A British assault failed to dislodge them from the Dover-Canterbury road, while on the other side of the cathedral city the Germans

233

reached the ominously named hamlet of Dunkirk on the A2. Canterbury was all but cut off, and that night the Luftwaffe bombers subjected it to a severe raid. The plight of the city became a matter of increasing concern to Britain's strategists. It was not a place to be abandoned lightly.

Along the southern flank of the British corridor, the Germans were engaged in turning their 17th Division round. They were aware of its vulnerability, but not of the extent of the attack to which it was to be subjected. 35 Division's progress into the Vale of Kent was also slowed down to avoid becoming separated from 17th. They had encountered British tanks in the Weald on their left. These were the tanks sent in to strengthen 45 Division's position in Hastings between the two halves of the German army. They had already worried the Germans on each side of them.

They were the reason that the German advance north west from Bexhill slowed down. Uckfield was captured but there was no further progress there. Lewes was encircled and the large British garrison trapped. But an attempted assault on the town failed. Above Brighton the British were increasingly established on the summits of the Downs. Also the Germans were making no progress at all beyond Hove along the coast, were even starting to find it difficult to hold onto their existing positions.

One of the Luftwaffe's distractions from the movement of British troops was the presence of the Home Fleet at anchor in the Medway. Two days of daylight raids failed to hit the surviving battleships. Repairs on *Nelson* proceeded well. In addition to precision and dive-bombing by daylight, Goering ordered a night raid on Chatham too. The town was set on fire, but the fleet and the harbour installations virtually unscathed. Goering was irritated, and complained to the Führer that the Luftwaffe was overburdened. Hitler brushed aside his worries.

"As long as you are protecting the Newhaven landings, my friend, that is all I ask of you. As long as those Panzers cross safe . . . "

The first tanks of 7 Panzer were swung ashore during

the night of 29th September. They were a token force to protect the landing of engineers and equipment. Rommel was taking no chances. He had sent over a staff major, Heidkamper, to supervise the proper preparation of the little harbour to receive his Panzer division. Special additional units of engineers had been made available on the orders of General Paulus acting on the direct authority of the Führer. He and Rommel conferred in Le Havre about the assembly of transport — barges commandeered from other units' reinforcement programmes. Their only concern was that the convoy should be given the maximum possible escorting force. They were heartened when they woke up on the morning of the 30th to see four German cruisers in the harbour in addition to the destroyers. The plan was to move the entire tank strength of the division, two Panzer regiments, plus as much as possible of the transport for the lorried infantry regiments during the next two nights.

The thoughts of the British were also preoccupied with armour. 1st Armoured Division was well on its way to the eastern flank, and 1st Army Tank Brigade had already completed its deployment in the centre. In the west, Brooke was worried about his relative weakness in tanks. He asked for and was given an additional reinforcement. He had already begun to move the 22nd Armoured Brigade through Southampton by train. Now 21st Army Tank Brigade would follow as well, also by rail. Their movements would be given priority. The transport and logistics were complicated. The result should be a tank attack in two waves through the Vale of Sussex while the infantry attacked along the coast through Brighton. (The town itself was not considered suitable 'tank country'.) This was the other claw of the pincers. With the additional tanks it looked as formidable as its opposite number on the eastern flank.

* * *

Soon after nightfall on the 30th, the ships of the Home Fleet sailed from Chatham. The following day's attacks would find an empty harbour. *Nelson* and *Rodney* were making a painful eight knots, the flagship's best speed after her hasty repair, northwards for the Humber Estuary, the screen of twelve destroyers strung out round the battle-ships. Four cruisers and the remaining destroyers were moving eastwards, out past the Isle of Sheppey, and then round the North Foreland into the Straits of Dover. They were the eight-inch-gunned near-sisters, *Norfolk* and *Suffolk*, and two new ships, the six-inch Colony Class *Jamaica* and the AA-Cruiser *Charybdis*. With the escorts they were under the command of Admiral Wake-Walker.

The ships ran swift, dark and silent, the gloomy mass of the French coast away to port, to the starboard the crackle of gunfire and thump of bombs as Dover and Folke-stone were visited by the Luftwaffe. As they came abreast of Hythe the first enemy shipping was encountered, invasion barges towed by tugs, moving at night to escape any risk of attack from the air. Searchlights flicked on aboard the British ships. This time it was the men of 17 and 35 German Infantry Divisions who experienced the might of Britain's navy. The heavy guns of the cruisers opened up first, and wherever the six- or eight-inch shells hit, an invasion barge was destroyed. The British gunners began to make meticu-lous and devastating practice. Then the destroyers went in, their lighter guns increasing the havoc.

The German airwaves crackled with anguished demands for air and naval support. And another battery of search-lights cut through the night, swept round, passing over the scatter of barges, then locking on the larger shape of a British destroyer. Heavy guns thundered out. The destroyer captain suddenly found himself sailing through a shattering barrage of waterspouts, his ship shaken by the impact of the near-misses.

"We're British, you fools," he yelled into the night. Then the second salvo fell onto his ship, and this time the gunners made no mistake. Shells sliced through the flimsy plating into the magazine, and HMS *Mashona* blew up in the water. These events were witnessed at close range by Wake-Walker on the bridge of the *Norfolk*. Still believing it might be some ghastly error, but filled with sudden apprehensions, he snapped the order,

"Put up star shell!"

"Radar reports large vessel to the south, Admiral".

"Then that's your direction for the star shell," he answered.

The great guns elevated, and crashed out, and moments later, high overhead the star shell burst like a series of spectacular fireworks.

"Enemy ship, sir!" Recognition was immediate as all the officers peered at her through their binoculars.

"*Hipper* Class, sir!"

Wake-Walker knew better.

"Gentlemen, that is a pocket-battleship. It looks to me very like the *Admiral Scheer*."

All eyes fixed on the admiral. He glanced down at the compass in the binnacle.

"Well, if they come on like that, we're already across their T," he said, deliberately loud so that everyone knew his thoughts and intentions. He turned to the Flag Captain. "Make to *Suffolk*, *Jamaica* and *Charybdis* — 'Cruisers follow me!' By semaphore and W/T please, the transmission in clear. Oh, and you'd better add:- 'Prepare to engage enemy pocket-battleship!' Then the men might care to hear the news on the tannoy, Captain."

A cheer rang round the bridge. *HMS Norfolk* went to full speed. *Suffolk* was already in line astern behind her. Eight turrets, each with two heavy guns, were already bearing on the pocket battleship as she came up fast. *Scheer* was not standing back to rely on the longer range of her eleven-inch guns. Only her forward triple turret could engage as she approached the British line at the worst possible angle, but she was firing with great rapidity, and on her third salvo achieved a straddle of the *Norfolk*. Then the sixteen guns of the two British heavy cruisers crashed out, almost in unison. There was only a single hit, but the weight of the attack seemed to have shaken the enemy commander. At once the *Scheer* began to turn to port, to come onto a parallel course with the British squadron.

In fact, Admiral Krancke on the *Scheer*'s bridge had believed his opponents to be destroyers rather than cruisers until he closed with them. Conscious of Admiralty instructions not to risk his valuable ship against a superior force, he was now preparing to break off the action. The *Scheer* had only been got ready for sea a day ago. Her mission, unbeknown even to the Führer (who believed her repairs would take additional weeks) was to provide the long-stop for the crossing of 7th Panzer Division. Raeder had sent the other four available large ships into the Channel already. They would provide the convoy force. The pocket battleship would patrol on their flank, looking out for stray British raiders, and helping to protect the rest of the invasion routes at the same time.

"Destroyers to launch immediate torpedo attack, and then begin laying smoke," he ordered.

But as the three German destroyers came out from behind the *Scheer* they were met by no less than eight British destroyers. A fierce little fight between the small ships began, with no doubt as to its final outcome. *Scheer* had turned away from the British line, but the heavy cruisers followed her on parallel course. Both had been hit. The flagship was on fire astern, and *Suffolk* had lost B turret. But the *Scheer* was also burning from several minor hits on her superstructure. After thirty minutes of the engagement, Wake Walker signalled,

"Light cruisers to take independent action!"

Jamaica and *Charybdis* fell out of line, and began to pull across the *Scheer*'s stern. The pocket battleship continued to concentrate all its fire power on the two County Class cruisers, and was rewarded by a decisive hit on *Norfolk*, penetrating her thin armoured skin, and exploding in the engine room. At once the flagship's speed was dramatically reduced. As *Suffolk* came sharply round to starboard to avoid her sister ship, Admiral Krancke suddenly swung his ship northward in a great sweeping curve, heading almost directly towards the slowly moving shape of the *Norfolk*. Though crippled, *Norfolk* could still fight. Her guns engaged the fast-approaching enemy. *Scheer* took more hits on her high forward superstructure, and the fires on her upper decks spread. She was now engaging *Norfolk* with her forward turret, and *Suffolk* with the guns aft.

No hits were scored on *Suffolk*, but as the pocket battleship swept past *Norfolk*, shell after shell was pumped into the British flagship. Three of her four turrets were now out of action, and she was stopped in the water. *Suffolk* and *Jamaica* had also turned now, taken by surprise at Krancke's daring manoeuvre, and were chasing *Scheer* to the north.

The two cruisers, and five of the British destroyers continued the chase through the Straits and into the North Sea. On the way they disposed of the one surviving German destroyer, but they did not catch the pocket battleship. *Scheer* finally found safe refuge in the Scheldt, but she was no longer operational. Her bridge and built-up military mast had been virtually destroyed, and her after turret was out of action. *Suffolk*, *Jamaica* and the destroyers were ordered to put into Harwich. *Charybdis*, meanwhile, had managed to get a tow on board the stricken *Norfolk*, and was proceeding slowly down the Channel aiming for Plymouth, screened by the rest of the destroyers.

During the night they crossed the path of a German flotilla conveying substantial units of 7 Panzer Division, including an entire regiment of tanks, to England. The two convoys did not encounter each other. Britain had won a useful naval success, but the Germans might regard the crippling of the *Scheer* as an acceptable price for the safe crossing of their tanks. Particularly as the damage to the British ships meant that on the following night Rommel's Panzers would once again cross unchallenged and unscathed.

The crossing proved less fraught with difficulties than the disembarkation. Makeshift cranes had been rigged up along the main breakwater to lift the tanks ashore, but the volume of armour to be put through the tiny port in the space of two days and nights provided the Germans with an operational nightmare. In addition to the tanks themselves there was all the transport of the attached infantry regiments, a regiment of field artillery, and all the necessary support and back-up formations. Had the R.A.F. struck at the port by day or night (for Rommel had personally ordered the unloading operations to proceed at night by floodlight, despite the risk from aerial attack) they might have removed the Panzers from the equation of battle at a stroke.

Goering was true to his word and round the clock air cover was provided. The Luftwaffe also provided substantial diversions in the form of heavy bombing raids on British positions in Kent. Not only were the coastal towns attacked, but also the troop corridor, the now vital communications centre at Ashford on the landward end of that corridor, and the east-west railway link from Ashford across to Redhill and ultimately Guildford. The German bombers engaged in some of these raids by day were severely mauled by Flight Command's fighters. Their own fighter escorts were off protecting Newhaven.

Further distraction was provided by the continuing successes of the 7th Parachute Regiment. On 1st October the Germans reached the North Kent Coast at Whitstable Bay. After fierce local fighting by the Home Guard stiffened by the arrival of 8th Battalion, Royal Fusiliers, the Germans finally forced their way into the town of Whitstable. This, combined with the continued bombing of Canterbury, had now led Churchill and the generals to believe that an assault on the cathedral city would come in the immediate future. For reasons of morale and propaganda, the Prime Minister was not prepared to abandon the city to its fate. There were sound military arguments as well. The northerly 'back door' route to the key coastal positions had now been lost, leaving the 'corridor' as the only route for troops and supplies. It was agreed to divert 1st Canadian Division to relieve Canterbury and teach the German paratroops a lesson before the great assault could begin.

So the Canadians deployed to attack, and the enemy paras melted away before them. General Crerar reported back the Canadians' conclusions to Churchill:- that the enemy paratroops might be a considerable nuisance, but they were so thinly spread that they were unlikely at the moment to constitute much more. By October 3rd Whitstable had been retaken, and on the following day the Ashford-Canterbury route recovered. The containment of the audacious Germans was completed by troops of the Royal West Kent Regiment who cleared the line of communications from Dover to Canterbury. The British had acted decisively and produced the required results with apparently very little trouble. They had even been aided by intermittent local air superiority. Apart from anything else, a singular boost to morale had been provided.

The mood was further reinforced by the steady deployment of 1st Armoured Division into the 'corridor'. The organizational difficulties in Ashford were horrendous. Three divisions passed through it in the course of a week. And the town itself now containing three divisional H.Q.'s. Despite the activity of the Luftwaffe, the British coped very well. Preparations for the big push gathered momentum steadily. It looked as if Brooke's planned date, 7th October, would be met. The operation had now got a name — or rather three names. The eastern attack was *Operation Lemon Squeezer*; the western, *Operation Coffee Grinder*. The whole grand design was graced with the name of *Mangle*.

Growing British confidence was not paralleled on the other side among the troops of General Busch's Sixteenth Army. They had encountered British armour in widely different places. The advance had slowed to a series of probing patrols and the development of strongpoints to protect the flanks. In Strauss's army, morale was better, and the advance had continued into the early days of October, though also at a slower rate. Nevertheless, the progressive capture of Wealden villages had brought the Germans close to Tunbridge Wells. At the same time progress through the scattered wood and moorland of Ashdown Forest was threatening East Grinstead. Neither centre was itself of prime strategic importance, but the fall of either or both would bring the Germans closer to lines of communication which undoubtedly were vital.

On 3rd October, after a valiant defence, the surrounded town of Lewes was stormed. Another British pocket, that of Eastbourne, was further squeezed by the capture of the road and rail junctions north of the town. In Brighton itself, however, German progress was nil. The British build up around the town in preparation for *Operation Coffee Grinder* was already beginning to put the Germans through the mill. But whatever the successes or failures of the two German field armies, the event which most mattered was behind their front lines, in the tiny harbour of Newhaven, where there was now a complete, fully equipped Panzer Division.

General Brooke also had the movement of his own armour for the western half of the pincers well under way. He had encountered serious difficulties in the provision of sufficient large flat cars, for the movement of the two brigades by rail simultaneously. He was also faced with continuing problems about the route, partly caused by destruction of track through enemy air raids, partly by the apparent bloody-mindedness of the railway operating authorities. Eventually Churchill dealt with the Railway Executive in person, and some progress was made. The Great Western Railway's vehicles which had brought 21st Army Tank Brigade as far as Southampton were commandeered for the rest of the journey.

22nd Armoured Brigade was already on its way, by a distinctly circuitous route. It would travel up the mid-Hants line to Guildford, then eastwards on the cross-country line of the former South Eastern and Chatham Railway as far as Redhill. From there it would be brought straight down the Brighton main line as far as Hassocks, under the shadow of the Downs. This was its start point for the great sweep along the Vale of Sussex, due east through the heart of the German army, ultimate objective — Hastings. 21st Army Tank Brigade now followed it by a different route, along the coast line, cleared after a series of enemy attacks on its stations, through Chichester, then up through Horsham as

far as Three Bridges. There it too would be reversed, and
brought down the Brighton line to Burgess Hill, just north
of the rest of the armour. The plan was that both armoured
formations should reach their positions on 5th October,
ready to commence their part of *Coffee Grinder* and *Mangle*
at dawn on the 7th.

During the evening of 3rd October, the last units of 7
Panzer were moving out of Newhaven. The miracle of
organization had been achieved. In his command vehicle in
the forward columns, Erwin Rommel was satisfied with the
way things had gone. And supremely confident of the way
he intended them to go in the following few days. At the
same time, 4th Panzer Division was beginning to arrive at
Le Havre. The Führer had been delighted with the success
of the 'Newhaven Ferry' (as it was known from the General
Staff down to the tank crews who sailed; its official name
was *Rhinemaiden*). The generals were appalled that Hitler
proposed to repeat what they still regarded as a very risky
business, and rely once again on luck to save them from
British intervention.

"You cannot win your battles without armour. The
British have armour, and they will not be slow to use it,"
Hitler told them. "Also, you overestimate the risks. You
are obsessed with risks. All war is a risk, it is merely a
matter of calculating which are worth taking. Not a matter
of making sure your own professional backsides are protected."

To reinforce his point, he went on to announce the
promotion of Friedrich Paulus to Lieutenant General. The
staff officers may have felt suitably snubbed at the advance-
ment of this relative newcomer to their exalted ranks. They
were no doubt equally glad that he remained in charge of
the transportation of 4th Panzer across the Channel. They
regarded that as a poisoned apple, particularly as the Panzers were to be followed up by a motorized division. This
would bring the whole of 9th Army's Second Wave over to
the one little port in German hands.

Rommel's Panzers had a difficult journey through the

night. Their route of necessity involved crossing the recently captured and largely destroyed town of Lewes. It had only fallen that day, and the first part of Rommel's orders dealt with his part in its capture. Beyond that now superseded task, his orders were vague:- co-operate with the infantry in securing the western flank of the invasion; then move against the British armour in the Hastings salient. The orders, prepared by his own Corps Commander, General Hermann Hoth, were deliberately open to interpretation. Hoth was a good Panzer general, and trusted Rommel to exploit the possibilities that were open to him. In fact Rommel intended to open a few more.

His study of the maps revealed that the best way to relieve pressure on the Germans in Brighton was to come round on the British build-up from behind. With any luck he might encircle a couple of entire divisions. Accordingly he now deployed his tanks on a start line formed by the green track of the ancient Roman road running north of Lewes and west of Uckfield.

Rommel began his advance at 10.00 hours on the morning of Friday 4th October. Above him on the left was Ditchling Beacon and the heights of the Downs behind Brighton, still in British hands. Before him, the open country of the Vale of Sussex. What no German commander knew about was the glittering prize that now fell into Rommel's hand. For as his tanks swept into Haywards Heath and Burgess Hill, rolling back the remnants of the Royal Welsh and Royal Scots Fusiliers before them, an astonishing sight met them on the London to Brighton main line. On the section of railway they now overran there were twelve trains, all running southward, operating as close together as the signalling system would allow. The Germans had found 22nd Armoured Brigade.

The tank commanders could not believe it, as they saw those endless processions of flat cars, draped with camouflage netting that could not begin to conceal the unmistakable shapes of the tanks beneath. Above the railway cuttings on each side of Haywards Heath station, the Panzers drew up and swung their turrets to the side. With guns at maximum depression, they opened fire on the British beneath. Rommel had a mixture of Panzerkampfwagen Marks II, III and IV. The armament of the Mark II's in particular was deficient. At this range even that did not matter. Even the 2cm and 3.7cm shells could smash the wheels and tracks of the British tanks, and penetrate the armour of the Light and Infantry tanks which still formed part of the British equipment. The newer Cruiser tanks fared little better.

The tanks on the flat cars were unmanned, yet each had ammunition loaded, and each was fully fuelled. This step had been taken to ensure that they would be ready and fully prepared to go into immediate action. In the result, it meant that they exploded and burnt well beneath the merciless German shelling. The three trains in those cuttings were obliterated in the space of half an hour. The troop train in the station between them, the train containing their crews, was next to go, as the Panzers moved down onto the railway tracks themselves.

The men in the next troop train southward heard the sounds of destruction just before German tanks arrived on the road beside their stopped train. This time they were on an embankment, and the German guns had to elevate. The British were a perfect target. The carriages were smashed to matchwood by high explosive shell, while other German commanders found the two trains of flat cars just ahead, and shot the British tanks off their wagons and over the side into the gully beneath. It was like a fairground shooting gallery. The Germans had never known anything like it.

In the station at Burgess Hill the same happened as had at Haywards Heath. The flames of exploding petrol tanks set the station ablaze, while the shells and machine-gun bullets erupting into the sky marked the scene of the carnage for miles around. The Brigade Staff of 22nd Armoured Brigade had got out of their train, stopped on the long embankment south of Burgess Hill that ran into the village of Hassocks, to try to find out what was happening. They were machine-gunned for the most part, by German light tanks racing along the flat country beside the railway above. German lorried infantry at Hassocks completed the operation by the capture, intact, of two trains of British tanks all ready for battle.

By two o'clock in the afternoon the Germans possessed the railway from the Downs to Haywards Heath. Eighty-nine British tanks had been destroyed completely or rendered inoperable, forty-one had been captured virtually undamaged. Rommel radioed back for his reserve tank crews to man them. They would be a useful adjunct to his own forces. He had been fighting for three hours, and had wiped out as utterly as if it had never existed an entire British tank brigade. His own losses in material amounted to one lorry and two tanks. From the bodies of the officers, lying beside the charred remains of their train on a desolate railway embankment, were brought him a copy of brigade orders for an operation called *Coffee Grinder*. By two thirty his tanks were moving again.

Their axis of advance was shifted a little, as their commander acted on the information about the enemy's plans now in his possession. He had separated his two Panzer Regiments to form two spearheads. One was to move up the approximate line of the railway in the general direction of Crawley and the important junction at Three Bridges. 25th Panzerregiment would find the going there quite difficult. The ridges of the Weald and the extensive stretches of wooded country did not provide the best tank country, and there was a shortage of good roads. 66th Panzer Regiment had an easier objective, the market town of Horsham.

Pennants flying, the victorious tanks sped along the country lanes, and the winding "main" road provided by the A272. Now it was really like France all over again. The tank commanders stood up in their turrets, watching the villages speed by. There were minor local difficulties. At the village of Cowfold they encountered a strong rearguard of the Royal Sussex Regiment, in the process of abandoning its base there and moving south to take part in the great offensive. The arrival of the Panzers came as an unexpected blow, and the movement southward turned into a British withdrawal, as frantic messages flashed down the line to the British units massing for the kill round Brighton. There was some sporadic interference from other isolated regular units and the Home Guard. Rifles and Molotov cocktails for the most part. The tanks hardly used their cannon. Most of the opposition could be dealt with by machine gun. Most of it was straightforwardly overawed by the abrupt and overwhelming evidence of German might.

At Cowfold, the confident Germans split their forces again. The bulk of the regiment turned north on the direct road to Horsham. But a flying column continued due west, to cut off the town, and encircle it if necessary. Rommel himself was with the main part of the regiment's armour, which entered Horsham at five o'clock. Even he found it hard to believe that his luck could have provided the same opportunity, the identical, ideal entrapment of enemy armour twice in the same day. In later years, as Commander-in-Chief of the German Army, he held that it was this sheer good fortune which had founded the legend and assured all his future successes.

One in the station, one just south of it, two trainloads of the tanks of 21st Army Tank Brigade unknowingly awaited the arrival of the Panzers. They were as indefensible as those already destroyed. Rommel himself watched as his tanks moved down the railway tracks, the barrels of their guns roaring blasts of flame and destruction at the lines of enemy armour. The news of a "battle" between tanks "in the vicinity of Haywards Heath" had been relayed to the 21st. But the possible arrival of the Germans a mere dozen miles to the westward in Horsham had apparently not been taken into account. By the light of blazing British tanks, Rommel heard of the capture of more British tanks in the quiet village of Faygate along the railway towards Crawley. That boded even better, for that was the direction in which his own second Panzerregiment was moving.

At seven o'clock, Rommel fought his first genuine tank battle on British soil. In Christ's Hospital, just outside of Horsham, the British had managed to have tanks and their crews together in adjacent trains. That, together with the presence of 21st Army Tank Brigade's commander, Brigadier Naesmyth, provided the first opportunity for real resistance. The fighting began on the playing fields of the Bluecoat School there, and spread into the southern outskirts of Horsham itself. Naesmyth was able to deploy eighteen tanks with reasonable speed. Only half a dozen faced him. Three of them had been knocked out and the rest were pulling back into the town by the time Rommel ordered up reinforcements. The British also had some reinforcements available. A second trainload, another dozen tanks, was being unloaded at Barns Green, farther down the line.

At first Rommel was concerned at British strength, and the dispersal of his own forces. However, it became increasingly apparent that in total the British had no more than forty tanks available. Rommel could speedily concentrate more than twice that number. The arrival of his artillery in the town served to provide added firepower against the point of British advance. Naesmyth on the other hand had just learnt that the rearmost train-load of his tanks, well to the south at Billingshurst, was under fire from German armour. They would not be coming to his aid. Seeing the risk of encirclement looming, and increasingly hard pressed by superior numbers, Naesmyth withdrew in good order westwards. He had salvaged for Britain out of the wreck some thirty tanks.

A few more escaped from Three Bridges on the far right of the second prong of Rommel's thrust, as the Panzers descended on them from the hills. There was another engagement at Crawley. There once again some at least of the British tanks were brought into action, and not wiped out like sitting ducks on their railway waggons. But by nightfall, 7th Panzer Division had advanced distances between twelve and twenty miles and occupied a triangle of 150 square miles of territory. They had wiped out all the available British armour, two entire brigades, on the western end of the front line, and had established themselves all along the flank of British positions on the coast. Furthermore, they now seemed poised to complete the total encirclement of those positions. Rommel had already received reports of German tanks rolling south through Pulborough towards the Arun Gap — and the sea.

"What we have seen today is a triumph of the National Socialist spirit," Hitler told the four ranking generals of the German army, Keitel, Jödl, Brachitsch and Halder, as they drank the health of Erwin Rommel in the ornate setting of Schloss Ziegenberg that evening. The generals sipped their champagne, and did not venture to suggest that luck might have had a great deal to do with it as well.

"What the hell is happening?" Brooke was asking Naesmyth at the same sort of time. Through the day he had begun to piece together the elements of the disaster. He already knew he had lost one Armoured Brigade from his line of battle, and was facing a Panzer Division which he had believed was still somewhere in France. Now he learnt that a second brigade of tanks was effectively destroyed. He put down the phone and turned to Dill and Ismay, with him in the War Office. It did not take long to impart the news.

"I think I'll have to stay here, gentlemen. Would you explain matters for me to Winston and the Committee."

"What are you going to do, Alan?" asked Dill, the C.I.G.S.

"Try to get through to Montgomery at V Corps, and Swayne at Chichester."

"And tell them to scrap *Coffee Grinder*?"

"Tell them to be prepared to withdraw," Brooke answered, his voice grim and tired. "Will you support me at the Committee, if Winston plays up?"

"You can rely on us to do that," said Hastings Ismay. "It would be madness to try to press on with it now. But what do you feel about the rest of *Mangle* — the *Lemon Squeezer Operation*, I mean?"

"With your agreement — and with the P.M.'s — I want it to go ahead."

They left him to take the news to yet another emergency

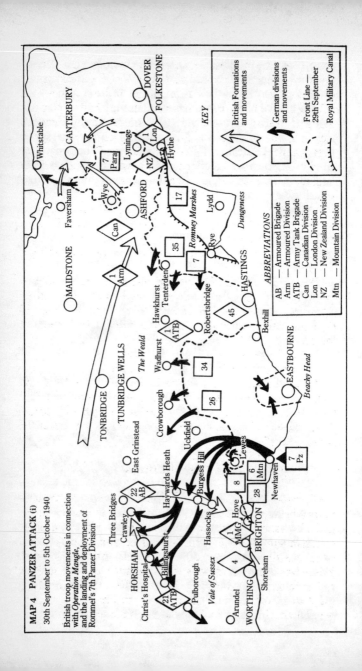

MAP 4 PANZER ATTACK (i)

30th September to 5th October 1940

British troop movements in connection
with *Operation Mangle*, the landing and
deployment of Rommel's 7th Panzer Division

KEY

British Formations and movements

German divisions and movements

Front Line —
29th September

Royal Military Canal

ABBREVIATIONS

AB — Armoured Brigade
Arm — Armoured Division
ATB — Army Tank Brigade
Can — Canadian Division
Lon — London Division
NZ — New Zealand Division
Mtn — Mountain Division

session of the Committee of Home Defence. Brooke remained, to prepare his commanders on the Sussex coast for withdrawal. Withdrawal from the positions they had defended so well. Positions from which they had so recently hoped to roll up the German line and fling the invaders back into the sea. As the evening wore on Brooke spoke to Brigadier Burrows, the commander in Worthing, and twice to Major General Swayne, the new commander of 4th Infantry Division. On the second occasion, Swayne told him,

"Brigadier Barber — 10th Brigade — has reported enemy tanks at Amberley — little place north of the Downs. Barber's in Arundel at the moment, at least his Brigade H.Q. is. He's expecting the enemy down the Arun tonight or tomorrow."

When Brooke finally put the phone down, he looked carefully at the great wall map of South-East England — *Operations Area* as it was now called. Then he rang 10 Downing Street and asked for Dill. The C.I.G.S. came to the phone.

"How is he taking it?" Brooke asked.

"With a display of fireworks, I'm afraid."

"Would you tell him I would like to come over and address the Committee, if the session can continue. Tell him I intend to demand the withdrawal of all British forces on the Sussex Coast to new positions behind the line of the River Arun."

"I see," answered Dill.

"I hope he will too," replied Brooke.

Rommel too had been consulting his maps, at his temporary headquarters in the Station Hotel at Horsham. He had also taken the opportunity to obtain his subordinate commanders' opinions over a glass or two of champagne which, with good reason, they all felt they had earned. There was much talk among the Germans too of completing the envelopment, sweeping down to the coast and cutting the British off. When the jubilant officers had gone, the general continued to look at the maps alone.

The temptation was certainly there for all to see. He had no doubt that the British would be well aware of it also. They had suffered two serious reverses in the course of the day, what would they do now? How would he respond if *he* were the British general directing this battle? It would not be a stupid man, he reasoned, though it might well be a cautious one. Knowing the British, it might be a committee. Then again, what would the famous Winston Churchill require his generals to do? He stood up, and glanced round at his batman, the only other left in the room.

"If I was the British commander, Franz, I would think about withdrawing. And now I am going to bed."

He rose early to hear the latest reports from his widely spread forces. The enormous sweep of his 'front line' from beyond Crawley to the Downs above Arundel was secure. He had issued orders that there were to be no further advances without his express consent. He needed to consolidate the position, and establish some sort of order. He needed his infantry to come up, and be concentrated ready to support the next phase of the action. He also needed to know what the British were up to. He had telegraphed Hoth, his Corps Commander, asking for extensive reconnaissance. Hoth had told Paulus, and Paulus had told Goering. Knowing how much it would please the Führer, Goering saw to it personally. Rommel got his reconnaissance, plus a personal message from the Reichsmarschall offering maximum air support. For some days now the Luftwaffe had been engaged in building its own airfield in England, near Dungeness. There were already fighter aircraft operating from it. Rommel had only to ask, and these would be available for the Panzer's dash to the coast. Goering was a little surprised by Rommel's reply.

At one o'clock he met with his regimental and other commanders again.

"The position, gentlemen, is this. What some of you last night told me was a spearhead is in fact the trailing left wing of an over-extended front line." He pointed at the positions held by the few tanks beyond Pulborough. "Behind that line, in this whole area here" — this time he indicated the Vale of Sussex stretching back to the Panzers' start line — "there remain numerous British units, pockets of local resistance. There is also the distinct possibility of reinforcement from the commanding heights of the Downs which are still in British hands."

"Now we could of course turn ourselves southward. Race to the sea, and cut the British off. It would look like another Panzer corridor, as in France. It would look like the British corridor to the sea on our right flank, about which you have heard. But the reality is that it would leave us on the coast, with all our communications through a narrow valley, stretching back thirty miles behind that across largely unsubdued country. The British could break out behind us if they chose. Or decide to try to cut us off. We are only one division, not a whole Panzer army. It is not quite like France. Not yet."

"So we are going to surprise them again. I cannot promise you a brigade or two of tanks to wipe out this time, but I think that we shall see some real action. They expect us to race for the sea. So we will leave a screen of armour down here beyond Horsham on our left flank, and they will go on thinking that. But we are going east. We are going to look for these tanks which have so worried our divisional commanders in the centre of the front. Our first objective is here. A place called Tunbridge Wells. About ten miles to advance through hostile country. I want us in position for a start at dawn tomorrow. I have your detailed orders here. Major Heidkamper will run through the operational details. I would like to be in this Tunbridge Wells place for lunch."

There were cheers from the eager young officers, perhaps some of the National Socialist spirit Hitler had boasted of. Their general looked round at them, pleased with what he saw. The massacres of the day before had raised their morale to unconquerable heights.

"Do you mind if some of us have lunch a bit farther down the road, Herr General?" someone called out. More laughter, in which Rommel joined. It was the spirit of the chase that was really animating them. The scent of the kill.

"It is a railway we are following, not a road, gentlemen," he announced. "And if you see a tank on a train, it is one of theirs." They shouted their approval. "But don't let me find any of you getting too far ahead of me, or there will be trouble. I think I am entitled to be the first into Dover."

The meeting broke up. Surreptitiously the greater part of the tanks beyond Horsham to the west fell back during the day. They left only a thin screen with orders to make its presence felt by shooting up villages. Even so, Rommel was being provident. As soon as the captured British tanks were manned, they would come into this sector of the line. The rest of his Panzers were regrouping between Horsham and Three Bridges. This time they looked like a spearhead. He spent the afternoon inspecting and supervising, joking with young men with cropped hair and silly grins who cheered him from their tanks. He was at Crawley when the first detailed reconnaissance reports reached him. It appeared — though surely it could not be right, as a cautious Luftwaffe intelligence officer had scribbled in the margin — that the British were starting to pull back some units along the coast, away from their strongly held positions in Brighton.

"I wonder if that *is* what I would have done?" said Rommel to himself.

Brooke and the Generals had persuaded Churchill, in the end, that the risks were too great. *Operation Coffee Grinder* was abandoned. Brighton was abandoned. Worthing and all the rest of the coast back to the River Arun — abandoned. And it was done for fear of a division of German tanks that were already beginning to drive away in the opposite direction. At the decisive moment, faced with a severe military setback, the British had taken the path of caution. Their will to win had not been strong enough.

Chapter 18

CAPTURED

It was just before dawn on Sunday 29th September when Don finally collapsed onto the bunk in the cellar and slept at once. It was the untroubled sleep of utter exhaustion, and he did not awake for eighteen hours. When he did stir, he felt strangely fit, almost cheerful. He knew at once where he was despite the complete darkness. The memory of everything that had happened was immediately clear before his mind's eye. He knew he had slept a very long time. He fumbled for the torch, found it beside his bed, and ventured back upstairs. Not surprisingly he discovered his limbs were stiff and protesting. Every move he made revealed a new ache and pain.

It was dark again. He guessed he had slept the clock round. What did that make it? He tried to work it out; time was already becoming hazy. — The night of the 29th. Still cautious he set about moving what he would need down to the cellar, only using the torch when he had to. The sky was bright and cloudless, though there was no moon up. The sounds of battle were only sporadic, drifting from a good way away. He took all the food and drink, real drink too, for there were bottles of home-made cider. There was another torch in a kitchen cupboard. The people had obviously been provident. There were candles and matches too. Just in case, he also brought down a good amount of bedding, risking a visit to the upper storey to fetch it.

Upstairs, the damage to the house was more severe. One side of the roof was smashed open and hanging off. The stairs themselves felt far from safe. He looked out of the windows, but there was little enough to see. The ground floor too was in a worse state than he had thought. It looked as if one end of the house could come down at any moment. But it was the opposite end to where the cellar door lay, so there was little risk of being trapped by fallen rubble. And it made it less likely that inquisitive Germans would come prying around.

The cellar itself was sound and dry. Once had made sure the window was really light-proof, and had blacked out the door himself with blankets, he felt confident in putting on the light there. He had even found a book or two to read. Of the house's occupants there was no sign. Perhaps they had run when the Germans landed, or fled when their house was damaged. He remembered the streams of refugees he had seen. They might have been among them. Wherever they had gone they would not grudge him now the comforts of their cellar or the provisions they had left behind in their haste.

He had decided that he would spend at least that night there, and possibly the next day, so that he could see the lie of the land. He still planned to push on across the Downs, but it would have to be by night, and how he managed it would depend on the Germans. When day came and he did venture outside, it was to an unpleasant surprise. The road was full of German vehicles. Back inside, from a precarious surviving upstairs window on the wrecked side of the house, he saw that the fields beyond him, the hillside on the right of the road, contained a vehicle park and tented encampment. There must have been a dozen troop lorries there and on the road, and perhaps a hundred tents. He counted them carefully, suddenly thinking that the information might be needed by someone . . . if he ever had the chance to deliver it.

He was faced with the growing certainty that he had escaped across the hostile city only to land on the edge of an enemy camp. There were a hundred and twenty tents.

Six-man tents, he guessed. So that meant over seven hundred Germans. What would that make it? A battalion, maybe — if they had the same organization as the British. Among everything else he had found a notebook and a pencil. Now, back in the cellar, he jotted down his 'intelligence' information. The tense excitement of his night-time flight had mellowed into a sensible realism. He was not forgetful of the danger, but compared with the pressing, heart-stopping danger he had been in before, it held few terrors for him. He reasoned that sooner or later the Germans would move on, or be pushed back. Until then, he had a safe refuge in his cellar. Everything he needed to live was now there.

He made a careful inventory of his food supplies, and calculated that he could last for two weeks if he was careful and rationed himself properly. The Germans were obviously not interested in a ruined house. Even if they did come, they would probably not find the cellar. He always barricaded the door firmly when he was inside. And at night he could prowl around, relying on the cover provided by the hedge and the shrubs in the garden. Perhaps even slip into the field beyond, watching the enemy from the coppice that ran up to their camp. His notebook now contained the information that there were tanks with the Germans — only two though.

He found himself thinking mostly about his family. By now his mother would have been told he was missing. "Missing believed killed," was what the official information would be. He could visualize the scene. She would not accept it, would complain. Protest that he was only a boy, only a Home Guard, had no business being there. He found the contemplation distressing. He tried to dismiss it from his mind, and concentrate on his own precarious position. But it remained, nagging at his mind, a constant worry. Would she be all right? How would she cope?

As the days trickled by in a curious mixture of intense boredom compounded with an ever-present undercurrent of excitement, he learnt that the war had not receded far. Only once had the Germans come near the house. Two of them, probably no more than taking a short cut, had paused to lean on the wall close by Don's cellar. He could hear their voices plainly, like those voices in the dark streets of Brighton. The next time he went outside after that, the big camp was being moved away. There were still Germans on the hillside, and military traffic on the road. He had noted the presence of a camouflaged position not too far away. And those tanks were still around.

Then the fighting seemed to be coming closer again. He knew by the sound of artillery that there was activity over among the hills. There had been a lull, but now the intensity was renewed. By night he could see the explosions. His spirits leapt in anticipation. It could only mean a British counter-attack. For the first time he could see signs of the action, over on the hill opposite, visible from the front bedroom window. There were running figures over there, rifle fire and a machine gun. He could make out the machine gun post. They were all grey-clad, so it was still Germans, but surely the British were just beyond the hilltop.

The following day the firing was renewed. The sound of it woke him up. He risked going out in the daylight, hid close under the hedge at the north end of the garden. He looked up towards the German camouflage tent, past where their camp had been. They were shooting on the hill to his left again. He strained his eyes to see the hoped-for khaki figures come over the top. He calculated that, counting the Sunday when he had slept all day, he had now been five whole days in his hiding place. Surely today was the day when it would all change . . .

Shellfire had opened up near by. He could see the bursts on the far hill, where he had fixed his hopes. He froze in horror. There were German soldiers, running up the road, a matter of yards from where he lay. He realized that they might well decide to use the house, the trees, the hedge which concealed him, as cover themselves. He was running a hideous and unnecessary risk. Far better to wait in the cellar. Skulking till the army gets here, he thought. He had already decided to stay where he was and watch. Apart from anything else, he rationalized, it was probably more dangerous to move.

A car went by, up the road. A motor cycle in the opposite direction. He continued to watch. Then suddenly there were artillery shells bursting in the field above, scooping out showers of earth and stones and grass. A straight line of bursts, followed a little after by the sound. Now he *must* get inside! Then, despite its netting and camouflage, he saw the German position hit. He watched fascinated, unable to move. He could see an armoured car on fire amid the torn netting. Another scout car, and a lorry. More shells were coming down, and the shapes of the Germans were running between the explosions. One of the petrol tanks went up in a burst of flame, and a great dark column of smoke marked where the Germans had been. It was almost like watching a film at the pictures. But it wasn't the pictures. The realization arrived that to stay here any longer had become plain stupid. He began to work his way back on all fours towards the house and some measure of safety. After everything, it wasn't going to be a British shell that killed him, he was damned sure of that.

He heard a car on the road again, and flattened himself on the ground by the gate. Then there was another explosion, this time only yards away, showering him with a fine rain of earth from the blast. A second followed, before he had time to recover from the shock. So close that at first he thought it had hit the house. The ground shook under him from the impact, and the shock waves of sound deafened him for a moment, so that he lay there gasping. Then he staggered to his feet.

There was a column of dust and smoke rising over the road, just beyond the hedge. He half noticed that the top of the hedge had been blown away too, leaving a ripped tangle of branches. He risked a glance round the gate. The back of a car was sticking out of a shell hole, jutting up into the air, wheels still idly revolving. Knowing he was a fool and worse than a fool, he opened the gate, checked the road was empty, and ran down towards the crashed vehicle. Somehow, with constant fearful glances around, he struggled to haul out the young German who had been driving, the only person in the car. He also salvaged the rifle that lay on the ground.

It took agonized minutes to drag the unconscious form inside the gate. Only then could he pause and rest, before making the last effort to get him into the house, and down the cellar stairs. At the end of it, he was damp with sweat, gasping as much from relief as from the frenzied effort. He risked putting the light on, and looked at the pale face and short blond hair above the Jerry uniform. The bloke was breathing alright. What a fool he'd have looked if he'd gone and rescued a corpse! Outside there came another explosion.

"Well I couldn't not go. And I couldn't leave him there," he muttered to himself, though a voluble voice at the back of his mind told him this was no way to win the war.

"What the hell shall I do with him now?" came the next thought.

In the end he sat him in the chair, tied his hands together behind him — there had been some useful cord in one of the cupboards — and also tied his feet. He bathed the man's head with a flannel and cold water. Smeared some vaseline on the brownish white lump there, the size of an egg. But that seemed to be the German's only injury. Then he waited, in the darkness once more, for the man to come round.

* * *

When Adolf did come to, his senses were hazy, and his first thought was that he was going to be sick. His head still reeled from the blow, though the last minutes before the crash were vividly clear in his memory. He knew he had gone into the shell crater. Now he would not be delivering the Major's message, that had meant so much to him as he was dying.

He opened his eyes, blinking several times, shaking his head softly to try to dispel the pain. He was in darkness. He stirred, trying to move. His hands seemed to be trapped, held tight behind him, caught up in something. He couldn't move them, or his legs, and his wrists hurt. He wriggled round, shaken and confused. Fought back the bile that rose with panic into his throat, as the conviction seized him that he was buried alive beneath the car in the shell hole. He thought he heard something, and held his breath. The light that shone in his face was so unexpected that he cried out.

"Be quiet!" came a voice at once.

For a moment he couldn't understand at all. Not words, just jumbled sound. Then he realized. The voice was speaking English. The light slowly resolved itself into the beam of a torch, shone onto his face. He could make out a dim figure behind it. His brain grappled for the right words. He had been a good student of English at school, but the pain in his head and the sickness did not help.

"Where am I?" he managed.

"You're my prisoner," the Englishman answered. "I've got a gun pointing at you."

So now he knew. He was a prisoner of war. The full import of it didn't register at once. He found himself thinking of Rudi and Hans, and how they would mock him. "That'll teach you to volunteer." He could hear Rudi's voice saying it now. He tried to move again, then understood that his wrists were tied behind him. His feet were tied too.

"Is it the night?" he asked haltingly.

"No. You're in a cellar," came the surprising answer. Adolf dredged from his memory the English word "cellar". It didn't make sense though.

"There's a light down here," his captor continued. "If I put it on, will you keep quiet? If you don't, I'll have to gag you."

He didn't understand "gag", but the rest was clear enough, though it made no sense. If he was a prisoner of war, why did he need to keep quiet? Why the fuss about putting on the light?

"I will be quiet," he answered.

The click of the switch filled the room with a pale yellow light, still bright enough to blind him at first. As he got

261

used to it, he looked at the man in front of him. A young man, the same age as himself, maybe even younger, with dark hair and a curl that fell onto his forehead. An anxious open face, quite handsome, but the nose a bit out of shape. He was wearing khaki, scruffy and caked with dirt. From the fighting, of course, Adolf assumed. But there was something wrong. He glanced round at the cellar — musty with old wood, a decayed table in the corner, glass bottles hung with spiders' webs on a shelf, an oil can. The only window seemed to be blocked off; there were stairs at the far end. Looking back at the Englishman, he noticed there was something familiar about the rifle he was holding. It was German. He screwed up his brow, guessing the answer. He took the chance.

"We are behind German lines, Tommy. — Is it not so?"

The Englishman's mouth fell open, off guard for a tiny moment before he recovered himself. He didn't say anything, but Adolf knew now that it was true.

"What makes you think that?" the enemy soldier had regained his composure.

"If really I was a prisoner of war, we would not be in the cellar, careful about the light, I think." He sorted out the complicated sentence carefully, hoping he would get his meaning over. "Also, you have only a German rifle. It is my rifle perhaps? Also you have tied me. That you do not do to a prisoner of war."

"Clever little bugger, aren't you?" said the Tommy in evident annoyance.

For no real reason Adolf smiled. He recognized the swearword. He had carefully taught himself the English swearwords, like any schoolboy learning a foreign language. For a moment the irritation remained on the young man's face. Then, suddenly, he too half-grinned.

"You're not that clever though — 'cause you're the one tied up."

Adolf worked out the gist of it, and shrugged his shoulders.

"Yes, I admit it that I am your prisoner, Tommy. What are you going to do with me?"

"I don't know yet for sure, Adolf," came the answer in a more confident tone. Adolf started in surprise.

"You have found out my name?"

The other looked puzzled.

"I called you Adolf after your flipping Führer," he answered.

"So my father did. My name is Adolf Mann. — And you are called Tommy, yes?"

"Don Gibbard," came the answer. He stretched out his hand, only to pull it back in sudden realization. They both grinned again.

"I am pleased to meet you, Don," said Adolf.

★ ★ ★

Don shook his head. It still seemed wrong, even after a few days. Here he was, sitting in some dusty cellar, a refugee or something like it in his own country, chatting away to one of the enemy. Adolf Mann didn't behave like the Huns in Churchill's speeches, the popular impression of the brutal German. Images left over from the Great War, now coloured and enlarged by the facts of Nazi cruelty that had seeped out of Germany. These were Don's images of the Germans. Naturally, for he had been offered no others. But there was no denying that Adolf was a different kettle of fish.

On the other hand, you never could be sure. Don remained a little wary of his prisoner. The first day he had refused to untie his hands to let him eat — which had meant feeding the man himself. They had both ended up laughing. Don's attempts to feed him first an apple, and then beans from a tin, had been less than successful. The following day, Don had relented and untied his hands to let him eat, tying them again after. Adolf made no attempt to escape or even to make a row. At first Don thought it was the threat to gag him. He had also made him give his word. Adolf had sworn "as a German soldier". Don was unaccountably impressed, remembering that *he* was not an English soldier, well not quite.

If it had been a British counter-attack, it had failed. The place was swarming with Jerries again. So Don retired to the cellar once more, only risking a recce once each night. For the rest of the time he found himself willy nilly talking to his German. Sometimes they argued. Don had not realized till now the pent-up bitterness in him at what had happened. Not so much to him personally, but to his family, his neighbours, his whole country. Adolf made no attempt to defend the invasion, or even explain it. He simply clammed up when Don railed at him. With dawning understanding and surprise Don began to realize that this young Nazi was embarrassed to be here in someone else's country. Maybe had no wish to be part of it at all. Or if he did, wanted only the glory and the excitement.

"We never wished to attack England, my friend," he said to Don. "We wanted England to be our friend against all the rest." It was a common view in Germany, extending to the Führer himself.

In fact Don's dawning understanding had come near to the truth. Faced with this curious, scruffy, hunted Englishman, who had saved his life and taken him captive, Adolf did find himself embarrassed about his country's invasion. The arguments that had been so compelling among the Hitler Youth, that had sounded so right and proper in the mouths of Hitler and Goebbels, were obviously no answer to this man, to anyone in England. And so, by tacit consent, they talked of girls and holidays and their families. Don told him about Gwen 'his latest'. Adolf produced a battered photo of his mother and father in a family group. Both were faced with the prospect that their parents were now mourning their deaths. They shared the worry, or exchanged jokes, all the burden of translation falling on Adolf, for Don had no German at all. They seemed to teach very little in English schools, Adolf thought. In fact, however, he was glad of the opportunity to practice his

English. Don tried in a self-conscious way to instruct him, and even picked up a word or two of German in the process.

More days trickled by, and though they remained enemies, one tied up for some of the time at least, the other always with a gun to hand, the residual hostility faded, and a curious friendship sprang up between them. They had much in common. Don gained the impression that Adolf had had more opportunities than he. Adolf began to see that Don had always had more — and more genuine — freedom. The last of their imposed emnity died when they put into words for each other the reasons it should continue. Don told Adolf about the attack on the station, remembered for him the faces of his friends, lying in their blood. Then Adolf told him about the British ship that had gunned down the helpless Germans in the water. About *his* friend too: Willi who had made it to the boat, only to die there of exposure and exhaustion, another dead face staring up.

The food was finally reduced to apples, though the stock of them was inexhaustible. Don had held Adolf prisoner for five days. Through that time the problem of what to do next had increased steadily — that and what to do with his half-friend, half-captive. At last he faced the choice.

"I'm going to have to make a run for it," he told Adolf. "Even though your lot are still swarming like flies. Trust me to hide right beside the main road to the front line! . . . Anyway, I can't stay here any longer, just hoping it'll be all right, and some chance'll turn up, because a chance hasn't."

"You are right, Don. There will not be a time when it is better. Perhaps you will do it, and reach your side."

"What would you do? If you were in my place, I mean."

"I would go." He smiled, sidelong. "But I am not sure what I would do with my prisoner."

"Oh shut up! You know I can't leave you here."

"Or kill me . . . Yes, it is a problem, is it not?"

Don looked at him cautiously, weighing up the possible answers to what he was going to say.

"I . . . I thought of untying you. — Or you letting me

have a start, a few hours or so. Then telling them after I was well away."

"I am glad you trust me so much," answered Adolf after a pause. "I am glad we are no more enemies. — But I would have to tell them as quickly as I can. You see, I am still a German soldier, although I am the friend of an Englishman." He looked at Don, his clear blue eyes troubled. "You would not act so, I think," he added.

"No, I suppose not. We don't make such a thing of being a soldier, and duty and all that — and I'm not really in the Army anyway."

"Oh but you are still a soldier," Adolf answered. "Also, I have an idea, I think. Take me up into the house. Leave me there, securely tied to the chair still, but do not lock me in. It will take quite a while to wriggle my way to the road. But I will come to it at last. Like a good German soldier, you see. Then I will speak to the first Germans I see. And I will tell them the story of you."

Don stood in thought.

"All right, then. We'll do it that way, Adolf. It ought to work. It'll give me a while anyway. . . . "

He got no further. There was a bang above their heads, the sound of feet and voices. Several men were there, speaking German. Don picked up the rifle and pointed it again at his prisoner. Too late to do anything, he realized that the light was on. Some of it, only a chink or two maybe, but some, would spill out round his blackout on the edges of the door. He heard the handle being tried, an exclamation, then a thud against the wood. The cellar door crashed open, and a big burly man stumbled through.

"Drop the gun, Don! For God's sake drop the gun!"

Without a thought, he obeyed Adolf's anguished shout. He heard his prisoner speaking in hasty German. The soldiers, a patrol of four, came down the steps. One of them picked up the rifle. Another caught hold of his arm — not as roughly as he had expected. The corporal nodded at him, apparently in some sort of approval, and said in broken English,

"Well done, Tommy."

"I told them you saved my life," said Adolf, in English. "It is the most important part for me — eh, Don?"

As the soldiers untied him, Adolf watched his former captor, now himself a prisoner, led away up the steps.

Chapter 19

FIGHTING BACK

Through the night of 5th October and the day of the 6th, the British army on the South Coast began to fall back from its bitterly contested and long-held positions overlooking Brighton. Transport congested the bridges, both the original and that restored after German air-raids, across the River Adur at Shoreham and Bramber. Above them was plenty of fighter cover. Spitfires were brought down to Tangmere in strength again. North of them, across the Downs, British bombers were vainly searching for German tanks to bomb in the obscure villages and market towns of Sussex. By and large they had to content themselves with smashing up road and railway junctions in order to disrupt the communications of the mysteriously absent Panzers. The only German tanks destroyed were two in Horsham, at the cost of much of that town's ancient centre. Another armoured patrol was sighted by a reconnaissance aircraft between Pulborough and Amberley. But the mass of armour, which had wiped out two brigades of British tanks and been so evident across half of Sussex had gone.

The units of British 1st Army Tank Brigade stationed in Tonbridge and Tunbridge Wells knew where the Germans had gone. From eleven o'clock in the morning they were engaged in a bitter running fight with heavy formations of enemy armour. The Germans were pushing eastwards along the railway from the general area of East

Grinstead. Brigadier Watkins reacted fast, moving elements
of his own armour farther back to encounter this threat
from an unexpected direction. Unexpected or not, his tanks
were in prepared positions, chosen for their advantage over
an attacker from any direction. Nevertheless, it rapidly
became apparent that he was heavily outnumbered. And he
was running the risk of envelopment, as the Panzers nudged
towards his flanks. He telephoned his operational commander, General Schreiber of 45 Division. Schreiber
immediately offered to transfer some of his artillery into
the southern end of Watkins' line. This would release more
tanks for the battle. Then he rang London.

"Mr Prime Minister, it is General Schreiber from Hastings. I would like you to speak to him in person," said
Brooke, after he had heard the news himself. Schreiber
repeated it to Churchill.

"I see, General. Will you hold the line a moment
please," he said, when he too had been told. Then he
turned to Brooke. "Another Panzer Division? It can't be."

"It may be," Brooke answered. "Unless it is the same
one, operating in two directions at once."

"No . . . not possible." Churchill shook his head, the
heavy jowls waggling, almost a comic figure at any other
time. "It must be a different one. Reconnaissance reports?"

"Some sightings of German tanks in the western end
of Sussex this morning. Failure to find concentration of
armour . . . Two tanks destroyed in Horsham bombing
raid."

"So they're still there. Or some of them at any rate."

"There is one other thing," Brooke added. "A stay-
behind unit on the coast has positively reported tanks landing at Newhaven."

"They must be bringing them in there," muttered
Churchill. "Get a raid mounted on the harbour facilities.
Right now . . . "

"Right now, sir, I need to tell General Schreiber what
to do," Brooke answered.

"Well — do so then." He handed Brooke back the
phone.

The Commander of Britain's Home Forces looked at him for a moment, as if expecting instructions. Then spoke down the phone.

"General — you are to continue to offer full support and reinforcement to 1st Army Tank Brigade. The line at Tunbridge Wells should be held. So long as that is consistent with the preservation of the majority of our armour. If it cannot be held without excessive loss, you are to instruct Brigadier Watkins to withdraw south onto your own forces. You yourself are to be prepared to withdraw from your position on the coast, and if necessary to break out across enemy-held territory to your north."

He listened for a moment to the reply, then replaced the receiver.

"Couldn't have done better myself," growled Churchill.

Relations between the two men had been strained since the "Day of Disaster" as Churchill called Friday 4th October. The debate which ended in Brooke and his fellow ranking generals getting their own way and withdrawing from the Brighton front had been long and acrimonious. Churchill had come close to calling the generals cowards. They — or Brooke at least — had in so many words called him a fool. The same stresses were there as between Hitler and his generals. Churchill, like his opposite number, had his intuitions. He did not want to pull back from Brighton and the Downs. He still believed it was wrong. But faced with the resignation of Brooke, Ismay and Dill, he had backed down.

"You realize you are now contemplating the evacuation of the coast in the centre of the line as well?" He couldn't resist the jibe at Brooke, for all that he recognized the good sense of the orders he had just given.

"I hope to avoid it. I intend to move Forty-Second Division, which has already come round as far as Dorking, farther south. To try to come across the rear of these Panzers. They are notorious for leaving supply lines trailing in the air. We may yet turn this to our advantage, Prime Minister."

"Have you thought of bringing the Aussies up in support behind them, Alan?" Dill asked. "We might also use them to probe towards this perimeter the enemy have established down from Horsham."

Brooke nodded his agreement.

"Yes, there are possibilities there certainly. Particularly as Naesmyth and his surviving tanks are still hovering just beyond Horsham."

"It might please the Prime Minister of Australia, if we were to place those tanks under direct Australian command," interposed Churchill.

"It would also make good tactical sense," Ismay added.

"Good! Then let us turn to the destruction of the enemy's harbour, at Newhaven," said Churchill. "Air Chief Marshall, this is a matter for you, I think."

"I can organize a series of intensive raids by day, if the fighter cover can be released, Prime Minister. If not, then it will have to be night attacks. And, I have to tell you this, the attrition rate of fighter aircraft is mounting alarmingly again. Squadron strength of Strategic Air Reserve has started to fall. Now they're flying from an English field, the Me109's are an entirely more serious threat."

"Well haven't you taken out this damned Dungeness airstrip yet?" demanded Churchill testily, flinging his cigar down as he turned away from the map table.

"It has been damaged once, but is now operational again," answered Dowding.

"Concentrate on it then!"

"Sir, I am running out of men and machines by the hour. In the attempt to achieve local air superiority on the Kent coast, we have exposed our *only* reserves to the most appalling wastage. It is not just fighter aircraft. It is bombers as well, and above all it is aircrew. I have already received orders today to divert substantial forces to west Sussex. Now further orders to launch heavy attacks on Newhaven. And all in addition to protecting our troop build-up in Kent. Sir, it cannot be done, not by me or you or anyone."

Churchill had gone pale at the vehemence of the verbal attack. For a moment his face showed a childish petulance, thwarted rage that all his captains were turning on him. They could see the effort as he bit back the angry response, and forced himself to control his temper.

"Is the eastern half of *Operation Mangle* still to go ahead, despite these German tanks near Tonbridge, Alan?" he asked, his voice quiet, but shaking a little.

"I believe that we should launch *Lemon Squeezer* tomorrow, on schedule. If it succeeds, it will solve our tank problem for us," Brooke answered.

"Air Marshall, I would be obliged if, in the light of what Brooke has just told us, you would continue to give the protection of the army in Kent the first priority among your many, onerous tasks. . . . I am sorry, gentlemen, I am tired. We are all tired. And I do not like losing."

"Well at least he admits he lost to us," Dill said to Brooke as the meeting broke up.

"He wasn't talking about losing to us," Brooke answered.

In the centre, the British line held. After the first, unwary attack, Rommel had held back his commanders. He had not expected to find British tanks this far north. He knew of two British armoured formations operating in Kent and Sussex. This might be the one which had reinforced the British in Hastings, and which he wrongly believed to be of divisional strength. Alternatively it might be the armoured division correctly identified at the eastern end of the line. Either way it was well-prepared, and its commander was responding with vigour and good sense. In the initial encounter Rommel had lost seventeen tanks. He suspected the British had lost a quarter of that number.

He edged his right flank southwards, probing the forested country. At first things looked promising. Contact was made with the forward units of German 34th Infantry Division, now firmly in possession of the Wealden hamlet of Crowborough. But the message that came back to the Panzer General was that the 34th had been pushed out of Wadhurst, farther to the east two days before. Pushed out by British tanks. In the maze of hills and woodland that marked the northern edge of the Weald, Rommel did not want to begin a complex and unprofitable battle against prepared British positions. There were hills north of Tunbridge Wells too, but cutting through them was the valley of the Medway. The valley led straight to the town of Tonbridge, the centre of a spider's web of British communications.

He launched the flanking movement in mid-afternoon. After a day which began so well, with the flying advance they had come to expect, this was proving less profitable. He found himself being irritable to his staff. The substantial force of nearly fifty tanks which engaged on the deployment to the north was halted long before Tonbridge. British armour and artillery ambushed them in the hills. It was apparent they were not being engaged by heavy British forces, and it was tempting to push on. On the other hand, the British might be tempting them deeper into a trap. Rommel decided to pull back, and wait. Brigadier Watkins' *eight* tanks in the hills had served the British very well, for the time being.

By evening the Panzers had received the reconnaissance reports they required, and the message had reached Goering that the Luftwaffe support already promised was now required. In the fading light, the Stukas came in first, hitting at the tanks and artillery exposed on the hilltops. Then they blitzed the centres of the two towns of Tonbridge and Tunbridge Wells to disrupt British communications. At the same time Rommel's tanks were beginning to move foward again. As before he had divided his two regiments. One struck northward, along the Medway Valley once more. This time they stormed the hills as well, paying little attention to the remnants of the half dozen tanks they encountered on the way. The other, led by the General himself, struck due east, determined to batter its way into Tunbridge Wells. As darkness fell, the Luftwaffe switched to heavy bombers, and a full-scale air raid on the town. The Stukas had already marked the targets with incendiaries.

In the engulfing darkness the fighting was as fierce as it was confused. The British now knew they were outnumbered — massively so. Five to one, locally ten to one. Losses began to mount, as the tank shells screeched eerily through the night to vanish into the woods concealing the British positions, or burst in sudden flashes of fire on the hillsides. The British started to fall back. The withdrawal was in good order. The tanks from Tonbridge retreated eastward. The larger force in Tunbridge Wells withdrew southwards onto the main body of British armour. 1st Army Tank Brigade remained intact. In fact its strength on the now shortened northern flank was being built up. In the blazing ruins of Tunbridge Wells, still pounded by the Luftwaffe, the advancing Germans found themselves harassed by continuous infantry attacks. By the morning of the 7th, Rommel was at last in possession of the town. And by then he knew that his presence was desperately required elsewhere.

On 7th October the British were retreating from Brighton in the west and fighting a delaying action against advancing German armour on the edge of the Weald. But on the eastern end of the line, *Operation Lemon Squeezer* had begun on schedule. The attack opened with a dawn naval bombardment of the German beach-heads along the East Roads from Dungeness to Hythe. Six destroyers and an elderly light cruiser had come down through the night from Harwich, slipping along the coast undetected. The bay was crowded with transports, also arriving at dawn. The leading formations of the German Second Wave.

On the beaches the fuel dumps, now well established and extensive, went up amidst the running men, amidst the transport desperately churning up the sand and shingle to escape. Blazing lorries in an obliterated convoy turned the sea wall above Dymchurch into a line of fire. Through the flames the shells of the naval guns crashed upon those troops who had already scrambled off the devastated beaches. Among the barges and steamers, the Royal Navy once again reminded the Germans that the sea was Britain's element. The fragile craft were blown apart before they could disgorge their troops, and the bodies floated on the sea amidst the wreckage that lay grounded in the shallows.

The fires made an excellent marker for the R.A.F.. As the Navy turned away eastwards, unmolested by any German ship or plane, two squadrons of Wellingtons came in low from the seaward. They had come down across Folkestone, then turned back in onto the coast. Over them were five fighter squadrons. For the necessary quarter of an hour Britain had total air superiority. One Hurricane squadron broke away to strafe the troops and supply columns behind the beaches. The Wellingtons comprehensively bombed the Germans in Hythe. Then bombed the beach-heads and transport concentrations, the dumps of stores and the landing barges. At the same time Spitfires coming in from the north took out the Germans' only airfield in England at Lydd, just as the Me109's were scrambling into the air. Few of them got off the ground safely. Those that did found they were climbing into the paths of the Spitfires which fell upon them like hawks, cannon blazing.

By the time the Luftwaffe arrived from across the Channel, the British bombers were already heading for home with their fighter escorts still close around them. A brief running dogfight developed, decided conclusively by the arrival of two additional Spitfire squadrons from Britain's exiguous reserve. Their fuel running low, the Germans went back to France. The Spitfires did not pursue them. Instead they remained to guard the advance of the British army beneath.

The naval bombardment along the beaches had already been joined by a creeping barrage from British heavy artillery, positioned along the length of the 'Corridor' from Ashford to the sea. The fire was of an intensity the German army had not encountered before — not in this war. The British had prepared well. They were attacking German dug-in positions on the ridge that runs to the north of the Royal Military Canal. The slopes were easy and did not present a serious problem to the British attack. For the Germans, possession of the heights proved more a drawback than an advantage. They found themselves dangerously exposed to British fire. Only at the end of the line facing Ashford did they have the benefit of cover from the extensive woods.

The barrage stopped abruptly after an hour and fifteen minutes. Then the first and often the last thing the cowering soldiers of the 17th Division saw was the British infantry advancing on them out of the smoke. Figures from the set-piece bloody battles of the previous war. On the coast the Germans were swept away from their last footholds on the edge of Hythe by the 1st Londons, their opponents since the invasion began. Their comrades holding the crater-pocked airstrip of Lympne melted away before the charge of the New Zealand Division. The dugouts in the woods south of Ashford were overrun by the Canadians. All along their line, the German 17th Infantry Division found itself falling back.

On its right wing the rout was most decisive. 1st London continued the push along the coast. The Germans contested stubbornly, but to no ultimate avail. The beaches won so dearly were re-taken by the British, amid all the carnage and destruction of aerial and naval bombardment. Surviving second wave units struggled ashore into the muzzles of British guns. They were forced to contest again a landing ground won on *S-Day*. Their losses just as catastrophic. The 17th's destruction as an effective resistance was ensured by the New Zealanders who swept them down the slopes and cliffs onto the edge of the canal. The New Zealanders followed up with an unstoppable attack, overrunning the waterway, and pushing on into the marshes. By early afternoon the Royal Military Canal was in British hands as far as Ham Street, that unimportant junction which had fallen by chance to German Paratroops back in the dawn of *S-Day*.

The most spirited German resistance came in the woods north of Ham Street. Here, the retreating Germans could call on support from 35th Division in the line next to them, and as yet unscathed. General Reinhard, Commander of 35th responded immediately with two infantry regiments.

The defenders, though still outnumbered, were not at the three or four to one disadvantage they were along the rest of the line of the British attack. They held on until 1st Armoured Division struck.

Like everyone else, Brooke referred to the armour as the spearhead of his attack. But in fact he had not launched it in the opening phases. It did not begin to move until noon. Then it advanced steadily westward sweeping the remnants of the Germans before its tanks. The tanks began to pivot, holding their left flank on the canal with the New Zealanders, pushing their right forward in a wheeling movement supported by the Canadians. The last resistance of German 17th Division crumbled, and the troops of 35th sent to assist, found themselves caught up in the general retreat before the steady progress of the tanks. The German's own armour consisted of some fifty submersible or 'floating' tanks, the remains of the force allocated to them for storming the beaches. Many more had been lost when their waterproofing had proved to be less than waterproof. Now they were far too few to resist an entire armoured division, deploying three hundred and forty tanks.

As the khaki-coloured tanks with their pennants flying rolled through the villages, everywhere the people appeared from their hunted, hermit existence. They came out into the open to cheer them, lining the country lanes, throwing the last flowers of late autumn, weeping and hysterical in their gladness. The tank crews and the infantry were caught up in it. How could they not be? Even back in London the spirit began to communicate itself to the generals. The gloom lifted a little from the meeting of the Committee of Home Defence. This overshadowed all other news. This lifted other dreadful fears. The tantalizing question of what the German armour would do in Sussex, the problems of the withdrawal from Brighton, the news of the fierce tank battles round Tunbridge Wells: none of this would matter if the Army of Kent flung the Germans back into the sea.

And that was beginning to look like a possible outcome. At nightfall the British halted to regroup in order to prevent the advance becoming ragged and the lines of communication jammed. 17 Division's Headquarters at Dymchurch had been captured. General Loch and his staff were British prisoners. First London and the New Zealanders were fighting their way through New Romney, to the edge of the damaged enemy airfield at Lydd, where the H.Q. of 35 Division lay. 35th's forward echelons had been forced out of Tenterden, and the whole division was retreating south onto Rye. At Rye the Germans were desperately trying to establish a defensive perimeter. Perhaps, as the British dared to let themselves hope, perhaps to prepare for evacuation. The whole of General Busch's Sixteenth Army hovered on the brink of defeat. The Paratroops were now hopelessly cut off, miles behind the new British lines, the other divisions were in headlong retreat. And behind them lay only the sea.

Hitler was told of the British counter-attack at ten o'clock in the morning. By noon, the full gravity of the situation was beginning to unfold. The Luftwaffe had now been committed in strength to providing air cover for the hard-pressed German army. But from somewhere, from nowhere according to Goering, the British had produced reserves. The skies over the battlefield belonged to neither contender, and the Messerschmitts and Spitfires fought it out as bitterly and doggedly as the embattled armies beneath them. Hitler spared Goering any sign of rage. He expressed his disappointment that the tide of battle could not be turned by the Luftwaffe. He urged Goering to greater efforts. The Reichsmarschall went to speak to Kesselring and Sperrle, the commanders of Luftflotten Two and Three, on the telephone.

"My Führer, I feel we must prepare for the worst," said Halder, when Goering had gone. Hitler's eyebrows raised.

"In what way do you mean, Herr General?"

Halder had already discussed what he intended to say with Brauchitsch and Jodl (though not with Keitel, Hitler's lackey).

"I feel we should prepare to disembark the survivors of

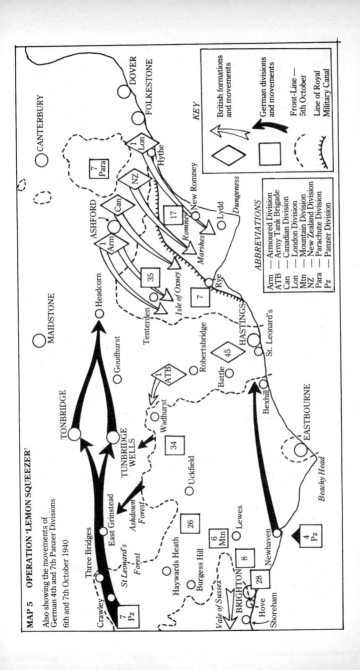

MAP 5   OPERATION 'LEMON SQUEEZER'

Also showing the movements of
German 4th and 7th Panzer Divisions
6th and 7th October 1940

KEY

British formations and movements
German divisions and movements
Front-Line —
5th October
Line of Royal
Military Canal

ABBREVIATIONS

Arm — Armoured Division
ATB — Army Tank Brigade
Can — Canadian Division
Lon — London Division
Mtn — Mountain Division
NZ — New Zealand Division
Para — Parachute Division
Pz — Panzer Division

the three divisions of Sixteenth Army from the coast of Britain."

"And the Parachute Division?" Hitler asked innocently, knowing already that they regarded it as lost, and an irrelevance to their plans. "No, do not bother to explain. . . . I understand your plan very well. I am sure it has its merits. I do not doubt you would succeed in saving a large part of the army by evacuation. Just as the British did. When they ran away."

Once again he had not raised his voice at all.

"Sir, it is not running away. The army might be landed again on different positions on the British coast. . . . where we have had more success . . . " Jodl stopped short in his explanation as Hitler stood up. He had a piece of paper in his hand.

"This, gentlemen, is a note of reports *I* have obtained this morning. *I* have spoken to the Commander of Army Group A, General von Rundstedt. I have also spoken to General Paulus, in Le Havre. Are you aware of the Army Group Commander's opinion?"

He paused, knowing they were not, well aware that his interference with operational matters was neither reported to them, nor within their control.

"General von Rundstedt has asked me to release troops from the control of Ninth Army, and transfer them to Sixteenth Army. I have given him authority to make the necessary transfers. I have instructed him to issue orders to General Busch that reinforcements are on the way. Sixteenth Army will retreat no farther. Its troops will stand and fight, and die if need be. But they will not fall back. They will not be driven into the sea, and they will not run away."

"Then they will be wiped out," snapped Halder, anger overcoming the habit of obedience. "There are no reinforcements."

"As I said, my second report was from General Paulus," said Hitler, silky voiced. He did not need to slap down Halder's moment of insubordination when he could destroy him with the facts. "He tells me that General Steuer has reported 4th Panzer Division now ready for action. There are your reserves. And the reason they are there is because *I* put them there. My decisions have given us two Panzer Divisions in England. Have enabled us to wipe out a division, perhaps, of British armour already. General Steuer is already moving east out of Newhaven. Our Panzers will punch through the British on the coast here at Hastings. And then on! On to rescue Sixteenth Army, that you want to run away. On to defeat the British armour. . . . Well, what is it?"

Keitel had just received a telephone call, now he stood with the receiver in his hand, his face agitated.

"General von Rundstedt wishes to speak to General Brauchitsch, mein Führer. The General is on the line now."

"Take it, Brauchitsch!" snapped Hitler.

The Commander-in-Chief of the Army listened for a while, then said,

"Please wait, Herr General. I am in the presence of the Führer now. He must be told." He turned to Hitler. "My Führer, Generalfeldmarschall von Rundstedt reports that Generaloberst Busch is unable to accept responsibility for ordering the troops of Sixteenth Army to stand firm. Generaloberst Busch feels there is no alternative but to withdraw to the sea and evacuate."

The Generals glanced at each other in triumph. Hitler's pale face may have blanched. They expected him to rage and rant, but this time they thought he might see reason.

"Who is General Busch's Chief of Staff?" he asked suddenly.

Brauchitsch fumbled with papers. He had forgotten for a moment.

"Generalleutnant Model," he replied, looking up again.

Hitler reached out his hand for the phone.

"Von Rundstedt, I address you as the Supreme Commander of the Armed Forces of the Reich. You will accept General Busch's immediate resignation. Generalleutnant Model will replace him with immediate effect as commander of Sixteenth Army. My orders remain unchanged. The army will stand fast. Panzer reinforcements are on their way. I rely on you, Herr General, to carry out my orders in all matters."

He listened to von Rundstedt's expressions of loyalty, then put the phone down.

"You may go!" He dismissed all the commanders of Germany's great war machine with a wave of his hand. Outside the door of the Conference Room at Giessen, Halder turned to Brauchitsch.

"I calculate that 4th Panzer has a day or so to travel fifty miles, through the middle of a British infantry division in prepared positions supported by armour in at least brigade strength. Then it has to stop an advancing enemy army in its tracks. An enemy army of four divisions, one of them armoured."

"It cannot make it, if that is the real picture," Brauchitsch answered. "It can only arrive in time to be destroyed itself, after the rest of Sixteenth Army has already gone. You are telling me the war against England is lost, Herr General."

"It may be. But I still have one or two hopes to pin on a man that our Führer seems to have omitted from his calculations."

"Who is that?"

"General Rommel, of course."

Chapter 20

PANZER

"So the balance has swayed back our way, then," said Churchill. He stubbed out the remains of his cigar, and immediately began to prepare another. It was the evening of the 7th October, a day of triumph for British arms.

"How soon before we have the swine ready for the slaughter?"

They were used to Churchill's sudden outbursts of bloodiness, product of his fierce hatred for the Nazis, a hatred which now extended to everything German.

"It is not impossible that tomorrow may be the day of decision," Brooke answered calmly. "I would say the balance is level at the moment, Prime Minister. If our advance continues, the Germans will soon have nowhere left to retreat to."

"Is there anything else *we* need to do?" demanded Churchill.

"I do not believe there is anything we can do to influence the outcome of this battle now. It is in the hands of our soldiers."

"And by all means let us trust them. They will see us through." Churchill puffed away contentedly for a while. "So let us look at the wider picture. There is a second German army to defeat. What news from that front?"

"In the centre we now have positive identification of the enemy armoured unit engaging our tank brigade," said

Brooke. He had already broken the news to Churchill earlier, before the Committee of Home Defence began its formal session. He had also agreed in advance with Churchill what action should be taken. Now he restated the position for the benefit of the others.

"The Germans entered Tunbridge Wells and Tonbridge this morning. There are two enemy tank regiments, and together they make up the 7th Panzer Division. The commander is General Erwin Rommel. Not a lot of information on him. But it is definitely the same division which was active in west Sussex earlier." He paused. They all knew that its 'activity' had wiped out two British tank brigades, and caused a full scale strategic withdrawal along the coast from Brighton. "It is now apparent that the bulk of this enemy armoured division has in fact turned east. So there is no possibility of enemy tanks breaking through to the sea in Sussex. We believe that there may be only a thin screen of German armour there."

"Pray tell us what action you propose," said Churchill, accepting the tactical defeat with equanimity, since a far greater victory seemed about to be won.

"In fact our withdrawal has been slow. General Montgomery commands the sector. He has evidently taken his own view of the situation, and directed that the line of the Adur rather than the Arun be held, together with the Downs above Worthing. Accordingly that is what he has done, and for once we can be thankful for a degree of insubordination, gentlemen. He also reports that enemy advances into evacuated territory have been tentative and sluggish."

"No wonder, if they haven't got an armoured division over the hills to help them out," put in 'Pug' Ismay. "But what is their armour doing, Alan?"

"Can I come to that in a moment . . . On the western sector still, I now have 42nd Division getting into position for a counter attack into Horsham and Crawley. I hope to commit the Australians too. I have good hopes of squeezing out this entire enemy salient. Now, the question of 7th Panzer. Our tanks hung on to Tonbridge and Tunbridge

Wells till this morning, then withdrew in good order southwards onto a line here." He pointed to the map by which
he stood. Churchill came over to look.

"Brigadier Watkins is still in contact with the enemy.
There has been intermittent fighting all day, but they are
not pushing him hard. The Germans have of course made
contact with their infantry. Watkins believes that the body
of enemy armour will now be committed on this central
front against our Hastings salient. He is anticipating an
enemy attack from the north tomorrow. He and Major
General Schreiber of our 45th Division are hopeful that
they can hold the line till we can provide armoured
reinforcement."

"Which means," said Churchill, "till our tanks have
smashed through the centre of the one German army, and
are ready to deal with the other. Panzers or not! Brooke
and I are happy enough as things stand. Comments, gentlemen?" He looked around belligerently.

"It looks sound enough," said Dill thoughtfully. "I'd
like to be a bit more sure about what that Panzer commander was up to, though."

*   *   *

In the course of the same morning "that Panzer Commander" had been engaged on probing towards the positions of the retreating British. He had established they had
not gone far. In the two captured towns of Tunbridge Wells
and Tonbridge he was beginning to get his own position
sorted out. As usual the tanks were a long way ahead of
their supporting infantry, but their degree of exposure was
greatly lessened by contact now established with 34th Infantry division. He had even met General Behlendorff, as the
two commanders inspected their front lines in the course
of the day. Rommel had outrun his own direct communications with the High Command. It was Behlendorff who
told him of the unfolding disaster to Sixteenth Army. The
infantry general urged him to bring 7th Panzer down onto
34th Division's front, and launch a frontal attack on British
45th Division and 1st Army Tank Brigade. The aim would

be to break right through the British Hastings salient and come to the relief of the retreating Sixteenth Army before the British swept it into the sea.

Rommel expressed polite interest, then returned to his latest temporary headquarters in Tunbridge Wells. Behlendorff's news *was* interesting, and even allowing for possible exaggerations, action was obviously called for. He had received no direct orders either from Paulus, who apparently was the Führer's personal agent in all matters of tanks, or from his own Corps Commander, Hoth. Given the complicated route such orders must come, that was hardly surprising. But it left him his own master. He studied his maps, and rejected Behlendorff's sensible and undoubtedly practical solution in favour of something more daring. If Sixteenth Army really was on the brink of disaster, there was insufficient time to fight his way through a British tank brigade which had already proved its mettle against the Panzers.

Orders now began to issue from the temporary headquarters. A thin screen of tanks was established southwards, probing at the British armour's new positions, then withdrawing. Rommel rapidly obtained a clear picture of the line through the village of Goudhurst. He left enough tanks facing it to convince the British they were still engaging a Panzer Division. He spared a few tanks for another screen, northward of his two captured towns. He did not have many to spare though. There had been the inevitable losses and breakdowns. There had also been the tanks left behind in west Sussex to preserve the deception. If his recent captures were to fall to a British counter-attack it was too bad. He was not concerned with possession of territory, only with enemy armies. And that was what he was now going to look for. With his armour in position for their next move, he despatched messages to Generals Behlendorff and von Förster to bring up their infantry to cover his rear. Then 7th Panzer set off, due east.

He estimated he had nearly twenty miles to cover. He did not know the nature of the enemy forces — if any — that lay in the country he intended to traverse. He did not know the state of the battle to which he now intended to commit his Panzers. In effect he was merely marching to the sound of the guns. The orders which arrived from Hoth and Paulus, many hours after he had gone, were to endeavour to break through British positions and relieve Sixteenth Army. In the event, Rommel was going round the back of those British positions.

His tanks rolled steadily through the darkening night. It was not a reckless, rushed advance. The strategy was bold but the tactics cautious. The main bodies of the Panzer regiments were advancing, once again, down each side of a railway. This had once been the vital lateral line of communications for the British. Now its centre section was in German hands. Flanking the route of the advance, Rommel had put out patrols, both tanks and infantry. Some three miles ahead was an advance guard of tanks. When serious resistance was encountered, the advance slowed. The strength of the enemy was carefully probed before men and tanks were committed against them.

Resistance was not great. There were residual units of British regular forces in the area. Mostly the Royal West Kent Regiment. There were engagements with local Home Guard units. But there were no British tanks. The only serious delay came at the village of Headcorn. There the German advance guard encountered the British Number Four Armoured Train, apparently holding the crossings of the River Beult. In a brisk engagement the guns of the train succeeded in destroying two tanks before it was put out of action.

It was at Headcorn that Rommel turned his tanks south. As usual he had a railway to mark his route, the eccentric trailing branch of the Kent and East Sussex Railway, too obscure even to have become part of the Southern Railway. The path of the railway would take him across the stretched-out fingers of the Wealden ridges, and into Tenterden. The tanks were closed up into four flying columns. Rommel now knew his judgement had been proved correct. He had got round behind the British. He expected to find them in strength at Tenterden, though. He intended to launch his attack before dawn.

He could not have come upon a better line of attack if he had drawn up the British deployment himself. The exposed flank of the entire British line was strung out in front of him. Its communications stretched back all the way to Ashford. Its front was facing the battered and crumbling German 35th Division, against which Britain brought to bear the full weight of the Canadian Division and 1st Armoured Division. The British faced south. Rommel struck them from the north.

The lines of communication went down in the opening minutes of the battle, as the Canadians' forward H.Q. at Tenterden was overrun. 1st Armoured's forward H.Q. was at Woodchurch, a fact soon known to Rommel, since the current positions of British forces were now available to him in the documents captured at Tenterden. He sent a squadron to ensure its speedy capture too. The main body of his tanks fell upon the rear of 1st Armoured amidst the marshy wasteland of the Upper Rother Levels, as they prepared for the morrow's assault on the fleeing German infantry. Those Germans on the Isle of Oxney now became the anvil against which the British were hammered by the assault of Rommel's Panzers.

As dawn broke, General Norrie, the Commander of 1st Armoured Division, was able to survey the flat marshland of the battlefield from his command post on a hump of ground called Chapel Bank. North of him was McCreery's Second Armoured Brigade, strung out across the marshes of Shirley Moor. Many of its tanks were stationary. The Brigade was cut in two by the lines of fast-moving grey tanks of the Germans. Smoke was blowing across the battlefield from burning vehicles, most of them British, the khaki now blackened. He counted forty for certain, compared with five or six of the enemy. To the west along the line of the unpleasantly named Reading Sewer he did not have such a clear line of vision. From the sound of the tanks' cannon the fighting was heavier there, if anything, as the

Germans engaged Brigadier Rimmington's 3rd Armoured Brigade.

In fact 3rd Armoured Brigade had not been so badly affected by the surprise attack, and had in some measure been able to turn on its own axis. Rommel's tanks came up against fierce resistance, and for the first time his losses began to mount alarmingly. For 2nd Armoured Brigade, however, the day was already lost. Many of its tanks were now bogged down in the marsh, where they had been forced back before dawn. The Germans had punched through the middle of the British armour, and even as General Norrie watched he saw the Germans come up onto the road beneath his vantage point. He could see surviving British tanks begin to pull out of the battle, down the road towards Appledore on the Royal Military Canal. Sending a messenger to try to rally them and prevent a general retreat, he now committed his own headquarters tanks to the battle taking place before him. He was killed when his tank took a direct hit, outside the ruined inn where the road crosses Reading Sewer.

Brigadier McCreery was captured in the buildings of Shirley Farm, where the last couple of dozen tanks under his command put up a final defence, gallantly supported by the infantry of the Canadian Division. The Canadians had become interspersed with 1st Armoured in the course of the preceding day's advance. Now they were caught up with them in the disaster. Their divisional commander and his staff had already been killed at Tenterden. Their division dissolved into its individual regiments, then local formations, each fighting desperately, but with no overall direction. Since there was no-one to tell them to fall back from the carnage, they fought on where they stood. The wrecks of Britain's tanks blazed around them, in the destruction of half of the armoured division.

The other half, and the rest of 1st Canadian Division, fought on through a dreadful morning. Brigadier Rimmington finally extricated his troops from the increasingly unequal battle only in the late afternoon. They struggled away westward toward Hawkhurst and the comparative safety of the woods and hills of the Weald. Rimmington saved about a quarter of his tanks, due in no small measure to the Canadians. Once again they formed the rearguard, sacrificing their lives against the relentless advance of the Panzers. In the end they were swamped by the counter-attacking German infantry of 35th Division, who came down from their high ground on the Isle of Oxney. 1st Canadian Division and 1st Armoured Division had vanished from Britain's line of battle. The first real tank engagement of modern times had been a crushing victory for General Erwin Rommel's Panzers.

As the British survivors contrived to disengage themselves, and Rommel began to collect together his own tanks, sprawled across the battlefield, General Steuer's 4th Panzer Division rolled across the little brook and gentle valley that separate St. Leonard's from Bexhill. The Panzers began to storm the positions of British 45th Infantry Division that had held onto St. Leonard's and Hastings since the invasion began. The British had a dozen tanks to help in their defence. The first wave of the German assault was a hundred tanks. The British fought well. Their artillery and anti-tank weapons took a higher toll than the Germans had expected. But the line buckled, then gave. The Panzers swept on, across the prepared positions on the railway track, through the dug-outs on the hillsides above, along the beach road and into the centre of St. Leonard's. Through Warrior Square, past the railway station. Up along London Road they came, and along Grand Parade overlooking the beaches where 1st Mountain Division had landed and then withdrawn; on to Hastings pier. In the centre of Hastings itself the advance slowed again. Violent house-to-house fighting developed. The Luftwaffe came over to ensure that the tanks did indeed carry out the Führer's orders and break through to the rescue of Sixteenth Army — an army that another Panzer Division had already rescued.

* * *

Through the day news of the unfolding disaster trickled

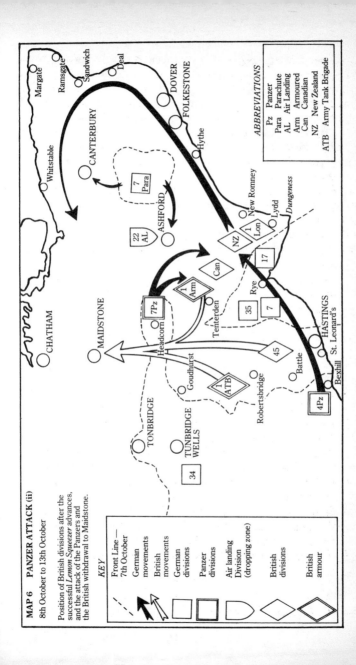

MAP 6 PANZER ATTACK (ii)

8th October to 13th October

Position of British divisions after the
successful *Lemon Squeezer* advances,
and the attack of the Panzers and
the British withdrawal to Maidstone.

ABBREVIATIONS

Pz	Panzer
Para	Parachute
AL	Air Landing
Arm	Armoured
Can	Canadian
NZ	New Zealand
ATB	Army Tank Brigade

KEY

Front Line —
7th October	
	German
movements
	British
movements
	German
divisions
	Panzer
divisions
	Air landing
Division
(dropping zone)
	British
divisions
	British
armour

into London. The pre-dawn attack on 1st Armoured by the Panzers. The destruction of the entire division, and the prized Canadian Division with it. Then the assault on Hastings by yet another enemy armoured division. Churchill remembered his earlier guess that there must be two enemy armoured divisions, and used it now to berate his generals. Brooke was not there to listen. He had gone down to Ashford early in the morning — to watch over the continuing attack. He found himself a helpless spectator of the ruin. He had no reserves available to commit, nothing with which he could change the course of the battle. In the evening he told the New Zealanders and 1st London Division to begin falling back. They had taken the German airfield at Lydd and pushed forward across Walland Marsh. When the order reached them they were three miles from the centre of Rye.

From London, Churchill issued the orders to 45 Division personally, telling Ismay to inform Brooke if and when opportunity presented itself. He instructed General Schreiber to pull his division back from the coast. Hastings was to be abandoned. Schreiber's task was to coalesce with 1st Army Tank Brigade, and then with all the available armour to break out through the German cordon to the northward, taking a new defensive pose around Maidstone. Schreiber could hardly believe it. He was prepared to make a fight of it for Hastings for a long time yet. And Maidstone was thirty miles away, almost on the *north* coast of Kent. The divisional commander sent a radio message to London:-

"Have received orders to withdraw north using tank support to break through encircling cordon. My troops still undefeated in Hastings. Reinforcement of Hastings position by our armour possible. Submit that enemy advance be resisted with all vigour here on the coast."

Churchill chose to regard it as rank insubordination. He ordered sent back:-

"Your submission cannot be accepted. You are unaware of grave situation elsewhere on front. Carry out my orders without further question. Churchill."

He also told Ismay to arrange for a staff officer to fly

down to make sure there *was* no local initiative to stay put. But Schreiber was already carrying out Churchill's peremptory demands. He disengaged skilfully, continuing the running fight from house to house, with two battalions of the Devonshire Regiment fighting a useful rearguard action up through the suburb of Silver Hill, north of St. Leonard's, and Blacklands on the edge of Hastings. By dawn on the 9th October, the entire Division was withdrawing in good order and relatively unscathed northward. Brigadier Watkins' tanks had already punched a hole through Rommel's thin cordon. General Schreiber was not there to supervise the successful implementation of his hasty plans. The car carrying him was hit by bombs from a Stuka as he drove up St Helen's Road out of Hastings. The General was killed immediately.

The rescue of 45th Division and 1st Army Tank Brigade out of the ruins was the only hope amidst the awful wreckage of British plans. The infantry and tanks slid away through Hawkhurst and Goudhurst; back across the East-West railway where Rommel had brought his Panzers by night round onto the British rear; and finally to the outskirts of Maidstone, far to the north. Back on the south coast, the destruction of Britain's 'Army of Kent' was being completed.

The New Zealanders began their withdrawal from the edge of Rye in good order, holding off enemy attempts at spoiling pursuit. More difficult was to hold the line of the Royal Military Canal on their flank against Rommel's first probing attacks. Screened by the New Zealanders, 1st London also began the dismal trudge back along the ground so recently won in such a glorious campaign. By noon they were back in New Romney, steadily retreating towards their start-point at Hythe, destroying stores and transport and communications as they went. The New Zealanders were still astride the Canal, but Rommel had forced the crossing at Appledore, and was now also advancing against them on both banks. The New Zealand Division was falling back on Ashford. So it thought.

For over Ashford, in the afternoon of 9th October, a

swirling snowstorm of opening parachutes began to descend. All around the town in the open fields, across the flat stretches of stubble where the corn had been harvested, fat ungainly gliders thumped and ground their way to an unsteady halt. Without even bothering to inform O.K.H., under whose command it was, Hitler had transferred 22nd Air Landing Division to the command of the new chief of Sixteenth Army, General Model. The Führer instructed him that the airborne troops were to be committed immediately. Model ordered them to attack Ashford, recognized by him and his predecessor Busch as the pivot of all British communications in the area. At the same time he ordered General Putzier, whose 7th Parachute Division had been hemmed in by earlier British counter-attacks, to break out in force southwards, and co-operate with 22nd Air Landing in the capture of Ashford.

The town, which had been safe enough for a visit by the Commander-in-Chief of British Home Forces the day before, fell to the Germans with relatively little fighting. The Germans had again achieved surprise. Though the casualties incurred by 22nd Air Landing, parachuting or landing in gliders in enemy territory, were high, the cost was well worth while. The New Zealanders now had nowhere to retreat to. Through the 9th and 10th of October the forests and copses between the Royal Military Canal and Ashford saw the end of New Zealand's gallant division, broken into fragments by the German armour. They fought on to the last in unrecorded engagements:- Longrope Wood and Faggs Wood; Priory Wood and Dicker's Wood. Little battles that would never figure on any battle honour. First the Canadians, then the New Zealanders. The Dominions were paying dear for the defence of England.

1st London Division went down before 4th Panzer, pushing on through Rye to engage the British infantry in the wastes of Romney Marsh on 10th October. 1st London had been heavily engaged since the first day of the invasion. It had fought the Germans to a standstill and saved Folkestone and Dover. It had led the advance back across the territory won by the German Sixteenth Army. It had come to the very brink of sweeping that army away. Its destruction by the Panzers was speedy and total. The body of General Liardet, the commander, was never found. He had died somewhere among his troops in the ruins of Hythe, which his men had defended so long.

On 11th October, 4th Panzer Division entered Folkestone. Then pushed speedily up the coast, sweeping away the remains of four British divisions before it captured Dover. The port installations were badly damaged, as much by the Luftwaffe as by the few demolition charges set in the ruin and chaos of Britain's greatest defeat in all her history. The Germans now had the port they had needed all along. The Panzers rolled on. Round the coast, through Deal and Sandwich to Thanet. Up the Canterbury road and into the Cathedral city. They were just beaten in its capture by units of 7th Para, the battle-stained young paratroops waving their flags from the towers at the west end of the cathedral as the tanks rumbled by beneath.

In Ashford, Rommel read his telegram from the Führer. It was promotion from Generalmajor straight to Generaloberst, missing out the intermediate ranks. But far more than that. The Führer intended to constitute a new *Panzerarmee England* for the conquest of London. Rommel was to have the command. From Division to Army in one jump. He sat down to compose a letter to tell his wife. He did not include Hitler's ultimate tribute:-

"In these few days, you, General Rommel, have become the saviour of the German army."

That, and the destroyer of the British army.

Chapter 21

PRISONER OF WAR

"After the explosion, I realized the car was going into the crater. There was nothing I could do about it. — I am not sure if it was the explosion, or the impact of the crash that knocked me out. But after that, I remembered nothing, Herr Leutnant." Adolf paused in his report. The lieutenant looked bored, and nodded.

"Yes, yes, carry on."

"When I came to, I was in the cellar of the house tied up. The English soldier had pulled me out of the car and taken me prisoner. He saved my life I am sure."

"Yes, Private. Since the petrol tank of your car evidently exploded after you were carried away to safety. No doubt you would still have been there when the explosion occurred." The other soldier in the room, apparently for the purpose of taking notes, sniggered at the lieutenant's sarcasm.

"Proceed then!"

Adolf gave an account of his days as Don's prisoner, trying to tell this pencil-twiddling fool of an officer and his supercilious clerk that he had been well treated. Twice he was told not to be irrelevant. If this was the intelligence service, then God help the Germany army, he thought.

"Then finally the patrol that was looking for me came to the house."

The lieutenant gave a short harsh laugh.

"You flatter yourself greatly, soldier. We do not send patrols looking for missing privates. When the burnt-out wreck of your car was found, you were listed as dead."

"But there was no body . . . " Adolf stammered.

"There was very little car." The lieutenant laughed at his own joke, and the toady joined in.

"Well then, you have wasted enough of my time. I am satisfied that there is nothing against you." (At the start he had had the cheek to suggest that Adolf had been running away when it happened). "There are too few intelligence officers available to squander on this sort of thing, I may tell you. I am satisfied that your Englander friend is not a saboteur. If he was, he would have killed you. In fact he seems to be precisely what he claims — a rather dim-witted member of their militia."

"Saboteur? What do you mean?" In his surprise Adolf dared to question the officer for a change. The lieutenant fixed his eyes on him.

"Oh yes. That is the whole purpose of this waste of time. The British have left such units and individuals behind our lines as agents provocateurs. Their function is to disrupt communications, ambush transport, destroy supplies — and kill stray and unwary German soldiers. They wear no uniform. They are shot as spies when captured — if captured. We would dearly like to ask a few of them some questions first though, young man. It is a pity your friendly Englishman is not one after all." He stood up, obviously deciding he had wasted enough time on Adolf.

"Probably thinks I'm dim-witted too," Adolf thought. Then he asked, standing too, and coming to attention,

"Sir, what happens to me now?"

"That is hardly my problem. See the orderly sergeant."

Adolf returned the Nazi salute as snappily as it was given. Then he went to see the orderly sergeant, glad to be out of the company of that particular officer.

"Intelligence — Abwehr, I suppose," the sergeant told him. He was a large Bavarian who had somehow fitted himself behind a desk designed for ordinary mortals, and seemed about to propel it across the room with his belly.

"But if you ask me he's not army at all, not any sort of army." His voice sank to a conspiratorial whisper. "If you ask me, he's Gestapo. — No business dressed up in uniform, if you ask me."

Being a Bavarian himself, Adolf had found favour with this sergeant, a new arrival since he had last been in the Grand Hotel, Brighton. But then, that had been nearly a week ago. It was no longer Divisional H.Q. of 28th. The division had moved down the coast, so the sergeant told him. Now it was much grander, VIII Army Corps, and its General, Walter Heitz. And in due course he would be joined by the High Command of the Army itself, Generaloberst Strauss, and his staff. Or so the sergeant confidently affirmed. There was apparently a whole suite of rooms, a whole floor of the hotel, being prepared for the general's arrival.

"Here, you can have coffee." The sergeant took two mugs from the private who brought it round. "Real coffee too, captured I wouldn't wonder — You realize it's NCO's privilege this. I spoil you my lad."

"I have mentioned in my letter home that there is a sergeant here who has looked after me. My mother in Munich will be relieved . . . "

He had every intention of continuing to butter up the sergeant. Apart from anything else he was a decent enough bloke, and in a position to hand out favours.

"Ah, not any more, Private Mann," said Sergeant Hausser, as if responding to Adolf's train of thought. "I have got your papers here somewhere. They've found you a nice little number though. No great exertions involved." He ruffled through a sheaf of papers before finding what he was looking for, then read out the one of a hundred similar orders, postings, directives with which his desk was littered.

"Guarding prisoners!" exclaimed Adolf when he heard what the 'nice little number' was. "But I'm a soldier, Sergeant." He looked in dismay at the large man behind the desk.

"None of that, my lad," responded Hausser, obviously

feeling that Adolf was not showing the proper respect for a superior officer. "You'll be a soldier in the guardhouse if you answer me back." Then he relented a little. "You youngsters just don't understand about obeying orders. Your orders, written down here in black and white, just like I've read out to you, say you're to report to the new prison camp for captured British soldiers — other ranks that is — at this place called Lev — ess." He failed utterly to pronounce the Sussex town of Lewes. Adolf realized there was no point in arguing, or falling out with his erstwhile benefactor.

"Yes, Sergeant Hausser. Sorry, Sergeant," he said with suitable signs of contrition.

"Oh, travel in style these days, Mann. Military convoy this afternoon."

"Do you know why I got picked for this job, Sarge?" He decided that didn't constitute insubordination in the ranks. It obviously didn't. The large face had gaped into a great Bavarian grin.

"To give you your own back, Private. After you've been a prisoner of some mad Tommy holed up in a dirty cellar. Now you can lord it over them. Of course there's also the question of you not being attached to any unit in particular. 100 Grenadierregiment, then 7th Regiment with a different division. — To be honest lad, it's the ones we don't know what to do with who get this sort of job." He laughed uproariously as if it was a huge joke, and Adolf dutifully joined in.

It was a pity he would not get a chance to see Rudi and Hans again for a while. They were still getting the random guard duty jobs that came up; this time somewhere down the coast — guarding the generals, apparently. That was a better job than the one he was getting. He had persuaded Hausser to send a message down to them though, immediately after his rescue. Rescue! — He wondered how Don was getting on. He had no wish to lord it over a whole bunch of captured Tommies. That was one thing he knew for certain. Still, as the sergeant had said, it was orders, and there was not much he could do about it.

"What's the latest news, Sarge?" he asked.

"Come on, come on! Shouldn't you be getting your kit sorted?" The annoyance was entirely feigned. Hausser was an incorrigible gossip, and any soldier prepared to act as a respectful audience full of praise for the sergeant's knowledge could obtain a reasonably up-to-date report on the progress of the war in England.

"Is the enemy big push still going on?" Adolf ventured.

"Ah, well there's a thing." The sergeant tapped his bulbous nose. "General Rommel again. Put paid to that, once and for all."

"That's the bloke who smashed through the British tanks near here."

It was now 11th October. Adolf had learnt that snippet of news, the destruction of two brigades of British armour, from the same source the day before. But the sergeant had said that there was also worrying news of a big enemy attack over on Sixteenth Army's part of the line. Talk of big British advances, possible evacuation, all that sort of thing.

"General, not 'bloke'. Let's have some respect. Yes, strikes me he's the man who's winning the war for us."

Though the sergeant could hardly know it, that was much the same way it had struck his Führer.

Adolf stayed and chatted for a while, then went and got his gear together. The convoy was assembled in Grand Parade. Adolf reported himself. It was a fine day, though starting to get colder now as autumn wore on. He found travelling the few miles to Lewes and a little beyond in the back of a horse-drawn cart a thoroughly enjoyable experience. His companions were for the most part from 8th Infantry Division, landed at Brighton and now going up line to join their regiments. They were all third echelon troops, either from 84th Infantry or 8th Artillery Regiments. Adolf found himself the veteran. Even the corporal in his wagon was almost deferential.

He dispensed the news he had gleaned from his fat Bavarian sergeant friend:- the big Panzer victories, the brilliant General Rommel, a British offensive halted. He also found himself telling of the destruction of his own regiment, his whole division, on the crossing. Then of the British sniper that he had shot, by luck more than anything else. Of the attack on the command post up in the Downs, the death of the major beside him. Finally his capture and strange captivity in a cellar under a ruined house.

They were new troops, just landed after an uneventful crossing. A crossing made at least partly by daylight under the ever-present eyes of the Luftwaffe. They hadn't seen a British ship. They had experienced nothing of the war yet. Their hopes were high, their humour good to hear and to join in. They were eager to listen to his stories. To them that was the real war. Adolf felt a fraud, as he told them. His experiences were not the real war, not as he had begun to perceive it. Not the war of unceasing gunfire, of living every moment in deadly peril, seeing your friends and comrades gunned down, waiting for yours to come.

He had spoken to enough men to know that exactly those things were happening to ordinary Germans like him and these chatting, unblooded soldiers. Happening all along the front line they discussed so blithely. He had just been on the edge of it, learning enough to be able to imagine what it was like, seeing enough for himself, just those couple of times — on the hillside amidst the bursting shells, and alone in the sea. Enough to be able to tell them of a grimmer reality. Yet they would be in it in a day or two, some of them dead by then. And he would be guarding prisoners, safe and sound, a long way away from the sound of gunfire. Adolf still found himself envying them in his heart of hearts, knowing that really they should be envying him. They passed through the shattered ruins of Lewes, and the time came for him to leave. He was sorry to see them go.

"Those yarns you told us! Don't know where you get them from, son," said the corporal as he tossed him his kit down. "Went down well with the lads though."

Feeling distinctly dispirited, he trudged up the dirt track where he had been directed. His first sight of the camp was from a low rise overlooking it. A stockade was

the main feature. Tall posts and wire, with huts inside it.
Flimsy looking affairs. They were still being built out of
ramshackle wooden sections that looked as if they had been
dismantled from some other camp somewhere else. There
were not many prisoners apparently, and it was they who
were assembling the huts, and doing the building work.
There were some corrugated iron huts too, and a great heap
of rusty sheets. Other heaps of materials lay about, and
there were cement mixers working, again operated by prisoners. German guards stood over them with guns. There
were other guards all round the perimeter. More guards
than prisoners, he thought. And the enclosed area seemed
to be enormous.

Adolf went down and reported himself at the little clus-
ter of huts outside the wire — the command post, guard
house, and the Germans' living quarters. They didn't look
much of an improvement on the prisoners' barracks from
the outside. Yet another desk sergeant — it seemed to be
the main function of sergeants in the army — asked him
the usual questions, and made the usual remarks.

"There's a whole batch of them arriving tomorrow,"
the sergeant told him. "You can get a bit of experience by
helping me to check them in. I suppose you can read and
write."

Adolf smiled to himself. The sergeant was obviously
dissatisfied with his task. There might be an opening as his
assistant. "I'd rather push a pen than watch over a wretched
bunch of P.O.W's," he thought.

"I don't suppose you got as far as learning any of the
lingo at your school?" Adolf returned his attention to the
sergeant.

"English, sergeant? Yes I can speak it a bit." — A bit
more than he had learnt at school too, since his informal
instruction tied up in a cellar!

"Of course English! What do you think I meant,
Chinese?"

He went and stowed his kit in the new quarters. Quite
a come-down from the Grand Hotel. He supposed he'd
seen worse. The rest of the day was his, to watch the

construction work, strike up the beginning of friendships with some of his fellow guards, start to make a niche for himself. The prisoners already there had started off in tents. So had their guards. The first real load of prisoners were those coming tomorrow, now there were enough huts built. He saw the sergeant again, and wheedled his way into some sort of a desk job. Assistant to the assistant it amounted to. But it reduced the time standing guard by half.

The next day he found himself seated at a desk across from the sergeant, typed lists in front of him. His job was simply to allocate the new arrivals to huts and make a record of the allocation. He had watched the column being marched in. It had been exactly as he expected, as he had dreaded. Tired men dragging their feet, khaki uniforms dirty and uncared for. What was there to care about for such as these now? And there were the grey faces, bitter some of them, hating him as he watched their plight. The flicker of fear in so many eyes, as they shot quick glances at their new prison. They would have heard stories about other camps in Germany. Just as Adolf had. He felt the urge to go up to them and tell them that it wouldn't be like that. They were prisoners of war. They would be properly treated. This was the German army, not the Gestapo.

It was almost a physical blow when Adolf heard the name "Don Gibbard" spoken by the man who stood before the desk. He had not even seen him among all those faceless figures the day before. Now he looked up into Don's face, and saw the same dreadful greyness as the other captives already written there. He realized that this was not like his own captivity — that strange game enacted by two children playing at war in an old cellar. Unthinking of what he was doing he wrote down the details, told Don his hut and number.

"I'll try to talk to you," he whispered, trying to smile at him.

"Thank you." Without any answering smile. Then he was gone.

Now the dreary October days slid by for both men. For

Adolf the duties were boring and repetitive. The same routine of stints in the guardhouse, filing and typing lists, was only interrupted by shivering spells wrapped in greatcoat and muffler with the more poignant misery of others to watch. Off duty he had nowhere to go. The captured towns were still under martial law. The entertainments available to a German soldier were limited. Everything for them had to come across the Channel, and there were more urgent things to be brought. Their only consolation was that the food was still good. Basic rations were shipped over from the continent, but they were supplemented by the contents of captured British stores. Efforts had been made to keep the troops supplied with the small luxuries. Tobacco and chocolate were regularly available.

Adolf didn't smoke. He had given his first packet of cigarettes to Don. In the curious world they had inhabited together, Don had bemoaned the lack of tobacco, telling him how he acquired the illicit habit as a boy. Adolf had laughed, and advised him to use the opportunity to give it up. Now Don took the cigarettes, mumbled thanks, and retreated into the scruffy khaki mass.

"What did he want you for?" demanded a probing Scots voice.

"You took something from him," said another, a cockney, wheedling.

"He gave me these, to share out amongst us," Don answered.

Amid the chorus of disbelief the cigarettes were handed round. One of them had a few matches. As they inhaled deeply, then breathed out with expressions of forgotten ecstasy, Don was patted heavily on the back, and told to stay friendly with that Jerry.

"I never thought I'd see a decent kraut," said one of them.

"He is," said Don quietly.

In fact few of the Germans guarding the growing collection of English prisoners did go out of their way to be unpleasant. They were soldiers themselves. None of them had volunteered for this job. They knew in the back of

their minds that this could easily have been their fate —
possibly could still be. Adolf was not the only guard who
passed on the occasional cigarette, or was prepared to talk
to his captives.

For the P.O.W's the main feature of their life was the
unremitting monotony. During their first week they were
employed on helping to put up the remaining huts. There
were complaints that they were being put to work. "Against
the Geneva Convention, that is mate", Don heard someone
say. But the complaints were half-hearted. Most welcomed
the diversion, and were glad of something to do. After that
there was nothing. They made what pastimes they could —
played desultory games of football, read the few books that
were about. (The German Commandant had raided a library
in Lewes to supply them with some.) A couple of them
began to carve chess sets out of old pieces of wood. They
were planning on a long stay.

When they talked, it was nearly always about the war.
Though they were in their own country, news of its fate
was lacking. There was no wireless. What they heard came
from new drafts of prisoners. There were many of those
through the third week of October. Their news was avidly
received, sifted and discussed. The new arrivals provided
a grim picture for them of a great disaster. Whole regiments
and divisions gone, Canadians and New Zealanders as well
as British. Entire armoured formations wiped out. Cities
captured. The Panzers sweeping all before them. Don asked
Adolf about it.

"It is what our news tells us too. Four of your divisions,
and all of your tanks wiped out by the Panzers. Of course,
you do not know how much of it to believe. I expect that
is true for English news bulletins also, Don? — Here I have
something for you again. It is good of you to share it with
the other men."

Don took the proffered cigarettes, and went back to
distribute them, and his precious gleanings. Even German
news was better than no news. But to hopes founded on
straws of rumour, the new confirmation of what had
befallen came as an icy gust. Though they had only been

captives for a matter of days, before them now seemed to stretch an immeasurable span. They could not count the days for there would be no limit on them. Minds went back to the appalling duration of the Great War. It still had its hold on the imaginations even of young men. And that was the best of their hopes, that it would be a long war in which the tide would turn. The prospect of England's utter defeat was the alternative, leaving their fate a plaything of the victors. Unconsciously, they all began the process of wrapping their spirits in webs of tattered hope, against the chill winter of despair. A winter blown to them on the wings of the news.

Eyes scanned the skies for British planes, for they were the tokens of those last hopes. Once they saw a whole squadron of heavy bombers, Short Stirlings, great four-engined machines, and escorted by Hurricanes. They cheered and waved and shouted. Once a lone Spitfire was sighted above the Downs. Some of the men said it had waggled its wings to them. They were glad to believe the story. The other perpetual worry of all the men was about their families. Whether they knew. Whether (in this war fought, like no other, here in England) they were themselves alright. It was worst for those whose people lived in Kent and Sussex, or London. Don had asked Adolf to help. He did not want to make demands on the friendship between them, but was driven by the force of his own anxieties.

"I just want them to know I'm alive, that's all," he told him. "Is there any way of checking if they've been told."

Adolf's own family had been notified of their son's death. He did not need Don's halting explanation.

"I am sure they have, my friend." he told him seriously. "The camp office here, you know, it is better than most. What is the word? — Efficient. I have helped to prepare the lists which go to the Red Cross. It was more than a week ago. Not long after you arrived. — But I will see if I can discover for certain."

The next day he called Don over to the wire, waving

and shouting out, earning the disapproval of the corporal of the guard.

"I have checked, Don. You can tell all the Tommies this. The notification has gone to the Red Cross authorities on your side, and it is more than a week since this was sent. This is true now for all men here. Their families have by this time been informed that they are living and prisoners of war."

"You're a real pal, Adolf. — If only all your lot were like you . . . "

To Don it was a chance remark, part of his gratitude. To Adolf, almost a sudden slap. He thought of his friends, from the Hitler Youth, from his school and childhood, from the army — some dead now.

"We are mostly like me," he answered.

"Of course. I'll go and tell the others."

He ran back to one of the huddled groups, with a crumb of comfort for them to feed on and savour over the long days to come.

★   ★   ★

Mrs Gibbard sat sipping tea in number 3, the Renoufs' house, just a door away from her own.

"There'll be news in time, dear. Not to worry. After all it's not certain he was . . . " Mrs Renouf, plump, bustling Edith, who couldn't stand the bombs, lapsed into silence.

"Shut up, woman," Ralph, her husband, told her, sharply for him; he never raised his voice. She looked offended, and retreated into the kitchen, muttering,

"Well, I'm sure I was only trying to help."

"There is a faint chance, Mrs Gibbard," said Ralph, "but it's no good getting your hopes up and pretending it's more than faint. That officer who came round, he didn't give much reason to think — to think Don might have survived. Don't give up hope, love. Never do that. But don't expect too much."

"He was such a nice man — a Captain Sawyer it was. He came himself too. He said if there was anything he could do. . . . " She began to sob again.

It was six o'clock in the evening, Saturday 19th October, over a fortnight since she first heard. The news that her only son was missing in action had come like a thunderbolt to her, something she had dreaded before the event in an abstract way, but which when it happened overwhelmed her in a flood of anguish. The officer with him had come himself to her door, told her with care and gentleness, made her tea while she sat there stunned. He stayed a long while, and finally, when he had to leave, had gone to fetch her neighbours to look after her. She had asked for the Renoufs.

In the end, she had calmed down a little, at least outwardly, with Ralph's help. But Gwen had spent that night and the next two round there to be on the safe side. Her desolation had not ceased since then. She had continued not believing, needing reassurance where there was none, seeking any word of help that anyone could give. That evening she had come over more than an hour before, distraught again, still refusing to accept.

"That officer should never have taken him," said Gwen bitterly, also near tears. "He had no business to."

"All right, love." Her father turned to her. "No point in getting worked up about it. . . . "

"Mrs Gibbard!" Nancy, the younger Renouf girl burst in. "There's a telegraph boy at your house. Telegram for you. An official one, I asked him . . . "

She saw the way things were, and stopped at once, suddenly aware of the implications — either way. Her father stood up immediately.

"I'll go out and get it for you. You just sit there." He patted the weeping woman on the shoulder, then hurried out.

"Oh, Ralph, you don't think . . . " his wife began as he hastened through the scullery. He just shook his head.

When he returned he was running, and he didn't run very often.

"Mrs Gibbard, he's alive! Your Don's alive!" He paused to get his breath. "Taken prisoner. . . . Here, it's all in the cable. From the War Office."

He thrust it into her hand. Her whole body shook as

she read it. Then she put her face in her hands, weeping again, shaking in her relief.

"It's a miracle," Gwen said. "A real miracle."

Only the tremor in her voice betraying her own returning happiness.

Chapter 22

THE CAPTAINS AND THE KINGS

After the storm of the great battle, a curious lull descended upon the field of war. In Kent and east Sussex, where the fighting had been, the two opposing armies were hardly in contact with each other. The Germans paused for breath, and to take stock, clutching their gains almost in disbelief. The British had in effect been wiped out. The survivors had fallen well back, leaving the Germans to their conquests, themselves as yet untroubled by the conquerors. The two rival warlords, Churchill and Hitler, both responded to the events of the great battle by reorganizing their armed forces. Hitler did so in response to the manner in which the fruits of victory had been won, Churchill because the heart had been ripped out of the British defence. A new defence, a new army, would need to be created, ready for the time when the Germans attacked again.

Hitler's immediate promotion of Rommel to General-oberst, after the destruction of the British 'Army of Kent', was only the beginning of the changes the Führer now personally imposed on the organization of the German armed forces in England. Rommel's victory, followed by the intervention of 4th Panzer to complete the triumph, had proved once again that he, the Führer, knew better than the generals. It would have been difficult to deny the assertion. Without Hitler's driving will neither formation would even have been present in England. Without his insistence that the retreating divisions of Sixteenth Army stand firm and wait for the relief to arrive, there might now be no Sixteenth Army. On the evening of 11th October, he retired with only Keitel. Faithful and reliable, or a snivelling lackey, depending on the point of view. Together they reorganized the German army, in the middle of the war. Hitler announced the changes at a Führer Conference the following day.

The new Panzerarmee England, under the man of the moment, General Rommel, was to consist of the two Panzer Divisions already landed plus 20th Motorized, already beginning to be shipped across, and the two badly battered infantry divisions, 17th and 35th, taken from Sixteenth Army. The two divisions which had withstood the full fury of the original British attack. This had the effect of reducing Sixteenth Army, now under General Model, to a single division. Model's task was to re-organize and reform his army. It would take its place in the front line again only when its second and third wave divisions, together with a reconstituted 1st Mountain Division, had come over. There was one exception to this role. 7 Para and 22nd Air Landing were to be constituted into a new I Air Corps, under the command of Luftwaffe General Kurt Student. The corps would be attached to Sixteenth Army, but would operate independently as a front line unit.

The biggest surprise for the generals came in the proposal for the formation of another Panzerarmee, to be placed under the command of the brilliant Panzer general, Heinz Guderian. Guderian had written the original text book of armoured tactics, *Achtung Panzer*. He had commanded a Panzer Division in the victories over France and Poland. His new army would consist of a Panzer and an infantry Corps, formerly allocated to Sixteenth Army, together with two additional motorized regiments, Grossdeutschland, and SS Adolf Hitler Bodyguard Regiment. The result of the reorganization was to leave both Ninth and Sixteenth Army much reduced, and without any armour. Their new role was to provide support for the two

Panzer Armies. Model was more than happy with this. Strauss was happy to keep his job.

Von Rundstedt offered his resignation, but it was rejected. The Führer had considered replacing both him and Brauchitsch, head of O.K.H., but had decided against it. Instead, von Rundstedt's role, and effectively O.K.H.'s role, was dramatically reduced. For the two new Panzer Armies would form a new army group, Army Group P, named after its head, Generaloberst Paulus. Paulus was the only general who had spoken up in support of his Führer. He was the general who had organized the transporting of Rommel's original conquering Panzers. Paulus would continue to report direct to Hitler. The formalities of army commands were not for the warlord and his trusted captains. The generals gave in. They did not try to argue. Not only was their own case weak, but they also knew that General Busch was even now under arrest, for high treason and cowardice in the face of the enemy. These were the new names for questioning the Supreme Commander's orders and resigning from office.

"The attack is to be renewed, gentlemen, as soon as 1st Panzerarmee is brought up to strength. My orders are that the reinforcement of the two infantry divisions assigned to General Rommel is to be given priority. That and the transportation of his motorized infantry. The general's objective is simple. He is to strike for London, utilizing the speed and mobility of his forces, employing enveloping movements against the remaining British troops."

He made expansive gestures with his arms as he strode before them. Paused to stab at the great map with his finger. The light flickered in his eyes with an almost manic quality. He seemed to be living the advance, willing it forward.

"The attack on London will be aided by First Air Corps. I have spoken in person to General Student, and he will go to England immediately. I have spoken on the telephone to General Model, and he has sworn his fullest co-operation. General Paulus is here in person to answer any questions you may have."

"What will your own role in these operations be, General?" asked Halder, an intelligent question, forseeing the possibility of disagreement between Rommel and his new chief, both decisive leaders.

"My role will be to ensure that General Guderian's army comes into existence and arrives in England," replied Paulus. "Neither I nor the Führer himself intend to direct General Rommel as to his operational strategy."

"Thank you, Herr General."

So that had been worked out as well, Halder mused. He was unhappy about this division of the army into infantry and armour. So was Brauchitsch when the two discussed it later that same evening. On the other hand, the Panzer generals were not fools. Far from it. It might well be that Hitler had stirred the correct mix again.

"It might even be that the man is what he thinks he is," said Halder in a low tone as he saw Brauchitsch to the door. "A military genius of the first water. . . . "

"Since Frederick the Great — or only since Napoleon?"

"Spare me any more Frederick the Great!"

Halder went back inside.

"Knowing when to take the risks. That's what it comes down to. When to take the risks," he muttered to himself.

* * *

"We took a risk. All military operations have an element of risk. We miscalculated that element. I accept responsibility for the error of judgement. Now I must insist on your accepting my resignation."

General Brooke finished what had been a lengthy address to the Committee of Home Defence. He had outlined the full facts of the disaster, stated the position of the British forces now, and made his recommendations. The Committee was larger than usual. Attlee and Halifax were present, together with all the chiefs of the three armed services. Later that day Churchill would put the results of their deliberations to the War Cabinet. It was beginning to seem that there might be some question whether he maintained the confidence of his cabinet. And there was

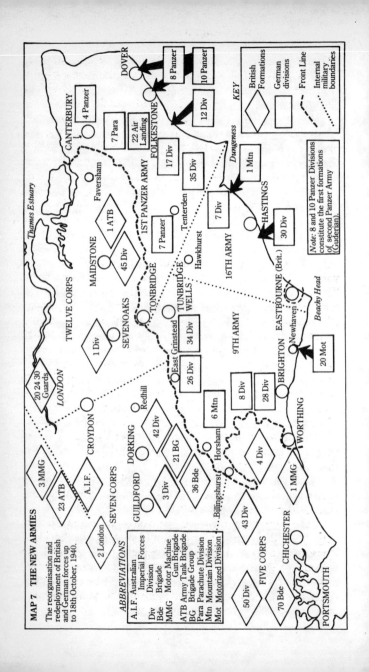

MAP 7 THE NEW ARMIES

The reorganisation and
redeployment of British
and German forces up
to 18th October, 1940.

ABBREVIATIONS

A.I.F. Australian Imperial Forces
Div Division
Bde Brigade
MMG Motor Machine Gun Brigade
ATB Army Tank Brigade
BG Brigade Group
Para Parachute Division
Mtn Mountain Division
Mot Motorized Division

KEY

◇ British Formations
□ German divisions
— Front Line
–·– Internal military boundaries

Note: 8 and 10 Panzer Divisions constitute the first formations of second Panzer Army (Guderian).

DOVER

8 Panzer
10 Panzer
4 Panzer
7 Para
22 Air Landing
12 Div

CANTERBURY
Faversham

FOLKESTONE

Dungeness

17 Div
35 Div
1 Mtn
7 Div
30 Div
Tenterden
Hawkhurst
7 Panzer

1ST PANZER ARMY

HASTINGS

16TH ARMY

Thames Estuary

MAIDSTONE
1 ATB
45 Div

TWELVE CORPS

LONDON

20 24 30 Guards

SEVENOAKS
1 Div

TONBRIDGE
TUNBRIDGE WELLS
East Grinstead
34 Div
26 Div
6 Mtn

9TH ARMY

EASTBOURNE (Brit.)
Beachy Head
Newhaven
BRIGHTON
20 Mot

CROYDON
3 MMG
23 ATB
A.I.F.

2 London

SEVEN CORPS

GUILDFORD
DORKING
Redhill
42 Div
3 Div
21 BG
36 Bde

Horsham
Billingshurst
43 Div
4 Div
8 Div
28 Div

WORTHING
1 MMG

FIVE CORPS

CHICHESTER
50 Div
70 Bde

PORTSMOUTH

talk of a no confidence motion in the House. Prime Minister MacKenzie King in Canada already faced just such a motion after the utter annihilation of the 1st Canadian Division. The government of New Zealand had actually fallen.

"If you resign, Alan, then I shall resign too," said Churchill. "There are enough of them eager to see the back of me. Let's see if the yapping dogs can do better themselves." He looked at Halifax. The antipathy between the two men was obvious. Halifax might have been Prime Minister in Churchill's place. Churchill believed he still cherished the ambition.

"I trust we can avoid the issue degenerating into a personal squabble, gentlemen. Now is not the moment for the Prime Minister and the Foreign Secretary to fall out. I feel it is also not the moment for resignations." The calm voice of Clement Attlee served to ease the tension a little. "It is the intention of the Labour Party to remain in the National Government, Winston, and to support you personally if this comes to a motion of no confidence. Which I doubt that it will, once our intentions are known. I also do not think any useful purpose will be served by the resignation of General Brooke. As I understand it, the decisions that mattered in this terrible affair were taken here in this committee. I was invited to be present myself for some of them. I also feel that to remove the Commander-in-Chief of Home Forces would shake confidence even further."

"American confidence is already rock bottom," interrupted Halifax. "I have seen Kennedy today. His advice is that we should come to terms."

"Fortunately cowardice is not a characteristic of all Americans," snarled Churchill. His views of the American ambassador were hardly a secret.

"The remark is unworthy of you," answered Halifax icily. "Nor do I think that you would wish to call President Rooseveldt a coward. Yet the president has cancelled the delivery of destroyers due under your lend-lease arrangements. The whole agreement seems likely to be abandoned. American public opinion and, more to the point, opinion on Capitol Hill is not favourable to us."

"Wars aren't won by anyone's opinion," Churchill snapped back. "And the best way to influence public opinion, on Capitol Hill or a Clapham omnibus is by starting to fight back. If you've anything useful to say, Lord Halifax, on that point, let's hear it!"

Halifax was pale with anger.

"If you wish to force *my* resignation, Winston, you should know that I will not go alone. You will split the party, and the country. And you may find your vote of confidence harder to win than you suppose. You are not a natural leader of the Labour Party. And you would do well to consider the case of Mr MacDonald, when he changed sides. . . . Not that changing sides is a new thing for you!"

"At least any side I change to will be English," Churchill answered. "I am not thinking of changing sides to the Germans. . . . "

"Mr Prime Minister, I feel it might be for the best if you were to withdraw that remark." It was Pound, the First Sea Lord, who broke the silence that followed. Churchill's fury had already abated, and he knew very well how far over the mark he had stepped.

"I withdraw it unreservedly, and tender my apologies."

Halifax sat down slowly, with jerky movements.

"My loyalty to England has *never* been questioned," he said, in voice in which the anger shook through every word.

"Sir, may we take it you accept the Prime Minister's apology?" This time it was Sir Charles Portal, new Chief of the Air Staff, trying to pour oil on the troubled waters.

"Yes! — For what it's worth." He spoke after a long silence, but it was apparent that a new bitterness towards Churchill now animated him. In the wake of military defeat, hidden personal rivalries were coming to the surface to create a spirit of dreadful acrimony among Britain's leaders, with all the dangers to her war effort which that implied.

Brooke did not resign, nor did any one else. His proposals, after discussion and some modification, were accepted. Three former corps were to be abandoned, three new ones created in their place. These three corps were to become the order of battle of a new army, given the title

First Army (in preference to Churchill's suggestion of Army of Home Defence).

The new V Corps would hold the right, or western end, of the British line. 4th Infantry Division, and 1st Motor Machine Gun Brigade were already there on the coast and doing the job. An extra division from reserve would be added to them immediately. The new corps would have its own reserves, brought up from the West Country and stationed directly behind its front line.

The new VII Corps would take the centre of the line, due south of London. 42 Division was already in place there, and 36th Independent Brigade was moving up. To these were added some reserve troops and another division (again from the west of England, rapidly emptying of troops). Corps Reserve was provided by a division, brought back from the Welsh borders, and the Australians. Brooke had originally allocated them immediately to the front, which they were already near. The politicians could not take the risk of committing yet another Commonwealth contingent to the battle so soon after the destruction of the Canadians and New Zealanders. Much to their own annoyance the Australians were held back.

The new XII Corps would hold the line in Kent. In addition to 1st Army Tank Brigade and 45 Division, the only formations rescued from the disaster of *Lemon Squeezer*, one infantry division would be spared from East Anglia. The Corps Reserve was provided by the three Guards Brigades holding London itself.

The Army itself would have a substantial reserve, still to be known as G.H.Q. Reserve, but to be under the immediate orders of the army commander "in an emergency" (these words were inserted by the Committee, as if wishing to create doubt and confusion at the outset). The reserve was to be based in London and on the Thames Valley. It included a brigade of tanks from Western Command which was added to 2nd Armoured Division. This division had been minus the detached brigade wiped out by Rommel at the beginning of his armoured rampage across southern England. Now the deficiency would be made good.

On paper Britain had re-created a credible defence. But the weakness in armour was immediately evident. The country was being stripped of troops to provide the army that would now have to fight the battle for London. If 2nd Armoured Division went the way of the 1st, there was no more armour left. If this army was defeated, there would be no troops to form another. If London fell, then Britain must fall too. The commander assigned the task of fighting the battle for London was 54-year-old General Bernard Montgomery. He had commanded a division in France, and brought it safe out from Dunkirk, where his personal courage had been made apparent. Since then he had commanded V Corps and held the western end of the British line with vigour and determination. He was known as an individualistic commander, very concerned for his men. He was not likely to throw their lives away, but likely enough to show nerve and initiative. The idea was originally Brooke's but Churchill had taken it up enthusiastically. Other names were considered, but they had little to offer except greater seniority. It was a gamble of course.

"Prime Minister, there is one other matter we must discuss," said Brooke, at the end of all the detailed debate of troops and armies that had gone on long into the night.

"I hope it is to be the last," sighed Churchill wearily.

"It is a matter on which the Service Chiefs have agreed in advance, and on which we now feel we must insist."

"Insist?" Churchill's eyebrows raised.

"I refer to the safety of the King and the Royal Family. London is now, for certain, the immediate enemy objective. It is imperative that the Royal Family be removed from the city."

Churchill sighed.

"I have anticipated you, Alan. — The Chiefs of Staff have raised this delicate matter before," he explained to the two politicians present. "We have once discussed it in the War Cabinet. — I have been to see His Majesty today."

That was a shock for them. Churchill allowed himself a moment of enjoyment.

"His Majesty is adamant on this point," he continued. "Neither he nor the Queen will leave London. If the fight comes to the city, I believe that His Majesty intends to take his place at the head of his army. However, he has, after very great pressure on my part and a certain amount of what the Americans call 'tough talking', finally agreed to send the young princesses away. A safe house is ready for them, and they will be escorted by troops of Captain Coates' mission."

"It was not to be expected that he or the Queen would go," said Attlee. "I think that the Chiefs of Staff must be satisfied with this."

It was at least a concession to the looming uncertainties of the future. All of them there had now to contemplate the possibilities of defeat. Despite the slogans they did exist. The unthinkable now had to be weighed up. Strange possibilities that the war might go on even if England fell, fought from Canada or ultimately the U.S.A. Britain had sent her treasure away for safe keeping beyond the seas in the earliest days of the war. Now she must look to the preservation of the dynasty, and the crown.

★   ★   ★

The morning of Sunday 13th October was cold, a warning of the winter to come. King George VI, wearing the ordinary uniform of a colonel in the army, accompanied by the Queen, also soberly clad, stood on the platform of St. Pancras Station. Aboard the two-coach train were their young daughters, and the soldiers who would guard them on their journey. Above them the air raid sirens were wailing. For the last three days the bombers of the Luftwaffe had turned their attentions to London again. There had been two indiscriminate night raids, and hit and run attacks by day. Both Kings Cross and Euston had been knocked out during the preceding night, the West End had been hit, and the houses in the streets of Camden Town and

Islington. From the royal car they had caught a glimpse of Oxford Street still burning.

"Sir, I must insist that Her Majesty and yourself leave the platform now. We must get into the shelter." Captain Coates' hand rested lightly on the King's arm.

"Let us wave the children goodbye, Captain," said the Queen.

There was the sound of exploding bombs, quite distantly, a sound so often heard, not a sound to disturb any Londoner. King George and Queen Elizabeth were Londoners. The engine on the train whistled, an L.M.S. *Royal Scot* Class, far more powerful than the two carriages befitted, but there to speed the royal passengers away. Wheels slid, and steam escaped from the cylinders. The King and Queen stood and watched as the train began to pull away. Then both turned, ready to go to the shelter. The sound of the falling bombs was suddenly much closer, dangerous now. The whine of their fall mingled with the unmistakable scream of the Stuka. It was the first time there had been Stukas over London for almost a month. They had been given a specific mission, beginning the previous day:- to impair communications, and in particular troop movements by road and rail.

The engine emerged from the great curving roof of the train shed into the sunlight. Out of that sun came the Stukas. Two went for the station itself, two for the train. The first bomb hit the engine, destroying it completely, and flinging the coaches off the rails, slewed across the other tracks. They remained upright at first. The King had turned at the flash of the blast. As the sound reached him he was already running back down the platform. The Queen and Captain Coates had started to follow him when the second bombs hit the train. Everyone on the platform stood still — the railway staff, the soldiers, the officials. In the blinding flash the two coaches were ripped apart in a moment. The royal Princesses were already dead within the tangled wreckage, as the bombs from the remaining Stukas smashed through the glass of the station roof.

The first explosion was on the far side of the station,

but the blast swept through the scattered group, knocking them over like figures of cardboard. As men fell, the King managed to catch hold of his wife. Then the other bombs came. King George was struck by flying splinters, piercing his back and entering the side of his head. His body shielded the Queen as he fell protecting her. He did not know that both his children, the Princesses Elizabeth and Margaret Rose, had died instantly when their train was hit.

Seriously injured, he was rushed to hospital. The Queen, who had escaped with cuts and bruises, accompanied him. As the ambulance raced through the streets of London, hardly noticed in those days, desperate efforts were under way to dig the bodies out of the wreck of the train. There were only three survivors. The bodies of the two girls were conveyed in army vehicles, in the greatest secrecy, back to Buckingham Palace. The King meanwhile was undergoing major surgery to remove some of the shrapnel. His wounds were appalling. Jagged splinters of metal had torn apart one lung, and ripped through his spine. His lower body was paralysed. He had regained consciousness for a moment or two when they reached the hospital.

"Inform all the Family. They must be told. Tell my mother. . . . Tell them, . . . that I will die." As the Queen held his hand, he asked, "How are the girls?" Weeping she told him they had got out alright. Told him they were well. She knew they were both dead.

Churchill was called from the War Cabinet to hear the news. It struck him harder than any disaster to Britain's arms by land or sea. He had regarded the Royal Family, and the King in particular, with a passionate loyalty and devotion. And now the royal children were dead. And the king was unlikely to live, certainly not to live as a whole man again. And they had gone there to the station on that day at his urging. Had they remained in Buckingham Palace, the disaster would not have happened. He returned to the cabinet, and told them in a few words, his voice broken and weary as was his spirit.

"I have sent my King to his death," he said, then left them.

He gave instructions for the members of the Royal Family to be informed, as the King himself had bidden. He directed that they should be summoned to the King's bedside. Those few others who must needs know, he arranged to be told. Otherwise, he ordered the secret kept. Then he retired alone to his study, seeing no-one, unable for a while to play any part in the war.

Queen Mary, the King's mother, had already joined her distraught daughter-in-law at the hospital. The two Queens waited as the gloom of evening gathered, and the bombs fell again across London. The Dukes of Gloucester and Kent came to join them, and the Princess Royal. The surgeon to the Royal Family finally came out to them at nine o'clock.

"Your Majesties, Your Royal Highnesses, the King is sleeping now, and in no pain. He may be able to speak to you tomorrow morning."

"He will live, doctor?" asked Queen Elizabeth, taking hold of the surgeon's arm in a sudden fierce grip.

"Ma'am, I can promise you nothing. At best the hope is no more than a faint glimmer. I will have to operate again tomorrow. I must ask you, all of you, to be prepared for the worst. I hope against hope to save him, but as things are now. . . . the King is dying."

"It is another son lost to me," said the old Queen. "First David, who failed in his duty. Now Albert . . . " She turned to the Duke of Gloucester. "It will be you they take next — to wear this poisoned crown."

Far away in the Bahamas, the island's governor was reading a telegram, reading again and again the simple message. The instructions of the King that all members of the family be informed had been carried out. The Duke of Windsor, who had been Edward VIII and was now banished to this tiny outpost of empire as governor, finally put the telegram down. He looked at his wife, Wallis, who had been Mrs Simpson, and was now Duchess of Windsor. He pushed the flimsy paper towards her, and she picked it up and read.

"I am going back. I am going to be at his bedside."

"They won't want you, sweetheart. None of them! Even Winston won't have you in England now."

"Nevertheless, I am going. It is time I did something, Wallis. Time *I* made the decisions, instead of 'them'."

By the following morning, the day after the tragedy at the station, the Duke had arranged for a private aircraft to take him to the United States. By the same afternoon he was in America, and within hours airborne again, flying into the approaching night, heading for Britain. He had not consulted with any of his staff in the colony, or with any British embassy officials in Washington. The news of his brother the King's injuries and the sight of the telegram, was enough to persuade the American authorities to speed his passage.

In Britain, too, his arrival was not expected. There were other things to think of. Though official reports and notifications were on their way, other news received priority in the decoding rooms in the days of Britain's crisis. The authorities at Hendon soon rectified the matter when the plane touched down. But they had no power to detain the Royal Duke. He went straight to the hospital, driving an R.A.F. car appropriated at Hendon. The King was still alive after the second operation, but very weak. He shewed no signs of improvement. The doctors had failed to remove all the splinters from his brain. The Duke looked at the ashen, twisted face of his brother, sleeping fitfully. Then came out into the anteroom. His mother met him there.

"Why have you come here, David? Why now?" she asked him.

"Because my brother is here. . . . because he may be dying."

She looked at him closely.

"You are not trying to come back?"

"How little you know me, mother. How little you really understand. I *have* come back. I will not leave England again. I will serve my King and his lawful successors here where I can be most use. In time my wife will come and join me."

"It should have been you in there, David."

Queen Mary looked at her eldest son, her eyes glistening with tears.

"But for you, mother, it might have been."

He turned on his heel and went. He had become steely in his resolve. At the door of the hospital he was met by a staff officer and taken straight to the bunker beneath Downing Street that was Churchill's war headquarters. The warlord awaited him, dressed in a blue siren suit, smoking the invariable outsize cigar. The only other person there was General Brooke. The Duke recognized him, knew he was Commander-in-Chief of Home Forces. They shook hands. Churchill indulged in no further polite formalities.

"Your Royal Highness had no business returning to England and abandoning your responsibilities and post without the permission of His Majesty's Government."

"I apologize for the lack of consultation. My responsibilities and my post in the Bahamas can, as you are aware, be filled by any tin-pot civil servant. And I am here because my brother is dying and his children are already dead. So spare me any more talk of duty, Winston. I am sick of it."

Churchill sat back down on his bunk.

"I have officially made H.M.G.'s displeasure clear. — I know why you've come. I suppose I would have come, had I been in your place, though there is nothing you can do for him."

"I haven't seen the doctors. What do they say?"

"The King is dying. They have eased his pain, and prolonged his life. But only for weeks, months at best. They will continue to try."

Edward sat for a long time in silence.

"Can you tell me how things are going in the war?" he asked eventually.

Churchill told him, tersely and to the point.

"I will not go back to Nassau, Winston," said the Duke. "It is not only that I wish to remain near my brother — at his side if he is to die. . . . I intend to stay and fight for my country. If you won't find me employment in the field, then I'll put on a private's uniform, and go and fight regardless."

"You are very full of martial ardour. That was how I felt once, a long time ago, different war . . . "

"It is not martial ardour. It is what I conceive to be my duty. It is my turn to use the word now. My mother has already told me that it should be me lying in that hospital — dying."

Churchill got up and paced the room. Brooke till now had been a silent witness of these events. Finally he spoke.

"Prime Minister, it would be possible for His Royal Highness to play a part — perhaps on my staff. . . . "

"No! — I have come to fight."

"The officer commanding 45th Infantry Division was killed in action," said Churchill. "Alan, who is in command pro tem? Remind me please."

"Brigadier Watkins of 1st Army Tank Brigade is acting senior officer:- the two formations are effectively combined at the moment."

"No new appointment yet?"

"We had a man in mind. Brigadier Morgan."

"Would you excuse us a moment, Edward, I wish to talk with General Brooke."

Churchill and the General went out into the corridor. They were gone some time, and the Duke heard raised voices. When they came back, Churchill said,

"Your Royal Highness, you will be offered a resumption of your former commission as Major General in the British Army. You will be given the *joint* command of 45th Division, together with an experienced soldier, Major General — formerly Brigadier — H. Morgan."

"You think I need a real general to help me, Prime Minister?"

"Yes, damn it! Do you think I have divisions to throw away? You will do what your colleague in command tells you. He will have seniority. And he will trust you as far as he can throw you. Until you prove otherwise."

"I'm sorry, Winston. You're quite right. . . . Will you

tell me one other thing now? — How much do the people know?"

"Nothing much, yet. They know there was an 'incident' and the Royal Family were involved. — It is too soon after the defeats. Those they know of. I have spared them nothing of our disasters."

"Tell them this too, Winston. It is their King who is dying and his heirs who are dead. They have the right to know."

"Yes. . . . I will tell them."

After the Duke had left, Churchill turned to Brooke.

"You know my views on this appointment, Prime Minister, so I will not lecture you again."

"I know you don't trust him."

"I am afraid he may crack under the strain. Especially in view of . . . the King."

"You promised me no lecture, Alan. The man is an old friend. That is why I am sending him to probable death in the forefront of his people's army. — What better place for one who was King and Emperor?"

Chapter 23

ESCAPE

For the Prisoner of War Camp, Lewes, it was a day like any other, a cold morning, the prisoners muffled in scarves, the guards as chill as they in their tight-buttoned uniforms. The drone of aircraft grew steadily more audible, coming in from the north. For the first time it failed to break the spreading apathy. Some of the prisoners went to the wire. The guards glanced up. British planes — probably not going to pass very near. Just the same, a whistle was blown. Germans came out of the guard-house, sauntering towards the two machine gun emplacements, cursing the nuisance that made them abandon their warm stove.

The engine roar was louder. Adolf looked up. Though he was off duty he was outside. He had been standing close to the wire, talking to Don. A snatch of conversation, a word of reassurance to his friend on the other side. The two planes had peeled off from their flight path, and were approaching the camp on separate courses, diving fast and low, a pair of Hurricanes. In their sights the pilots saw only another enemy camp. The attack had happened before anyone knew it was coming. Tracer cut through the barbed wire, flashes of silver. The whole of one side of the perimeter fence was cut down, metal and concrete fragments flying. The prisoners scattered.

Adolf too turned to run, tripped and fell. Picking himself up quickly, he saw the men in the machine gun post just in front of him as they swung the ponderous weapon round. He also saw the track of angry spurts of dust and soil flying up, their line scything in towards the men. Then the line of shells had ripped into the emplacement. Bursts of sand and dull thuds from the cushioning sand bags, and the screaming of one of the men. The other had died at once, unprotesting. Blood ran down from his head as he lay over the parapet of split logs, then dripped down and mingled with the spilt sand. The other man had fallen backwards, flung aside by the force of the bullets entering his body. Adolf looked around him, wild-eyed. He could only see one of the planes, making another pass, straight for the huts. The prisoners were hiding under them or in them, or lying on the ground, hands over their unprotected heads.

"They are your own men! Your side! English!" Adolf found himself screaming in vain at the aircraft. He was stood up, a perfect target, waving his hands, caught in an overpowering fury. Then he was running to the machine gun. He seized the heavy weapon, and swung it on its rotating tripod, fired almost before he could aim. The gun shook in his hands like a drill, and the sound almost deafened him. But he had the plane now, and he held the bucking barrel firmly on it. It banked steeply, and came at him.

Again he saw the spurts rush across the ground, the twin tracks of the plane's gunfire, straight at him. The Hurricane was now filling his entire vision. He continued to fire, up to the moment he felt a sudden blazing pain in his arm and side, and a hammer blow that spun him round, away from the gun at last. His eyes were still on the aircraft, and there was black smoke surging out from the fore part of it. He fell onto the ground, supporting himself with his good arm, and watched it fly straight into the hillside. Amidst the dazzle of the explosion, he felt an arm under his shoulders, saw a face. Whose was it?

"It's me. It's Don."

The words didn't make sense. — Yes, of course, English. He made the effort to speak, puzzled by the fact that the words would only come with difficulty.

"You had better take your chance, my English friend. Perhaps you will make it all the way this time."

For a moment he saw the hesitation in the other's eyes.

"Do not worry about me. — Run!"

Don let him down softly, half stood up, and looked around him. There was chaos and confusion everywhere, men running and shouting — lots of Englishmen outside the wire, much of the wire down, hardly any Germans. He saw the guard house was ablaze. So he ran, without any conscious decision to do so, without any thought about why or where. Not down the track, but northward, the direction the planes had come from. Down a hillside, across a hedge, through another, into a coppice, stumbling and gasping for breath. But never ceasing to run. He didn't know how many fields, hedgerows and walls he crossed. His mind kept repeating,

"Treat it as a race. A race. A cross-country. . . . Got to win. Can't rest! Got to win!"

He was trying to keep his direction right, keep the watery sun behind him all the time. It was just before midday, so the sun marked the south. And he was going north. His route was downhill, sharply at first, a steep slope he had to scramble down. Then it was gentler, through some sort of park, and then the fields and farms. He crossed a deserted railway line, and a brook, minor roads, but no main roads yet. He avoided the farmhouses, and the occasional larger house. Stayed clear of any sign of a village or hamlet, stayed always in the open country. Two more streams, and the first road with any sign of life, a car or two, easily avoided. Then a larger wood of beech and oak closed about him. Only then did he pause to rest.

He leaned, shaking in exhaustion and tension, against the trunk of an oak tree, trembling as he fought to get his breath back. He let thoughts form in his mind for the first time, to push aside the one overpowering thought of escape. There was Adolf, blood seeping into the grey, torn serge of his uniform, face pale like a ghost's. But Adolf couldn't be dead. It was only his arm, wasn't it? And Adolf had made the chance for him, told him to go. And now he was away, free and running, but not safe.

Thoughts of pursuit crowded back in. He had never paused to look round as he ran. Never dared, because he knew that if he looked he would see them there, after him already. Now it seemed there was no pursuit. After a while he crept cautiously back to the edge of the wood, and looked across the country he had covered, rolling little hills, patterned with fields and lines of trees, the rounded peaks of the Downs beyond. He had seen almost no-one in his run. He wondered how far he had come. Five miles? — No. More than that. Perhaps as much as ten. It had not been a straight line, though.

On the road near by a man was walking along uncon- cerned — a farm labourer, with old, brown, country clothes. Not the uniforms he was looking out for. He watched the man until he was out of sight, gone to the village marked by a church spire away to Don's right. He was beginning to accept the fact that he was not being followed, not yet at any rate. He turned back into the wood, and started to make his way through it. He was no longer running, but making as good a speed as he could.

"Must save energy," he said to himself. "Must go care- fully now. No more running across open ground. Must do it like I did in Brighton." He realised he was talking aloud, half smiled, and said, still aloud, "Shut up, you fool!"

The edge of the woodland brought him out above a river, with a railway alongside. This was not just a stream. He decided against swimming across. It was cold, and he did not want wet clothes. He made his way cautiously along the edge of the wood, staying inside the screen of trees. The bridge when he came to it was beside an inn. There was no sign of life anywhere. He took the risk, and darted across. Under the railway bridge, and then there was more woodland. Pine trees mingled with the bare-branched oaks and elms, making better cover.

He was obeying his own good advice now, keeping away from open fields, sticking to the hedgerows and where possible to the woods. Increasingly the countryside was wooded as he followed the line of a little stream, back up into new hills ahead of him. These were to the north, he was sure, so they were not part of the Downs. Not the South Downs at least. They had been left far behind. He wracked his brain for any scrap of knowledge of this part of the country. Wondered if it might be the North Downs already. Or were there other hills in between?

Coming out of the valley for a moment to spy out the lie of the land, he saw a farmyard over to his left. Conscious that he was getting hungry, he approached closer, wondering about asking for food. Was it worth the risk? But the place was deserted, no sign of people or stock, except a few chickens pecking in the farmyard. The thought of staying there, of going into hiding again, crossed his mind. He decided against it. Even when well hidden he had been found once before. This place was too large and there was a road nearby. Better to pass his nights in the open, and press onward. It was getting on towards night now, the evening shadows lengthening. He looked round for the sun in the west.

"Damn it!" he muttered. He had been keeping the sun behind him without thinking what he was doing. Not bothering to think about it. "Must think! Must take better care!" he told himself, wondering if he had strayed very far to the east. Probably not he decided. The main thing was to be well clear of the coast, but he knew there had been a German victory in Kent, so he didn't want to stray that way. If anything north-west was probably the best route. But it would depend on the way the land lay. As he turned things over in his mind, he was cautiously and thoroughly searching the farm house for food. This time water was no problem. The stream he had followed was a perfectly clear, icy trickle. And there would be other streams. The quest for food was less rewarding. There was almost nothing — useless mouldy bread, a goodish hunk of cheese and a store of apples.

"Cheese and apples again," he thought. "I'm sick of cheese and apples!"

He did not take the couple of tins of food he discovered. "Don't get too heavily weighed down," he said.

He did take the carving knife from the kitchen drawer, though, and a coat — just an old gardening coat.

"They won't mind," he thought as he knotted the knife into the coat's belt. "This isn't looting. No more than the stuff I used in the other house. . . . " And who was there to know or care now, anyway? The larder was cleaned out, though no apparent damage had been done. Nothing else seemed to have been touched.

"Perhaps it was the Germans."

The thought spurred him to action. Best not to hang around too long, not with that road over there. There *might* be someone who would come back. He emerged cautiously, returning to the safety of the trees. There he ate an apple or two, and chewed on the cheese, hard and old but very welcome. His first food since a meagre breakfast. He fell asleep almost without realizing it, cradled between the roots of a tree, wrapped in his heavy coat.

When he awoke, it was with a start, gazing wildly around, so utterly alien were his surroundings. He had dreamt he was at home, and a cold draught was blowing in; he would have to get up and close that window. Now he shivered, somewhere in the open, presumably in Sussex but in unknown countryside, and completely alone. The mood took a while to pass. Finally he stood up, went to the edge of the trees and looked up at a clear night sky. The stars blazed with frost, and the Milky Way dusted the blackness above. He grimaced in the tranquil night. He knew enough about the patterns of the constellations, learnt as a Scout, to steer by them. On a night like this it was easy, especially as all he wanted was to go due north. He could see the Plough off to his right, sparkling and vivid. He followed the Pointers up to the Pole Star. Then, stretching his limbs and working the stiffness out of the joints, he set off.

Now, in the night, he skirted the wood, but keeping it close in case he needed to return to cover again, still wary in the starlight. He crossed one road, silent and safe. Found another line of trees to follow, rising up the hillside to his left. To the right there was cause for more caution, a road, and getting closer to his route. He slid back into the trees. They came right down to the roadside. A cross roads in fact, two main routes, and another road as well. There was a large building, a pub or hotel. His eyes took it all in carefully. He was absolutely still. For there were German troops — a column marching. Starlight glinting on their helmets. Their voices were muted. He saw the occasional glow of an illicit cigarette. For some reason he had not expected them, but his mind and body were in such a state of alertness that he ran no risk of accidental discovery. He hid lower, moving slowly, wary of every movement, like an animal distrustful of human voices. They paused at the building. In the night air he could hear the German they spoke, even the rustle of the maps. Then the column marched on where the road went, due north. He waited a long time, but there was no-one else.

"Our lot will all be inside, obeying the curfew," he reflected. "Everyone who moves at night will be an enemy."

He decided he could not risk following the Germans. He would have to change direction, at least for a while. He decided against the steep wooded slopes behind, and struck off to the right, crossing the now empty main roads. He ran over an open stretch of moor, and then into the forest again. Came down into a new valley with another gentle brook to follow, until he saw a church spire ahead. That meant a village, and even by night he intended to avoid villages. Again he found himself deflected to the right, eastwards. He passed through a park overlooking a fine country house. There were another two roads to cross, but neither presented any problem, and a railway line, as he tried to get back on course, until dawn brought him safe and utterly exhausted to another woodland. Even the cold could not keep him awake any longer. In eighteen hours he had paused for only the two or three when he had slept before. This time he slept for most of the day.

It was afternoon when he awoke, to the greyness and drizzle. His body felt unutterably cold and stiff, full of aches, so that he found he could hardly walk. But the thick fir trees had sheltered him from the day's rain. Behind him, as he looked out from the cover, he could see signs of habitation, a road, and what looked like a railway junction. As he watched a train jolted and rattled through, the old engine wheezing with the effort. It was a goods train, and he was sure he could make out guards on the flat cars. Germans of course. Or was it so certain? He did not know how far he had come. Well over twenty miles, he was sure of that. Probably that was not far enough. He was faced with another question. Which way now? He thought the train was coming from the south, but there was no way to be sure. There was no sun, and did not look like being any stars in the night. He decided to go on through the wood, while there was still light to see in the dense growth of pines.

He came out unexpectedly onto a wide metalled road. It was empty of traffic, and the forest continued on the other side. He did not wait to weigh it up, just ran, straight across, back into the safety of the awaiting trees. Something went by on the road. A car, or what? He lay in the shadows and didn't look up. The engine receded into the distance. He had not been seen, though it must have missed him by a matter of seconds, appearing round a bend in the road, just as he reached cover.

"Don't do that again," he said, hearing the tremor in his voice, but comforted by the sound. "Be careful. Always be careful!"

He wished he knew where he was, wished there was some way of finding out. All the road signs had gone, taken down to confuse the enemy. But the enemy had maps. He continued through the wood. It was getting darker now. This was the most extensive tract of forest he had yet found, and he was glad of it while he moved by day. At night he would need more open country. He kept the rising ground on his right; in that direction the forest seemed deeper. There was another main road. This time he was more cautious, watching and waiting while a German motor cycle sped by. Even so, he almost failed to notice an elderly

couple, walking along the forest edge, almost close enough
for him to reach out and touch. Though they were plainly
English — he heard a few words, about the war naturally
enough — he would take no risks. He waited till they were
out of sight. Once over, he made his way to the edge of
the wood, and looked out. He was inclined to think he
might be looking north.

If he was, the prospect that greeted him was disappoint-
ing. There was a hill with houses on it, looking like the
edge of a town. There was no going that way. In the last
of the light he continued to skirt the wood, then in the
newly fallen night, cloudy and safe, he struck across the
open country. Followed a watercourse again, then abandoned it to get past a railway embankment. For a while he
found himself on a golf course, dangerously exposed. He
knew by now that there was a sizeable town on his left,
and he had no choice but to skirt it. His journey seemed
to grow harder all the time, more woods, and an uphill and
down dale path through them. Sometimes in darkness so
utter that he was feeling his way along between the trees.
He began to think he was going round in circles.

Finally he stumbled upon a barn, almost too near to a
house, but shelter. The rain was coming on hard, and he
was soaked and dispirited, utterly lost, all sense of direction
gone. He went in gladly, ignoring the risks, pausing only
to conceal himself a little in the straw before he slept again,
longer than he had planned. He awoke in the half darkness
of his resting place, conscious of sunlight through the cracks
in the wood. There was the house nearby, and people there.
But they did not see him vanish round behind the door,
safe again among trees. He guessed it was afternoon. The
sun was quite high, so he knew roughly where south was
again. As far as the lie of the land permitted he took the
opposite direction.

The main road that finally faced him was the worst
obstacle yet. It seemed to run roughly east-west, across
his path. Along it flowed a steady trickle of refugees. He
remembered those he had seen so many days before when
he drove the motor cycle for that mad captain. There was

also military traffic, enough to show this was a German supply line. The refugees hastened to get out of the way, as a horse-drawn convoy passed, laden with oil drums. Then they continued their listless journey. He saw the handcarts, and the pathetic bundles of possessions, felt the anger rising in him at their plight, and cursed the Germans who thrust them aside, uninterested.

There would be no crossing this road. He sought for yet another detour, and almost blundered into a village, perhaps even a small town. Deflected again, he continued the painful journey over hedgerows and round beside fields, till nightfall brought him to a new resting place in a wood above the ruins of an ancient castle, nestling in its moat beside a river. He did not sleep long, but pushed on into the wood, cursing the tangled undergrowth. Crossing a road gave him a brief sight of the sky. He seemed to be moving east still. In the cover of new trees, he turned north, sure that he was now safe to do so.

Out of nowhere a hand clamped over his mouth so tight that he could hardly breathe. Another hand thrust something sharp at the small of his back, hard enough to cut through his coat and nick the flesh. A voice said something in German. Even in his horror he knew it was speaking with a strange accent. Not the way Adolf had spoken, or the guards. He had no idea what it meant, but he knew there was no point in trying to resist. He let his body go limp, after so long tensed up. His legs felt like water, and the bile rose into his throat. Unresisting, the blade pressed into his back, he allowed himself to be half marched, half dragged through the bushes and undergrowth.

It went on for a long while, across another road, occasional glimpses of the sky, then deeper into the woods. Then heavy hands were pushing him down a sudden flight of steps. Yet it was still in the forest. He couldn't make it out. It seemed as if a trapdoor in the ground had suddenly appeared out of nowhere. He stumbled and almost fell. As the door was lowered above, there was utter blackness. Another voice spoke in German.

"I'm sorry, I don't understand," he said, voice shaking in fatigue and fear. In that moment he was convinced that these were the Gestapo, and he would be tortured. There was a muffled exclamation. A match was struck, and some-one lit a tilly lamp. In its flame three faces stared at him. His arms were no longer pinioned, and the knife had been withdrawn, but the man who had brought him in jerked off his old overcoat. The carving knife in his belt clattered to the ground. Another of the men pulled at his uniform to read the shoulder patches, then looked back into his face and abruptly, unexpectedly, laughed aloud.

"Well I'll be damned. A bloody Home Guard. And a long way from home too. All right, son, squat on the bench, and let's hear the story."

"You . . . you're English," Don stuttered.

He looked around him. He was in some sort of dugout, its walls lined with shelves, all neatly stacked. Tin upon tin of food, ropes, cans of petrol. And more sinister equipment, grenades, a machine gun, sticks of dynamite. Behind the three men a big wireless set stood on a table. Slowly he sat down on the bench. His original captor came round to look at him.

"Sorry if I hurt you, mate, but it's kill or be killed out here. Cold night, so it's cocoa. All right for you?"

"But what is this? Where am I?"

He still could not understand.

"All you need to know is this," said the man who had first spoken. From his accent, Don guessed he was the officer. "We are well inside occupied territory, and we are in the County of Kent."

"Kent!" Don interrupted in a near wail. Now he knew for sure that he had come too far east. He had probably been walking into enemy territory, not away from it! The officer ignored the interruption.

"This is what is commonly known as a 'Stay-behind-unit'. More than that it would be very dangerous for you to know. — Now, from you I want a detailed account of how exactly you come to be wandering through my wood in the dark."

Don gulped. These were saboteurs, English agents behind German lines. Sneak attacks and guerilla warfare! No wonder they were not wearing uniforms, beyond the army berets. Strange that he had at once recognized them as soldiers. . . . The mixture of awe and confusion on his face showed. The officer type smiled encouragement, and, sipping his scalding cocoa, Don told the story. At first with some difficulty, then in a rush, the events came tumbling out. He omitted nothing. These people would be trained. They would know if he lied or tried to hide anything. And they were English, his side, the right side. He was sure of it. There was no trick.

"So now I've got to carry on northward, until I can cross the lines and then. . . . " His voice trailed off.

"Well, I'm damned," the officer said for the second time. "It's the best story I've heard in this war, Private Gibbard of the Home Guard. If they believe it when you do make it, they'll be giving out medals I shouldn't wonder."

"I'll tell you one thing, mate," said another man, engaged on scraping hot stew out of a can into a mess tin. "No-one could have made that little lot up, so it's got to be true."

Don ate ravenously, the presence of the food awakening his dormant hunger. It was the best he had tasted for a very long time. They even managed to offer stewed fruit and custard to follow the stew.

"I'd rather keep you for a week than a fortnight," said the soldier, grinning. Don grinned back.

After the meal, he was taken deeper into the hide-out. For the rest of the night, and most of the next day, he slept on a bunk, warm and dry and well fed. He was hidden from any pursuers in a strange tunnel, burrowed out of the soil and lined with railway sleepers, beneath the woodlands of Kent.

He woke up to more food, and another long-lost luxury — a shave.

"Well, Private Gibbard, Home Guard, I'm going to let you go on. I'll take you out tonight myself. I have some business of my own to attend to. — You'll be blindfolded for the first part of our little journey. Not because I don't trust you, but because if you don't know, you can't tell — whatever happens. . . . I will put you on a road. I know you've been avoiding them, but this one will be safe at first. When you come to the main road, use the diversionary routes you're so good at. You'll need to cross the river. Be on your guard. Once you're over it, you should be nearly safe. You are making for Maidstone."

"When you get to the town, you should find British forces in strength — though my information is now a little out of date. Go carefully. They may be pulling back soon. And I'll tell you now that there are probably enemy tanks in the area. If you come across any fighting, wait till night. There's not much more I can tell you."

"No-one *is* likely to ask about us if you are caught. If they do, you will know precisely nothing. Now look at this. It is a traced map of your route. I am not going to let you take it, because if you're caught it will excite instant suspicion. You have to learn it by heart. So study it now."

Don learnt the map. Evening came, and blindfolded he clumsily clambered up the steps. He heard the whispers,

"Good luck mate!" and

"You'll make it!" in his ears.

It was hard going with the blindfold, though the officer guided him skilfully. Also it was not a "little journey", or not a little part of it anyway. It seemed interminable. He fell several times, though without doing himself any damage.

"The mud will add to your nondescript appearance," the officer told him with a chuckle. "We might have given you 'civvies', but you're safer in uniform if you are caught."

Finally the blindfold was removed. They walked on a relatively short way, Don blinking as his eyes grew accustomed to the darkness of the night. It had been raining for an hour, and he was wet and uncomfortable. They came down a hill and into a black and silent hamlet. Don saw they were at a crossroads.

"Which way is yours?" the officer demanded. Don looked all around, then pointed at the country road he must take, the memory of the map clear in his mind.

"Well done. My way is there."

The officer's hand clasped his tightly.

"Good luck," said Don. "I wish I knew who you were, to thank you properly. . . . "

"That is the only thing not secret," came the answer. "The Germans know the name they want me by. It may help you to see the commanding officer in Maidstone too. Give him the regards of Captain Robin Sanders. — Now, good luck to you."

Then the man had gone, setting off at a run. Don turned, and hurried down the dark lane.

Chapter 24

THE LONDON ROAD

Despite the lull on the ground during the 3rd week of October, in the air the fight never ceased. The Germans were repairing their advance airfield at Lydd, and hurriedly getting the devastated field at Lympne ready. Now they also had Hawkinge and Manston. By the end of that week they had twelve England-based fighter squadrons, with more arriving as facilities became available. Their bombing offensive was concentrating on British communications and troop movements. And on softening up the next, and ultimate, objective, London. The resources of the R.A.F. continued to dwindle. Every attempt to interfere with the Luftwaffe's activities only tilted the balance of attrition still further against the British. Only in bombing the enemy's newly conquered ports in Kent, and returning tit for tat in attacks on supply lines, was some small measure of success won.

The Royal Navy had not returned to the Channel, despite Admiralty requests that it do so. The Admiralty's assessment of the affects of the Home Fleet's activities on the Germans was different from Churchill's. The Prime Minister believed that no more than nuisance value had been obtained, and that at excessive loss. Though he was wrong, his view prevailed, at least for the time being. As a result the crossing of new German divisions and reinforcements in men and material for those that had suffered in the fighting, continued at a growing pace. By the end of that week troops were being landed in small numbers at both Dover and Folkestone — troops and tanks. For this was the beginning of the formation of the new Second Panzerarmee of General Guderian.

In Kent, the mopping up of the survivors occupied Rommel and the airborne troops. Towards the end of the week tentative thrusts were made north and west. The British 45th Division, with 1st Army Tank Brigade and the few surviving tanks of 1st Armoured, had prepared a strong defence. Rommel withdrew his armoured scouting groups, and once again the British sat and waited. With increasing good cheer as 1st Infantry Division began to arrive to reinforce them.

In Sussex, the tanks Rommel had left behind to hold the long and utterly exposed salient stretching from Horsham to the edge of the Downs found their task increasingly hard. They were steadily reinforced by captured British tanks (though German crews found these distinctly unsatisfactory) and infantry support. But the British withdrawal along the coast had halted just behind Worthing. The heights of the Downs above the town remained in their hands, and so did the open country beyond across the Vale of Sussex up to Horsham. And, far from a docile retreat, the British were now mounting an increasing series of miniature offensives. They cleared the Sussex countryside, and left the enemy salient more and more exposed. The Germans fell back. As 43rd Division started to arrive on the British front, the German position looked potentially dangerous.

The stiffening of British opposition after the disasters was due in some measure at least to the arrival of General Bernard Montgomery as the commander of what was now British First Army. In the first two days of his appointment he had contrived to visit 45th Division and 4th Division at opposite ends of the line. He had also made his presence felt in the movement of the reinforcing divisions to the front line, cutting through some of the red tape. Churchill, despite early doubts about his appointment, gave him substantial assistance. Together with the C.-in-C. Home Forces, Brooke, they formed a workmanlike team.

The British plan of campaign, with Montgomery in charge, was not entirely defensive. As superiority in numbers was available on the western end of the front, he now proposed a continuation and development of the rolling offensive there. The aim was to push the Germans out of Horsham, and at the same time back along the coast towards Brighton. Montgomery was also more than conscious of the presence of the Panzer Divisions. Contrary to military advice he was already bringing Second Armoured Division through the heart of London. They were ready to deploy south of the River, to hold the front at any point the Germans attempted an armoured breakthrough in strength. There was no doubt in British High Command that such an assault would come. The balance of opinion expected it in the thinly-held centre of the Front before Dorking.

The British expectation of an attack in this sector was well-founded. The Germans were aware of the British weakness from their own reconnaisance reports. General Strauss of Ninth Army had obtained the consent of von Rundstedt to launch an offensive using four of his five infantry divisions. The objectives were Croydon, Dorking and Guildford. The current German front was everywhere at or beyond Army Group A's initial objective. This new advance, with its general north-westerly axis would be the logical next step towards O.K.H.'s 1st Operational Objective, a line roughly from Gravesend to Portsmouth.

34th Division began the attack on Saturday 19th October, pushing forward from a start line to the west of Tunbridge Wells down from the Weald into the valleys of the Eden and the Medway. The British were not well established in the wooded hills, and began to give ground. On the following day the attack was extended along the Front. British 36th Brigade, newly in position on the escarpment of the North Downs towards Guildford, put up a spirited resistance. And the enemy found themselves harried by the few surviving British tanks in the area. Fighting was also hard along the A24 towards Dorking.

After three days, the Germans had not made significant progress towards their objectives. They had, however engaged the full available strength of 42nd Division under attack on both its flanks.

On the third day of the attack, with General Willcox already appealing for reinforcements if he was to hold his line, he was attacked in the centre as well. This time the Luftwaffe joined in. After twelve hours of heavy fighting north of Crawley, the Germans broke through in strength. 42nd Division was split into two pieces, both of which began to crumble away under continuing German pressure on the flanks. By the night of Wednesday 16th October, the Germans had pushed up the A23 into Redhill. In the course of that night Reigate fell. The remaining British positions farther east collapsed. By the following morning Dorking was under heavy attack. 42nd Division had effectively ceased to exist. The Germans were advancing fast towards Croydon, less than seven miles away.

As these events unfolded, Montgomery saw in them the beginning of the great offensive which he expected the German High Command to launch against London. The attack towards Croydon was following the most direct and obvious route, and was plainly in strength. There had been no armour committed as yet, but he had received confirmed reports of German tanks moving westward towards Tunbridge Wells. He anticipated that Rommel's tanks would soon be brought into play, taking over from the infantry for a final armoured punch at the heart of the capital. He acted accordingly.

On the morning of Thursday 24th October, the advancing German infantry ran full tilt into Second Armoured Division on the Croydon road, and after a bloody engagement were repulsed with losses. In the afternoon of the same day, British tanks were back in Dorking. 23rd Army Tank Brigade had arrived from the West Country to add to Montgomery's armour. He also now had 3rd Infantry Division available. If necessary, whatever the politics might be, the Australians were directly behind his front. He was confident of holding the Panzers off, when they came.

Montgomery's error was entirely reasonable. He had limited armour available, and had to commit his reserve where he saw the threat developing. Croydon lay on the main road to London, and it must not be allowed to fall. So the British tanks went in. On the same day, Rommel struck. While the German infantry were shoving at the front door, he kicked in the back.

4 Panzer under Steuer hit first, a frontal assault on the well defined perimeter that 45th Division and its associated tank brigade had developed screening Faversham. The British defences held, but once again started to draw in reserves. Particularly since an infantry attack also began to develop on the southern part of 45 Division's front. British resistance was to be worn down by the relentless pressure on two sides. The new British commander in the field called on the recently arrived 1st Infantry Division on his left for help. It was the same day that the British armour was committed in the defence of Croydon.

The new British commander of 45 Division was His Royal Highness the Duke of Windsor. He had taken up his new appointment less than a week before, and he had a 'proper' soldier to keep an eye on him. He had arrived to find a unit still high in morale after its successful defence of the coast at Hastings. But the men were confused and unhappy with the order to retreat thirty miles when still undefeated. Enemy air attack had added to the inevitable confusion of any withdrawal. And this one had involved breaking through enemy positions. Nevertheless, the division and its tank brigade were in good shape.

Their new commander was received with initial disbelief, and not a little doubt. Within a day of his arrival he had acquired a reputation for roughing it which his upbringing would not have suggested, and another reputation for coolness under fire and in the face of the enemy. He insisted on visiting the most advanced positions, and surveying the dispositions of his brigade commanders in detail. He developed a nervous but eager comradeship with his men. Once they had sorted out their own feelings, officers and men rallied to their commander. They were caught up in a feeling of privilege that they had been chosen to be led by a royal general. That the former King had been placed in their care. The Duke lived up to their confidence in him. When the Germans attacked he held a well-prepared and strongly defended line. But he held it with one division and one tank brigade, against four enemy divisions, two of them armoured.

On Friday the Germans broke through at Faversham, and 4 Panzer began its advance along the North Kent coast towards Sittingbourne, which fell during the night. Then on to Chatham and Rochester on Saturday 26th. The British recoiled southwards, still in good order, still holding their perimeter round the headquarters at Maidstone, and resisting the infantry attacks from the south. By that Saturday the fate of 45th Division and its tank brigade was already sealed. For when 4 Panzer broke through the day before, Rommel also launched the entire strength of his own old division, 7 Panzer. He did not strike at the well-defended British front. He attacked north-westward, from Tonbridge, full upon the still scattered forces of the British 1st Infantry Division.

The single infantry division was ill-prepared and disorganized. It had already been called on to reinforce 45th. Without the time to prepare proper defences it was smashed through by the Panzers in the course of a single day. On the Saturday, Rommel's spearhead was in Sevenoaks. By Sunday in Orpington. Montgomery had managed to get some of his army reserve across the Thames to stem the tide a little. But he had no armour with which to face the Panzers. The infantry were told to contest every inch against Rommel's tanks. In effect it was an order to die where they stood. Over the next few days they obeyed to the letter, and the tide was slowed a little in its flood.

On Saturday night the fires of the blazing naval dockyard at Chatham, the stores and warehouses, the building slips and repair yards, a base not threatened since the Dutch Wars of the 17th Century, lit up the skies for miles around. The explosions of the charges set by the Royal Engineers under the Medway bridges rocked the night. The last

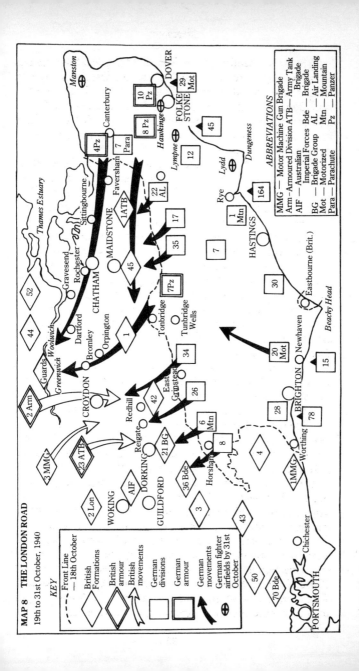

MAP 8   THE LONDON ROAD
19th to 31st October, 1940

KEY

- Front Line — 18th October
- British Formations
- British armour
- British movements
- German divisions
- German armour
- German movements
- German fighter airfields by 31st October

ABBREVIATIONS

MMG — Motor Machine Gun Brigade
Arm — Armoured Division
AIF — Australian Imperial Forces
BG — Brigade Group
Para — Parachute
ATB — Army Tank Brigade
Bde — Brigade
AL — Air Landing
Mtn — Mountain
Mot — Motorized
Pz — Panzer

Thames Estuary

Manston

DOVER
FOLKE STONE
29 Mot
10 Pz
Hawkinge
8 Pz
Canterbury
7 Para
4 Pz
Faversham
22 AL
Lympne
12
45
Dungeness
Sittingbourne
Gravesend
Rochester
CHATHAM
Dartford
MAIDSTONE
1 ATB
17
35
45
7 Pz
Lydd
164
Rye
1 Mtn
HASTINGS
7
Woolwich
Greenwich
Guards
52
44
Bromley
Orpington
CROYDON
1
Tonbridge
Tunbridge Wells
30
Eastbourne (Brit.)
Beachy Head
2 Arm
3 MMG
23 ATB
Redhill
34
East Grinstead
42
26
20 Mot
Newhaven
2 Lon
WOKING
AIF
DORKING
Reigate
21 BG
6 Mtn
8
Horsham
15
BRIGHTON
28
78
Worthing
GUILDFORD
36 Bde
4
1 MMG
3
43
50
70 Bde
Chichester
PORTSMOUTH

British warships that could escape were already steaming out past Sheerness into the North Sea. It was not until the Monday that 4 Panzer forced the crossings of the Medway, against a rearguard defence that had acquired the characteristics of heroism. On the same evening they reached the Thames at Gravesend. The tank crews cheered and celebrated the race won against their comrades of 7 Panzer.

The suburbs of south London were not the best tank country. Rommel encountered a continual guerrilla struggle as he pushed on northward through Bromley and Lewisham. Finally on Tuesday 29th October he reached Greenwich. The General had accompanied the leading tanks himself. In the darkening evening he and his tank commanders looked out across a river that flowed the colour of blood. Across from them Silvertown and the Royal Docks were ablaze from end to end, as the Luftwaffe poured incendiaries into them. Now London was the only target, and at last Goering had his way to the full. The Isle of Dogs too was ablaze, and across from Millwall the flames were met by those of Rotherhithe and the Surrey docks. The twin curtains of fire reached out in a vast arch to join above the dazzling waters, and create a tunnel of flame, a hundred feet high above London's river.

The inferno burnt through all the following day, and the two German divisions watched and waited for it to die. 4th Panzer edged forward through Dartford, and made contact with 7th Panzer at Woolwich. Rommel re-organized the twin spearheads to resume the attack. 4th Panzer would press on along the riverside. 7th would fight its way through the suburbs farther south, aiming to break through into the West End. Far behind them in Kent, 45th Division, and the tanks of 1st Army Tank Brigade that had not been destroyed by the Panzers, remained. They were hopelessly cut off but undefeated, under the command of their general, the Duke of Windsor.

As the fires in London finally began to die down, the Panzers ground forward again. Artillery fire echoed through the narrow streets south of the river. The monstrous snouts of the tanks nudged round ruined houses and along scenes of abandoned desolation. All those who had once dwelt there had fled. For days the bridges over the Thames had been unusable by the British army, as the throng of frightened refugees fought their way across. South London, the City itself, and some of the surrounding boroughs were placed under martial law. Montgomery insisted that the bridges must be closed to civilians, and obtained Churchill's agreement. There were ugly scenes on the roads towards the bridges. English soldiers fought with Englishmen. Someone gave the order to open fire. There were refugees killed. The Luftwaffe, at the urgent request of General Rommel, had been ordered to refrain from bombing the bridges. The charges under them had been placed there by the British.

The German bombers moved their attention forward from the docks and south London. The bombing raids advanced like a creeping barrage ahead of the grinding progress of the Panzers. The City of London itself was the victim of three days of attack by night and day. The Germans relied heavily on incendiaries, and the resulting fires were far beyond the scope of any of the fire-fighting and civil defence services which had never fully recovered from the earlier experiences of firestorm. One after another the institutions of British civilization went down into the ruin. The Old Bailey and the Inns of Court had been burnt. The Bank of England and Somerset House were ruins. King's College and the Guildhall were gone. The National Gallery, empty of its pictures, had been gutted. At the same time the lesser buildings and institutions which enabled the capital to function were being lost. The stations at Charing Cross and Blackfriars had been reduced to ashes. Smithfield Market and Barts Hospital were destroyed. The GPO sorting office at Mount Pleasant was burnt down. Gas and electricity supplies were at best intermittent. South of the River they had almost vanished.

The sinews of national government too were being withered. Whitehall had been the subject of repeated raids, and most of the ministries were already wrecked. In the courtyards of the Foreign Office and the Home Office there were new fires from burning documents. The people of

London knew now, in the course of those few fateful days, that the capital was doomed. Those that stayed put, and suffered the hardships of food shortages, of no light and no power, had unpleasant sights to see and a grim new existence to discover. There were the German tanks overlooking the Royal Dockyard at Woolwich, and grey-clad soldiers on guard outside the Woolwich Hospital. There were German artillery emplacements in the ruins of the Royal Naval College at Greenwich, German officers strutting in and out of their temporary command post that had been Deptford Town Hall, German vehicles parked on Millwall's football ground, the Den. Where the Germans had not yet come there were worse things. As food supplies broke down there was looting and then violence. Once again English soldiers fired on Englishmen, and women. These were the Camberwell Food Riots. The people who could no longer flee attacked each other. Finally they attacked their own country's troops.

On Monday 28th October, Parliament met, defiant of the nearby enemy, in the Palace of Westminster. Across the river Lambeth Palace was on fire, the Archbishop of Canterbury already interned by the Germans. St. Thomas's hospital presented a blackened, ruined front, its roof gone, most of the patients killed in the raid that had gutted it. County Hall was largely undamaged, but manned only by soldiers. Artillery emplacements were at both ends of Westminster Bridge. In New Palace Yard and on Westminster Pier, on the terrace of Parliament itself were machine gun posts.

The business of the House began with what would once have been unthinkable. Now it was put as a government motion by the Home Secretary, Herbert Morrison. He proposed that the debate be broadcast to the nation. The microphones and technicians were ready and waiting outside the chamber. The members were not entirely happy, but in the face of a united Front Bench they agreed. The equipment was brought in, and the Honourable Members debated the conduct of the war. The microphones could just pick up the distant rumble of artillery fire, as the enemy closed in.

Churchill did not speak first. His address came at the end of the day. There had been little criticism of him personally, much criticism of the "conduct of the war". The mood throughout was sombre and muted. The Prime Minister kept to none of the parliamentary conventions. He addressed the people, not the Speaker of the House.

"People of England, I speak to you today from the Mother of Parliaments here in the heart of this beleaguered capital city. It may be I shall never speak in this place again. In the distance we can hear the sounds of fighting in the streets. Above us, the Nazi air force holds sway. Our own gallant fliers, who have fought and fought, are dead now. Their aircraft are destroyed, there are none to replace them. In the field of battle, across the countryside of Kent and Sussex, our soldiers have fought to the bitter end, and fighting, died where they stood. For great heart and human flesh and blood avail nothing against steel and armour plate."

"Even so, we are not defeated. For all its grievous losses, our army remains in being. We fight on. Though we have been forced back by superior numbers and weight of equipment, though our divisions have been destroyed fighting for the counties where the Nazi jackboot now stalks, yet we fight on, here in London itself. Our army is in the field. The spirit of our soldiers is unbroken. Though its losses have been terrible to bear, yet our Navy endures."

"For the Nazis to proceed with the conquest of these islands will yet cost them dear in men and matériel and treasure. For we shall contest every inch of our soil. There will be more divisions and brigades to counter every new attack. No English regiment will surrender to the Nazi hordes, not though they be ten thousand times stronger. Each private soldier will be his own captain in England's war. Each man will be his neighbour's brother, all private quarrels forgotten in the greater cause. No Englishman will withold his strength and courage, his hearth and home, his very soul and life in England's cause."

"Though London fall, yet Londoners, those gallant hearts, will never fail nor fall. They will fight on behind the Nazi lines. The soldiers will hide away their guns and uniforms, but will never forget they are soldiers. Ordinary men and women will take up arms. They will harass the enemy amidst his conquests. They will make every window a sniper's position. They will burn his supplies. They will destroy roads and bridges and railways that he needs for his war effort. They will be the victims of savage reprisals from a brutal and inhuman foe. They will see all they hold dear defiled and ravaged. Their children will be snatched from their arms, their wives and daughters misused, their homes taken away. Yet they will fight. London will become a great running sore amidst the army of the Nazis, costing them tens of thousands of troops to try and hold it down. Our spirit will not be broken. And we will never surrender!"

He said more, and the people heard his message broadcast to them. When he sat down in the House there was some cheering, some shouting. But it was no ovation. The government carried the day, but Churchill, the skilled parliamentarian, knew that something was very wrong. He had misjudged the mood of the House, but far more had he misjudged the mood of the country. Especially of that part of it which suffered most. The spell of his rhetoric had cracked. Faced with the realities of invasion, people found it hollow. It belonged to a different time, a different age, a different world.

It had been a decision of arrogance to have his words broadcast. The people no longer wanted to hear of unending, unendurable sacrifice, of fight to the finish amid only ruin and death. They were pulling in on themselves. Each family was becoming a unit of endurance, determined on its own survival in the general ruin. In their minds, perhaps in the minds of women more than men, was a growing conviction of horrors to come. Evil times to be softened by any means at hand, but not to be courted, not to be exalted into a cause. Those things Churchill had spoken of were already real to the people of Kent, Sussex, Surrey and London, and for many others beside. They already had experienced the suffering and sorrow, the deprivation and

loss of all they held dear. But they were preparing to conserve what little was left to them, in the dreadful ruin of
all their hopes. And the preservation of that little did not
lie in going down amid a welter of blood and destruction.
Its preservation did not lie in guerrilla war, with no end in
sight, while the country bled to death around.

On the day of the broadcasting of parliament and the
Prime Minister's speech, the third operation on King
George VI to remove the splinters from his skull failed.
One fragment had worked in too far. As the breath of life
began to weaken in the stricken King, so the spirit of the
country faltered and began to fade. And as the thrusts of
the enemy spearheads neared its heart in London, so the
signs and omens of death were visible. In the army, morale
had never failed, though now it was become a grim resolve
to do one's duty, fighting on while there was something to
fight for, but not beyond. The army would not fight on
once the war was lost. Britain had fought on the beaches
and in the hedgerows, in the fields, and finally on the streets
of London — and had lost. The instruction to "take one
with you" was losing its point. The boast that "we will
never surrender" rang hollow now.

Also on that day, 28th October, the balance began to
tilt against the valiant defenders of the Maidstone pocket
in Kent. There 45th Division, 1st Army Tank Brigade, and
the shattered remnants of other broken formations, were
fighting on. At first they fought against 35th and 17th
German Divisions. Then against Student's Corps of 7th
Para and 22nd Air Landing Division as well. It was there,
cut off, already discounted by British High Command, that
the last of the old spirit still breathed fire. Against massive
odds, under the leadership of the man that had once been
King, the resistance continued. But on the 28th, the first
unit of General Guderian's Second Panzer Army had completed its landing, and was ready for battle. Guderian
offered it for the destruction of the stubborn British pocket.

When Churchill returned, unhappy, from Parliament,
it was to a pre-arranged meeting with Admiral Pound.
Ostensibly it was a report on the naval situation. The Prime

Minister listened to the news of unsuccessful Luftwaffe attacks on Devonport. He heard of the build-up of Britain's fleet there, *Barham* back from Freetown, *Warspite* from the Mediterranean. He heard of the difficulties of the log-jam of convoys in the Western Approaches, now that the Channel was closed and the port of London lost, but also of the absence of any serious U-boat depradations. Finally, Pound asked once again for permission to use his battleships to try one final time to contest the Channel. Churchill finally agreed to support him, and to push the issue before the Committee of Home Defence the following day.

"With half of London in German hands, Dudley, the loss of another capital ship had suddenly lost its power of fascination for me," he wearily told the admiral. But it was not the naval situation that had so depressed him (for things were not so bad on that front). Not even the battle for London, not even the unsatisfactory reception given to his stirring words. When Pound had gone and he was alone, he picked up again the telegram from his desk. It was from President Rooseveldt, on the subject of Britain's fleet. It was a plea that Germany should not be given Britain's battle fleet in the peace treaty.

"So the Americans are already sure," he said to himself. "They believe that Britain's war is lost."

Chapter 25

CONVALESCING

When he came round, the room seemed all wrong. There was a window behind him that shouldn't be there. The bed was the wrong way round. He couldn't make it out. This wasn't his room. He wasn't at home in the quiet suburbs of Munich on the Dachau Road. He realized hazily that there were other people, sounds of quiet conversation, and many windows, not just one. It seemed strange to be in bed in a room with other people. He moved his head, half sat up, and a bolt of pain shot down his right side. He gasped and lay back, as the broken fragments of memory tumbled through his mind.

Above all, the sight of the plane appeared before his eyes. Perfect in every detail, so that he could see the smoke from the engine and the rivets on the cowling, all enlarged to giant size as it came at him, twin flames marking its roaring cannon. He had been sure that he was going to die in that moment, but he had not been afraid of it. He remembered that distinctly. He lay back, letting the pain ease. So there was the proof that he was a true German soldier. He felt unaccountably pleased with himself, and, forgetful, tried to move his arm. Again the pain made him groan. He may not have been killed, but he had been wounded. His mind leapt in alarm. How badly? Had he lost any limbs? Was there internal damage? Frightful possibilities, familiar as everyday things to any soldier in wartime. He moved his legs a fraction, then his left arm. He turned his head, trying to look at his right arm, which now ached with a steady dull throb.

"Hallo there, mate! Woken up at last?"

He looked round to see the face of the man in the next bed. — Yes of course. In hospital. Till then he had still not realized. The man was eying him with patient concern, half-grinning, cheerful eyes in a typical Prussian bullet head.

"Where is this?" he asked the man, surprised at the dry croak which was his own voice.

"Central Field Hospital, Ninth Army," came the reply.

"Not in Germany?"

The man shook his head sadly, killing the sudden note of expectation in Adolf's voice.

"Sorry, pal, still in England. Brighton. Not a bad place though. Used to be a hospital you see, before the war. So they've got all the gear here."

Adolf lay back, as his senses returned more fully and the sensation of pain also became more apparent. He winced at every movement.

"You copped a good few," the cheery fellow next to him observed, almost as if he was congratulating him. With the returning soreness, it was not how Adolf saw it, not yet.

"I know that very well," he replied, a little irritation coming through in his voice, but regretting it almost at once. The fellow was only trying to be friendly, and was injured himself. Also Adolf wanted to know exactly what he had "copped".

"Do you know how many times I was hit?" he asked.

"Four big 'uns in you, mate. From a 'plane they said. You're lucky to be alive at all, you are. — Nurse coming now, not that she'll be able to tell you much. Dunno why they couldn't get some of our own girls over."

Not really understanding, he glanced along the neat row of beds. The nurse looked like all nurses, starched apron, sober uniform, white cap. A good figure too. Perhaps that was also compulsory for nurses. Her dark hair was cut short and she bore a determined serious look — that and a tray of medicines. She gave a jump as she saw Adolf's eyes on her. She had not been expecting him to be conscious. Putting the tray down, she turned and came over to his bedside. Her cool hand felt his brow, then she took his wrist and checked her watch.

"My pulse is all right nurse, but my arm and side are very painful," he told her in that same croaky voice. He was also going to add that he needed a drink badly, preferably schnapps, but water if it had to be. The nurse frowned and shook her head at him.

"It's no good, mate," announced the man who had spoken to him. "Like I just told you — English. All the nurses here are. You see what I mean. No good at all for us, none of them understand a word. Can't chat them up."

Adolf tried to gather his thoughts. His English had improved talking to Don. — Don! He had forgotten all about him. He didn't even know if he'd tried to make a run for it, or if he had been killed by his own side's fool of a pilot. Seeing the nurse looking at him, he pushed the problem away. Struggled to remember the right words, construct the phrases:—

"My body is painful, nurse, here on the side. Also my arm."

Her eyebrows raised, and a smile almost came to her lips.

"You speak English! Good, then I can tell you what to do. Open your mouth please."

Obediently he suffered the insertion of the thermometer under his tongue.

"Not much above normal," she concluded. "And pulse quite normal. I'll be back with you in a moment."

"You're doing well there," the next man told him. "Wish I could speak the lingo."

When she returned it was to change his dressings. He groaned and winced, though she was in fact very gentle with him.

"How many wounds have I suffered?" he asked. "Please tell me if any wound is serious." He wanted a medical opinion on his case rather than the word of the man in the next bed.

"You were hit four times. Two in the right arm, and two in your side. But I don't think any of them were all that serious." She smiled suddenly. "Try not to look so disappointed at the news!"

He smiled too.

"No. I am happy really. When can I rise?"

"That's for the doctor to say, but not just yet, I'm sure. Aren't you thirsty, or hungry? I'm supposed to bring you some nice hot soup now you've woken up."

He didn't feel all that hungry, surprisingly as he had plainly been unconscious a good while. Nevertheless, after she had helped him drink some water, he let her go and fetch the soup. When it came, hot and thick with meat and vegetables, he found he did want it after all. She fed him, at first with some spillage, and a certain amount of laughter.

"It is the most good, no, the *best* soup, I have tasted," he said, as she wiped off the stains. "What do you name this English soup?"

"Scotch broth," she replied immediately, and laughed again. Then tried to explain the joke to him.

"You do not behave like my enemy," he told her suddenly.

The guarded look that she had when he first saw her returned. For a moment her face was bleak and angry, though her voice betrayed little.

"You are a wounded man like any other. It's my job to care for you whether you are English or German, friend or enemy. Does it make a difference to that?"

Adolf shook his head. He had had this conversation before, with Don. Now he felt impelled to say the same things again to this woman that he had only just met.

"No, perhaps not. But my people are in your country. Does not that make us enemies?"

"Oh, yes," she replied at once, eyes fiery with that same suppressed anger. "We will never forgive you for this. You and your Nazis and your vicious little swine of a Führer. Never!"

As she turned to go, he called after her,

"What is your name?"

For a moment she hesitated, then called back,

"I'm Nurse Johnstone . . . Christine."

He lay back, feeling entirely contented. Even the pain had largely eased.

The doctor did not come to see him till the next day. A German this time and a military man. He worked methodically along the row of beds, finally arrived at Adolf's, studied the chart and nodded approvingly.

"I'm glad to see you wide awake, Private. I cut two bullets out of you, you know."

"Thank you, doctor."

"I might add that you're a very lucky young man. Another six inches for any of those shells and you'd have been downstairs on the slab, make no mistake about that!"

There was something to think about — but not now. The doctor was talking on, as he undid the dressings without much compassion for Adolf's soreness. Adolf concentrated on what he had to say, keen to know more.

"Yes, two of the shots were no problem, straight through the flesh. One here in the arm. Had to do a bit of sorting out of your muscle there, you know. And the other one up here broke your humerus. Clean fracture, I'm pleased to say. Hm, now let's have a look at these two in the side. There's the flesh wound. Quite trivial, no internal organs touched. And there's the one that glanced off your ribs. Only two broken, well, not much more than cracked . . . " He replaced the dressings, then straightened up. "You're a very lucky soldier."

"How long before I'm released, doctor?" Adolf asked.

"Keen to get back already, eh? — Well, I've heard tell of the sort of thing you've been getting up to, so I'm not surprised. But that arm will be in plaster for a good while, and a sling after that. And the ribs will take their time. No, my lad, I think you are going to be out of luck as far as this war is concerned. You'll be sent back to Germany for a period of convalescence — and by then everything will be over."

And then he was gone, busy with the next patient on his rounds.

The days in hospital passed slowly, and Adolf found himself more and more dependent on the company of his nurse, the dark-haired English girl. She spared him what time she could, and they talked and argued, and she teased him. It was his only release from the boredom. He hated being inactive, hated having nothing useful or serious to do, was eager for news. For some reason the German newspapers, now apparently available to the ordinary troops, were excluded from the hospital. As a result rumours were rife. Everyone said the battle for London was on in a big way, and that if the Germans took the city that would be the end of the war. Even Christine believed that. Again Adolf found himself wondering if Don had made it to his own side. Back home to be an engineering apprentice again, or perhaps to fight on as a member of the British army. He recalled those strange days in the cellar almost with fondness, already coloured by nostalgia. It seemed to have happened an immeasurable time ago.

The first visit he had was part of a great occasion for the hospital and its patients. There was the usual fuss before an official visit, the patients shaved and washed, their linen changed. Christine, harassed, had briefly told him why.

"It's a general, the general in charge of one of your armies. Some big brass hat from what everyone says. Come to boost your morale, I expect."

Just before the arrival of the exalted personage they were told officially that it was General Strauss, the Commander of Ninth Army himself. When he came into the ward, at first Adolf wasn't sure which one he was amidst the collection of staff officers passing from bed to bed. He realized at once when they paused at the foot of his own bed. The only one not wearing his cap stepped forward and deliberately offered him his left hand. They shook hands, firmly, left handed. The general nodded smiling his approval.

"Now, you are one of the fellows, I have particularly wanted to meet today. Private Mann, is it not? Formerly of 1st Mountain, but now a part of. . . . well, a part of Ninth Army, eh?"

"Yes, sir, of course."

Adolf was somewhat taken aback by the interest in him.

"That was a fine thing you did there. The sort of thing the army relies on."

Adolf wanted to say that it hadn't been like that. He hadn't had time to think, and if he had, then he would have been too frightened to move. But there was no way he could tell the general that. Even generals needed their illusions.

"It was the only thing there was to be done, sir. . . . " he muttered lamely, thinking it sounded a dull and stupid answer as he said it. He wondered why there should be such curiosity. British planes were being shot down most days, though maybe in not such dramatic circumstances.

"Ach! Do not belittle your courage. Most men would not have done this, and it is a fine thing which will never be taken from you. I have seen the pictures in the papers as well. You will have to become used to being a hero."

"Pictures? In the papers. . . . They don't allow us newspapers in here, sir. To avoid demoralization."

He was unsure whether to be pleased or horrified by what the General was apparently telling him.

"And no-one could have taken a picture, sir," he added.

"What? Not allowed the papers. This is a foolish regulation. I will have changed at once."

"It's not anyone's fault, sir" Adolf interrupted, not wishing to fall out with the hospital authorities. They had been very good to him. The general waved the problem aside.

"I will personally have the Berlin and Munich papers — you are Bavarian, are you not? — sent in, so that you may see yourself. The Führer himself is aware of your heroic action." Adolf realized that the General had raised his voice. This was now a conversation intended for other ears as well as his own. "There is no question of demoralization among our troops. We do not need to hide things away. Not when we are winning. We have them beaten already. It has been hard fought, but victory is in our sights. Most of the men here will not even come out in time to take part in the final great push."

Adolf did not grudge the general using the 'private' chat to give the rest of the ward a boost, though the references to his own "heroism" made him cringe now, and would later, no doubt, earn him sly comments and the usual jokes. He still wanted to know how there could be a photograph, though.

"Sir, about the photo. . . . ?"

The general had already turned to move on.

"Taken by the sergeant of the guard, through the guard-house window," interrupted a staff major, distinctly fussily. "— There is one other matter, concerning this man, sir," he added to the general.

"Oh yes", said Strauss. "I made a mistake when I met you, Mann. I called you private. Congratulations on your promotion, Corporal!"

Adolf let his mouth hang open, and only just managed to stutter, "Thank you, sir," as general and entourage swept on. Then he lay back, and despite the nonsense about being a hero felt very satisfied. He had always wanted promotion, always wanted to work his way up. He was well aware that he would rather be a corporal than a hero any day. And this was a good way to get promoted, better than being rewarded for pushing a pen. "Just let one of those clever blighters in here make a joke about heroes, and I'll have him on a charge, sooner than look at him," he thought. He felt like laughing aloud.

When Christine came round to change the dressing and give him an injection (an operation which reduced any feelings of heroism drastically) she was not smiling.

"I've been told what you did. Everyone has. They say you're a hero. — Come on now, turn over, please, and let's not have any fuss this time."

"I don't feel like a hero . . . Ow!" He rolled back, grimacing after the injection. "Is something the matter?"

"You killed one of my people. The pilot of that plane was an Englishman. You didn't tell me before."

Adolf nodded. He spoke slowly, making sure he said
what he wanted, hampered by the foreign language.

"That is what they mean by being a hero in war, you
know." He kept his eyes fixed on hers. "It means killing
people you never knew, and who have not harmed you,
because they are your enemies. The pilot was not the only
one. There was another man also. Both times, by a chance,
I was the lucky one, if you can say lucky. Both times I
killed, and I was not killed. It may have been the other
way."

She returned his steady glance.

"I'm sorry I was short with you. . . . I've got a minute.
You'd better tell me the story. — Not about this other
time, not now at any rate. Just the bit they're all talking
about."

Rather grudgingly Adolf told her. At the end she stood
up and collected the tray of medicines and dishes and syr-
inges.

"Yes, I think you were rather brave, perhaps very
brave," she said. "— But don't get big-headed about it,
just 'cause you're a corporal now. And don't boss the other
patients about."

The next day brought him two more visitors, Rudi and
Hans, with a bundle of German newspapers, and the gossip
of half the German army, gleaned from continuing cushy
numbers in Corps or Army H.Q. in Brighton. The papers,
as Hans explained when he handed them over, were not
the lads' idea. They had been waiting for delivery to the
new corporal in the hospital lobby. Apparently compli-
ments of some general or other, or possibly from the Führer
himself. Hans wasn't sure what circles his old friend was
now moving in. Rudi laughed uproariously at Hans' heavy
repartee, and was reprimanded by a doctor. Adolf was so
glad to see them both that he willingly forgave them the
jokes at his expense.

He looked through the national papers, and saw the
accounts of his shooting down of the British plane (wrongly
described as a Spitfire of course; to those at home all British
fighter aircraft were Spitfires). They were only short col-

umns, but the *Völkischer Beobachter* had included it in a
column labelled "Feats of the National Socialist Spirit",
and featured the photograph very large next to it. He
squirmed a little. Anyone could see why the photo had
achieved such prominence. The plane and the machine gun
post with its solitary figure shewed up to excellent effect.
He might have been consoled by the fact that his face was
not visible, had they not found a photograph of him —
presumably from his army records — to go with it.

"It makes me look like a baboon," he groaned, slapping
the paper.

"Good likeness, I reckon," remarked Hans.

"A bit unfair to the baboon though," Rudi added.

Adolf tried to swat him with the paper.

"Careful, Rudi, my lad," warned Hans. "The corporal
will have you doubling round the square in no time."

"You can cut that out too," grumbled Adolf. "Well, I
suppose record card photos all look like that. Pity they
didn't keep it where it belongs, in a filing cabinet."

"I don't think this concern about your looks shows
much National Socialist spirit," remarked Rudi, safely out
of range.

"I give up!" muttered Adolf, and turned back to the
papers, as his friends chattered on. He glanced idly over
the headlines and the pictures. He would have plenty of
time to read the stories later on.

"Look at that one of London on fire!" Rudi leaned over
to point at the double page spread in *Das Reich*, a spectacular aerial photograph. There were others, pictures labelled
"landmarks of England", famous buildings with German
troops outside them, or in ruins. Hans made a point of
showing him the famous one of Canterbury cathedral with
the Swastika on it.

"They say we'll soon be flying the flag from their Parliament building," said Rudi.

"Then you two lazy lumps will be home before me,"
complained Adolf.

He glanced at the map in the *Frankfurter Zeitung*, not
one of the 'government' papers usually. It showed the

campaign in detail, southern England criss-crossed with arrows, little swastika signs beside fallen towns. British troops cut off somewhere in Kent under attack. And the arrows going on right into the heart of London.

Chapter 26

OUT OF THE FRYING PAN

After leaving the enigmatic Captain Sanders, of the stay-behind unit, Don followed the route he had memorized from the map. For the most part it seemed to be through little-frequented country, based on the line of a country road. It provided plenty of woodland cover if needed. Don was surprised at so much forest this close to London, but glad of its protection. He had two railway lines to cross, both empty of traffic, and one village centre to skirt. It seemed easy going compared with his earlier journeyings, but they had been a headlong flight across unknown country. Now he knew where he was heading, and it speeded his progress. By dawn he was over the river. For once he knew its name — the Beult. And he had avoided the hamlet of Yalding. According to what he had been told he should now be inside the British perimeter.

In the early light he saw the road coming in from the east towards its junction with his own route. It was visible from a distance, fortunately. For on it were the unmistakable shapes of tanks, the ugly muzzles of their guns raised. He watched from his vantage point on a hillside, ready to retreat into the cover if need be. There was a column of twelve of them, and as the light broadened any doubts in his mind were dispelled. They were German. A convoy of lorries arrived and pulled up alongside, completely blocking the road. The oil drums they carried were being unloaded.

Heavy and awkward work. The shouts and curses of the soldiers drifted up to him. There was plainly no way forward there. He called the map to mind again, visualising the position of the town. It would be best to edge to the right where woods had been shown. If he was to get round the tanks.

And so he disappeared into the wood, welcomingly thick. (Much of his cover lately had only been orchard or plantation.) Also the trees ran down to the edge of the road he wanted to cross. Several times he came to the edge to reconnoitre. In each case there was military traffic visible, and there were German soldiers as well, in larger numbers than he had seen before. The presence of the infantry was disconcerting. They presented a far greater danger to a fleeing man than tanks or supply convoys. In the course of the morning he managed to get over another main road, going into Maidstone, he knew it must be. But towards the town there was once again too much traffic on it. A sense of unease about the situation grew in him.

For the first time for a long time he could hear firing, off to his left, as well as ahead. But ahead was also reasonable cover. More orchards, a stretch of parkland, some thicker woods. His crablike progress continued, the way north towards his goal in Maidstone always barred by that same road which had now become an enemy thoroughfare. Only after he had waited for over an hour to get across another of the radial routes into the town, detouring to avoid a more sizeable village in the process, was he able to swing north. For a long time he had been moving along the flank of an extended hillside ridge. Now, as the cover grew momentarily less, he was able to look towards the line of woods on the hilltop. There was a road with soldiers on it. Grey shapes, so Germans. Flashes of momentary light as they fired. For a moment it did not register. Then the full realization came. This must be the front line.

He crouched beside the hedgerow and watched and listened, the excitement rising in him so that his mouth was dry and his legs shook. The loud crackle of machine gun fire broke out in long bursts below. From the woodland beyond, on the further slope, he recognized answering rifle fire. Heavier guns, several of them, were in operation away to his left. Towards the town, that would be. This was the moment it had all been for. But what to do?

He hadn't envisaged what a front line really might be. He had been near the fighting before, that time on the Sussex Downs. So he knew it would not be trenches and no-man's land, like everyone's picture of the Great War. But there would be German positions, and he would have to get past them. Spy it out by day, move by night, he decided. Somehow he had always envisaged making his final run by night. To his surprise he was hardly afraid at all, as if the risks had become an acceptable, even a natural, thing.

There was another road away to the right, leading down into the valley, clear of any troops. More fruit trees provided the cover, and there was a ruined house. He decided to make use of this road to get nearer, to make the distance he would finally have to run through the darkness as short as possible. No sooner was he on the road, than he realized there were troops in the ruined house. They had to be Germans. He struck on into the trees, not pausing, though he was sure they had not seen him. The ground was falling steeply now, as he came out to the edge of a ploughed field. The next cover was beyond. He would have to take the risk of a run. He could feel the excitement mounting, almost impelling him to risks.

He took a step or two up out of the gully beside his last hiding place, cautious, then moving fast. He must have walked a couple of dozen yards before the cry from behind him spun him round like the impact of a bullet. Back on the edge of the fruit trees, about a hundred yards away he saw a man standing up in a sort of dug-out or burrow. Metal glinted behind him. After the first second of unrecognition, he knew what it was. A heavy gun under netting — and the round steel hat of the soldier, and the grey uniform.

Don began to run. He ran as he had never run before. There came a second shout, then more distantly a stream of German, and then the first shot. He had no idea if it was close, where it went. Two more followed. He was in a ploughed field, striking across the line of the furrows. He ran clumsily, stumbling repeatedly, just managing to stay upright. It was uphill, and only now did he realize just how tired his legs were. He forced them to work faster, to carry him on through the clogging soil.

Louder reports sounded behind him. A compartment of his mind was telling him that this was rifle fire. The first shots had been a pistol. He dared to look back, over his left shoulder, where the rifles were. There were running men. A dozen, probably more. A German patrol. They were after him. The dread of being caught again after all this time filled him with a physical sickness. He tried to go even faster. The trees were near now, looming up before him, and the slope was easing too. Shots rang out. — Ahead! From the wood. But he couldn't stop. He plunged into the shade of the branches, convinced that he was running into the waiting arms of other Germans.

"Get down, mate! Get your bloody head down!"

He felt himself seized and dragged to the ground. Bullets whined above him, and cracked against the bark of trees. From nearby a machine gun opened up. The voice in his head was saying, "They're returning the enemy fire." And the man that had spoken — it had been English!

"Is this British territory? Have I crossed the lines?"

The words stumbled out. He turned to look at the face of the soldier lying on the earth next to him. The familiar khaki, the shallow British tin hat, like a big soup plate, over a broad tanned face.

"Come on, matey. Our first job is to crawl back from this little lot. And if this ain't British lines as you calls it, then I'm in the wrong bleeding army."

They crawled back some distance through the wet humus, then ran, still crouching, though the firing behind them had died away. In a clearing Don found himself telling his story, or some of it, to a sergeant.

"Can you fire a gun then, laddie?" the sergeant asked, his voice with the Scots burr of the borders.

Don nodded.

"Aye, well you'll need to. For you've jumped out of the frying pan straight into the hottest part of the fire." He turned to the soldier. "Better take him up to the C.O. It will be a good story to cheer a cold night for him, and the man will be wanting to hear it."

Don followed again, obediently, but increasingly bewildered. He had found the British army, but nothing seemed to be quite right. One thing *was* clear — he had landed smack in the middle of the fighting. They arrived at a collection of khaki and camouflage tents, a few lorries, small piles of stores.

"There you are, mate. Divisional Headquarters, 45th Infantry Division of the British Army."

Don stood, not sure whether to be even more puzzled, or to assume he was being ribbed in the normal way. The soldier had entered an unprepossessing tent, unguarded by anyone. He emerged after a few moments.

"Commanding officer will be out to see you, mate."

Then he hurried away, back towards the renewed shooting.

Now Don knew for sure he was having his leg pulled. He might not be a professional soldier, but he had seen a divisional headquarters, with Captain Sawyer, back in Chichester. This looked like the forward post of a company, perhaps just a platoon. It would be a captain at best, more likely a lieutenant in charge here. He realized with a guilty jump that the officer had emerged. He was a slightly built man, not tall and now stooping a little. His face was pale, and his short fair hair was plastered across his forehead by rain or sweat. His features were finely cut. It was a face Don knew. His uniform bore the usual badges of rank. Don was no expert, but as far as he was concerned the red tabs did mean a general. He looked into the clear eyes of the man again, and remembered where he had seen the face before.

"Good God. . . . " The words were spoken involuntarily. The general's face twisted into a half smile, used to such moments.

"To save time, private, I will tell you that I am Major

General the Duke of Windsor. Yes I was King Edward VIII. You call me 'Sir' or 'General' as the other men do, and please do not spend the next ten minutes in embarrassed silence. — Sit down!"

He pointed to a tree stump, on which Don sat at once. The General pulled a battered canvas chair out of his tent and also sat down. For the first time Don noticed the crackle of a wireless set from one of the other tents. Saw another officer sitting at a makeshift desk inside a third. Two soldiers chatting in muted tones as they changed a tyre on one of the trucks. Their presence almost seemed to add to the unreality of the scene. He had never thought in all those days of flight what he might find once he had made it back safe. He had never dared to set his sights on any target beyond that of simply making it. Now the strangeness of events after so close a brush with capture — or death — left him dazed.

"Right! I'm told you have an interesting tale to relate. Since we have nothing to do here except wait for the inevitable, I'd like to hear it."

Yet again Don recited the sequence of events that had brought him there, wherever 'there' might be. The general listened intently, asked questions once or twice, and Don's confidence grew. At the end, the general offered a wintry smile.

"Well, well! It would seem that you have had a more interesting war than most Home Guardsmen. — I would imagine they will want to decorate or promote you."

Don gaped again, and tried to think of something appropriate, suitably deprecating, to say, though he didn't know what. He was not accustomed to talking to generals, not to mention ex-Kings, and did not find the experience agreeable. The general solved the problem, cutting him off before he could get a word out.

"No, I know you had no such thing in mind. You were acting as seemed best to you. And very right and proper too. . . . But I must tell you something now. You are talking to a general because I am one of the *two* surviving officers here. This is Divisional Headquarters of 45th Infantry Division and 1st Army Tank Brigade. It is all that is left of the division. About two hundred men in all here. Another few hundred cut off from us now in Abbey Wood. They may still have a tank or two. There may be a hundred left fighting in the town, but isolated, just snipers. . . . "

Don realized that he was talking because he had to. Don was the first person to arrive from outside. Therefore he was the one to hear the account of the disaster from this man who had been at the heart of it, and had suffered most cruelly from it.

"We are cut off, in a wood in Kent, ironically named King's Wood. It is one of the last of our remaining pockets. They are chopping us up, bit by bit. Tomorrow maybe, or in a day or so — then it will be our turn. We will be killed or captured, like all the rest. — I'm so sorry, my boy. . . . " Don could hear the catch in his voice and did not look up, not wishing to embarrass him, not wishing to see. He had risen, taken a step or two, placed his hand on Don's shoulder. "So sorry you came so far for this," he murmured.

Don also stood, still searching for the right words, trying to speak formally, with propriety, and yet say what he felt.

"It's a privilege to fight beside you, Sir. . . . "

It sounded lame enough, but he meant it. He swayed on his feet, as the tension of his long flight ebbed, and left him weak and helpless. He was given a mattress, and slept, privileged indeed, in the back of a lorry. He slept untroubled by the stray small arms fire and the more distant artillery as it pounded another remnant of 45th Division into final submission.

In the morning he was given breakfast and a rifle, and joined the line of men in their position along the forest edge. He had slept the best part of the afternoon and all night, and felt better than he had for a good while. There was no feeling of let-down. No thought that it had all been wasted. Only a strange and indefinable exhilaration. The general — the Duke of Windsor — joined them too, lying on the ground, rifle in hand like a common soldier. Don had heard the muttered protests of the sergeant, and the reply: —

"There's no point pretending I'm a general with a division to command now, Sergeant. None of us is more use than any other here and now. All ranks are levelled."

The attack began on another sector of the wood's perimeter. They heard the firing, and at regular intervals the explosion of shells, as the artillery opened its barrage. Then there were also running men, Germans racing across ploughed fields away to the right of where Don lay. Other fields just like that he had run so hard across to where he now awaited his enemies. The attacking infantry were right at the edge of range, and there was no point in opening fire on them. But they saw Germans fall and the attack falter. Then the tanks came up, only half a dozen. Just out of their reach to offer any help, their comrades were overwhelmed by the German attack.

"Moving forward in front of us, sir."

They had been waiting at the ready for over three hours. Now it was their turn. Elsewhere there was some fighting still within the wood. Other than that, they knew they were the last. Don was close to the sergeant, and heard him speak in clear measured tones, unworried. His eyes fixed on the grey-clad shapes rising out of the ditches and hedgerows, he also heard the general's answer: —

"Give the order to open fire only when they're in good range. No wasting ammunition now."

"It doesn't matter any more. Waste it! Shoot it off at them . . . " Don heard his mind babble on volubly, anything but concentrate on the agonizing wait as the attackers came on.

"Fire!" The sudden cry. The ragged volley rang out. It was the first time Don had ever shot at a person. The figure he had aimed at fell. Perhaps it wasn't his bullet that did it. Perhaps one of the others had picked the same target. Perhaps he had made a mistake, it was a different man who had fallen, perhaps. . . . The thoughts clogged his mind, and beneath them all, he was sure that he had just killed a man. Killed, like his friends had been killed on the station, a world away. The next two shots had already been fired, his hand and eye operating automatically. He no longer knew if he was hitting any of the enemy. He was aware of the splatter of bullets on the tree bark above, aware of the man next to him, stood up clutching at his throat, with a hand that oozed blood from round its white, long fingers, aware of the Germans almost at them, machine guns, and shellfire, a tank coming out of spreading smoke in the distance.

"Come on! Back!"

Someone almost dragged him up. He turned and ran with the others. Very few, it seemed. They passed a second thin line of British soldiers, kneeling or crouched behind trees, or lying in the bracken. Then they were at the head-quarters — a dozen men or so.

"Right, all of you, listen!" The sergeant was speaking quickly, but with that same precise clarity. "I want all insignia of rank, unit, the lot, *off* those uniforms. Rip 'em off now! Don't be shy! That goes for you too, if you please, General, sir!"

Everyone obeyed, hurried fingers fumbling, general included. The sergeant was pacing, eying the men, apprais-ing them for something. There was a renewed volley behind them, in the trees now. The screams of the dying rose suddenly shrill for a moment in the silence that followed. There there was the shooting again, more sporadic.

"Get in a line!" The sergeant ordered, and they obeyed. Another swift glance. "Right! It'll have to be you, laddie." He pointed at Don. "You're the only one with the right build. I would like you, General, to change uniforms with this man." He had turned to the general now, explaining the plan. "They'll still recognize the officer's uniform, you see, sir. So this might throw them off the scent."

The Duke shrugged.

"Very well, Sergeant Steel."

"The rest of you, get into position round the trucks!" The sergeant was already dealing with the next military matter, clearly in command now, making his last dispo-sitions. "We'll give the bastards one last going over!" he told them, and they grinned and cheered, and let the knowledge that they were about to be taken into a hopeless captivity, or killed, or maimed, have no hold on them in their last fight.

Don and the General, the Duke, looked at each other, and both began to laugh. They stripped still laughing, and donned each other's uniform. The men shouted their jests, caught up in the bizarre humour of it. At the end the Duke saluted Don.

"Any orders, General?" he asked.

"With respect, sir, get your bloody head down," yelled Sergeant Steel, as a bullet whanged into a tree above them.

The final fight did not last long. The Germans came from the sides as well, and there were too many of them. Don saw men fighting hand to hand, tried to struggle to his feet himself to use his bayonet, and was kicked flat by a heavy boot. Something hard and round was being pressed into the small of his back. There were men with their hands up now. He saw the Duke among them. He let go of the rifle, a prisoner again.

Chapter 27

PLAYING POLITICS

The War Cabinet met on the last day of October. It was two days since Churchill had allowed Parliament to be broadcast, and delivered his "No Surrender" speech to the nation. Since then the Prime Minister's political position had been steadily crumbling, eroded by forces at work both within and without. Militarily, the battle for London still hung in the balance. General Montgomery had slowed the advance of the Panzers to a crawl, redeploying what little armour he had to meet the new threat, and letting the battle suck in all of his remaining reserves. The Committee of Home Defence had acceded to his demands for the provision of a new reserve. Churchill had complained that it left no possibility of defence in depth in the Midlands, the West or East Anglia, but had bowed to the military necessity. Surviving units could always withdraw to those areas. Montgomery and the service chiefs had a different perspective. They regarded the battle for London as the last battle, from which there could be no withdrawal or regrouping. They also still believed it was a battle that could be fought to a stalemate. Or, just possibly, won. On the field of politics, a different battle was being fought.

Before the meeting of the War Cabinet there was another, private meeting. It was attended by Ernest Bevin, Arthur Greenwood, and Clement Attlee, the three Labour leaders in the War Cabinet; and by Lord Halifax, Foreign

Secretary and Leader of the House of Lords. Halifax was an arch-Conservative in the old style. The Chamberlain style. The animosity between Prime Minister and Foreign Secretary had not abated since that earlier meeting of the Cabinet when Churchill had called Halifax traitor to his face. Churchill had let it be known that he wanted Halifax replaced by Eden. He had suggested that he be sent off to the United States as ambassador. In the circumstances not so much a demotion as a humiliation. Halifax, on the other hand, had let it be known that the Prime Minister's powers must be curbed, before his excesses destroyed the country.

In both Conservative and Labour parties there was a growing disquiet at the conduct of the war by Churchill and the generals. The mood of high optimism that Churchill had tapped earlier in the year, a few short months before, had been ground down by the attrition of events. It had never been a logical mood, based, as it was, on a series of unprecedented disasters, culminating in the precipitate flight of the British army from the continent at Dunkirk. In Churchill the British people had found a great war leader in their hour of need, but his strategies had been insufficient to prevent the German victories continuing.

Had the British side had more simple luck, had the German side made one or two more strategic blunders, then things might well have gone very differently. But once the Luftwaffe had won the air war, it had always been hard to see how, ultimately, the Germans could fail. Churchill's rhetoric had helped to keep the people going, but it could not win battles. The army Britain had rescued from Dunkirk minus its equipment was still, at the end of September, ill-equipped and badly organized. Its leadership had seen the German application of the Blitzkrieg, but had failed to apply those lessons — or had lacked the material to apply them. The imaginative use of armour required thought patterns not common in the middle and upper echelons of the British army. It was not merely the lack of tank generals. The army commander now directing the defence of London was apparently such a general. But Britain had possessed only two full armoured divisions. Possibly the equivalent of another one and a half when the separate tank brigades were taken into account. Blitzkrieg required the concentration of armour in strength against enemy weak points: the concentration was never there.

Britain also lacked another essential to be able to use German tactics against Germany. The strategic initiative. Germany had held the political initiative since 1936. Throughout the war the Germans had also held the military initiative. In the course of *Operation Sea Lion* this had been most tellingly true. All the British had been able to do was react to Germany's actions, presenting what was largely a linear defence to the enemy's attacks. General Brooke had made his effort to seize the initiative back. In the two halves of *Operation Mangle* he had come near to doing so. It had all the seeds of success, but miscalculation of enemy strength, misjudgement in the deployment of forces, and ultimately failure of will had destroyed much of its logic. Even so, the half of the operation which was launched, *Lemon Squeezer*, came within an ace of victory.

On the day, it had all come down to the preparedness of one German tank general to use his armour like cavalry. To ignore the frontiers of division, corps, even army. To fight the enemy wherever he found them. To obey Napoleon's dictum and march to the sound of the guns. In this way Rommel's Panzers had ranged as freely across the hills and plains of southern England as the Mongol cavalry across the plains of Europe and Asia. The result was that he had always had surprise on his side. He had always been ready for combat when his enemies were not. And he usually had superiority in numbers. Once Brooke's offensive had been defeated, Britain had no option but to fall back onto a linear defence, bringing more and more divisions of a dwindling army into a line that receded ever nearer to the capital.

The politicians could see what was happening. Churchill's offer of war to the end, on beyond London, through the Midlands, into the hills of the North, Scotland and Wales, had ceased to be acceptable to many of them. They questioned Brooke's generalship, because in effect he had lost his battle. They questioned Churchill's generalship because, in the last analysis, he was no general. Confidence in the army itself had also been terribly shaken. The old talk of Brass Hats who cared nothing for the lives of their men, of Colonel Blimps interested only in regulations and procedures, was current again. For the most part it was unjustified, as most of it had been in the earlier war.

The British generals — and admirals and air marshals — were doing what they could in 1940 with armed forces broken by the politicians of the 1920's and 1930's. It was less than reasonable for the military men, and particularly for Churchill, to be held responsible for the failures, the weaknesses and the treasons of the Conservative appeasers, and Labour's disarmers. The policies of those years had seemed to be discredited when Churchill took office, but they had never sunk far beneath the surface. Now that defiance had failed, war to the knife, even against the Nazis, was not going to be acceptable to the politicians. The men of Munich, and the men of Geneva, were about to take on a new lease of life.

"Prime Minister, I think that we should begin by listening to what the Foreign Secretary has to say." Attlee began the meeting. He did not give Churchill the opportunity, but jumped in quick in a manner entirely uncharacteristic of the reticent Labour leader. "I feel he has something important to tell us. Something concerning the whole course of the war . . . " He began to flounder, as if needing to justify himself. Churchill gave him a quizzical look, suppressing his annoyance. He was nobody's fool, and knew how weak his own position was. He knew he had misjudged the mood of the House the other day. The information coming in that he had misjudged the mood of the people was less palatable, and he still refused to believe it. He shrugged, and turned to the Foreign Secretary with a smile on his lips, and his distaste for the man openly to be read in his eyes.

"Well, Halifax, what is this mystery you have to unfold for us?"

"Prime Minister, gentlemen," Halifax spoke formally, and he had stood up, never the custom in the Cabinet, "I have to read to you two telegrams. The first is from the President of the United States."

Churchill stiffened. His jaw set in the familiar line, and now his eyes glinted with real anger. But he said nothing as Halifax read.

"To the Prime Minister of Great Britain, and the Ministers of His Majesty's Government, from the President of the United States of America: —

'In your hour of trial my thoughts are with the entire British people. Great Britain has fought alone and valiantly against overwhelming odds. The goodwill of the whole American people is with her. I call upon you to consider using that goodwill.'

'The time is past when America can aid Britain with matériel and the supplies of war. The time has come when America can be of inestimable service to Britain by the exercise of moral suasion and of diplomacy.'

'The threat of American power inherent in American displeasure is not lost on Herr Hitler. I am prepared to make it clear to the German President and Chancellor that the United States will not tolerate the enslavement of Great Britain or the possession by Germany of Great Britain's fleet and the British Empire.'

'Accordingly I am sending this message to you, and another, different, message to Herr Hitler. I implore you, gentlemen, to take up this, my offer of mediation, while the influence and power of the U.S.A. may still be brought to bear upon the survival of Great Britain.'

'Signed Franklin Delano Rooseveldt, the White House, Washington."

Halifax sat down abruptly.

"Why did he not make this communication to me directly?" growled Churchill.

He was used to conducting his increasingly delicate diplomacy with the American president man to man. He had not told any of them about the earlier telegram concerning the disposal of the fleet. He had replied to it personally, hedging his bets, hinting at an outcome that might frighten the Americans into real support. Now he wondered if he had misjudged another situation. This was not the response he had wanted or expected.

"He has sent it to all of us because it is a message to all of us, Winston," Attlee answered his question. "It naturally came by way of the Foreign Office."

Now it was Churchill's turn to stand up, his fists clenched, knuckles white on the table.

"Because it is a message telling us to surrender. Because he knows I will not countenance it. Because he knows that if we fight on, sooner or later he will have to join us!"

"Winston, I don't think there is any 'later'," said Kingsley Wood, the Chancellor.

"And the Americans are not going to join the war on our side with the German army in London," said Halifax. He also stood up again, facing Churchill across the table. "*You* will not countenance. . . . Just who do you think you are, Winston? This is not a matter for *you* to decide. It is for us, and for parliament, and if necessary for the people."

The debate was more bitter than any before. Churchill felt betrayed by Rooseveldt, and by his own cabinet. When he was told of the meeting between the Labour leaders and Halifax, he told them how he regarded such collusion. He still had some measure of support from Wood, Sir John Anderson, and Beaverbrook. They too disliked Halifax's approach to the other party. But they would not stand with him in his wholehearted opposition to any talks. Anderson suggested at least listening to the Germans' response to the American offer. Wood suggested Britain should put forward her own terms. Churchill saw that, in the end, they were nearly all prepared for some sort of compromise.

Also, Halifax had a second offer of mediation to put on the table. King Gustav of Sweden had written both to Adolf Hitler and to King George VI — the letter now placed before the Cabinet. The Swedes called on both sides to proclaim an armistice and to meet in Stockholm to arrange a permanent peace and European settlement. It was less significant than the American approach, but another straw in the wind. The members of the Cabinet wanted negotiations. Many of the people would agree with them. To

Churchill merely to talk with Hitler was an impossibility. He saw negotiation and surrender as much the same thing. When he was outvoted he repeatedly offered his resignation. That also was unacceptable. For him to go now would be ruinous to British morale. His presence was necessary, and that was his only bargaining counter. He must be granted something towards his position.

All could agree with him that while London stood, England stood. It was also apparent that England still existed even if the capital were to fall. There would still be something to negotiate for and negotiate with. It was accepted that all available troops would be committed to the defence of the capital, as Montgomery had demanded and the Committee of Home Defence agreed. And there would be no withholding of the remaining fighter aircraft of the R.A.F., even if it meant their final immolation. The bombers too would be sent unescorted over the battlefield and the Channel, in a last attempt against the crossings.

Admiral Pound's wish to try conclusions for the last time with his remaining battleships of the Home Fleet was to be granted as well. In the past it had been Churchill who had refused this. Now he was converted. Halifax questioned the decision. He saw the fleet as a weight in the balance at the peace conference. Churchill had his way. He also retained direction of the war via the Committee of Home Defence. And it would be Churchill that replied to Rooseveldt, though the Cabinet insisted on the inclusion of certain specifics. For Britain was — cautiously and tentatively — to accept the American offer of mediation. A similar answer was to be given to the Swedes.

By the time the Prime Minister saw his colleagues to the door he had recovered something of his composure. Still in the Cabinet Room, he sat and composed a short telegram, which he sent to Rooseveldt at once:—

"Mr President, be assured that Britain fights on. Britain still needs all the help the United States can give her in real and material terms. As you must know, we are near to the limit of our resources, and in such straits we may not reject any offer of help or mediation. Nor would we ever reject the mediation of that other free people, the people of the United States of America."

"At the moment, Mr President, the frontier of the U.S.A. is no longer on the Channel. It is on the Thames. I pray you to use all your strength, both in word and deed, to ensure that Great Britain and her Empire are not permitted to go down, and to ensure that in her ruin, the frontier of the United States be not withdrawn to the very Atlantic coasts of continental America."

★　★　★

In Berlin, Hitler had received a different telegram from Rooseveldt. It was carefully worded to avoid giving direct offence to the Führer. The Americans even referred to him as "Führer" in their telegram. For Rooseveldt was well aware of Hitler's moods and tantrums. Nevertheless, the underlying threat was there, veiled in diplomatic language, but not to be mistaken. Ribbentrop, the Foreign Minister, who received the telegram, certainly understood its import:—

"The United States has no desire to become involved in European wars or to interfere in the affairs of soverign states. At the same time, the government of the U.S.A. has a duty to defend its own people against any possibility of attack or aggression. To carry out this duty, this administration is determined to ensure that the countries of Western Europe, and in particular of the Atlantic seaboard, are preserved in their independence and to prevent the subjugation of the colonial empires of those states by any single great power."

"We are well aware of the success of Germany's arms, and we acknowledge the existence of many past grievances and injustices done to Germany. It is for this reason that the United States of America makes this appeal to Germany. We seek to persuade the Reich government that the creation of new injustices *by* Germany against her present enemies can only lead to yet a third great war, into which the United States will inevitably be drawn on the side of Germany's opponents. Now is not the time for a new *Diktat*, given

383

in the spirit of revenge, but rather for magnanimity in victory."

"It is for these reasons, and for the overriding reason of ending this conflict and sparing innocent lives, that the United States government now offers its services as mediator between the warring nations. As mediator, the U.S.A. can offer the benefits of her commercial and industrial strength equally to all the war-damaged nations of Europe. With the U.S.A. as a combatant in a resumed and more bitter war, that same commercial and industrial strength, converted into overwhelming military might, could only lead to the ultimate subjugation of the entire European Continent to American power. We wish neither to exercise such power, nor to enter into such a war. Our only desire is to mediate between the warring nations to ensure that a strong, free and independent Europe continues to play its rightful part in the affairs of the world."

It was a long message, and von Ribbentrop delivered it to Hitler with some trepidation. He did not want his Führer to descend into a rage and declare war on the U.S.A. The aristocratic foreign minister was also well aware that the Austrian corporal did not like him. Hitler might well decide that Ribbentrop was to blame for the news from America. Perhaps because he was the aristocrat, and Hitler the commoner, Ribbentrop had entirely misjudged his Führer.

Through the early stages of the invasion Hitler had been afflicted by constant jitters and doubts. His lack of confidence in his own generals had led to his constant interference, and increasingly to his personal direction of the campaign. Even so, he did not trust himself entirely. His intervention in the Panzers' drive to the coast in France had not been helpful. By contrast his "stand and die" decree in response to the only British counter-attack, and his decision to send over the Panzer divisions early had together been deciding factors in Germany's victory in England. Now, with those Panzers fighting their way through the sprawl of south London, Hitler found the ultimate victory in his grasp. He did not know quite how to handle it.

He had long regarded the English with a provincial mid-European awe. They represented what he was not, and what (at least as he saw it) Germany was not. They were the world's aristocrats, the effortless rulers of empire, naturally and easily superior. The Germans by contrast were the crude commercial parvenus. For all their successes, they were always a little out of place at the top table, or in the country house or the garden party. Now the Panzers were at the garden party, and Hitler would soon be sitting at the head of the table. The temptation to smash it all up was submerged in the desire to be part of it.

Hitler did not, deep down, want to destroy Britain. He had never wanted to invade. Now he had invaded, and was on the point of victory, he still wanted his opponents to come to terms. He wanted a compromise whereby the arrogant, lordly British would welcome the thrusting, vigorous Germans as equals. They had lost. Let them now be humiliated by Germany's magnanimity. Then, suitably chastened, let them line up alongside Germany in the National Socialist Crusade against Bolshevism and international Jewry. Germany would make a resurrected Britain great again, as a new (subordinate) partner in a bigger and better Axis.

Ribbentrop was subjected to two hours of these aspirations. Nevertheless, it all came as a relief to him. All except the talk of the coming war with Russia, currently Germany's friend and ally. Hitler authorized his foreign minister to respond in favourable and measured terms to Rooseveldt's approach. To make it clear that Germany did not wish to be vindictive, would not destroy Britain, would not threaten the U.S.A. by massive aggrandisement at the expense of the British Empire. Ribbentrop was instructed to ask Rooseveldt (and also the King of Sweden, whose offer had been received the day before) to appeal to the British to come to the conference table. Germany was prepared to talk, and prepared to grant an armistice — quite soon.

When the Foreign Minister had been ushered out of the door of Schloss Ziegenburg, Hitler rushed over to Giessen, summoning his commanders to meet him in a joint conference. He normally preferred them individually and in small doses, but this was to be short and to the point, and the Führer did not require any debate. He had an order to issue. The German army was to cross the Thames and complete the occupation of England's capital in the space of the next seven days — by the end of the first week in November. The battle of London was already well under way. Now it was to be won without delay. Germany was on the brink of the ultimate victory, and England about to fall as France had fallen. All Germany's strength must be put forth to give the final push. This was to be the order of the day to all of Germany's soldiers, sailors and airmen.

* * *

As October merged into November, the fighting in London was reaching a new pitch of fury. Few prisoners were taken and every house was the scene of a bitter conflict in miniature. Montgomery had proved his worth as general. He supervised on the spot the extrication of the British armour from the front line between Dorking and Croydon, where he had committed it in response to the initial German threat. Then he had moved his tanks laterally across the front to confront the Panzers in the London suburbs. He had the infantry to support his tanks as well. Rommel lacked it, though a motorized division had now landed at Newhaven and was on its way to join him. Also the cramped and criss-crossed streets were not proving the best tank country. As Hitler's order of the day reached him, Rommel's advance was slowing down to a crawl.

But the infantry he needed would soon be available. The trapped and cut-off British in the Maidstone pocket had been providing a valuable contribution to the British war effort. They tied down Rommel's two infantry divisions, and also the crack Air Corps of General Student.

On the night of 28th October Guderian sent in General Kuntzen's 8th Panzer Division.

The Duke of Windsor also proved himself a good general in these extremities. The German tanks were ambushed by most of the surviving British armour on the Maidstone-Ashford road. A fierce tank battle developed through the night, and initial German losses were high.

The following day brought the Luftwaffe in strength, and Britain had no planes to spare for the desperate sideshow far away in Kent. The Panzers punched through, and with troops of 7th Para entered Maidstone. The British position collapsed into isolated fragments. The last of the armour was sought out and destroyed by the German planes and tanks. The German infantry were already marching off the field, hastening to support Rommel in south London. They left the mopping up to the Air Corps. The last organized British resistance was overwhelmed on the 30th. No news came to London of the fate of the Duke of Windsor. Another burden for Churchill to bear.

Montgomery's movement of his armour to counter Rommel's attack into the heart of London had also left the front in Surrey dangerously weak. When General Strauss launched his four available divisions in a renewed attack on 2nd November, he encountered little resistance along the front line between Purley and Dorking. General Montgomery had deployed 3rd Division to prevent any advance through Croydon, and there the Germans made no progress. Second London Division barred the way to the Thames around Kingston, and once again they were able to stop short the enemy advance. The Germans could not be kept out of Guildford. But then they came up hard against the Australians holding prepared positions. A British counter-attack in the flank deep in Sussex gave them further pause for thought. Montgomery had conceded territory, but the attack was now spent, and there had been no general enemy breakthrough.

Again the balance was poised. In the United States both British and German responses to the call for an armistice had been received. On the 3rd November, both Britain and Germany would make their last decisive throws on the field of war, to determine whether there would be peace, and if so, on whose terms.

Chapter 28

BERLIN HIGH SOCIETY

"You have given your name as Gibbard, Herr General. Yet I have here a document you will no doubt recognize. — The British *Army List*. I can find no record of such a general. You have given me a number which does not exist. You have stated your age as thirty years, and I do not know of any general aged thirty years in any army. Yet it is indeed true that you do not look older than thirty years. In fact, General, you look younger."

Don fidgeted uncomfortably on the chair as he faced the German. He was all too conscious that this man who spoke so softly, pedantically almost, as if lecturing an obtuse audience, was one of the Gestapo. Don's whole body was tied up into knots of fear. Fear of the unknown possibilities. His imagination had already rehearsed them a hundred times. The terror that gripped him now was infinitely worse than the simple fear of capture or death. It was a fear compounded by the knowledge that he was in the hands of men to whom his existence was nothing, who might use him, break him, twist his mind. . . . above all might torture him.

A voice at the back of his mind continued persistent, "Tell them, tell then now. You'll have to in the end. Why not tell them before they start? What good will it do to suffer for nothing?" He was sure he would tell, in the end, certain he could not take it. Yet he said nothing, as the chattering voice condemned his silence, and the grisly images of his fate rose up to make the anticipation more hideous than the reality.

After their capture, the last survivors in King's Wood had been brought back to Dover. It was there, in the castle, that Don was now being interrogated:— his second session. The ill-hidden insignia, torn from their uniforms by all the men before capture, had been found in the wood by the Germans. Don was duly identified as the general, as the sergeant had intended it. Since then, he had been separated from the other men and kept under close personal guard. They had come down through Canterbury. They travelled in open trucks, a convoy bound for the coast, no doubt to pick up supplies.

Now he wondered how it was they hadn't seen straight through his claim. The whole idea had been stupid from the start. As soon as the Gestapo had got hold of him it was all over. He didn't look like a general, anyone could see that. He didn't look thirty for that matter. How could they have failed to guess the uniform changing trick? He desperately wanted to blurt it out and get it over with, but somehow he said nothing.

"Very well, General!" Don gave a start. He realized that the Gestapo officer had been sitting staring at him for some minutes while he said nothing. "My men will have to work on the soldiers in your command. Since you find yourself unable to co-operate, I will endeavour to. . . . *persuade* them. I trust I make my meaning clear to you — General!"

Without pausing for a reply he went out, slamming the door. Don understood exactly what he meant. They would torture the other men now, and when they found out, it would be his turn. He would have to stop it happening. He would have to tell. It was not to protect his own skin; it was everyone, he told himself. No sooner had he made the decision than it fell apart in his hands. What if the others kept quiet? Then he would have betrayed his trust, betrayed the Duke and let them suffer for nothing.

The door opened, and Don swung round to face the

Gestapo officer. The Duke was with him. He spread his hands in a gesture of resignation, his face grey with weariness. Suddenly lined like an old man's face.

"I'm sorry young man, but they threatened to torture you. They would have found out sooner or later, so I have told them. Told them that I am the commander of 45 Division."

He stressed the last sentence. Don nodded slowly. That was *all* he had told them.

"I am reasonably satisfied that you are in fact the officer who commanded 45th Division, now annihilated by the German army." The German was addressing his remarks to the Duke. "That much may well be as you claim. I have checked the name you give, and I find in the British *Army List* there is indeed a brigadier, now general of course, named Morgan. Nevertheless, you and this man" — he nodded towards Don — "will both be taken to Germany, for further questioning. I would advise your fullest cooperation. My colleagues you may find less meticulous in their observation of conventions than I am. . . . "

The man's voice trailed off. He was looking fixedly at the Duke as he stood with his head and shoulders silhouetted against the window.

"Perhaps you would be so good as to come a step or two nearer to me, General," he said after a long pause. The Duke obeyed, and once again the Gestapo man studied him closely. Then he shook his head.

"I will arrrange for your transport to the continent as soon as possible," he said. "On the journey to Berlin, the false general may act as the real general's servant. I will leave this matter for you to sort out yourselves, gentlemen." Then he left them. The door was locked behind him. They knew there was a guard outside.

"Well, do you mind being a general's servant instead of a general?" the Duke asked, sitting down heavily.

"No, sir, 'course I don't." Don shook his head emphatically. At that moment his only feeling was relief. Relief that it had not come to the point where the choice was his to betray his trust or let other men suffer. Relief that the threat of torture which had suffocated him up till those few moments ago was suddenly lifted. He was back in a world of ordinary anxieties and fears, all of them beyond his experience or conceiving before the invasion began, all now known to him, and stripped of their terrors by that knowledge. But there was another matter.

"Sir, I think that Gestapo man may have recognized you."

The Duke rubbed the stubble on his chin.

"Yes, I am afraid he may have. . . . I'm not sure though. In the end he seemed to change his mind. We may still be in luck. — After all, it would be an unlikely thing for anyone to notice. Why should he be familiar with the faces of former English kings?"

Don looked doubtful. He had regarded the Gestapo man as no fool. And Edward Duke of Windsor's face had been plastered over every paper in the world not so long ago.

It was just after dawn, when the sudden eruption of shell-bursts awoke Don and his companion from the sleep of exhaustion. Through the window, the pale light was interspersed with brilliant flaming reds and oranges. They both ran over, and as they looked out the heat and the blast struck them at once. They were flung back from the window, struck by an impact which had also almost blinded them, and yet was utterly silent. Until the sound came, with a shattering roar. The ancient stone of the tower seemed to be swaying. Don sat on his bunk in the cell, and watched as the Duke, looking almost nonchalant, strolled back to the narrow window.

"Ammunition ship in the harbour, I should think. You'd better come and see this, Don Gibbard. — It may be the last time it ever happens."

Don came over. At first his eyes focussed on the tower of smoke rising straight up through the drizzling rain into the air above the harbour. He took in the fires beneath it, the other fires and spouts of fire in the town and harbour. He heard the dull continuous roar of the blaze, and heard the lesser thunder of repeated smashing, hammer-blow impacts amidst the crowded shipping and on the crowded docksides. There were German transports blazing beside the jetty. He saw tanks from a line of tanks picked up and hurled over the quayside into the water, other tanks in the line erupt in fire. And all in miniature, like watching a battle in the cinema or from an aircraft.

"Out there, look at them, man!" The Duke had hold of his shoulder and was pointing out to sea. Don looked up beyond the blazing harbour, and saw the cause of the destruction.

Still huge and dominating though they were a mile or two out, he saw the great grey shapes. They were ugly in the dawn light, their massive fo'c'sles dark against the sea, their gun barrels marked by sudden flashes of flame, rippling for a moment. Then there came the screech of shells, and the massive salvoes were crashing down upon their targets. Around the two big ships were others, several of them also heavy vessels, though none as large as the two leviathans in their midst. Don correctly identified the destroyer screen and the protecting cruisers, and knew enough about Britain's navy to recognize the battleships, unmistakable with their high bridges and all their guns forward, the *Nelson* and *Rodney*. He found himself cheering, and waving, hardly noticing that the Duke was cheering too.

"That's a sight for sore eyes," he yelled, as the great vessels continued slow and untroubled on their way across the front of the town, pouring destruction into it as they went.

"It's the Home Fleet! They'll show the bastards!" Don heard the Duke yell.

They didn't notice the rattle of keys in the lock, or see the guards until they were seized from behind, and marched down into the depths. They could still feel the castle shaking as the sixteen-inch naval shells ploughed into the ground.

"My apologies for spoiling your entertainment, Herr General." It was the Gestapo officer again, down in the cellars. — The dungeons, Don thought — "But the activities of your navy are likely to curtail your own lives, as well as those of Germans."

As if to fulfill his prediction they heard a series of louder crashes above. Stone crumbled from the walls even down in the depths, and somewhere up in the castle was the dull rumble of falling masonry.

The bombardment did not continue for long, though they passed the rest of the day in the dungeon, confined in a narrow dirty room that fulfilled all the requirements of a cell, with the guards edgy and unpleasant. By night they returned to their accommodation up above, still spartan but a great improvement, and apparently undamaged. In the darkness they could see fires burning in the harbour area below. The next day their journey to Germany began.

They were driven through the streets of Dover, and saw for themselves the effects of the war on a town which became its victim. The Duke had already seen something of the devastation during his brief stay in London. Don had only seen the results of a few limited bombing raids. Dover lay in ruins, and amidst those ruins the real consequences of total war, close-up and vivid, were brought home on both men. The streets for much of the journey were marked by piles of rubble. Occasionally rows of houses, an elegant crescent, pleasant town houses, some larger buildings, were left standing, as if to point the contrast more starkly. They passed through one district that was relatively untouched, then came to the centre of the town. There all was ruin.

"It's been wiped out," said Don quietly, thinking of how he had exulted in the firing of the guns yesterday — British guns. The Duke till then had sat silent and impassive beside him.

"Not just the ships," he said as if reading Don's thoughts. "Bombing as well, over the weeks. First theirs, when we held the town, then ours when they had taken it. It's not an English town any more now, you see. Just a German base, to be pounded down by British bombs and British guns."

Don heard the bitterness of the contradiction in his

voice, and tried himself to absorb what had become reality in a world of contradictions. They pulled into the harbour. At first sight it too was wrecked. There was a half-sunken cargo vessel ablaze by the breakwater. The invasion barges of the enemy lay awash and smashed like man-made rocks across the whole expanse of water. Tanks and lorries stood burnt out on the dockside, and there were still some bodies. The Germans moving about amidst the carnage, trying to sort something out from it, appeared listless and defeated.

Nothing seemed to have escaped damage except, at the end of the breakwater beside a burnt-out supply dump, the squat incongruous shape of a Channel ferry, still looking much as it must have always looked. This was the vessel they boarded, in an unreal atmosphere like a day-trip to France. She had come in that morning, and the Germans manning her had not shared the horrors of the bombardment. Don had never been abroad before, and despite the circumstances he found the crossing exhilarating. He was obliged to stay close to the Duke, and a guard always accompanied them, but by and large they were allowed the run of the vessel. Most of the other passengers were German wounded. Food was brought to the cabin, and it was obviously that provided for German officers. Nor did it show any sign of being rationed. Don found himself regretting the journey did not take longer, particularly as the rest of it would not be so pleasant.

From Calais they were taken by train for three days across the congested railways of Holland, Belgium and Germany. They were always kept under close escort, even escorted to the toilet. The blinds of the carriage were usually pulled down. Now the food was snacks and sandwiches only. Don was more than glad to arrive in Berlin. The weight of his experiences over the preceding month had begun to dull his senses into an acceptance of what came. He preserved an underlying confidence that the Duke would not now let anything happen to him. This took away the need to fight his own war any longer. Above all he was overcome by tiredness. After the effort of will in his long escape and flight, it left him a passive spectator of events he was too weary to influence.

From the train they were taken by car through the German capital, unlike a city at war. Just as the towns and villages of the North German Plain (what they had seen of them) had shown no signs of battle. It was a grim contrast to their last sight of England in the ruins of Dover.

Once again the two men found themselves alone in a room with a German. He was a civilian, a man in a dark suit, a man who spoke perfect English. He had sent the soldiers outside, pleasantly offered them seats across from him. Then he leaned over to face Don, and said:

"You are an imposter, and very possibly a spy. You have forfeited any rights you may have held under the Geneva Convention. I intend to have you shot."

Don sat frozen in his chair, the verbal blow so utterly unexpected that the force of it could not penetrate. But the Duke spoke almost at once.

"This man is a private soldier in the armed forces of the Crown. His name is Gibbard, and he was in fact my valet. He changed uniforms with me on my orders, and I insist on his protection."

The man sat back, a large man, but not fat. He smiled to encompass them both.

"Good, then we have that matter settled once and for all, and there is no need to shoot anyone. You are obviously used to giving command, General, and I really did not doubt for a moment that you were the real officer. . . . Though, it does seem a little odd you should speak of this man as your valet. Surely the correct military term is 'batman'. — I fear you are more used to the civilian mode of address, Your Royal Highness!"

It was Don who gave those words all the confirmation they needed, a sharp intake of breath, stifled too late. The German opened a drawer and produced a sheaf of photographs. He spread them across the desk. Photographs of the Duke as King Edward VIII.

"I believe that you were indeed the Commander of

British 45th Division, Your Royal Highness, but that is hardly *all* that you are."

"I am Edward Duke of Windsor," said the Duke flatly. The German stood up.

"I am honoured to meet you, Sir. Your name is held in high esteem among the German people. Your abdication from the throne of England was a tragedy for both our nations."

The Duke looked narrowly at him.

"I am the King's man," he answered, "my brother's man."

The German inclined his head.

"Your Royal Highness will remain as our honoured guest, despite the unfortunate circumstances. I will see this other man is properly treated . . . "

"I would like to keep him with me," the Duke interrupted. "I could use a valet, or should I say 'batman', who is my own countryman."

Again the German gave his little half-bow of acquiescence.

"As Your Highness wishes. I will now, with your leave, go to make the necessary arrangements for appropriate accommodation for you."

He went out, pausing to bow again, this time with the click of the heels in the Prussian manner.

"Like all the bloody Germans, obsessed with titles and etiquette," muttered the Duke.

Don felt himself jolted back to a reality that had vanished when that suave, cool and deadly man had threatened to shoot him. Gratitude for the Duke's intervention, his two interventions, flooded over him. He stumbled over the words,

"Thank you, sir . . . I mean Your Royal . . . "

"Don't you start," snapped the Duke in exasperation.

* * *

Don was not a natural personal servant to any person, however exalted. Nevertheless, being a careful, even meticulous young man himself, he contrived to get the

Duke's possessions into some sort of order. Those possessions of course were supplied courtesy of the Germans and included a full dress British uniform among assorted formal and casual clothes. Since Don acquired the Duke's rejects, he found himself dressed more expensively than ever in his life. He was provided with a large room, a bathroom, excellent meals and a high standard of comfort. All that and boredom. His only real function was to talk to his ex-king, to try to amuse him, to keep his spirits up.

The strangeness of the situation was not really brought home to him. Because of the circumstances in which they had met and been together, Don *could* talk to Edward, even on first name terms in private. He told him the humdrum details of his life, his family, his ordinary hopes and fears. He heard in return Edward's reminiscences of a glittering youth and grooming for privilege and honour — the greatest honour the world had to offer, to be King of England. And he heard of how it had been thrown away. There were bitter recriminations in dispirited moments against false ministers and hypocritical churchmen. And the ever-present worries about his wife, now on the other side of the ocean. Edward talked more than Don, but he seemed to want it that way, and it also seemed more the natural order of things. Don had always been a good listener and ready to learn. He slipped willingly into his new role of confidant to the former king.

Chapter 29

BREAKING POINT

The work of General Guderian's 8th Panzer in destroying 45 Division had been completed by the evening of 30th October. On the same evening he obtained Model's permission to borrow I Air Corps, fresh from the victory in Kent. Model's Army was still re-forming. He was prepared to allow Student's troops to provide the infantry for Guderian's offensive. Accordingly, as 8th Panzer started to roll westward across the northern edge of the Weald, and 10 Panzer moved out of Dover to follow it, the airborne troops began to entrain. They would take the cross country route which had once been a British life-line and was now repaired as an artery for the Panzers, from Kent to the front line at Guildford. Guderian had decided to emulate Rommel's earlier disregard of army boundaries, and launch his armour not against south London, but out to the west where the British would not be expecting it and would be unprepared. Strauss, in whose sector the new assault was to fall, readily gave his consent.

On 3rd November, 8th Panzer Division, supported by the airborne formations, struck at the line of the Australian Imperial Forces from Woking to Farnham. Guderian had concentrated the tanks in the centre of the line, his objective of the day being Aldershot, the home of the British army. The Australians resisted desperately, but there were no troops to be sent to their aid. By contrast, through the day more and more became available to Guderian, and by the evening the first tanks of 10 Panzer were also joining in the assault on the flanks of the line. The third and last of the Dominion armies that had been sent to the defence of Britain went down under the wheels of the Panzers. Through the night the tanks trundled across the parade grounds of Aldershot, and the supply dumps and ammunition stores exploded or were captured intact.

Leaving his infantry to consolidate, Guderian ordered Kuntzen and Schaal, his divisional commanders, to strike out north and west. The objectives now were the crossings of the Thames and the heights of the Chilterns beyond. Rommel had likened his adventures in the Weald and the Vale of Sussex to the battle for France, but this was more so. There were no British troops left in the Thames Valley. The newly arrived tanks of 10 Panzer took the westernmost line. They pushed up the course of the Blackwater into Reading, then along both sides of the Thames on through Goring Gap, beyond the Chilterns to within ten miles of Oxford. 8th Panzer fanned out northward, into the great bend of the river between Henley and Maidenhead. The tanks rumbled past Ascot racecourse, and through the streets of Windsor. 22nd Air Landing Division mounted a new guard on Windsor Castle, and General Kuntzen of 8th Panzer ate his dinner in Eton College. Whatever happened in London, the British flank was now turned. The Germans were on the Thames to the westward. Before them the West Country and the Midland Plain lay open and defenceless. If they did not choose to turn east and encircle the capital itself.

On the same morning, November 3rd, that Guderian launched his Drive to the West, Rommel committed all his forces in the last push for the City of London. He used 7th Panzer and newly arrived motorized troops to hold off the British armour in Dulwich and Camberwell and make any counter-attack impossible. Similarly he used his infantry to mount a feint towards Westminster which would and did draw in all the remaining British reserves. Then he ordered 4th Panzer to strike for the river crossings and the City itself. By noon the British had been smashed in Southwark. They had blown London Bridge and Tower Bridge. But Southwark Bridge was taken intact.

The remains of the three Guards Brigades put up what resistance they could in the City, but their force had been spent south of the River. Montgomery hurried reinforcements to support them. He was suddenly faced with the nightmare of having his armour and the core of his entire army cut off south of the River while the Germans debouched to the north. The British somehow stopped the Germans short of Waterloo Bridge on the Embankment. To the north they managed to halt the progess of the German tanks along the line of the Euston Road, and eastwards there was stiff fighting through Finsbury, Spitalfields and Whitechapel. The Swastikas floated out above the ruins of the Bank of England and the Tower of London. A Nazi banner hung down from the nearly undamaged cathedral of St. Paul's. For once the propaganda pictures which the Germans sent round the world meant what they said — not because the Germans had just about managed to thrust themselves across the River into the City of London, but because they had also outflanked the British to the west. Though his troops counter-attacked in London, Montgomery told Churchill that without the troops to resist Guderian in the Thames Valley he could not continue to hold the capital. If the army was to be saved, it must withdraw. Or Britain must come to terms.

The third decisive stroke of the 3rd September had been made by Britain. At dawn *Rodney* and *Nelson* and the escorting cruisers and destroyers of the Home Fleet loomed out of the mists off the North Foreland, making for Dover and Folkestone. The Germans had kept the remains of the civilian populations in the coastal towns, and let the British know that fact. In this, the final throw, Churchill decided they must take their chances. The fleet could only move at fourteen knots, the *Nelson's* maximum speed despite emergency repairs, after her earlier mine damage. It was dangerously vulnerable to air attack, but if need be Britain was now prepared to lose it. If only the supply line to the continent could be broken.

The sixteen-inch guns smothered the seaports. Nine shells in each salvo from each ship. Each shell weighed nearly two and half thousand pounds. Folkestone was crammed with the transport and supplies of 29th Motorized Division, arriving to join Guderian's Panzers. Four thousand German soldiers were in and around the town, many others were on the beaches down towards Hythe. The harbour, and the coasts were crowded with barges and other shipping. The great guns of the battleships and the weight of fire from the five escorting cruisers wiped out one eighth of Germany's available invasion transports there alone.

But the carnage was even greater in Dover. There the Home Fleet caught two Motorized SS Regiments, Adolf Hitler Bodyguard and Grossdeutschland, in the process of disembarking. In addition to the men and vehicles of these formations on the quayside there were still some tanks of 10th Panzer, others to reinforce Rommel in London, supplies and ammunition for the Panzers, a huge stockpile of munitions, and eight or nine thousand men. The giant naval shells ripped the tanks on the docksides to pieces, flinging the grey steel machines into the air, snapping the gun barrels like sticks. An ammunition ship exploded in the harbour, adding to the destruction, and raising a vast pall of smoke above the town. And the shells continued to scream down into the press of small craft, where the two elite SS Regiments were being ground into pulp before they could even take part in the fight. The blow to the invasion fleet, though, was the hardest for the Germans to bear. They had soldiers a-plenty. Their stock of shipping was beginning to run out.

The battleships came under concentrated air attack in the second hour of their bombardment, when they were off Folkestone. High level heavy bombers failed to hit either, though there were hits among the escorting forces. The Stukas fared better, but their bombs were too light to penetrate the armoured decks, and the only damage was to the superstructures. Only after the fleet had broken off the bombardment and begun to steam north again did the torpedo attack go in. The big cruiser, *Berwick*, was hit by two torpedoes. Her large virtually unarmoured hull split in half and the ship went down in the space of minutes. *Rodney* was hit, but the torpedo failed to explode. The destroyer *Sikh* was sunk, and an AA Cruiser badly damaged.

Then the *Nelson* was struck beneath the stern. The repairs to her mine damage were blown out, and both propeller shafts lost. Wallowing and stopped, she began to drift up the Downs towards the Goodwin Sands. Admiral Forbes, now flying his flag in *Rodney*, stayed by the stricken sister. He first tried to take her in tow himself, then offered protection to the cruisers and destroyers as they tried. As a second torpedo attack came in and more Stukas appeared, the undamaged battleship finally turned north, working up to her maximum available speed of 21 knots. Under fire and torpedo attack, the destroyers removed virtually all of the crew from the *Nelson*. Only late in the afternoon did heavy bombers finally manage to hit the ship with armour piercing bombs. Fires were started amidships, and began to spread inside the vessel, as she was finally abandoned to her fate. Even scuttling charges set by the British still failed to sink her, and the great hulk drifted up through the straits like a beacon in the night.

It was not the only German experience of British sea power that day. Pound had planned a two-pronged attack. In Plymouth he had *Warspite* from the Mediterranean, *Barham* from West Africa and *Ramilles* from the Atlantic. As the Home Fleet struck at Dover, so the Western Squadron descended upon German coastal positions from Worthing to Brighton. In the Bay and in Newhaven they caught the first stages of the landing of the two second wave infantry divisions for Strauss's Ninth Army. The three ships steamed up and down the coast while their escort stood off to permit them uninterrupted target practice. To the Germans they were a constant flicker of orange flames, fans of smoke rising from their funnels. Vengeance administered, they continued east, rounding Beachy Head to take a sideswipe at two more divisions in the process of disembarkation. Frantic demands for air and naval assistance flashed across the Channel, and Goering ordered the Luftwaffe to come to the protection of the beach-heads even if it meant abandoning the troops in action in London.

Raeder had already done all that was necessary. Between the Isle of Wight and Le Havre, six submarines were in position. *Warspite*, the one of the three aging ships with the greatest turn of speed, continued the bombardment. She wrecked conclusively the German facilities at Hastings and Rye, and came in close by Eastbourne to receive the cheers of the largely forgotten yet undefeated garrison there. The other two battleships meanwhile turned for home. The Luftwaffe achieved hits on both, and on the cruiser *Charybdis* which was put out of action. On the *Ramilles*, the fires which were started could never be got under control. The air attacks were continuous through the afternoon, and it was becoming evident that *Ramilles* would have to be abandoned.

Off St Catherine's Point the battleship *Barham* and the heavy cruiser *Edinburgh* were each hit by two torpedoes fired by U-boats within minutes of each other — though different boats were responsible for the two attacks. A major explosion tore *Barham* apart as she still steamed at full speed. The battleship capsized and sank under a great pall of smoke in a matter of a minute or so. The heavy cruiser lasted another hour, before she too went to the bottom. *Ramilles* blew up in the early evening when the raging fires finally reached her magazines. Aided by nightfall, the *Warspite* escaped with little damage, two of the cruisers and eight destroyers coming safe to Plymouth with her. The next day, when the Luftwaffe attacked the naval base to claim their final victim, the fleet had gone, this time sailing westward.

* * *

For the British, the Channel raids were seen as a great success, but a success too late. Their cost, no less than three capital ships destroyed, was huge, but had been agreed as acceptable in advance. At this stage of the war it no longer mattered. Coupled with the other events of the day, Churchill and the High Command were driven to the grim conclusion that none of the naval affair now mattered. Though the destruction of German resources, in both men and matériel had been massive, it now seemed that it could make no difference to the outcome of the war. For Guderian's Panzers had just smashed through the Australians into the Thames Valley, and Rommel had stormed the City of London itself. Montgomery asked the permission of the Committee of Home Defence to withdraw the British armour and most of the infantry back across the Thames. He believed that the fight could be continued north of the River, so long as the army was saved.

Churchill agreed. He knew now that the war was virtually over. On the following day he would meet the War Cabinet. Though the 'City' was not the whole of London, they would tell him that London had fallen, and the battle was lost. He looked at the maps when the generals had left him alone again, and saw the opportunities for encirclement which now lay open to the Germans. He counted their known armoured divisions against Britain's one. He comprehended at last that he had no arguments to put to his colleagues to make them believe otherwise. He glanced at the first aerial photos of the naval attacks on Dover and Folkestone — and dismissed them as an irrelevance.

His view was not shared by Adolf Hitler. By the end of 3rd November, Germany had lost between a third and a half of her available invasion barges, over a half of other shipping, and had seen plans for landing four to five divisions utterly crippled. Three of those divisions, caught in the act of disembarkation had suffered serious casualties. Two SS regiments had lost half their effective strength and all their transport. The losses in supplies, fuel and munitions, were enormous. And the facilities to replace those losses were slashed in half. Hitler's initial anger that Raeder and Goering had let it happen degenerated into a state of frenetic apprehension in the course of the following day. He heard the news of Rommel's capture of London as if it were a defeat, for Rommel reported that his effective strength in tanks was now down to half and requested urgent reinforcements. There were none. Even if there had been any there was no longer an easy way to get them to him.

Through 4th November, Germany once again had no port available in England. When Hitler heard of Guderian's dash into the open country, he told General Paulus that the Panzers must stop that night, whatever advantages or opportunities were offered. They must go no farther. No air cover would be given to them, and they must be prepared to withdraw. Rommel also was told that his air cover would be reduced, and given the same astonishing order to be prepared to retire behind the Thames. The German press that day carried none of the pictures of the swastikas over London. For the Führer believed that the British navy would return to the Channel, and that this time the life-lines would finally be cut. What use were the Panzers in London when their fuel ran out and their tanks broke down, if there was no way to help them? In the hour of victory, Hitler believed that he was suddenly staring at defeat.

He need not have worried. The battleships would never return. For the British fleet was now almost expended. The treaties and restrictions of the Twenties and Thirties had denied Britain the battlefleet with which she could have swept the Channel of any invader. In subservience to the opinions of American senators, or enslaved by the phantom of disarmament, or corrupted by the moral cowardice of appeasement, the British governments of those years had failed to build the Navy which could have ruled the waves of the Channel, and the Air Force which could have held the skies over Britain. Once the R.A.F. had been defeated by the Luftwaffe, it was only the Navy that could challenge the invaders. And now the Navy was used up.

Warspite and *Rodney* had left the Channel for good. On 7th November, in company with the brand new *King George V* and the nearly-finished *Prince of Wales*, with the aircraft

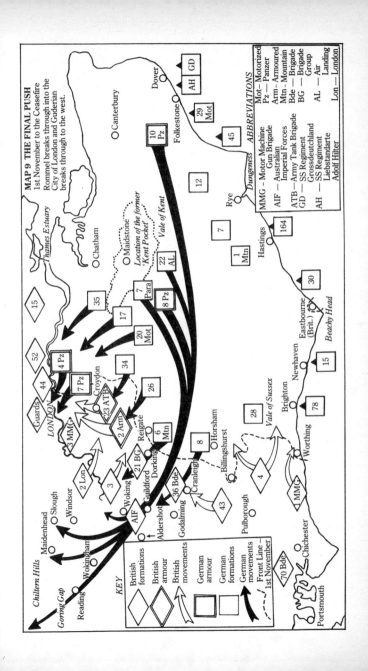

MAP 9 THE FINAL PUSH
1st November to the Ceasefire
Rommel breaks through into the
City of London and Guderian
breaks through to the west.

ABBREVIATIONS

Mot – Motorized
Pz – Panzer
Arm – Armoured
Mtn – Mountain
Bde – Brigade
BG – Brigade Group
AL – Air Landing
Lon – London

MMG – Motor Machine Gun Brigade
AIF – Australian Imperial Forces
ATB – Army Tank Brigade
GD – Grossdeutchland SS Regiment
AH – SS Regiment Liebstandarte Adolf Hitler

KEY

British formations
British armour
British movements
German armour
German formations
German movements
Front Line – 1st November

carriers that had played no part in the battle because their planes had been taken for the war on land, with the cruisers and destroyers, they put out from the shores of Scotland. Silent in the dawn they moved down the Firth of Clyde, past the Isle of Arran, rounding the Mull of Kintyre and out into the broad Atlantic. Churchill had given his promise to Rooseveldt that the Germans would never have Britain's navy, and now the fleets were sailing for the New World.

* * *

Both Britain and Germany had responded favourably to the American offer of mediation. On 3rd November, the day when the war was decided, the Americans replied by asking each for their terms. The German reply came almost immediately, on the following day. By prior arrangement it was leaked to Churchill as soon as it was received. Though neither the British nor Americans knew it, the response had been drawn up by Hitler himself, and was a response less to the appeals of the mediator than to his own panic at the naval disasters of the preceding day. Paulus had reported to him, inaccurately but not excessively so, that there was fuel in England for only three more days of Panzer operations.

The German conditions were simple. The British were to evacuate all remaining troops from the counties of Kent, Surrey, Sussex, and Berkshire — and from the County of London. Germany would then proceed to complete the occupation of Kent, Surrey and Sussex; and Berkshire up to the line of the Thames. London also would be occupied only to the line of the river, except for a quadrilateral of territory taking in the City which the Germans currently held. Britain would undertake to make no new naval or troop movements, construct any defensive lines, or deploy any new aircraft. Germany for her part would move no new formations across the Channel. Armed with advance knowledge of these proposals, the War Cabinet met on the evening of the 4th to consider their own proposal.

Churchill did not speak against accepting an armistice. He guessed, rightly, that Halifax would have prepared the ground in advance. He saw little gain in claiming that the battle of London could still be won. He had already told Montgomery to pull the British troops, and especially the armour, in south London back across the river. He had given him a single new military objective:— at all costs to keep the army in being. He had even sent a private telegram to Rooseveldt, telling him of his intention to sail the fleet to Nova Scotia. He had asked the President to exert every pressure at his disposal to make the Germans accept the British terms, when they were delivered.

Churchill proposed a British offer which differed from the German in only three respects. Germany's occupation of Berkshire would not extend beyond a line west of Reading. Germany would undertake not to base any additional aircraft in the occupied territories. And Germany would withdraw from London north of the River. Halifax argued against the last point, doubting that the Germans would ever agree to it.

"If you're right, then we shall drop it like a hot brick," the Prime Minister replied. "But if you are wrong, we will have won back the City of London at the cost of not a drop of our blood. Do you not think it is worth it?"

The rest of the Cabinet did think it was worth it. The British offer was sent that same evening, only three hours after Churchill was aware of the contents of the German proposal. Events were now moving fast, as the ending of the war became a thing of words not guns.

In America, a mood of mounting alarm in the Congress and among the people gave Rooseveldt an added spur to act on Churchill's demand to put pressure on the Germans. The Americans had persuaded themselves that they disliked the British presence in the Americas. Now they were faced with the prospect of a Nazi German presence in Bermuda or the Bahamas or the Caribbean, they suddenly found the British more acceptable. Worse still was the thought of the three thousand miles of undefended land frontier with Canada. There were newspaper articles talking of the cession of Canada to the Germans — a nonsense of course. The great Dominion was not Britain's to cede as so much spoils of war. But a Nazi-controlled Britain might take a different view of the Empire. The U.S. Chiefs of Staff on 4th November received instructions from the President to prepare contingency plans for the occupation of Canada — two plans. One where there was no opposition, another in which the Canadians resisted. As diplomatic activity between Washington and Ottawa intensified, Rooseveldt conveyed the British proposals for an Armistice to the Germans. With them he sent a telegram which contained the sentence: —

"If this war were now allowed to continue, with peace so close, it might become my duty to interpose the full might of the United States Navy between the two combatants."

Amidst the subjunctive mood and the conditional clause, Hitler could still recognize precisely what this meant. It was a threat to commit the American fleet to the Channel. Not between the combatants at all, but between the German army and its supplies. Germany would have no choice but to contest the crossings with the Americans, and Rooseveldt would have his *casus belli*. Meanwhile, the Panzers would have run out of fuel, and England would fight on. Hitler's contempt for the U.S.A. did not extend to inviting war — not yet. He instructed Ribbentrop to send immediately a conciliatory telegram, reassuring the President that Germany had no intention of prolonging an unnecessary war, and no wish to impose upon Britain any treaty which would affect the security of the U.S.A. The message was sent in clear 'by mistake', and the German embassy made quite sure that the press received the relevant leakage. On Wednesday 6th November, the headlines in the *New York Times* and the *Washington Post* were the same: —

"Germany Ready For Peace".

In fact the formal German response to the British terms was a compromise. British troops were allowed to remain in position in London north of the Thames, except for the territory held by the Germans. That must remain under German control. Nevertheless, the Panzers would be withdrawn from it, and Germany would undertake to station no more than two infantry brigades in the area. That much Hitler insisted on. The preceding day he had succumbed to the temptation of letting the German people behold the fruits of victory. The pictures of the captured city had appeared across front pages under the headline:

"Unser London" — "Our London".

Ready agreement was given to the British demands for the limit of occupation in Berkshire to be restricted, and for a ban on the importation of further German warplanes into the occupied counties.

The War Cabinet met to consider the latest German offer on the morning of the 7th. Churchill came armed with the news that Montgomery had now managed to extricate all the British tanks from South London, and virtually all of the infantry. He had deliberately retained only the bridgehead opposite Westminster. In the Vale of Aylesbury he had managed to deploy 24th Army Tank Brigade (the only armour not yet committed) together with one infantry division. In London north of the River, the line was being held. Neither in the Chilterns nor in London itself were the enemy pressing home their attacks. Somehow the line was being held.

Churchill was disposed to negotiate further, though the primary objective of ensuring the army was still intact, had now been won. His colleagues — rightly — did not believe the Germans would give up their hold on the City. The Cabinet voted to accept the latest German terms, subject to the approval of Parliament, which would be called in emergency session on the following day. Provisional acceptance was to be telegraphed to the Americans and Swedes immediately. A further undertaking was offered not to initiate any new military action prior to the formal signing, if the Germans would do the same.

When the news was relayed to Hitler at Giessen he called his commanders together and read the telegram to them himself, tears in his eyes.

"This is the greatest triumph of German arms in all our history," he told them. "This is the culmination of all our endeavours and trials. We are privileged to witness it. Privileged to have played our part in the hour of Germany's glory."

Afterwards, outside the door, Admiral Raeder remarked to Halder, Army Chief of Staff,

"You know, Herr General, on any day, in any hour, from the moment we set sail we could have lost this war on the waves of the sea."

Halder nodded judiciously.

"You know, Grand Admiral, I don't think you are quite aware just how close we came to losing it once or twice on the land as well. And I will tell you this, our Führer is breathing a little sigh of relief that they happened to throw in the towel just now."

Raeder's eyebrows lifted.

"Perhaps there is something of which I am not aware . . . ?"

"I think very few are aware that today the fuel supplies for four Panzer divisions are just about enough to keep them going for forty-eight hours."

"Wasn't it the Duke of Wellington," and he quoted in the English, "'A damned close run thing'."

* * *

Parliament met in joint, and secret, session on the afternoon of 8th November. Churchill had insisted that once again it be in the Houses of Parliament. The previous session there had been the last, so most M.P.'s believed. Now Churchill wanted to make his point. What he did not know was that Halifax's Foreign Office had let the Germans know (via the Swedish embassy) of the session. The Luftwaffe and the artillery were obligingly called off. Halifax was already treading the road of a new appeasement, the Germans already wooing a new potential ally in their enemy's camp. The M.P.'s and Lords already knew that a ceasefire was imminent. Such things could hardly be kept quiet. Many expected the Prime Minister to resign as well.

"Mr Speaker," Churchill began, opening the debate, "I have come to Parliament today to read to you terms proposed to His Majesty's Government by the Government of the German Reich for a cessation of hostilities — an Armistice."

He slowly read through the twelve clauses. The Chamber was packed to capacity, Members and peers crowding the aisles, and spilling out into the lobbies, the galleries given over to them as well, everyone craning forward to hear what Germany had to offer to Britain, all voices but Churchill's hushed and breathless.

"At a meeting of the War Cabinet held yesterday it was unanimously agreed that His Majesty's Government now has no choice but to accept the proposals of the enemy. It is that decision we place before you today for your approval."

He paused, and a long sigh echoed like a gust round the great vaulted room, the voices of many mingled in the same misery.

"There has already been much negotiation over these terms. My government and I believe they are the best to be had. They are the best *we* can obtain. It is for you to decide whether others might do better. It is for you to reject all terms, if you see fit, and choose to fight on, as once I wished to fight on. Be well assured that if that is your decision, I will serve to the best of my ability and strength, either as Prime Minister, or in any capacity and under any leader to further your will, the will of the Sovereign Parliament."

There were uneasy stirrings on the front bench. Momentarily the old fire had revived. They half suspected that he was about to appeal over the heads of the Cabinet, and ask Parliament to let him throw out the German terms and fight on regardless, as he had demanded a few short days before. They need not have feared.

"Let no-one doubt that it is *my* belief that we must accept these terms. Though we have inflicted grievous losses on the invader, though we have made him pay for every inch of English soil with his blood, yet, at the last, all our strength is done. The Nazi flags are floating over London. His tanks are in the streets. Everywhere he holds the line of the Thames. If fighting is resumed, as it may be resumed at any day or any hour, for this pause is entirely of the enemy's choosing, we have nothing to stop his encirclement of London. Nothing to stop his debouching across the plains of the Midlands to capture our industrial heartland. But above all, we will not be able to stop him destroying our army. Our last army. Our only army."

"In the air, all our pilots are gone. There are no reserves, trained or untrained. Our total fighter strength now stands at ninety fighter aircraft in the whole country. We could, if we wished, use them now in a last conflict, use them up, until all were gone. At sea, we have two or three battleships left of the Home Fleet. We could attack again, let them be sunk by the Luftwaffe after more great and gallant efforts. They could bruise our enemy; they could hurt him. They could not stop him. And on land, we could perhaps get some of our army, even most of it, back to a line from the Severn to the Wash. We could abandon the South-East, and fight our last battle on that line. The generals believe it might be done. They believe that in such a battle we would give a fair and valiant showing, such as men would talk of for many years to come. And then we would go down. And England, all of England, would be conquered."

"When I urged you, when I urged all our people, to eternal resistance I believed there was no alternative. I believed that come what may England would be enslaved, and that rather than slavery destruction was to be preferred. I think now that we may yet manage to salvage something from the ruin of our hopes. We are not yet defeated. We have an army in the field, and it fights on. The terms are negotiated, not imposed. We have our honour, and some measure still of our strength. We are losing, but we have not lost. The moment will not be with us long. Let us look to our survival."

"That this nation shall not die is not a matter for ourselves alone. Though we be lessened and diminished, yet England will remain. But if this struggle is further protracted, and made more bitter and unforgiving as the count of the dead rises, there will be no terms offered by the victor to the conquered. We will become a German colony. Our people, those that survive, will indeed be made into slaves. Our tongue will become the speech of the oppressed, its glories debased. Our Empire, left to fend for itself in a world of predators, will be swallowed up piecemeal into other dark empires. Slavery will be the lot not only of the ordinary men and women of these islands, but of the people of Australia and India, of the natives of Africa, and ultimately of the peoples of the New World also."

"The world is already a more evil place. We can no longer offer hope to the subject nations of Europe. We could offer them no better hope if we were to be subjected ourselves. Yet if we but remain a free people, if our laws be preserved and our democratic institutions continue, then we may still play a part in the succour of the oppressed. We have exerted our power, and failed. All we have left to exert is our influence. Germany wants us, so Herr Hitler says, to be her friend. A subservient friend, a complaissant friend — but not a slave. It is a tawdry role for this great nation, a demeaning role, and never think I relish it. But I tell you this, I will toady to, and lick the boots of, the most despicable men in the world if thereby I can save our army, the Dominions, our Indian Empire, one ship of our Navy, one yard of English soil. I would rather fight in the streets and in the hedgerows. I would rather die. But I have no right to exercise my preferences. None of us have the right to prefer brave words and defiant gestures. It is our country at stake."

He sat down amid an ominous and utter silence, his face heavy and unsmiling, the face of an old and tired man. Only in the hunched shoulders and the set of his mouth did the old determination still show. Somewhere on the Labour back benches an MP stood up and, contrary to all parliamentary custom, began to clap. Another followed, and then others, members and peers, until it was the whole of the chamber, steady waves of sombre applause, unmarked by any shout or cry. They were clapping honesty, not oratory. He had caught their mood once more.

The Commons vote was 541 in favour of the Armistice

proposals, 30 against. The decision was telegraphed to Germany that evening. Hitler had already stipulated the time and place of the Armistice. It was to be formally signed on 10th November in St. Paul's Cathedral, and to come into force on the following day, the 11th, at 11 a.m. Churchill was too tired and dispirited to argue.

In front of him was a personal letter from the King's physician. In terse sentences it informed His Majesty's Government that the doctors had now done all that was in their power to save the King. Their efforts had failed. At most he might live on for another two or three months.

"He is dying as the country dies," muttered Churchill. He got up and looked at the great map of England, with the flags of armies that no longer mattered. Also on the desk lay another communication, from the German Foreign Office, via the government of Sweden.

"The Reich Government begs to inform the Government of the United Kingdom that His Royal Highness the Duke of Windsor was captured on 1st November at the head of his troops in Kent. His Royal Highness is now being held as a prisoner of war in Berlin. The Reich Government wishes to assure the British Government that his Royal Highness is being treated with all courtesy and consideration as befits his rank and station.

Signed, Ribbentrop."

Chapter 30

PARTING SHOTS

It was the morning after Rudi and Hans had visited him. The sudden crash started him awake. He looked round, at first unable to make out what was happening. The hospital ward seemed exactly the same. There was the sound of gunfire outside. — There shouldn't be. They were miles from the front. He struggled out of bed, holding his side, still stiff and painful. It sounded like heavy artillery, down towards the town. Thoughts of a counter-attack by the English flashed across his mind. Yet the maps in the papers had shown them miles away and retreating. The other patients were stirring too. There were irritated demands to know what was going on.

As he reached the window, the whole building seemed to shake. He saw one great pillar of flying earth and grass blossom up out of the ground just below the hospital, and heard the crash and grinding roar of shattered glass and broken masonry. He saw the wall tremble in front of him, the shock waves running through his fingers. Farther along the ward a pane of glass smashed inwards. The entire hospital was filled with a low growling sound. He could just make out one of the wings, off to the side. Its whole front was slowly leaning forward, slipping away from the other walls, falling with increasing momentum, in one piece almost until it hit the ground amid a gushing cloud of dust and rubble.

Adolf looked upward, craning his head round. The skies were cloudy, empty of any planes. His eyes slid down towards the sea. He looked across the centre of the town, between the hills on which it was built, towards the grey triangle of water. On it, as always were the distant shapes of vessels, small from the high vantage point of the hospital. Not so small this time though. These were not the barges and light craft of the invasion flotilla, not even the German destroyers which occasionally put in an appearance. Adolf guessed that he was looking at British battleships.

For a while he watched, fascinated by the sight, taken up in the pure interest of seeing the famed British battle fleet, noticing the high masts and the squat powerful shapes, the ugliness of steel and armour transformed by distance into the beauty of line and speed. He could even make out the bow waves as the great ships cut through the rolling seas. And above, the muzzles of the guns were marked by the pin-points of flames, rippling down the line of three vessels, like old-fashioned broadsides from wooden ships.

His admiration was jolted back into reality by the concussion of an immense impact, apparently just beneath him. The floorboards buckled and twisted under his feet, the wood snapping. He felt a splinter go into his leg, its sting spurring him into action. The people had to be got out. They were under fire, and the hospital had been hit. He was not given the opportunity to speak, to call out his first orders as an NCO. The blast smashed all the windows at once, hurling the frames inwards as well, dissolving the glass and wood into deadly flying fragments. He was knocked flat by the force, flung underneath his own bed. In front of his eyes he could see numerous tiny pock marks of blood on the back of his hand. He reached up and touched his face. More blood there. His ribs ached from the fall. But above all he was conscious of the screaming. The ward seemed to be full of it.

Painfully he wriggled out, not sure how badly he was hurt. The floor was littered with rubble and debris. Where the window had been was a ragged hole. Other beds were turned over. He saw a man on the floor, the man from the next bed, who had spoken to him when he first woke up. A long knife of glass jutted from the man's throat. Blood had engulfed his face as his head hung down so that it was one mask of red. A steady drip trickled down from the scarlet matted hair. He looked up from the dead man, looked at his own body — a little seeping of blood through the arm of his pyjama jacket, a cut on his foot, a long scratch, little bubbles of blood on his hands. He picked up the cracked mirror from beside his bedside locker and looked at his face, oblivious of all around. The same pin-pricks of blood.

"Adolf! Adolf, what are you doing?" He turned at the voice, letting the mirror drop to the ground. Christine, Nurse Johnstone, was stood there.

"Doing? — Making sure I haven't cut myself shaving!" he abruptly screamed at her, realised he was shouting in German, and switched to English:—

"This is your British people who do this. Your ships out there! — Do they not know it is a hospital?"

Her face was frightened, almost as much by his rage as by the carnage all around.

"There's a red cross painted on the wall. . . . "

"They are probably using that to aim to," he snarled back, the memory of the British ships that had gunned down the men in the water now clear in his mind, the only image of war that mattered — that and the man beside them whose eyes stared out of a sea of blood.

"Are you going to help me take the men out? Or are they on the wrong side?" he went on, blaming her because there was no-one else to blame, and because she had always blamed him, and Germany, in the past. Because he had almost come to believe her.

They began, together, to clear out the men. There were others dead, others horribly wounded by the splinters and flying glass. Yet he had been standing by the window. It should have been him, ripped apart, lacerated and scream-ing like those they were trying to help. Now he was blaming himself for not being hurt, for always being the lucky one who escaped with a scratch or two or a flesh wound. Finally some solders arrived to help, and one of the doctors. He glanced at Adolf.

"You again, Corporal Mann! Always in the thick of it. You are supposed to be a patient, you know!"

The doctor seemed unperturbed by it all, treating it like part of the day's work. Adolf let his indignation overflow again.

"How can they do this? What sort of men are they that attack the wounded?"

"What sort of men. . . . ? They're the enemy, Corporal." He shrugged.

"We wouldn't do this."

"Look here, I don't suppose they could see our markings from out at sea. And if you think we wouldn't do this, then you're a damn fool. — I haven't the time to hold debates on the morality of war with junior NCO's, so shut your mouth. And if you are helping, then help!"

Adolf shut his mouth, his own flailing fury covered as if by a blanket by the doctor's more useful anger.

It took all day to get things sorted out in the hospital. They were not attacked again, though the shells had continued to fall in the town for several hours. Finally Adolf found himself sitting on a bed, in an undamaged wing on the opposite side of the hospital, as the same doctor removed the last tiny fragment of glass from his face.

"Well, it hasn't spoilt your looks, Corporal. You were lucky nothing went into your eyes. You must not worry too much about what I said to you earlier, you know. You worked hard, when plenty would have laid down and squealed. It will be another feather in your cap, I should think."

When the doctor had gone he lay back. His side ached abominably, and his injured arm, only put in a sling a day or two before, was throbbing dully. Repeated use had reopened the bullet wounds. His face and hands smarted from the antiseptic ointment on the numerous cuts. He wanted to sleep, but he wanted to see Christine, his nurse, first. He did not want things left as they had been that morning. He had worked beside her most of the day, and they had talked about the job in hand. Now he had other things to say. He started to get out of bed, to go and find her, as she came into the ward.

"Back to bed, Corporal," she ordered.

"I was coming to look for you."

"If it's any consolation," she said, as she fussed around the bed, "the two English wards, where the wounded prisoners of war were, have also been hit. There are plenty of men and nurses dead."

"No, it is not a consolation," he answered. "Do you think really it would be?"

"I don't quite know what to think. I know why you were angry. I thought you might still be. I thought you might want revenge for your people. . . . "

"Revenge by other innocent people being killed? Do you not know me better than that?"

"Yes . . . I suppose I do know you better than that. —"

* * *

"Goodbye, Nurse Johnstone."

Adolf held out his hand to her formally. His right hand still bandaged up and in the sling, but usable. She took it.

"Not Christine any more?" she asked.

"Of course, but. . . . you know I may not see you again."

"Best not to get involved . . . " She nodded as she spoke. "I'm glad we've been friends though."

"I am also."

It was a week after the naval raid. He had been in the hospital for three weeks altogether. Now in the cold November morning he was released, fit for light duties, but entitled to some leave first. Most of the rubble had been cleared up round the front of the hospital. He noticed they had painted larger, clearer red cross symbols. He had happened to chat to a petty officer from the Kriegsmarine who had reckoned they were ranging shots; there had been no intention to hit the hospital. From out at sea, no-one would have made out such small markings. Adolf told the news to Christine. She had shrugged, and said that didn't make much difference to those killed and wounded. It did make a difference, however, to his own perceptions, reducing it from hideous malice to mere wantonness such as characterized all of war.

He turned to go, doing up his greatcoat against the chill of the wind, paused on the hospital steps.

"I *will* come back to see you. To visit the sick, I will call it. That is a very good excuse, I think."

"Do you need an excuse in the German army?" she said, then abruptly was gone back inside.

Now he was discharged, Adolf found himself almost regretting it, though while he had lain in his bed he had fretted constantly and been bored by the inaction. In retrospect the times spent in snatched conversation with his nurse seemed far more important than the hours of idleness. And what would he be found to do outside in the real world. A desk job of course! All he was fit for now. And according to the papers the war would be over any day now. The British were asking for terms. He hadn't bothered to read the last couple of days. Despite everything, the prospect of the end of the war left him feeling flat and let-down. His strapped-up ribs still gave him a twinge as he walked, adding to his depression.

"Want a lift then, Corp.?"

He looked up to see a soldier — another corporal — leaning out of the window of a British car, its camouflage paint chipped and scored, one side window taped across where it had been broken. It reminded him of the car that he had once driven into a shell hole, and been dragged out of by a lone English soldier.

"Thanks, I wasn't looking forward to the walk." He got in.

"Typical of those inconsiderate bastards," the other man remarked. "If you'd been an officer there'd be transport laid on, don't worry. But the poor bloody infantry walks — wounded or not."

"Oh, I'm not that bad," Adolf answered. "I don't suppose there's much transport to spare anyway."

"Well there was this car and a driver to spare to bring

a Herr Major up here. And no doubt there'll be another one to come up and collect him some time."

The man was full of the usual soldier's moans. If it wasn't the pampered life his officers led it would be something else — shortage of women or quality of food.

"Have you got a time to report in?" Adolf asked him as they drove off. The man had already told him he was attached to the staff at Army HQ in the Grand Hotel. As Adolf would be himself according to his orders. The docket told him to report at noon.

"No. — Why? Want to go sight-seeing, mate?"

"Yes, I suppose I do. Well, one particular sight. I don't have to turn up till midday. — Are you sure you won't get done for it, though?"

"Not a chance. Just tell me where you want to go."

He directed the man — Bruno Pöhl his name was — round through the suburbs of Brighton. Then up onto the Downs, along the narrow, unfenced road up which he had once driven with a staff major.

"I've been up here before," said Corporal Pöhl. "There was a big infantry camp. 83rd wasn't it? If you've got mates in that lot they've moved on long since. The artillery's here now, 27th Regiment. Is it them you're after?"

Adolf shook his head.

"No. — Could you pull in there!"

They had almost passed it, the house where Don had taken him prisoner. Or where it had been. There was just a pile of brick-red rubble and splintered wood, still smoking where it had been burnt. He walked round the garden, sure it was the right place. In the fields running up to the Downs beyond there was a row of artillery field pieces parked, not even camouflaged. There was where the command post had been — where the shells had landed and the major was killed. He came back out onto the roadway. Rubble filled the shell crater where he had crashed the car. Pöhl leaned against the car smoking a cigarette, giving Adolf a long questioning stare. There was a man walking up the road, shabby in old civilian clothes.

"Hey, you there!" Adolf called to him. The man

stopped, eyes glancing to the side, warily. Preparing to run, Adolf thought. "Can you tell me something?" he asked quickly. "The house that was here, what happened to it?"

The apprehension in the face turned to sullen dislike.

"Where did you pick up the lingo?" asked Corporal Pöhl, new respect in his voice. Then he added, "If that swine doesn't answer you, just give him a kick."

"You should know." The man had decided to answer, his voice as surly as his looks. But then, hadn't he reason to be surly? "Your lot knocked it down with their guns. — Just for practice. Not content with bombing it, see. Had to finish the job."

"It was your house?" Adolf felt embarrassed now, unwilling to ask.

"No, but it was someone's."

"I'm sorry."

"Yes. Aren't we all?"

The man pushed past him, continued his solitary tramp up the hillside.

"You should have given him a taste of your boot, mate. Sour-faced bastard that he was. They don't know when they're beaten. Even now, they don't know."

"It was just a place. . . . I was based at, for a few days only," Adolf half-explained, not wanting to tell the story, as they drove back. Part of his war had gone already, knocked down by some artilleryman with nothing better to do, just part of the random vandalism of it all. He found himself wondering what he would be thinking and feeling now if his own regiment had not been shot up at sea, if he had not been left as an unclassified remnant to engage in his own private and exotic war. Perhaps he would be the same as this oaf next to him. But then, he was the same as him; finer feelings and sentimental regrets didn't make him any better. He turned to Pöhl.

"How near the end is it then?" he asked. The other shrugged.

"The rumour is that they're signing today. The top brass are looking like so many fat cats with their paws in the cream, I can tell you. Never known them so polite. Oh we've won alright — whether it's today or tomorrow or next week. Didn't you see the papers with the pictures of London. Even that Goebels couldn't invent that!"

"Yes, I saw it. . . . Thanks for the trip, Corporal. I'll do the same for you one day."

They were coming along King's Road now, the seafront. Adolf recognised the impressive façade of the Grand Hotel, the swastika banners hanging limply down above the doorway where he had stood guard a few weeks back. At least that was still here. They had smashed up the railway station; both piers were gone, and half the big old hotels. But not the Army HQ. He felt a momentary return of his anger towards the British ships that had shelled a hospital out on the edge of town and marked with red crosses, but had missed this most obvious target, with its German flags.

He climbed the steps, debating whether ordinary corporals were expected to do so, brushing shoulders with generals of the army. Then again, he had met the General of this Army. A gaggle of officers swept past him down the steps, laughing, one of their number shouting. Very much not the public face of the German officer corps. Adolf frowned his own disapproval as he walked past the guards on the door unchallenged. That wouldn't have happened if it had been him and Hans and Rudi there. Inside there was no orderly sergeant on duty at the desk. He was beginning to feel put out by the state of affairs, when a large hand slapped him on the back. He spun round with a cry of pain.

"Oh. I'm sorry, Adolf, Corporal, that is. I clean forgot. . . . Here, have a chair. Clumsy dolt that I am!"

"Clumsy dolt that you are," snapped Adolf. "You've put me back a week, I shouldn't wonder, Ah! It's made my whole rib-cage ache again. — What are you doing here, anyway? I thought you and Hans were on station guard."

"Oh, rotation of duties, I dunno," Rudi dismissed the tedious matter of guard duties with a wave of his hand. "Anyway, I'll get you a drink — that'll ease the pain of your wounds, my little hero. You'll have champagne of course?"

425

"Look, you great cart-horse, this may have the appearance of an English hotel, but it is really a German Headquarters. Swarming with officers, you know. You'll be in the guardhouse if you don't shut up, or the madhouse!"

"Official permission," replied Rudi — and did bring him a glass of champagne. "We've just had the news. — General's orders, personally given, everyone in HQ to celebrate." He paused, looking at Adolf's blank face. "You don't know yet! — No, of course you don't. Here, look at the order of the day, issued to all troops. They signed yesterday. It's just come into force. We had it through on the telegraph. Your fat Bavarian sergeant friend took it up to old Strauss himself, shouting and yelling."

Adolf read the words: —

". . . . armed services to cease all military actions on receipt of codeword 'Sieg'. Armistice to come into effect at 11.00 hours on Monday 11th November, 1940. . . . "

Rudi slapped the sheet of paper in his hand.

"Eleven o'clock, today. Half an hour ago. We've won, matey! The war's over. We've beaten the English!"

Adolf sipped the champagne, letting the silly grin spread unheeded across his face. Somehow he had never really planned for or thought of this moment, never let it come into his hopes. He'd always believed it would come, never doubted it would be Germany that won. And now it had happened. He read the words again.

"Armistice, 11.00 hours, 11th November."

Chapter 31

ONCE AND FUTURE KING

They had been prisoners in Berlin for about a week. Don had settled down to his curious role, while the Duke of Windsor chafed more and more at his enforced confinement. Above all he resented the fact that he was permitted no contact with the outside world. The Gestapo man visited every second day, to ask politely if all was well. Edward addressed his protests to him. He was met with a smiling courtesy, and regrets that the Duke's position made it impossible for any message to be conveyed to his wife or his family, or to the British Government. Don listened to these interviews — present because the Duke had insisted at the first one that he remain — and listened afterwards to the Duke railing at the Germans.

Above all he was concerned about his wife, her and the King. He believed his brother was dying. Don did what he could to comfort the man. He had his own worries for his mother, the rest of the family, and for Gwen, if she hadn't found someone else by now. But beside these great matters his affairs seemed trivial. He had tried to tell the Duke so at first, but Edward had rounded on him angrily. "Do you think it makes any difference what title you have or he has, when it's your brother that's dying? — When it's you that put him there?" It was the first time Don had contradicted his royal companion. "I don't think you put him there. I don't think anyone would say that. The Germans put him there, just like they put you and me here." Even from Don (who did not account himself someone who mattered) that assurance had apparently done something to ease Edward's mind.

It was a cold bleak Monday with a bitter wind blowing, when Don noticed the long black car draw up in the street beneath. They had been talking about escape, debating the risks and possibilities — the inefficiency of the guards. Don pointed out the car as a possible way out of the city: no-one would stop an official car. They were talking about it, half serious, half in earnest, when the visitor was shown in. It was not the usual man, but a tall thin fellow, with the same aristocratic demeanour that Don still noticed occasionally in Edward. In this man, for some reason, it provoked instant aversion. The man bowed and clicked his heels. Don allowed himself to snort aloud at what he saw as a caricature. He was pleased to see the quick glance of annoyance, before the fellow recovered his composure.

"Your Royal Highness, we did meet once, briefly, at a reception in Lisbon, when I was with the German embassy there. I trust they are looking after you properly."

"I am being treated better than most prisoners of war in Germany, I am quite sure." Edward's reply was icy. He showed no sign of recognising the man. "However, it is my intention to protest in the strongest manner to the authorities of the International Red Cross, if and when I am permitted access to them, against the deliberate and persistent refusal to permit me to communicate with my family."

Once again, for a moment the man was taken aback. Then he spread his hands in deprecation.

"I am sure that Your Royal Highness will understand that your own particular position is such that. . . . "

"That I am denied the right to have my country's government and my family informed of my capture. I would remind you that I am a serving officer of the British army, captured while wearing His Majesty's uniform."

"Yes, Sir. But hardly your own uniform!" That time the suave exterior had gone completely, the teeth bared as he spat out the response. Don suddenly realized that what he had taken for 'aristocracy' was just a veneer, a thin coating of civilization on the face of a gangster.

"At the time I had some reason to remain incommunicado. Now I have none. Nor do you, Mr Schellenberg. — You were not a member of your government's mission to Lisbon. You were sent to Lisbon specifically to entrap my wife and myself into some foul and despicable plot hatched by your unpleasant overlords in Berlin. Since you are what passes in this country for both policeman and hangman, I presume you are here today with the same purpose."

Don watched, grinning, as the man, evidently some bigwig called Schellenberg, made a positive effort to control himself. He must have seen, for he turned towards Don himself.

"This is a private interview, Your Royal Highness. . . . I must insist on this, this ape leaving."

"Then I will be leaving too. Unless you intend to call in the thugs now, to beat me up. That is the normal procedure is it not? — Stay where you are, Don. I want you here to witness what this person says or does."

"Very well. I have nothing more to say to Your Royal Highness except this. You will be conveyed to see the Foreign Minister of the Reich, Herr von Ribbentrop, this afternoon. I would advise you to be more co-operative there."

"I shall be delighted to see Mr Ribbentrop. You may tell him my man will be accompanying me. You may give him the reason, just as I gave it to you. . . . You can find your own way out?"

Don responded to the cue, and sprang to open the door. As the man walked past him, Don could see that his body was trembling with suppressed fury. Edward collapsed onto the sofa. He too was shaking. Don went and poured him a whisky — and poured himself one too. Previously he had stuck to beer. Only his exotic captivity had given him the taste for anything stronger.

"It was marvellous — the way you handled him, Sir . . . " Don began.

"My dear chap," — the Duke took the glass and deliberately held his hand to steady it before downing the drink in one gulp — "that man is a senior officer in the SS. He wields more power to do people harm than you can begin to imagine. *I* am probably a fool to taunt him. Make sure you do not join in. He would kill you out of hand just to annoy me."

"Sorry, sir. I didn't think of that. . . . It was the way you were sorting him out."

"I have never been so scared in my life," answered Edward.

"Do you really want me to come with you to see Ribbentrop?"

"Oh yes, if they let us. I meant exactly what I said on that point. I want someone else present to hear what is said to me. But far more I want you to hear what I reply. If I can manage it, I want to bring a witness back to England with me, to tell the truth of anything I may have said here."

"Sir,. . . . Edward," — Don tried to find a way to phrase the question in order not to hurt or offend — "if the King, if your brother, does die, do you think they will try to — put you back?"

"Well! You're no fool, my lad. I suppose it *is* obvious. They think I'm some sort of friend of theirs. It's what Winston will be wondering too, if they have told him. . . . Oh God, I wish I knew what was going on. I wish I knew how my brother was!" He stood up and paced the room in frustration.

The same car came for them after lunch. It was the usual officer who took them down to it. The SS man did not reappear. No comment was made as Edward firmly put his hand on Don's shoulder and steered him towards the door. The Duke winked at him. He had put on the general's uniform they had given him, for the occasion. Don felt out of place by comparison in a dark suit.

"I can hardly call for Home Guard's uniform to dress you up in," the Duke had announced. "And you'll make a reasonable showing as my personal detective."

As they drove through the streets, amidst the crowds

of ordinary people going about their business, glancing up idly at the car, with its two escorting staff cars full of Gestapo men, Don decided there was no possibility of an escape attempt. He nearly joked about it to the Duke, but saw his face was troubled. He was worried about what this Nazi was going to say, even though he pretended he was not. When they were shown into the sweeping state appartments on the Wilhelmstrasse, the tension had been buried. The Duke presented a cold, bland countenance to von Ribbentrop, as the German Foreign Minister rose smiling to greet them with the Nazi salute. Edward returned a military salute and took the proffered chair. Don took up position behind him, looking exactly like a bodyguard, he thought.

"Your Royal Highness, I am honoured to welcome you to the German Reich on behalf of the Führer. I can only add that I much regret the circumstances of your visit, and express the hope that they may soon change for the better."

"Why have you brought me here, Herr Ribbentrop?"

The absence of the polite formalities caused a pained look to cross the Nazi's face.

"Perhaps your young, er, friend would like to sit down. There is really no need for his presence, I do assure you. Nevertheless, we are more than happy to accord with your wishes."

The Duke turned his head, and nodded to Don, who sat down beside him. This time he was determined not to be fooled by the appearance of these people. He set himself to remember every last word, every inflection of the voice in all that was said.

"Your Royal Highness, my main purpose in requesting this audience" — the Duke stiffened slightly at the choice of the word — "is to convey to you certain information that it is important you should be told. Firstly, I know you have expressed your concern that your, shall we say, position be made known to the British authorities. You have my assurance that this has been done, by telegram, direct to your Prime Minister. It was done soon after your capture. — As soon as we were entirely sure of your identity."

He paused, still smiling. "Secondly, it is my duty to inform you that at 11 a.m. today an Armistice came into effect between the forces of Great Britain and the Reich."

"I don't believe it!"

"I have of course anticipated," Ribbentrop continued as if he had not been interrupted, smoothly as oil, "that Your Royal Highness will require verification of this statement. I am happy to provide these documents — British Government, official documents, as you will see. Tomorrow, and subsequently, I shall direct that the British and American newspapers be made available to you, should any doubts still linger."

"I have included here another document." He held the piece of paper in his hand. "It is from, shall we say, Swedish Government sources. We realise that Your Royal Highness must be concerned about the health of your brother, King George VI. — This is a current report on his condition."

Edward jerked forward, almost stood up. Don thought he was going to snatch it out of Ribbentrop's hand, but he controlled himself and sat down.

"Thank you — for your thoughtfulness," he said, only the faintest tremor in his voice.

"I will leave you for a little while, so that you may study the documents in privacy," Ribbentrop replied, suaver than ever in his little victory.

When he had gone, it was the medical report that Edward snatched at first, scanning the closely printed page. Don watched him anxiously. He hadn't had time for it to sink in yet. The news about an armistice still lacked any real meaning. Having shared Edward's company for the past days, he also shared his paramount concern.

"How is he?" he asked, speaking about a man's brother, not about a king. The Duke gave a long slow exhalation, subsiding, hunched, into the chair.

"Three months at the most," he answered. "Probably less."

Don tried to think of things to say. That was why they told him now, he thought. He cursed the smooth-voiced Nazi who was manipulating his friend. In the turmoil of

432

his anger, he regarded him as friend without thinking, in a way he could never have done consciously. And he had recognised the techniques of Ribbentrop for what they were. The need to intervene, to put something else into the balance, forced him to speak.

"You knew it would be that. . . . It might have been worse. And these doctors, they might be wrong. — It might not even be true."

"I think it is true. And yes, I knew it could not be good news."

"They've only done it now to get at you!"

"All right, Don, all right. I know that too. . . . Give me a moment, please. Then you can help me look over these other things."

Don went and looked out of the great ornate windows onto the broad street, trying to find his way through the tangles that beset Edward now. He had been thrust into the position of chief adviser to a man who might after all be king again. He had learnt enough in the past week to know that that was not how things worked, that it could not and should not happen. But if there had been an armistice — then things might change. To him armistice meant more than the end of fighting. It meant what it had meant at the end of the Great War — the imposition of a cease-fire by the victor on the defeated. It was the prelude to a victor's peace and a conqueror's triumph. It had all the overtones of surrender inherent in it to him, and to most people in England and Germany alike.

"I am afraid these documents are also genuine."

He had allowed his thoughts to wander away from Edward. Now he went over to the Duke and read the thing too. There was no way he could judge. But yes, it sounded like a treaty to him.

"I do not see what they would gain from the pretence," the Duke continued. "And I recognise the gloating in that odious man's voice. He wants to break me, and he knows he has the weapons to do it."

"I think you ought to get it in writing, from Mr Churchill." Don gave his advice.

"Yes, you're very sensible. — Well, Privy Counsellor, I suppose we wait and see what venom the snake has ready to pour at the next session."

"You asked me why you were here, Your Royal Highness," the German Foreign Minister began without preliminary when he returned. "Partly, as I said, to be told how things stand. Partly, now you are informed as to the realities, to receive an offer, an offer made by me on behalf of the Führer himself."

"Now it's coming," Don thought.

"I am a private individual Mr Ribbentrop. I am not empowered to accept any offer on behalf of His Majesty's Government."

It was like watching two swordsmen, circling, probing for the weak spots.

Ribbentrop leaned over the table, and spoke with a sudden intensity.

"His Majesty the King is dying, Sir. It pains me to speak so, because he is your brother, but it is the truth. And when he dies, there must be a new king. In the past you have shown yourself sympathetic to the cause of National Socialism. You also have little affection for the ruling classes of your country who stole your crown from you. — The Führer wishes *you* to be that new king."

"One moment," Edward interrupted. "Do not suppose that I have any sympathy for your loathsome regime. Do not suppose that I have any feelings towards you and your fellows except revulsion. Why do you imagine I was fighting with my country's army?"

"You were at the head of your army because that is were a king belongs," came the smooth reply, a strange echo of sentiments that Churchill had expressed when sending the Duke to his command. "We understand that at the moment you feel towards us as towards an enemy. But you have seen the armistice documents. — The war is over. And when the new England emerges, she will need her *rightful* king to set her on the path to National Socialism."

"You really believe that I am prepared to be some sort

of Nazi puppet?" For a moment there was genuine disbelief in his voice, then he had rounded on Ribbentrop. "Listen to me, you smooth-tongued murderer, when I was king some at least of my people loved me. If I went back as your gauleiter they would hate me to a man. And what's more they'd be right."

"I can understand Your Royal Highness's agitation," Ribbentrop continued, ignoring the insult. "However, I feel that you have not fully appreciated the situation. Your country has today surrendered. Any odium arising from these events will attach itself to Mr Churchill and his government, not to yourself. You might even acquire, in some small measure, the position within the English state which the Führer established for himself in the early days of the Weimar Republic. Nor do we require Your Highness to be a puppet ruler. The Führer does not, at the moment, wish to occupy the British Isles or to impose harsh terms on the British Empire. We are prepared — with your help — to work together in friendship with the people of Britain. Rather than destroy them. . . . "

"This conversation is pointless. I am a servant of the Crown. I can do nothing without the authority of my government, with which I have not been permitted to communicate. And I can assure you that you will get the same answer from the British government as you will from me. Be damned to you, and your offer, and your whole vile conspiracy!"

"You will write a letter to Herr Churchill, as soon as this interview is finished." The suave silkiness had suddenly vanished from the Foreign Minister's voice. "You may say what you wish, but you will be surprised at the answer that is returned to you by your government. They are perhaps more aware of other prisoners whose captivity is not quite so pampered, and whose release they desire. They perhaps want to recover the counties of England that we have occupied. They may not wish us to impose a regime upon the whole of England, to dismantle her industries and ship them to Germany, to deport her male population as labourers for the Reich."

"Slave labour, in death camps!" shouted the Duke.

"I see that at last we understand each other," returned Ribbentrop. "That is precisely the alternative. You will now return to your comfortable lodging, and write your letter."

He stood up abruptly, and indicated the door. Without a word the Duke turned and left. Don followed him. Up till the very end, he had thought all was well. Edward said nothing in the journey back to the hotel, and when they arrived immediately sat down and composed a letter. He did not read it to Don, and it was taken by the Gestapo officer. Only then did he speak.

"Don't you want to know what I wrote?"

"I should think you said the same sort of thing that you said to Ribbentrop."

The Duke sighed.

"Well you at least still trust me. . . . Yes, that. And I asked for advice on how to handle it."

Throughout the interview Don had watched the two men like a spectator watching a game. And then Ribbentrop had spoken the truth, and the game ended. It had been like the moment when the pleasant, polite Gestapo man had told him he was going to be shot. Only a threat, but made with such sureness and lack of concern, that it would not be doubted. He understood what defeat by the Germans could mean, and the word armistice acquired new connotations beyond those of the Great War. The Nazi Foreign Minister had not even bothered with denials about death camps. He had wanted Edward to know the truth, and to understand what the real choices were.

"Don, will you answer me a question, as honestly as you can?" Edward's voice interrupted his train of thought.

"Of course I will." He wondered if he was being asked to make the choice — would he accept Edward back as king? And how would he answer?

"I think it is possible that the Government will order me to do what the Germans want. . . . " He spoke slowly, weighing the words. "I do not think it likely, I hope and

pray it is not. . . . but you heard that man make his
threats. — I want to take the option away from them."

"I don't understand." Don could not see where this
was leading.

"I am not prepared to be their puppet king. I would
prefer to die honourably. . . . But I do not think I could
do it myself. Would you be prepared to do it for me?"

"Do it?"

"To pull the trigger."

"You mean you'd kill yourself. . . . You want me
to . . . to help you?"

"I want to take away their option of using me. If I had
died in battle they would not be able to propose this. I do
not know for certain that it will come to that. But I want
you to tell me now."

"You can't. The Government will never expect
you. . . . There must be another way — something else
you could do."

"Do you mean you won't help me?"

Don knew that the man was reading the panic and
confusion in his eyes. His mind complained that it was not
fair. It was wrong for him to be put in this position, given
these choices. But then it was wrong for the Duke too, to
be given such alternatives.

"I will never be their puppet," Edward repeated.

"I-I'll help you, if I have to." Don forced the words
out.

"It may be that all you will have to do is hold my hand
steady."

Chapter 32

ARMISTICE

Churchill was informed that the Führer would not be present at the signing of the Armistice in person. The delegation would be led by Deputy Führer Rudolf Hess. He would be attended by the chiefs of the three armed services, von Brauchitsch, Raeder and Goering. Goering would have the secondary role of keeping an eye on both his two colleagues and Hess. Military and Party were nicely balanced. Since the Führer would not attend, neither would the Prime Minister. The British contingent was headed by Lord Halifax, the Foreign Secretary. His number two, War Minister Anthony Eden, a Churchill supporter, also had the job of watching his chief. The only representative of the forces was Brooke.

It was a strange meeting that occurred in St. Paul's on the morning of 10th November. The great church had suffered some damage in the fighting, but the nave and soaring dome were untouched. From the crown of that dome, once the symbol of London's resistance, were draped huge swastika banners. Funereal palls of smoke still shadowed it on every side. Ringing the building was a cordon of German tanks. All up Ludgate Hill the approaches lay in ruins. Inside the cathedral the seating had been stripped out, replaced by tables taken from St. Paul's School and now arranged in a square before the undecorated high altar. It was a chilly, late autumn day, with a bitter wind under grey skies. An iron cold lay on the cathedral.

The Nazi dignitaries had landed at Croydon that morning, and been driven up through the devastation of south London with a heavy military escort. It was a new sight for them, the endless rows of rubble where the streets had once been. The Panzers had fought their way through here, house by house. Too many tanks had been lost to anti-tank fire, grenade or Molotov cocktail. The Panzers response was methodically to demolish the houses and shops, the pubs and churches, creating out of the ruins of a city a landscape more suitable for tank warfare. It was a desolate, eerie place, all colour reduced to smudged grey and brown, uninhabited but still deadly with snipers.

The route of the delegation had been notified to the British, and a safe passage guaranteed. The five staff cars, brought over specially, were all clearly marked, bonnets and roofs painted white. Despite the guarantee of immunity, German soldiers lined the route, and tanks lurked amidst the rubble. The soldiers had been told to cheer, and the Nazi chiefs acknowledged the plaudits. In fact the troops were weary and battle-stained. This had been a harder battle than that for France. Losses had been high, especially in London, and there had been cruelties and revenge on both sides. The men meant their cheers. The presence of those gold-braided uniforms, the polished leather and gleaming insignia, meant that the war really was ending.

"If Goering's here, there won't be any British planes about," they joked ironically. Goering's record as a flier from the Great War had been rather dimmed since he became head of the Luftwaffe. Perhaps more practically, there had been a suggestion from Raeder that they travel by a different route in unmarked vehicles.

"If I was Churchill, I wouldn't miss the opportunity to remove most of the High Command," he told Doenitz, the U-boat commander, today acting as his deputy. "We shouldn't be on this job at all. Foreign Office with a few staff officers are all that's needed here. It's a publicity show. Look at those carfulls of pressmen."

"I think the Reich can use the publicity," Doenitz answered. "Wars are not only won by battleships." He was a better Nazi than Raeder.

"Battleships!" snorted the Grand Admiral. "If I'd had one or two, this whole affair might have been a little less hair-raising. I can tell you, Doenitz, that for the Navy this cease-fire is only just in time."

They drove slowly over the hastily rigged metal span that the engineers had put up in the middle of the damaged London Bridge. Then on past the Bank of England, an empty shell, past the Headquarters of 4th Panzer Division in Saddlers' Hall; the direct route along Cannon Street had not yet been cleared of rubble. Outside the Cathedral, they posed for the film crews of U.F.A., making the Wochenschau newsreels to be shown in every cinema:— the glitter of the military, the silent muzzles of the tanks around, and above the pinnacles of St. Paul's, the giant flags on the dome, the drear ruins all around. No need for the propaganda department to edit these pictures. Then when a staff officer reported the cars of the British delegation approaching, the Germans went inside, and took their places round two sides of the square of tables. Goering complained of the cold.

The British had driven up from Horse Guards, past Trafalgar Square, where Nelson's Column still stood in front of the charred façade of the National Gallery. The Strand and Aldwych had been devastated by firestorm. The Savoy, the Lyceum, Somerset House, King's College were all gone, indistinguishable mounds lost amid a field of ash. As the car drew level with the flattened remains of St Clement Dane's, British Tommies in smeared battledress came out of the rubble. An officer, no more than a boy, ordered present arms. The cars crossed the front line from England into the Nazi empire — occupied London. Outside the gaunt gothic shell of the Royal Courts of Justice, it was troops in field grey that presented arms. And as they drove along the line of what had once been Fleet Street, there were the guns of tanks poking out from behind the broken walls. They were glad when they came to St. Paul's, awaited by German officers, immaculate in service dress and white gloves amidst the wasteland. They were shown in with studied courtesy and deference. The German delegates stood to greet them.

"Welcome, gentlemen, on behalf of the government and Führer of the Third Reich. Heil Hitler!"

His arm came up in the Nazi salute, a frosty smile on his square stolid features, grey-rimmed eyes fixed on the face of Lord Halifax. The matter had been discussed by the British in advance.

"Give them back their damned salute. Tickle their vanity. — It might be the little touch that saves us Gilbraltar!" So Churchill had said.

Reluctantly Halifax brought his arm up. The cameras turned, flashbulbs flickered. Tomorrow the German papers would carry the picture under the headline,

"Britain salutes the Führer".

As Raeder had said, the whole affair was largely a publicity stunt, appealing to the Nazi leaders' sense of theatre. The proposals for the armistice itself had already been agreed. Only the details needed to be sorted out. Or so it seemed to the British. Already, there was little fighting. In places the opposing armies were not even in contact. The formal cease-fire would take effect the following day at 11 o'clock. Over the subsequent ten days, withdrawal of troops by both sides to agreed positions would take place. After that stage, advances to agreed positions would occur. No opportunity of conflict between the two sides was allowed.

The British would be pulling out of Sussex, Surrey, Berkshire up to the agreed line west of Reading, and their last toehold in Kent. The Germans would fall back behind the Thames. In London the cease-fire line was drawn in detail along the streets, from Tower Bridge up past the railway termini at Fenchurch Street and Liverpool Street, then along City Road and Pentonville Road, past Euston almost to Regent's Park; then back towards the river down New Oxford Street and Kingsway at last to Temple Pier. The Law Courts, the British Museum, the University; the

Bank and the Tower of London, the Cathedral of St. Paul's — the heart of London — would remain German. The Palace and the seat of government in Whitehall, where the government had deliberately remained, Parliament and Westminster Abbey were left to the British. They would also retain the triangle of land south of the river from Waterloo Bridge down to the Elephant and Castle and back to Vauxhall Bridge, a bridgehead to mask and protect the City of Westminster. The streets down which the unnatural frontier ran were designated "The Red Line". Crossing them would not be easy. Outside London there would be a mile wide demilitarized strip on each side of the cease-fire line. In the capital, the armies would still face one another.

"I am instructed by the Führer to present these further documents for your approval." The details had been read through by lesser officials, checked off and agreed one by one. Now Hess rose again. "The Führer requires that the following paragraph be appended to Section Twelve of the Armistice Agreement."

The Englishmen listened to the translation, and read the papers they had been given.

"Both parties accept as a condition of the Armistice agreement that a Peace Conference shall be convened to settle finally all outstanding points of contention between the governments of Great Britain and the German Reich, and to sign a lasting treaty of peace between Germany and her allies and Britain and her allies. It is further agreed as a condition of the Armistice agreement that such a conference shall meet in the city of Nürnberg in the German Reich not later than 1st December, 1940."

"I am not empowered to consent to such a far-reaching addition," Halifax replied. "I must consult with my government."

The British were taken out, and ensconced in the headmaster's study at St. Paul's School. A phone line to Whitehall, where the Cabinet was in session, had been prepared in advance. As Churchill put the matter to his colleagues, and the delegates waited, a flight of Stukas escorted by ME110's flew low across Westminster. They made a series

442

of long sweeps, peeling off in dummy runs towards the ministries and the Houses of Parliament. No hostile action was carried out, but the message was clear.

"Argue against it, if you can," was the message Churchill returned to Halifax. "But I think the swine are looking for an excuse to provide us with a show of strength. If you can't get it left out, get it postponed."

"And if they insist?"

"Then give in."

"We cannot guarantee the presence of Dominion representatives at such short notice," Halifax told the Germans, back in the Cathedral. "Furthermore, we feel that it provides insufficient time for the drawing up of adequate documentation."

"I think that this time, we will be providing most of the documentation," said Goering.

The Führer's paragraph was duly included. Hess was too loyal a Hitler man to permit any of his leader's wishes to be thwarted.

"There is one last matter I wish to bring before the British authorities today," he announced, after the cameras had clicked again, and the documents been duly initialled. "I have received from the Führer the appointment of Reichskommissar for the Occupied Territories of England. I shall possess full authority over all German personnel, civilian and military, and over the conquered population of the territories. I am empowered to conduct all necessary negotiations between the Reich government and her occupying forces, and the British administration. I will require to meet regularly with your government to" — he spread his hands — "iron out any minor difficulties which may arise."

"In that case I would take this opportunity to remind the Reichskommissar at the outset of the provisions of the armistice document concerning the treatment of U.K. civilians and their property in the Occupied Territories." It was Eden who spoke. It had already been decided by the Cabinet that this matter would fall to him as Minister of War. "I have here a dossier of abuses which have occurred prior to the cease-fire."

"There have been abuses by British civilians against the German military as well," cut in Brauchitsch. Hess had not even looked at Eden. He addressed himself to Lord Halifax.

"I will pass this dossier of your colleague on to the appropriate section in my administration," he said. "It is the Führer's intention to have all his dealings with the people and government of Great Britain properly conducted, and given the highest priority. It is for this reason that he has appointed the Deputy Leader of the National Socialist Party to this position."

The Deputy Leader of the National Socialist Party sat back, his expression hugely self-satisfied. The ceremony was over. The British hurried to their cars, and returned through the silent city.

On the eleventh hour of the eleventh day, just as it had twenty two years before, the shooting stopped. Then it had been the end of four years of unparalleled, inconceivable slaughter, of immovable fronts, stalemate and attrition. It had ended in defeat for Germany, and destruction for her allies, a peace imposed by her enemies. And now the verdict had been reversed. In that war, Britain had been safe behind her dreadnought navy. There had been no rival to equal her on the seas, no airforces to tip the balance. Since then the British had let that great navy slip through their fingers like sand. And the airforce they needed had never been properly built. The door to invasion had been opened, by weakness and neglect.

And now, as the dull November days passed, South-East England witnessed the carefully regulated troop movements. Khaki-clad soldiers marched back into towns and villages from which they had retreated. Troops in grey moved across countryside surrendered to them, amid the recriminations and bitterness of the population. Though the people as a whole were not prepared to fight on, yet there were many who affected to see the armistice as a betrayal. Its announcement was greeted with dismay, a numbed shock which fell upon a nation unprepared to believe that at the last it had come to this.

There were the last of the columns of refugees, trying

to move out with the withdrawing army, and more anger and disillusionment, as British troops forced the fleeing, frightened people to turn back into the arms of the enemy. As some escaped across the fields and hedges, guard-posts went up on main roads to control the authorized traffic. It was the responsibility of the British to see that the civilian population of the occupied territories was fed. Their task was made harder by the extensive requisitions of the German army. Little of the produce of Kent and Sussex would reach the people of those counties now. Nevertheless, on the whole the Germans did not treat the people badly. There were instances of provocation, and of callous behaviour by soldiers, but there were no deliberate atrocities. The plans drawn up for the imposition of an unbending regime upon the whole of a conquered island had been quietly forgotten in the changed circumstances of the Armistice. Instead there had been instructions from Berlin that the behaviour of German troops must be impeccable. The generals were irritated. They replied to Berlin that such behaviour was required as a matter of course. England was not the same as central Europe. It was to be a show-piece. For now the Führer was concerned with world opinion. Which meant American opinion.

In that earlier war, as Britain had been inviolate from invasion, so had the safety of her rulers been guaranteed. In this war, her King lay dying in St. George's Hospital, not far from the Palace where his wife and mother awaited the daily reports, and mourned the death of the royal children. As other wives and mothers learnt to bear similar griefs, and the country as a whole adjusted to the facts of defeat and occupation, Reichskommissar Rudolf Hess had already requested a personal meeting with the Prime Minister, in private. The two men faced each other across the polished wood of the table in the Cabinet room. Churchill sat with pursed lips, suppressed anger showing at the mere fact of sharing the same room with this man. Hess had a fixed glassy stare that seemed to look through the other man at some visionary prospect. The German leaned forward, adopting a faintly ridiculous conspiratorial tone that the interpreter failed to convey.

"These matters are for the ears of none save the highest. They concern the fate of our two nations, and the dying King of England."

"The death of the King of England is a matter for his people alone, not for his murderers," snapped Churchill.

"Do not be offended, Herr Churchill. We understand the sanctity of kingship, and the awe which surrounds it. His death was fated, because he should never have been king. The Führer understands that. You must see it too. Destiny will not be thwarted. The rightful king will return."

Churchill looked at the interpreter, and said in a loud, clear voice: —

"Tell this gibbering imbecile that it has never been my misfortune to listen to such a mass of drivel before. Tell him the fate of King George, our only and rightful king, and of the Crown of England, is nothing to do with him or his bloody Führer. When the King dies — if he dies — there are rules of succession which will determine inexorably who follows him on the throne."

The interpreter, provided via the embassy of Sweden, conveyed the sentiments, but not quite the actual words of Churchill's statement. Hess stood up at once and began to speak without pausing, as the interpreter tried to keep up.

"Not so, Herr Churchill. The laws of succession were broken in 1936, when your rightful king, a man who was your friend, was deposed by the treacherous government of his own ministers. Those ministers were your enemies too. Of course you are loyal to your King George. But he is dying. When he dies, your loyalty can return where it belongs. To King Edward. The Führer wishes the rightful king to return. You must tell him it is his duty to do so. You who are his friend must tell him. He asks you what he must do."

From his pocket he produced a long cream envelope, and thrust it into Churchill's hands. The Prime Minister looked at it, guessed who it might be from.

"Excuse me. I wish to read this in private!" he said shortly, and went out, tearing it open with fumbling fingers as soon as he was outside the door. He read: —

"Dear Winston,
They tell me you have been informed of my status as a prisoner of war. I have now been permitted to write to you, having hitherto been denied any contact with British officals. I have been well treated, however. I trust this letter will reach you undoctored. It will not, presumably, reach you unread.
Pressure is being put on me by Ribbentrop and the Nazis to act as their puppet king in the event of my brother's death. I have told them that I am not their dupe, and will not be their puppet. I have pointed out that there are laws of succession which must now apply, and that my abdication was final and irrevocable. Nevertheless, they persist in regarding me as a possible, and desirable, occupant of the throne.
I write to assure you that I am and will remain a loyal and true subject of my brother, King George VI. As such, I wish to receive the instructions of His Majesty's Government as to my future conduct in this and every matter.
Please convey to the Queen, and to all the Family, my faith and love and prayers. Tell Wallis I think of her always, night and day.
I remain your friend as ever,
　　　　　Edward, Duke of Windsor."

The Prime Minister felt a heavy load lifted from his shoulders. "Good man," he muttered to himself, as he hurried back in, and slapped the letter down in front of Hess.

"Your candidate for King does not want the job!" he shouted.

447

Hess's florid face flushed further as he heard the translation. He spoke slowly and carefully this time.

"We have read the letter and know its contents. The Duke of Windsor is loyal to his brother. He is confused at what has happened to him and unhappy at his captivity. But we believe that he will provide the King that England needs to work together with Germany in building a new world. This has been a foolish war, a civil war. Now the time had come to stand together, against the evils of international Jewry and Bolshevism. Have you not fought all your life against Bolshevism?"

"I have opposed Bolshevism, and Nazism, and will oppose any creed that is evil at the heart."

"You will come to understand," Hess answered, unshakeable in his crusading fervour. "As you will understand the decision of the Führer. When your king dies, Edward VIII must return to his rightful throne."

"He is acceptable neither to Church nor Empire. And a puppet king controlled by Germany is not acceptable to Parliament or the people."

"He can be made acceptable to all. Times have changed now. The Führer does not wish to resume this war. He does not desire to destroy the Empire of Great Britain, to occupy your land, and make slaves of your people. You are Aryans and Teutons like us. I understand how hard it is for you to bow the knee — as we were once made to, before the coming of the Führer. Do not sacrifice your country and its future greatness for your pride, Herr Churchill. — Write to the man that Germany has chosen, and tell him he may return to his lawful throne. Do this for the sake of the friendship of the Führer."

Hess left. That afternoon, Churchill played to the War Cabinet a primitive recording of the 'private' conversation with the Reichskommissar. They were now forced to inhabit a new world of realpolitik. In it the Führer of Germany held hostage the counties and peoples of occupied England. And so he had acquired a voice in naming who might sit upon the throne of England. A letter was drafted to the Duke in his distant captivity, to be conveyed to Hess the following day. It contained the paragraph:—

"Though Your Royal Highness has no wish to resume the crown, and though the laws of succession might seem to make such a resumption impossible, it may yet become necessary, in the interests of Great Britain, her people and her whole Empire, to embark upon such a course. Be assured that His Majesty's Government reposes in you all trust and faith that in the hour of decision you will act in this as in all matters in true loyalty to Our Soverign Lord the King, your brother, and on the advice of his Ministers in Parliament."

Hitler The Kingmaker had received his answer.

In Berlin, as he read the words and the meaning under them, a resolve hardened in the mind of the Duke of Windsor, a decision to match the bleak winter that lay on the south-east of England and the spirit of all the people in the Island. Now the U-boat blockade was lifted the food situation began slowly to ease, but there was still stringent rationing that would remain long after its cause had gone. Much of the surplus food, provided by a United States Government generous too late, was funnelled into the Occupied Territories. Everywhere the country was full of refugees, homeless people with nowhere to return to. The capital was divided between two armies, much of it in ruins. The structures not only of government but of life itself teetered on the brink of collapse. Ordinary people spared little thought in those days to who should be king over them.

And the troops had not stood down. Carefully and properly, always within the terms of the Armistice, Brooke and Montgomery were reorganizing and reinforcing the battered and almost broken army of Britain. Tanks were still being built in the North and the Midlands, to bring the armoured division back up to strength. Guns and munitions were being delivered to the troops. The available stock of Spitfires was slowly mounting again. And in Nova Scotia, on the other side of the ocean, Admiral Forbes held sealed orders, which would bring the fleet back if fighting ever resumed. Among all the other contingencies it was something the British had to plan for.

The Germans planned too. Across the Channel, now more leisurely and untroubled by shells or bombs, the dilapidated barges and transports of the invasion fleet plied their crossings. No new units were conveyed, as the Armistice directed. But the existing formations were being brought up to strength. The Panzer Armies were receiving new tanks so that once again they outnumbered the re-equipped British armoured units by four to one in modern machines. Great supply dumps were being built up, the airfields prepared to receive whole squadrons of fighters from France and Belgium at a few moments' notice. If the war were to resume, it would not be a long one. Once the Armistice had finally been signed, the balance which had wavered so long had finally tilted decisively and forever towards Germany. The war was over. Only the peace remained.

Chapter 33

PEACE CONFERENCE

The Conference at Nurenberg was to be Hitler's great show-piece, the crowning achievement of his 'struggle', the final reversal of the hated Diktat of Versailles. He himself presided over the ceremonial set-pieces; his deputies over the detailed negotiations. Attending were the representatives of the defeated enemies of Germany, and her jackal-like allies and hangers-on. The date of the conference had been set by Hitler, despite British pleas for delay. The place was chosen as the spiritual heart of Nazism, a fitting scene for the triumph.

The German press was not slow to point out that at the Versailles Conference there had been no German delegation, while at Nurenberg the defeated powers would be heard. They would be heard but not of course listened to. Hitler, magnanimous in victory, did not want 'his' peace seen as another Diktat. He was already playing a different game. In it he needed to woo a restored Britain ar ι to drive America deeper into isolationism. Above all he wanted to begin the encirclement of Russia. The countries of mainland Europe were so much ripe fruit, for Germany to gather as she wished. On the wider stage of the world, the conference would take a different turn.

The opening ceremony was produced in a blaze of Nazi pageantry. The great arena of the Luitpoldheim filled with the ranks of the party faithful. The display of trumpets,

451

uniforms, and banners proclaimed to the world the power and the glory of Nazi Germany. Churchill had been constrained to attend, for the first time sharing a platform with Adolf Hitler. Pétain was there in the shadows, Mussolini in the reflected glory of the Führer. Even Stalin had consented to come, so that all the great dictators should be there. Only missing were the Americans.

Together the leaders of the world watched Hitler stride down the Road of the Führer, the drums of the party rolling, the blood red of the great banners darkening in the cold December evening. The fanfare as he assended the steps to the podium and took his place at the centre of all of them. The sudden white beams of the searchlights, like the columns of some immense, austere temple. The deep-throated cries of "Heil, Heil, Heil" from the massed thousands, the ecstatic faces of the worshippers, upturned, awaiting the words that would fall from his lips.

"At least they put on a good show," whispered Halifax to Churchill, their lesser feud forgotten now in their nation's defeat.

"Ours has been running longer," Churchill answered, face glowering and bellicose, his humour worsened by the fact that he was about to hear Hitler speak. He had loathed Hitler for years, and found his public humiliation all the sharper for that. Also he was accustomed to occupy centre stage. Second fiddle was for him an unaccustomed instrument. He yawned pointedly as the resounding heils died into silence, even then aware of the trivial level his protest was reduced to. No-one would notice; all eyes were on the Führer.

It was a long speech, rehearsing Germany's former wrongs, and the means by which he, Adolf Hitler, had righted them. He reminded them how he had brought the nation back from ruin and despair to her rightful place at the head of the continent. The enemies that had conspired to drag down the Kaiser's Germany, had now suffered the consequences of their actions. For the Reich which Hitler had built would never be defeated. Like all history, it was a partisan view, but what the huge crowd expected. It was interspersed with cheering and applause.

"Speech day in the monkey house," muttered Churchill, as the Führer finally came to his peroration.

"Do not think, my friends, that I am motivated by the spirit of revenge." He spread his hands widely, then half turned and wagged a reproving finger towards the rows of statesmen sat behind him. "No, I do not look to the past. The past is dead and gone. When Germany signed an armistice in 1918 it was the signal for her enemies to fall upon her broken body like a flock of vultures tearing away the flesh from the wounded eagle. Now the eagle has become a phoenix, and the vultures — they find themselves like pigeons in the cooking pot." He paused for the laughter and cheering to subside, smiling benignly across the sea of upturned faces. "At this conference all the peoples of Europe that wish to attend are here. No country is excluded, as Germany and her allies once were excluded. All may put their case. None have anything to fear from the German people. We will take nothing that is not ours by right, nothing that was not stolen from the Second Reich of the Kaiser or from the First Reich, the great ancient homeland of the German Volk."

"For someone who ain't looking to the past, this fellow sounds uncommonly like a history teacher — and a bad one at that," growled Churchill to Eden and Halifax, taking some comfort from his mockery of the arbiter of destinies. The only comfort there was to be had, unless you were German.

"Germany will require a fair and proper redistribution of colonial possessions. This is no more than just. We will not, as was once done to us, take all the colonial possessions of our defeated enemies. And Germany will require her proper and just living space in the heart of Europe, the ancient homeland of the Teutonic nation. Those peoples of Germanic origin, separated from the historic volk by old wars and unjust treaties, will return to the fold and resume their rightful place in the German nation. Lesser races on our borders will be given our protection and friendship.

They will join us in building a new order, free from the evils of Jewish plutocracy and exploitation, free from the curse of revolution. Free peoples, each in their own homeland, guided and directed by their friends, the people of Germany, the core and heart of Europe, the master race and the guiding race, the hope and bright star of the future."

Back in their luxurious state apartments, the representatives of the "lesser" nations, and of those countries unlucky enough to be deemed of "Teutonic" origin, gave their serious consideration to the contents of the speech. Amidst the rhetoric, the sprinkling of facts was carefully sifted, and the message they revealed was frightening. Hitler had apparently agreed to let them all be present at the conference to sign away their birthright.

The Conference was divided into three Area Committees:— Eastern Europe, Western Europe, and Colonial. Each of them was presented at the outset with a draft treaty document produced by the Wilhelmstrasse. Interested delegations could comment on these, hold discussions among themselves, consult the Germans. If they wished, they could make alternative proposals. At the end of this process the German government would produce a revised version to be discussed in plenary session. Further revisions might be proposed and incorporated at that stage. The Germans would then write the final, comprehensive treaty document, which all the participants would sign. Even in theory, the procedure clearly gave Germany a decisive role. In practice it would be a role of complete dominance. Such discussions as there were would always end in the Reich delegate announcing the German decision. That was what they called a negotiated peace.

The Eastern European Committee began by listening politely to the Finns — invited by a devious German foreign office — who condemned Russia's recent war of aggression against them. Molotov protested angrily. Ribbentrop assured him privately of Germany's support. Moscow was condemned by the world press — as Germany had intended. Protest groups from Estonia, Latvia and Lithuania were also given extensive publicity. Their countries had been swallowed up by the U.S.S.R. From the German protectorate of Slovakia on the other hand, there was only an "official" delegation, full of praise for the "protecting power".

The representation of Poland was also a sham. In 1939, after the blitzkrieg defeat of the country where the war began, Germany and Russia had annexed a huge slice of territory. In what was left Germany had set up the "General Government" — Nazi military rule. Now at the Conference, "Poland" was not the exiled government in London. It was the collaborators from Lublin. With Russia and Germany they affirmed the new frontiers of the rump of Poland. They also let the world know that the new Poland would be racially pure. Poles only — no Gypsies, no Jews. The Nazis, in their magnanimity, announced that their military occupation would end. Poland was to become another protectorate. Germany was eager to introduce the language of colonialism into Europe for the "lesser races".

One protectorate had already come and gone. The heartland of Czechoslovakia was now to be formally incorporated into the Reich. The Czech nation had ceased to exist. The representatives of Britain protested, but they carried little weight in the Eastern Europe Committee. The French were not even represented there. Germany gave assurances. The Czechs would surely gain by becoming full citizens of the Reich. In fact their language had already been proscribed, and their culture and literature was being systematically obliterated. Officials were busy assessing racial purity, and granting certificates to "ancestral Germans". Those without the required proofs, or the money, and those still stubborn in their pride could always choose to go to Slovakia or Hungary. Or they could stay as the serfs and menials of their conquerors. This was the country Britain and France had betrayed to Germany when they still might have fought and won against the Reich.

Hungary and Rumania were both in Hitler's pocket already, but they had received very different treatment. Hungary had already been given Rumanian territory via the "Berlin Award" a few months earlier. Now she claimed

much more — all that she had lost in that earlier war.
Again the ghost of Versailles was walking. There were
similar demands upon Yugoslavia. Rumania bowed to the
demands. The Yugoslavs, faced with Italian claims as well,
refused. There were Italian claims on Greece too. The
Greeks and Yugoslavs walked out. Their time would come.

The time of the Jews had already come. A deadly time.
Hitler told the nations that the "Jewish Question" must be
answered once and for all. He announced the establishment
of an International Commission on Jewry. He spoke expansively of possible solutions; hinted at the possibilities in the
British Mandate of Palestine. Perhaps some Jews allowed
themselves to hope. For those that understood, those who
perceived what manner of man they really dealt with, there
was only a sickening dread. "There must be a final solution," Hitler had said.

The German plans for Western Europe were announced
by Ribbentrop himself, his speech punctuated by gasps and
cries of disbelief. Germany was changing the map more
decisively then she had in the east. Beside this the demands
that the victorious allies had made of Germany in 1918
paled into insignificance. Denmark, The Netherlands, and
Belgium were to be expunged utterly from the map of
Europe. They would be incorporated into the Reich as
so-called autonomous regions. Alsace-Lorraine had already
been annexed to Germany; now the rest of Lorraine was
taken. Even Calais and Boulogne would become German
towns.

For France there was worse to come. Far worse. The
Germans proposed to rip out from the heart of France her
ancient eastern provinces — Burgundy and Champagne.
They were to become the centre of a new state, called
Burgundy. It was the revival of a very old state that had
once spanned the borderlands between France and Germany. Ribbentrop wanted a buffer state to keep the remains
of France at arm's length. Goering and Himmler wanted
an anachronism, where Nazi Barons would reconstruct a
heroic past of mist-shrouded castles and knights errant.
With a large population of serfs to provide for the needs

of their overlords. Burgundy was to be another German protectorate. So was Norway. The Norwegians might perhaps feel grateful that they were not to join the Danes and the Dutch as subjects of the Reich. Maybe something of their national identity might be permitted to survive.

For France, the final humiliation was the loss of territory to Italy. Pétain himself had come to the conference to speak against the whole of the German plan, to speak for France:—

"I beg you not to submit France to that humiliation which was once, wrongly, imposed upon Germany. We are a great and proud nation, the heart and the soul of European civilization. Do not still that heart. Do not let that soul stifle. Without France there can be no true Europe. Germany may be the driving force, the turbine room of Europe. Undoubtedly Germany is the sword of Europe, and none would challenge her military might. That ancient conflict between our two nations is over now. We no longer challenge the leadership of Germany. But let us work together. Let there be no more emnity. Do not give France cause to hate Germany, do not sow the seeds of bitterness and revenge that will flower into evil blooms to blight the lives of our children and grandchildren. Let there be no false and phantom state raised up like a spectre from what is and must always be a part of France. How could the people of France forgive such an act?"

It was a very serious mistake. Hitler saw the speech as a threat of *revanche*. Far from softening him, it opened his mind to those most determined to destroy France so utterly that she would never rise again. He replied in a speech made the following day to a youth rally at Tempelhof Airfield in Berlin. His words addressed specifically to Pétain and the French were a deadly thrust:—

"It is not Germany who made an enemy of France. France chose this war with Germany, and in the war has been broken and swept away like a reed before the flood tide. Even her former ally, Britain, has turned against her, attacking her fleet and invading her possessions. As I speak to you, the army of the Reich is in occupation of more than

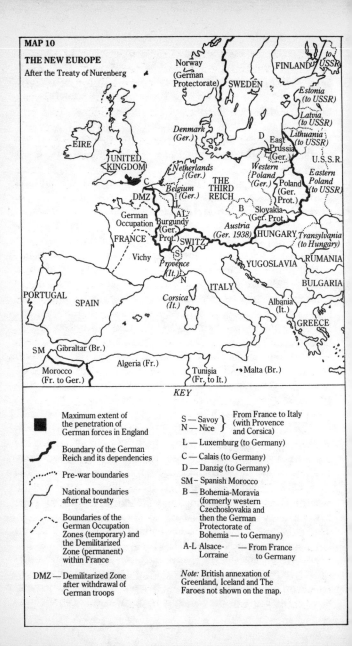

half of France. We might have elected to take more to ourselves. We could occupy all of the country. We might retain to ourselves those lands we now hold, ours by right of conquest. We might even choose to expunge the French from the roll of the nations of Europe. Such would be a fitting return for her ceaseless enmity towards Germany."

"In 1918, did France hesitate to plunder Germany? Yet where then were the armies of France? Not in occupation of half of Germany. Not in occupation of any of Germany. Now we see a true conqueror, whose armies bestride the foe. Enough of this whining from the French! Is France able to prevent us from taking *anything* we want? Perhaps Maréchal Pétain would prefer France's frontiers to remain as they are now? We are giving back territories to France!"

"I ask the Maréchal, how can France threaten Germany with her emnity? Where is France's army? There is none! Where is her airforce? Gone! Where is her navy? Run away! Or sunk by the British! France has only one choice left. To accept Germany's terms, and to become Germany's friend, willingly and gratefully. We hold in our hands the power to destroy France utterly. We have not used it. We have merely curtailed the boundaries and the power of France. We require her to return to the boundaries acknowledged by her ancient kings. St. Louis was content with those boundaries. Let Maréchal Pétain and the French people also be content!"

Mussolini telephoned the Führer to congratulate him on his speech. Earlier, Hitler had taken a great deal of persuading to let his Roman jackal gain territory from France. Now he consented to Italy advancing her claims up to the River Rhône. When Count Ciano placed these new demands on the table at Nurenberg, Pétain, in despair, refused to have anything further to do with the conference. It was left to the greedy and devious Laval to accept all the demands made on France. He also ensured that the blame for France's harsh treatment was attributed to Pétain's speech. The old Marshal found himself reviled in his own country for trying to save that country.

A mood of bitter, unforgiving resignation settled ever

more firmly on the French people. Refugees, not only from Alsace-Lorraine but from all the provinces of the new Burgundy, began to flock west and south in their thousands. Soon in their millions. It seemed the whole nation was on the move. The German army stood by and watched, or hastened them on their pathetic journeys. And France slipped deeper into ruin and despair.

The only thing the French people had to look forward to was the withdrawal of the army of occupation from those lands they had left to them. The withdrawal was to take place in three stages over a total period of just three years from the date of signing. It was a provision trumpeted abroad as evidence of German magnanimity. But it was in her treatment of Britain that Germany intended to fight and win her propaganda war. The Germans offered to remove all their troops from British soil as soon as all the colonial provisions of the treaty had been put into effect. It could be a matter of months, as Ribbentrop was swift to point out.

Furthermore, Germany would exact financial penalties from *none* of her former enemies. There would be no crippling reparations to blight the future of nations as there had been when Germany was the vanquished. Cynics might point out that this time many of the defeated nations had simply ceased to exist as independent countries. Nevertheless, it was an important matter for the French, and particularly for the British. In the Colonial Committee. Hitler chose to make in person another offer Britain 'could not refuse', and that not because of the Panzers in London. He began by dealing with the colonies of the French, Dutch and Belgians, which could be and were regarded as so much real estate to be redistributed. Not so the British Empire. The Führer approached the subject in a hushed and almost reverential tone.

Everyone had expected the demand for the return of the former German colonies. Now there were gasps of surprise as Hitler renounced his Southern African claims in deference to the Union of South Africa. He gave up the colonies and islands of the Pacific to prevent offence to

Australia and New Zealand — and Japan. Spain was to be denied her claim to Gibraltar. This was partly to punish Franco for his lukewarm support — Spain would be getting nothing. Nor would Italy acquire Malta. Britain must retain her naval bases, for the British fleet was a mainstay and defence of European civilization. There would be no naval demands made upon Great Britain. She would keep her fleet.

Even as Hitler spoke, the French were talking of betrayal. The French navy was to be handed almost in its entirety to Germany. The British must have done a deal. It was what Hitler had intended should be thought. The Italians were almost as bitter as the French. They did not gain the supremacy in the Mediterranean that Mussolini had set his heart on. Italy's colonial gains were a tiny morsel. The Reich swallowed up whole empires in Africa and the East Indies. Ciano asked who was the friend of Germany and who the enemy.

Hitler had become contemptuous of his ally, had decided that the British were a more worthy race. They were a Teutonic people. They would be Germany's ally in future. He had no plans to destroy the British Empire. On the contrary, he planned to build it up again. In Germany's image. In Europe, he even offered the British Iceland and the Faroes, and across the Atlantic, the great empty wastes of Greenland. All were the rightful property of what had once been Denmark. The Americans urged acceptance on the British. They had no wish to see the German Reich bestriding the North Atlantic. By accepting Britain became in some measure no longer merely a victim. She looked, just a little, like a partner in crime.

To serve his new end, Hitler had also insisted that the military provisions of the treaty should favour the British. There were some restrictions on the air force and army, but none on any troops maintained overseas, notably in India. Since Britain never maintained any but the smallest standing army in peacetime the conditions were not onerous. There were, however, also restrictions on the stationing of troops and planes in Kent and Sussex. Hitler might be ready to withdraw from English soil, but he wanted the option to come back if he felt the need. The French, by contrast, faced a permanent demilitarized zone in the north, and a massive reduction of their once mighty army.

In the suite of the British delegation Churchill told Eden and Halifax, his deputies, that he was not prepared to abandon France and the other allies. He intended to speak out. Halifax was not slow to inform him of the facts.

"Whatever you may be willing to do, Winston, you don't in fact have any option. You saw what happened to Pétain. *I* don't intend to let that happen to Great Britain."

"So you cast yourself in the role of Laval?" Churchill sneered, the old animosity flaring again. "Well I'm Prime Minister, and what *you* don't intend, don't matter. I am not planning on changing jobs right now."

"You are Prime Minister so long as the Germans choose, just at the moment. And when this is over, you will stay so long as the British choose. During your remaining tenure of office I will do all in my power to see that you do no more than the minimum damage to the interests of your country. You may possibly have been the right leader in the war. But the war is over, and we lost. And you are not the right leader here and now. So you won't be speaking up for France, and for Britain, you'll speak as the Cabinet agrees."

The Prime Minister sat silent for a moment. Halifax had never dared so much before. It was all the worse for Churchill because he was an honest man, and recognized the truth even from an enemy. He got up and walked away, so that they should not see his tears.

"I'll have to go after him," said Eden, his friend.

"And tell him what?"

"Tell him that you were right, but tell him like a decent man."

He found Churchill on the balcony of the lounge looking out at the night, across the roof-tops of the home of National Socialism.

"Well, what do *you* say then?" he asked Eden.

"I say that while we were fighting we needed men of

iron. Now we need men of putty. The time for heroes is over, Winston. Now is the time for cowards."

"I thought we'd tried appeasement. I thought that's what got us here."

"So it did. But we *are* here Winston. And we must make the best of it. You should have been in power then, when there was still time. *They* lost the war for you, and for all of us. Now they're in the driving seat again. You know damned well we can't start fighting again. You know they've given us better terms than we dreamt of. We can save the Empire, rebuild the navy, build a new air force. We can prepare for the next war. But just now, *all* we can do is appease."

"How can we save the Empire if the Dominions don't share your view?"

"They are being appeased themselves. You've seen the way Ribbentrop has played the colonial question. I've already heard the Australians saying that Germany in the East Indies is better than Japan. I don't think there is any stomach there to carry on the fight. . . . They've all lost terribly in the battle too, you know. . . . "

"And what about Canada? They will leave if the Germans insist on Edward returning to the throne."

"Winston, Rooseveldt has been working on them for the last three weeks. They won't have any choice. I was speaking to Mackenzie King yesterday. He has accepted the morganatic solution."

"You have been busy. . . . Have you spoken to the Duke by any chance? Because he will insist that if he is king, then Wallis must be Queen. And what's more he's bloody well right."

"He is in England, talking to her. . . . I think she wishes it, if it will help the country. And Edward will do what the government advises."

"I see. I did not know she had been brought to England. . . . How much else is there I do not know, Anthony?"

"I'm sorry, Winston. Sorry to deceive a friend, even if only by silence. The Duke will take *your* advice in the final reckoning. I think that you must tell him to return to the throne when his brother dies."

"Because that dirty little Nazi guttersnipe says so."

"Yes, precisely because he says so."

For a long time the Prime Minister said nothing, drawing on his cigar, savouring the tobacco, letting his mind deaden, grow numb so that he could accept.

"If need be, then, I will tell him he must return."

"And you'll make no fiery speeches here? No Nazi-bashing, no wounded pride?"

"I'll do as I'm told, Mr. Secretary for War. Just make sure that that man Halifax gets us the treaty we need. . . . something left to start again."

Britain would accept the German terms. Hitler had insisted the Conference last no longer than two months. In the event the treaty was ready to be signed on 10th January, 1941.

It had been a merry Christmas in the Reich.

Chapter 34

HERO OF THE REICH

Adolf had never believed that they would stay in England. No-one in the German army that he spoke to did. There had been talk of conquering and occupying the country in the early heady days before they sailed. But the war had not ended like that. England had been beaten, but not destroyed. There were plenty of men passing through HQ to tell tales of bitter resistance by the British army continuing to the very end. There was also talk of how precarious Germany's own position had been, with the Panzers almost out of fuel and the supply routes under attack from the British fleet. "We were lucky to get away with it," was the consensus. But now he and they knew that, sooner or later, they would be going home again.

Perhaps because of this there was little animosity towards the civilian population. Some, like Adolf, went out of their way to try to be friendly as the fearful people began to emerge again onto the streets. From most, Adolf got little response to his attempts at greeting them in English. Distrust and caution was in their eyes, faces veiled against his openness. There were those ready to associate with the conquerors; in places even enthusiastic collaborators. In the last days of the war a British position at Dial Post in west Sussex had been betrayed to the Germans by local busy-bodies, the entire garrison lost in the attack that followed. Those women had their counterparts now in the women who chose to prostitute themselves to the soldiers. There were also some whose hatred could not be contained. Like the guerillas who had blown up German supply dumps in Brighton three days after the armistice had been signed. Most treated the conquerors with an utter reserve, determined to keep them distant, as if by that means they would depart the sooner.

Adolf found those late November days the most dreary of his time in England. His duties were purely administrative, form-filling and pen-pushing. He had applied for leave in Germany, but been told that he was in a special category, and would be assigned his posting home at the appropriate time. At least it would be a posting home, not just a few weeks leave. But there was still the prospect of Christmas away. With Rudi and Hans he spent what time he had off duty chatting about the war they had had. All of them were veterans now. As December came they speculated about the momentous events of the Peace Conference.

They whistled over their beer or schnapps, as they read the three day-old newspapers announcing this or that provision, letting themselves echo the boasts of the editorials as Germany came into her own. Adolf was much the same as the others, the product of the same upbringing, the heir to the same natural patriotism turned in on itself by the propaganda of revenge. Now they had their revenge. As well as the draconian treatment of France and Germany's smaller neighbours, there was also the treatment of Britain to excite comment.

"I wonder why we bothered to come over here at all," Rudi announced. "They've got off scot-free."

"I don't reckon they were beaten at all, if we knew the truth of it. It might have been all arranged by the top-brass." Hans swigged his beer, nodding knowingly.

"I wouldn't recommend telling any of the top-brass that, if you see them around," Adolf interrupted the discussion between the other two. "You're getting as bad as Rudi, you know. And I don't reckon there was any agreement. They were beaten alright, but now we're trying to be friends with them."

"Well, I can't say I've found them all that friendly," answered Rudi. "Come on, drink up!"

Rudi and Hans got their Christmas leave. Adolf had to make do with a week off duty in England, with nothing to do and his closest companions gone. He managed to go and visit the cliffs above Hastings, where he should have landed with 1st Mountain Division. From high up he looked out past the debris of war still on the beaches below to the grey of the Channel. There his regiment, the lads he'd trained with, lived in close proximity with, laughed and argued with, had been torn apart by the British naval guns. He thought back to those hours adrift in the water, when he had expected to die. Less than three months ago. — He recognised himself as a different person, that day the first that had changed him.

He had inquired about Don. Gone back to the Prisoner of War Camp, and been fêted by the Commandant, spoken to a couple of his acquaintances among the guards. Yes, one prisoner had got away in the confusion. They hadn't found out till the following day. No, they had no idea what had happened to him. Probably made it back to his own side, they thought. For some reason, once he knew that Don had got safe away, he found himself certain that he would have made it.

On Christmas Eve he went to see Christine again at the hospital. The patients were English now, civilian victims of the fighting, though the hospital remained under the direction of the German military. They were singing carols, and he joined in, not made unwelcome there. The people tended every day by German doctors had had their enmity dulled. He sang *Stille Nacht* for them, consciously remembering the story of Christmas in the trenches in 1914. Now it was 1940, and the verdict of the Great War reversed. He took Christine for a walk in the cold clear night when she came off duty.

"I would like you to go out with me," he told her.

"Tonight! But it's too late . . . "

"No, not just tonight, often. I would like us to be more than friends."

She did not answer for a while. Finally, not looking at him, she said.

"I like you very much, Adolf. Another time and another place I expect I would go with you. But I can't."

He had expected her to say no at first, and was ready with his arguments.

"You must not be afraid of the things people would say. . . . "

She turned on him, eyes suddenly angry.

"I'd hate what people would say, but I wouldn't be afraid of them saying it. I'd only be afraid because it would be true."

"What do you mean?" He genuinely did not understand. "All this, the war, everything, it need not affect us."

"It does affect us, completely and entirely. . . . Perhaps one day, when your soldiers are gone, and England is England again — but not now Adolf."

"Do you really think that I am the enemy of your people, the enemy of you?" he asked.

"I know you are. I can see by the uniform you're wearing. It may be foolish. And I'm sure there are plenty of English girls going with German soldiers. I don't even blame them for it. But not me, Adolf. Not yet. I'm sorry."

She left him suddenly and hurried back towards the hospital. He caught her on the steps.

"I will come back and ask you again, when the soldiers have gone, when I am not in uniform."

She smiled.

"Yes, if you still want to, do come. — Goodbye, Adolf."

The rest of his Christmas was bleak. All he wanted now was to return to Germany. His time in England had become deadly. His release was not long delayed. The adjutant major had called him into the office, handed him the travel warrants, and the bundle of documentation that was necessary for any soldier to do anything. He was to report to a depôt office in three days time, on the 9th January — at Nurenberg. South Germany, Bavaria — less than a hundred and fifty kilometres from home!

He travelled by train. There were English trains operating again now, with reserved compartments for German troops. At Dover he had time to be shocked by the wrecking of the town, but then found himself on a German military steamer which crossed to Ostend. His warrant for the continental trains was made out for first class. He smiled at the error, more than willing to take advantage of it, since the trains were all crowded to capacity. At least he would get a seat. Nurenberg was also crowded to capacity. Soldiers, sailors, airmen and party officials naturally. Every unit in the Reich was apparently represented.

Adolf managed to report himself. With difficulty since there were a dozen or more 'receiving depôts'. He found himself hurried off at once to a 'briefing'. He tried to explain there must be a mistake. Corporals were not invited to attend briefings. But he was sent on his way in no uncertain terms by the harassed officer. So he found himself in a large hall with an assortment of other NCO's — many of them wounded, some badly. It was a full colonel that addressed them. Not an Oberst from the regular army, but an SS Standartenführer.

"The Führer himself, and the whole Reich, acknowledge the debt owed to you and to your brave comrades who have not returned to share your triumph," he began without preliminary. "The Führer himself has commanded that you, the wounded heroes of Reich und Volk, shall occupy a place of honour in the victory celebrations and parade here in Nurenberg, this sacred city of National Socialism, before the eyes of the watching world. — You may have wondered why your due decorations have not yet been granted." He smiled. "The Führer asks you to be patient. He intends to bestow them with his own hand."

He paused, then continued his voice lower, earnest and hushed, as if inviting them into some secret.

"It is my privilege to be an officer of SS Regiment Liebstandarte Adolf Hitler. You will have heard of us as the Führer's own bodyguard regiment. Perhaps you will not have heard that we too landed on the shores of England. That we too suffered, suffered more grievously than any other single formation. But the losses will be made good.

The Regiment will go on. The Führer has specially ordered that you, the bravest of the brave, should be offered the opportunity to take the place of the fallen. You shall form the heart and core of a new, reborn regiment, privileged to stand guard upon the hallowed person of the Führer, the most trusted of all men in the Reich. — Sieg Heil!"

Adolf was with the rest, those who could, springing to his feet, arm out in the Hitlergrüss, echoing the Heil. As he went to find his allocated accommodation afterwards, he already knew that he would be one of those to accept. There had been other inducements of course, after the appeals of glory. Swift promotion; officer training within the year. Better pay, even. He had thought of it before, but there had always been question marks over the SS. His mother had not liked the idea, though old Otto had been keen enough. But this was different, he told himself. This was the Waffen SS, the fighting elite. Not involved in the dirtier jobs. He let himself skirt round what the dirtier jobs really were.

Just as it was the glory that had really drawn him, that and a certain unwilling pride in being one of those chosen, so his doubts centred on his own worthiness. Now the elation born of the colonel's speech had died away, he questioned his own exploits, knowing there were others there with infinitely better title to be called bravest of the brave. To be honest, he had no claims, in his own reckoning, to any species of bravery. He was there because of the gesture of a moment. And then there were the men of his own regiment, the Hundredth Infantry, torn apart on that first morning. Wasn't it a betrayal of them, to abandon them now? Or was he no more than their representative, taking the laurel on behalf of all of them? There was a new Hundredth Grenadierregiment now, that he had never been part of. Better to go on, not back.

He found himself looking forward to the victory parade itself. He had always loved such ceremony, always been ready to be drawn into it. He had played a minor part in many other lesser occasions, rallies of the party or the Hitler Youth, part of any German's upbringing in those days. But he had never been to one of the great Nurenberg Rallies. And now this would be the greatest of them all. As the colonel has said, the world would be watching. It would also be the last time he would wear his uniform as a soldier of the old Army. The following day, he would be an SS man. Waffen-SS, sworn to die for the Führer. There was to be no period of training or anything so ordinary for the chosen of the Führer. He would don the black at once, and take up guard duties at the door of Adolf Hitler himself.

The ceremonies that had marked the opening of the conference were a pale prelude to the pomp and splendours of power with which the Führer sealed the moment of signing, when the men who had been Germany's enemies must gaze upon the display of her triumph. Even they must experience some of it, must see what National Socialism really meant written in the pride and joy of those countless thousands of young, uplifted faces, all caught up in the spell of Adolf Hitler. And Adolf Mann was one among the many, as spellbound as the rest. In those days the memory of a mud-stained, unkempt soldier who had pulled him from a burning car, even of a young, dark-haired nurse who had rejected him because of what he stood for, was faint and far away. They had been pushed to the back of his mind by more immediate images of a different reality. But even amid the power and the glory, there was one thought nearer his consciousness. This was the thought that he had survived, had come alive through the fire, seen death and ruin close up, and still come back. It was a thought in the minds of more of them there than he could ever have guessed, from the greatest to the least.

There was a series of grand events, not just the victory parade itself, nearly ten miles long, from the Luitpoldheim to the Märzfeld, but also the attendant rallies and celebrations, the state banquet and the receptions. Winston Churchill, the arch-foe, had not stayed beyond the first day, the minimum appearance he could make. Then he had gone home to the election the British were now having. There was talk that he was having a hard time. His anti-German propaganda no longer working, so people said. Now, after the defeat, the British version of National Socialism was also finally emerging. Adolf had been one of the few near enough to glimpse the man. He had seemed, above anything else, old. Goering twenty years on, Adolf had decided irreverently. Churchill went. But Hitler's designated heir to the British throne had to stay on. The British could not go off and sulk that easily. And there was Mussolini, and Stalin, and the galaxy of lesser leaders, all of them now insignificant before the slight, small figure of the Führer, the ordinary man come to greatness. So Adolf Mann saw him, and so Adolf Hitler would probably most have wished to be seen.

* * *

"You are indeed privileged, Corporal Mann," the stiff, sallow-faced young officer told him, arrogant in the uniform of Untersturmführer SS. A mere Second Lieutenant, Adolf thought, stood to attention for the last time as a corporal in the army. "You will attend the Führer-Reception for the Armed Forces in the Congress Hall. This is a singular honour for one not an officer. You and a group of what we must now call 'War Heroes' will there be decorated by the Führer. — Tomorrow, you will be sworn in to the Liebstandarte. You may find things rather different then."

Adolf recognised the reason for the officer's tone. It was envy. No doubt this SS-man was a thousand times better Nazi than he was, far more deserving in his own eyes to clasp the hand of the Führer himself.

"Will you be my officer in Liebstandarte, Lieutenant?" he asked in all innocence.

"Who your officers are is not your business. — No I will not!" The reply was snapped back. There was hierarchy of prestige even within the SS. This man was not in Liebstandarte. Newly-joined, he had not been to England, not fought. Victorious in his little encounter, Adolf left.

Nervous, he stood at the edge of the throng, talking to another corporal, a paratrooper who had captured intact two British tanks. An ordinary sort of man, thank goodness, glad to join Adolf, skulking out of the way of the generals and admirals, the marshals and politicians. He too had

472

taken up the offer, would be joining Liebstandarte. He told
Adolf he was glad of the chance. When they had jumped
into the night they had come down in trees. He had seen
friends shot as they hung there by the English militia. He
did not want to jump again.

The moment arrived when anonymity ceased to be possible. In a group of NCO's whose faces showed curious
mixtures of embarrassment and excitement, nervousness
and pride, he found himself stood stiff to attention, eyes
straight ahead, the model of a German soldier. One by one
the Führer awarded the honours of war to his selected
heroes. None of those too badly maimed, none of those
disfigured, Adolf thought, undeceived for a passing moment
even then. Hitler was pausing to speak a word or two to
each, and Adolf by chance was at the end of the line. He
caught his breath as the moment came, heard the adjutant's
words,

"Corporal Adolf Mann, the Iron Cross, First Class, for
heroism in battle."

He leaned his head forward, looking into the face of
that strange man, his Führer, Adolf Hitler. He knew that
most of the young men of Germany would have given their
right arms to stand where he stood. He felt the cross hung
about his neck. Then gave the Nazi salute, and came back
to attention.

"I read your story, my boy." Hitler's voice was soft,
friendly, concerned. Utterly different from the same voice
Adolf had heard so many times on the radio. Different
from the voice he had heard personally here at Nürnberg
declaiming from the great tribunal a few days before. "I
hope your wounds are no longer paining you." The concern
in the brown eyes was plain.

"No, my Führer, thank you. I am ready to serve in the
Liebstandarte."

The Führer nodded, smiling encouragement.

"That's the spirit. — A corporal, eh. — You know I
too received the Iron Cross, First Class, when I was a
corporal — just a corporal, they would say then!"

"I know, my Führer." He suddenly found himself smiling back at the great dictator. "I know all the events of my Führer's life . . . " It was no more than the truth — true for any conscientious product of the Hitler Youth — but he regretted it, not wanting to seem to boast, as soon as it had been said.

"Of course, of course," Hitler replied. "But now, we are comrades in arms, you and I. — Why, we have the same name, eh?"

"I was named after my Führer. My father was an early member of the party." Again unbidden. Hitler seemed to be exerting his renowned magnetism over him. He thought how glad his father would be when he related those words, spoken to the Führer.

"Ah, did you hear that, Reichsmarschall?" Hitler turned to Goering, hovering behind. "Here we have a true son of the party, from the beginning you see." Adolf caught the guilty movement of the fat Reichsmarshal's eyes. Goering himself had not quite been "from the beginning" — and had allowed his allegiance to waver. The Führer had taken his arm. Adolf allowed himself to be led away.

"You were in England, Corporal. What are they really like, these English? You saw them. . . . Tell me, did you speak to them, to the ordinary people?"

Adolf felt himself at a loss in this situation and sinking deeper. He wished he had kept his mouth shut. Now he stammered,

"Yes, my Führer. I did speak to them. . . . quite a lot. . . . To one or two of them. They are" (He gulped) "like us, really. — Ordinary people, as you said."

"There!" Hitler's exclamation almost made Adolf jump off the floor. For a second he was sure he had gone wrong, and a sickening misery gripped his stomach. But no, the Führer was lecturing Goering and any of the high officials unwise enough to be near by.

"Like us, you see. The Germanic blood will tell. This was an unnecessary war, a Jews' war. That is why I have spared the British Empire, to join us in the crusade to build a new Europe. . . . "

He stopped almost as soon as he had begun, the ranting

quality replaced as he turned back to Adolf. He was speaking now, Adolf identified it, as the old hand, the veteran, to the newly-made-up corporal.

"This man, Churchill, he is still calling me a warmonger, you know. But I do not think the British will believe him this time. You know I have here the man who will be their king. He was our prisoner, before. They are not so proud now, these British. When I have made him king, he will change his tune, him and Churchill and the swines of Jews that run his government . . . "

The flickering light in his eyes, and the sweat on his brow mesmerized Adolf. He realized that the Führer's hand was clutching his injured arm in a vice-like grip. The words were there of the great speeches, but the tone and the quiet voice revealed that this was Hitler himself, the man behind the public image. The same man, but with the pomp and circumstance and oratory missing. Suddenly for a moment of awful insight, he seemed no more than bitter, spiteful and still, despite everything, envious.

"I trust I will see this man among the troops of my personal guard," he observed to his entourage generally, suddenly letting go of Adolf's aching arm. "I tell you, gentlemen, one day he will be among the leaders of the nation, when we are all gone." Then, turning to the assembled throng he called out,

"Let us fill our glasses, and drink the toast, to the 'Heroes of the Fatherland!'"

As the toast was echoed by all, Adolf was glad to slide back into the relative anonymity of the ranks of "Heroes".

Chapter 35

HOME AND AWAY

"Your dad was ever so sorry to miss you, love, but he was only home a fortnight. — Of course, by then we knew you were safe, well a prisoner anyway. The funny thing is that your dad never even knew you were dead — oh you know what I mean!"

Don looked up from the lavish tea his mother had scrounged from goodness knew where. The front room was full of people. She'd got all the neighbours in. By the look of it they too had sacrificed a fair proportion of their meagre rations for his homecoming. He thought he ought to say something to thank everyone, but couldn't think of what to say.

"This is the best meal I've had since I've been away," was all he managed in the end. They seemed pleased enough with just that, laughing and slapping him on the back, some of them who hadn't really done more than pass the time of day with him before.

"I'll have a bet that those Jerries fed you and the Duke of Windsor a sight better than the Avenue can offer, if the truth be known," remarked Mr Renouf wryly.

"Oh, but that wouldn't have tasted the same, dad," his daughter Gwen replied, springing to Don's defence. Her hand rested lightly on his shoulder. Already the hint of possession.

"No, of course it doesn't," Don's mother agreed.

"And it'll all have been that German stuff. He won't have liked that. I don't suppose the Duke liked it either." Mrs Renouf added her contribution. Don decided not to spoil that particular illusion.

"Anyway, I was saying about your dad. He sends his love of course, and says he hopes he'll see you next time the ship's in, because by then we knew the war was over you see. . . . "

"Tell us about the Duke, then, Don," demanded Nance, Gwen's sister, interrupting the inconsequential flow. "We've seen it all in the papers. Here, look at this in the *Echo*:— 'Local Boy and Ex-King'." She handed him the crumpled cutting. Front page too! His eyes skipped down the column:— "Daring exploits"; "To be Decorated"; "Credit to the Town".

"It says 'To be decorated'," Nancy continued inexorably. "I suppose that means the V.C."

"Don't be silly, Nance," Gwen interrupted. "It'll only be something ordinary. They don't give Home Guards the V.C."

Don was thankful for that spot of sanity. He found himself decidedly unenthusiastic about all the fuss and nonsense of being given a medal. For a start he hadn't done anything particularly exciting, and was going to look a right fool when he tried to explain it to his mates at work. At the same time, he couldn't deny it *was* an honour, and he was pleased. "If it makes the women happy," he told himself, to justify his own pleasure. For now, he failed to escape the demands to tell the whole story again — with repeated interruptions for questions and opinions from his eager audience. They had heard most of it before, some of them, like his mother, several times. But then she obviously was never going to tire of it.

Release from the strange, gilded captivity he had endured in Berlin had come suddenly, one afternoon towards the end of November. He had been sitting in his own room, while the Duke read through letters from his wife, now in England. There had also been something official. Don hadn't asked. That was the procedure. He would be told soon enough, in Edward's own good time. For him there had been no letters. Apparently still no-one had been told where he was. He was feeling resentful and bored when the Duke called for him.

"Don, do you remember what I asked you — that time before?" There was only one thing he could be referring to in this roundabout way. Don nodded.

"Yes, of course . . . "

"If ever I have to hold you to it, will your promise stand?"

"I . . . I suppose so. — Yes it will!"

The Duke suddenly laughed aloud.

"Don't look so solemn. It may never come to that. It may come to something very different. — But I shall still need you, Don, when this is over. I think you're the only person I actually trust. You, and Wallis of course. — I suspect we'll be going home soon. The Cabinet has agreed to find a way round all the problems. It seems that I may be asked to resume the crown after all."

"Going home?"

"I'm sorry! I was so busy with all my worries . . . I'd forgotten you haven't even had a letter. — Yes, going home. You'd better pack some clothes."

And that had been it. Later on, the Germans had come and told them officially. There had been the guard of honour at the door, and official cars to Tempelhof. Civilian aircraft with Luftwaffe escort, to Croydon. Staff car with Nazi flags on it to take them through the Crossing Point in the heart of London. And finally, after the hours of questioning by his own side, they had brought Don home. Fortunately for him the story had been given to the papers a day or two before. He had arrived unexpectedly, unannounced, after it had died down a bit. He came in through the back door, as his mother was doing the washing up. Back into the real world.

Now as he told the story from the beginning, he could see that all around him these people from the real, ordinary world were utterly caught up in it.

"It's like a comic book happening to us," the woman

next door had said. He saw that that was how it must seem. Their war had been full of equally grim and fearful events, harsher realities in many ways than he had endured: — rationing, bombing, the constant dread of the tide of invasion sweeping over them and washing their world away. To them, his war had been a thing of high adventure with daring escapes and mysterious meetings, fairy-tale intrigue and exalted persons. He couldn't very well tell them how fear had dominated most of it, how unheroic it had seemed while it was happening. They didn't want to hear that, and he hadn't the words to express it. So he gave them the facts, and let them embroider their own mythologies around them. Once it was told — again — and the general debate on the conduct of the war was well under way, he managed to slide towards the edge of the circle, and finally through the door. It was the way all talk turned in any gathering of English people in those dismal days after the cease-fire, before the Peace Conference began. He had already noticed that no-one called it cease-fire, or armistice (the official designation, but too reminiscent of 1918). To everyone, it was "The Surrender".

"Do you fancy a walk outside? It's not raining now." Gwen came out of the kitchen. She had managed to get roped in to a great deal of the preparation and the clearing up, so it seemed. He grinned at her.

"Yes. I'm glad to get away from all that."

"Oh, don't mind them. There's not much to cheer us up, you know, and your mum's loving every minute of it. She'll be telling the neighbours how good you are for years now. — Don't worry, mine's every bit as bad."

"Come on, put your coat on, and we'll slip out the back door," he said. They strolled along the avenue, quiet now, no sirens, no threat — only the two bombed-out houses to show where the war had come and gone.

"Have you really been offered a job with the Duke of Windsor?" She looked at him suspiciously.

"Yes — with his household. If I want it. A month to recover, and get sorted out, then I could start in the New Year, if I want to."

"That's twice you've said that. It sounds to me as if you aren't going to take it up. What would you be doing anyway?"

"Oh, being his 'batman' again, I suppose." He laughed at the private joke that word had become for a while, between him and Edward.

"Well I don't know why you're laughing. Unless it's because it's a daft name for a job."

"No, I'm not laughing at anything really. It's a sort of cross between secretary and valet."

"Oh, I know what it is. I'm not stupid. . . . I suppose you really did become friends with him then, while you were prisoners. — It always sounds, well — like a bit you've 'improved on'. You know what I mean . . . "

"Yes. I suppose we were friends. He got used to me anyway."

"Hm, friend of a duke, eh. I'm not sure I approve of dukes."

He looked at her anxiously, then saw the upturn of her mouth.

"Oh, don't worry. I'm sure he's a special case. And he's a king really after all."

"Oh, you approve of kings then." Now they were both laughing.

"I thought he was a friend of the people when he was king. He should never have abdicated. It was all the Conservatives, you know. Baldwin and that windbag, Chamberlain."

Don wondered whether to say anything about what he knew — about Edward's reaction to the attempt to make him heir to the throne again. He decided against it. Perhaps it wouldn't come to that, as he had said.

"You sound like a red-hot socialist today," was all he said.

"Not really. — Well, a bit. I don't like the rich very much. Not when they haven't earned their money."

"I wouldn't mind being one of them!"

They walked on in silence for a while.

"It's a pity about King George though, and his little

girls." She returned to the same theme. "He didn't do anything to deserve that. That was terrible. But then, so are lots of people's stories. — I hate the Germans. . . . I suppose you do too."

"Some of them. Not all."

In his story, the public version, there were things left out. In particular his brief friendship with Adolf. He decided that now was not the time to tell it.

That December was a strange time in England, a limbo between war and peace. Mr Churchill had called a general election, with polling day immediately after the signing of the treaty. So that the people could give their verdict on it, he had said. The verdict Don heard most often was: "What can we do about it anyway?" No-one imagined the fighting could ever start again. No-one trusted any of the politicians. The shock of defeat had snapped the reed of their credibility. Churchill and Attlee both experienced being booed and heckled at meetings of their own supporters. Neither of them had any acceptable way forward to offer, and the voters were not so stupid that they could not see it. Many, very many, said they would not vote. Those who would looked for alternatives with a different message.

Christmas came and went. For Don it was a good time, as good as any he had known before the war. His father was home and the family together; and he had brought enough provisions to see that they were not short of anything. And now there was Gwen too, and her family. He and she were going out regularly. He got on well with her father and sister too, though her mother was a bit of a bind. She'd make a typical mother-in-law — when the time came for that. He was also aware that he and those around him were an island of relative contentment in a sea of suppressed anger. He had never known people to be quite as they were then. And as the New Year came, he knew that he would have to make up his mind about the offer from the Duke. He had gone back to his old apprenticeship in the meantime, still happy enough with it, still hesitant to take the plunge. On 2nd January, the headline in the morning paper was:—

"King in Coma"

They did not expect him to live more than a couple of weeks, so the paper said. There was a letter in the post for him too, from Windsor Castle where Edward and Wallis were living. It had been deliberately chosen at Edward's insistence because it was inside the Occupied Territories.

"I know you have not made up your mind yet whether you would wish to join my service permanently," he read. "But I would wish you, at least, to join me on my trip to Nurenberg, where I am attending the 'celebrations' following the signing of the peace treaty. I am relying on you for this."

So that was that. He went and told Gwen, catching her before she went to work.

"How many days before you have to go?" she asked.

"Six. A week, all but . . . We can see every picture in town in that time."

It was a good week, too. Now he was confident enough to tell her unbidden the parts of the story he had left out, about Adolf in particular. Of course everyone already knew that he had managed to capture a German and hide him in a cellar for nearly a week. That was a central part of the legend. What he had not told them was that the German, Adolf, had turned out to be an ordinary mortal, very much like themselves, neither a savage nor a fanatic. At the end, Gwen said,

"Yes, I can see now, there are good ones. Probably most of them are like that really. . . . "

"They can't change things, not the ordinary men and women, any more than we can," Don answered.

"But they've done some terrible things, haven't they? And they're still doing them, now there's no-one left to stop them. We'd never do that sort of thing, would we?"

He remembered what Adolf had told him, of the British ships shooting the survivors in the water.

"No I suppose not," he answered, not believing.

She shivered, perhaps at the thought she had raised, perhaps in the January cold. He put his arm round her.

"Fancy me coming out without a coat," she said.

"Well, make sure you don't forget it tomorrow night."

They both laughed, the transient mood gone.

"Is that supposed to be a sly invitation?"

Then it was time to go. He found himself nervous at the prospect of meeting Edward again — sure that things must have changed. He was even less eager to return to Germany. This time there was a proper staff, equerries and secretaries, advisers. As he had feared, Don felt out of place among them as they waited for Edward's arrival at Northolt. (This time at least they would be flying in a British plane.)

"Of course Winston will be there for the signing, but the Duke has to stay on for the rest," one of the secretaries told him, a supercilious fellow, clearly condescending to talk to Don. "It's partly an exercise in smoothing ruffled feathers as well. Some of dear Winston's election campaigning hasn't gone down too well with Mr Hitler."

"Why should the Duke be likely to calm him down?" Don asked.

The man produced a knowing wink, irritating Don even more.

"Well, there is just the hint of sympathy there, you see. It *is* the Germans' doing that our friend is likely to be returning to the throne, after all. I think you'll find Mr Hitler had reason to expect great things from his chosen king."

"And I think you'll find he's going to be disappointed," Don snapped back, angry because he knew better, more angry at the arrogant disloyalty of this man, supposedly on the Duke's staff.

"Er . . . why is it you're wanted, old chap?"

"Because the Duke and I were prisoners together in Berlin — old chap. I think he wants someone he can trust!"

He swung round to walk away, before he thumped the fellow in his smirking teeth, and cannoned into the Duke

himself, felt his hand taken in a firm grasp, and the muttered words,

"You handled that lounge lizard well enough."

Don frowned.

"Why have you really sent for me?"

The Duke only shook his head.

"Probably for nothing. — To make a change from the
likes of that fellow. Let's hope that's all it is."

He learnt little more in the course of the following days.
He had to admit he almost found himself caught up in the
great Nazi rallies, needing to remind himself that they
were the enemy, and that the pomp and majesty was in
celebration of England's defeat. He wondered what it must
be like to be a young German, brought up amid all this. —
Yet it had not seemed to have affected Adolf that much,
hadn't made him either monster or superman. He saw
Hitler for the first time in the flesh, was affected by the
power of the words that poured from his lips, despite not
understanding them, but soon became bored with the
interminable speeches. He amused himself by writing to
Gwen about it, and taking pictures with his box camera.
As they had said, Churchill had gone back home straight
away, for polling day. Don couldn't rouse much interest in
the election, and he was too young to vote. The Duke
remained for the round of receptions and 'celebrations'.

* * *

They had been there just over a week. In England the
votes had been counted. There in Nurenberg the leaders
of the nations were begining to disperse. The treaty had
been signed. The war was over.

It was the early morning of 16th January when Don
was shaken into wakefulness by the Duke himself.

"Would you get up please, Don, get yourself ready,
then come and give me a hand. — Oh, and get your own
suit ready. I shall be going out shortly, and I require you
to accompany me."

In half an hour Edward was attired in the full dress
uniform of a British general again. He had not worn uni-

form at all this time. Don had not seen him wear it since they were prisoners together. He himself wore stiff and uncomfortable civvies, and felt entirely bemused. It was only just after eight o'clock. Edward had hardly spoken, and he wore a strange, distracted look. Don darted sidelong glances at him. At one moment it seemed as he was going to cry, the next to laugh aloud. His eyes were wrong, fixed and unnatural, almost a glassy stare — like a dead man. The conviction grew in Don that something was terribly wrong. In the passage they were met by a man Don recognised as the new British ambassador, flustered, agitated.

"Your Majesty, I must recommend again, in the strongest terms, either that you do not go, or that I accompany you."

Edward shook his head.

"My mind is made up. I will go, and I will be accompanied only by an equerry and by my personal servant here. Has the coach they are sending arrived yet?"

"It is at the door, sir, but . . . "

"Then I bid you good day."

They hurried downstairs, met at the door by an equally distraught equerry. They were helped into an open, horse-drawn coach, by liveried flunkies, saluted at the door by a German guard of honour, officers with drawn swords. Before and behind the coach was an escort of cavalrymen, resplendent in ceremonial uniform. Don looked across at Edward, the inconsequential thought in his mind that it was too cold to travel like this today. He leaned across towards Don.

"Whatever happens today, I ask you to do nothing to hinder me. To help me if need be. You will be the only one near me. . . . If I fail, do it for me. You will know what."

Don was already sure he did know what, sure that Edward meant to die that day. He could only nod dumbly, held now inexorably by his promise.

Edward sat back, calm now, his face serene, a smile flickering faintly on his lips.

"We are going to see Adolf Hitler for the last time," he said.

Chapter 36

TELL MOTHER

There was little joy outside Germany and her allies in the Christmas of 1940. In England, hard times were eased slightly by the influx of food and fuel from America and the Empire. In much of the country the work of clearing the debris and rebuilding was beginning. In places little damaged the outward face of normality had already returned. But there was a strange mood about the country, growing out of the initial shock of defeat. The pent-up anger, which had flowed so readily against the Germans, now had no outlet. The people turned in on themselves, turned against their former leaders, and old ways of thought.

Strangest of all was the Occupied Territories. There the German army behaved with a scrupulous rectitude. Plans which had existed for a concentration-camp state in occupied England were swiftly and quietly forgotten. Instead, there was a massive propaganda campaign, mounted by Doctor Goebels' ministry and supported by German broadcasts from London itself. There were curious, unreal incidents. Two German soldiers were shot by the military authorities for looting shops. An Englishman who fired his shotgun and killed a German soldier was handed over to the English civil authorities and put on trial for murder. There were other gestures. The Germans began to repatriate prisoners of war, before the signing of the peace treaty.

By Christmas all Englishmen captured in France and Belgium had been returned. Goebels exploited this and similar gestures to the full. Many of them were carried out on his initiative — donations to hospitals, troops helping out half-unwilling old people, food parcels for children.

Amid it all was an election campaign. Churchill had announced he would go to the country (as leader perforce of the Conservative Party, rather than of a National Government) on the third day after the peace treaty was signed. It was a strange departure from practice since then, in mid-November, no-one knew when that signing would be. Most expected it many months removed. In the event, by Christmas the date had been fixed for 10th January. Hitler had no desire for a long conference, since he had already decided its outcome. So the election would be on the 13th. As the brutal stamping of the Nazi mark across the map of Europe unfolded in the polite phrases of the arbiters of Nurenberg, so too did the sparing of Britain and her Empire. To have lost the war was itself unthinkable. To have lost and *not* be subjected to the horrors of Nazi frightfulness was unintelligible. As people read reports of Nazi leaders vowing to preserve the integrity of the British Empire, the sustaining myth of a national crusade against the evils of Nazism itself began to crumble. By lowering the stakes after he had won, Hitler, led by his random intuitions and prejudices, had already begun to win over the one ally he really wanted in Europe.

Churchill's rhetoric against Hitler sounded to the people like the same old story. It had lost its point, since the war could not be fought again. Almost, he was resented because he was right — had always been right, but never believed until it had been too late. Also there was a more realistic thread of thought. This kind of talk would annoy the Germans. Now it was no longer sensible to annoy the Germans. Though there were many who would stick by him out of loyalty and sentiment, his popularity was already waning.

Attlee had announced that the Labour Party would leave the coalition. Churchill had wanted him to continue, wanted a National Government returned by the electorate to deal with the problems of peace. Attlee was too astute for that, and had the fate of Ramsay MacDonald as a recent warning. He wanted the Labour Party to fight on purely social issues, a welfare state, nationalization, social justice. From the start he was plagued by disagreements in his own party on foreign and defence policy. He was faced with a strong disarmament lobby, and he lacked any policy in dealing with the Reich and the New Europe. Isolationism was not going to be an alternative, and the voters knew it.

The election provided Churchill with an excuse only to attend the formal ceremonies of signing at Nurenberg, where Hitler would play the bountiful host to the heads of state. There had been an outbreak of royalism in the Nazi camp, for the crowned heads of the nations now absorbed as provinces or protectorates were required to be present. There was talk of the south German state of Bavaria welcoming back its old royal house. The crown of Burgundy, that strange revival, had been granted to the Kaiser's eldest grandson, Prince Wilhelm. But Hitler had not released his former Emperor himself from his captivity at Doorn in Holland — now part of Germany. Goering had instead made a speech urging the Führer to become Kaiser himself. For the moment Hitler was more concerned with organizing the succession to the crown of another country.

The English succession would not be included in the treaty. It was, naturally, an English domestic matter. Nevertheless, it had been settled in advance, in accordance with Hitler's wishes. The Führer was aware of the obduracy of his captive candidate, duly reported by Ribbentrop who regarded the whole business as a ghastly mistake. But Hitler remained convinced that Edward VIII would, restored at German hands, adopt a posture of friendliness towards the Reich. This would accord with the pro-Nazi sentiments he was (erroneously) thought to hold. Opposition from the Dominions had been worn down by Lord Halifax (who took to the task with a relish Churchill disliked). Only Canada had stood out for long, threatening to leave the Empire, until MacKenzie King's attitude had been softened by pressure from Rooseveldt. The Empire might not like it, but it would accept. The Archbishops, Lang and Temple, had been leaned on heavily — threatened even. In the Royal Family, the Queen blamed Edward for what had happened to her husband and her children, but was too distraught to care about the succession. Queen Mary was violently opposed to Edward's return. But the Duke of Gloucester, the next in line, would stand aside readily. Most important, Wallis, Edward's Duchess, had accepted that the marriage must be regarded as morganatic:— she would be the new king's wife, but never the queen.

Only when the succession of the Duke was promulgated did Hitler consent to release him from captivity. Interference with the order of succession was no new thing in English history. This time the method was necessarily convoluted. Verbal consent was obtained from the King. He was rarely conscious for more than a few minutes at a time and under constant sedation to ease the terrible pain in his head. His body lay half-paralysed and useless. After the consent an Order in Council was issued, and a resolution put through both Houses of Parliament. There was a substantial vote against in the Commons, and it was nearly lost in the Lords, but not quite. No Act was passed. The King would never sign any bill into law again. The country knew he would never recover. The long vigil of his wife by his bedside was more in keeping with the mood of the people than the chicanery involved in promulgating his successor, and the vituperation of the election campaign.

On the Grand Tribunal at Nurenberg, Churchill and the Duke stood together as Britain's representatives. They were on Hitler's right hand — Mussolini relegated to a position beyond them, Stalin to the Führer's left. Later, after the hours of unwelcome pageantry, Churchill described the Duke and himself as the ham in the sandwich. And then there was the signing itself. There were twenty-one separate copies of the treaty, each one bound in a vast embosssed leather volume, each to be signed by every head of state or national representative in seven places. Churchill regarded it as preposterous, and said so. He insisted on brandy and refreshments being brought to the table itself to revive him, and was glad to note the personal annoyance this caused the Führer. He was required to speak, and did so, briefly. No great oration, a hope that this peace would last, and the fear it would not. An appeal to the Führer that he use his subjects well, that Germany not abuse her power. Low key, as if he regarded it as pointless even while he said it. When he sat down he said,

"I have inherited the mantle of Chamberlain — and a flea-ridden, filthy garment it is."

Hitler spoke at length, as he would many times over the coming days, of the New Order in Europe, in which all must work together, under the leadership of Germany. He took up Churchill's points, and commended them, praised his old enemy. The final humiliation. Churchill went home the following day, to await the verdict of his people on him.

Before Christmas, he had almost decided to stand down and let someone else lead the party. It had been the Duke of Windsor who persuaded him not to. A curious reversal of the roles they had once played to each other. If he went, and the Tories won, it would mean Halifax as premier, rule from the Lords, and by a man he detested. He regarded Halifax as a worse disaster than Attlee. So he fought on, the wrong campaign. He denounced Hitler and Attlee in the same breath. He called up apocalyptic visions of the vanguard of Bolshevism and the Gestapo jackboot. He saved his most virulent obloquy for the revived British Union.

Sir Oswald Mosley had been a recent victim of internment, released like all internees as one of the terms of the Armistice agreement. In the course of the couple of months available to him, he had managed to scrape together candidates for no less than 280 seats. To do so he had accepted money from unnamed sources. . . . He returned to the message he had delivered before the war: that it had been an unnecessary war, contrary to Britain's interests. It was a message that now, abruptly, had acquired a ring of truth. It sounded well, coupled with a programme of social progress at home, co-operation with Germany abroad, and national revival. Mosley had always been a good orator. Now he organized from nothing a masterly campaign. He appealed especially to servicemen — "those who did their duty to the end, unselfishly, unquestioning, in this mistaken war". There was also a message for the people in the Occupied Territories. "My first policy is to see there are no occupied territories", he said. Both Churchill and Attlee regarded his appeal to these two groups as the equivalent of electoral suicide for a party which was, after all, Fascist.

In the event, the election provided a result no-one had anticipated. Churchill was neither endorsed nor rejected. The welfare state on offer from Labour convinced many: the Party's failings in foreign policy lost them others. Many turned to alternatives: the remains of the Liberal Party, Independents even, and to Mosley. By midday on the 15th the outcome was clear. The results for the main parties were:—

Conservative & Unionist	273
Labour (and I.L.P.)	269
Liberals	21
National Liberals (government supporters)	14
British Union	39

Twelve of the Fascist seats were in constituencies under German occupation.

For the first time since 1929 there was no clear majority, a hung parliament. There was also a constitutional crisis. For a fortnight now the king had been in a permanent coma. Though his condition was reported by the doctors as stable, there was no question that he would ever regain consciousness. Normally, the sovereign, acting on advice, would send for the party leader he deemed best able to form a government which could command a majority in the House. That meant, in these circumstances, the leader who could cobble together some sort of coalition. Mosley had already given out, the day before, that he was prepared to serve in a "patriotic government" with either major party.

Any such arrangement was abhorrent to both Churchill and Attlee. And there was no king to steer a course through the troubled waters.

At twenty-seven minutes past three, in the early hours of Thursday, 16th January, 1941, King George VI slipped quietly from coma into death. England had a king again. Still legally Prime Minister, Churchill called the Cabinet together in the night. The order went out that at sunrise that day Edward VIII be proclaimed King of Great Britain and Northern Ireland, and all the Dominions and Colonies overseas, Emperor of India. The new king, far away in Nurenberg in Germany, heard of this accession at five o'clock.

At eight o'clock in the morning a state landau of the government of the Third Reich arrived to collect King Edward, to bear him through the streets of the home of Nazism, to be hailed as King of England by the Führer of Germany. He was attended, at his own insistence, by only an equerry and a personal servant. The open coach, on that frosty winter morning, with its attendant guard of cavalry, attracted many curious gazes. The news of the death of George VI and the return to the throne of his brother, supposedly pro-Nazi, or at least pro-German, was not yet public knowledge. Few recognised the stiff upright figure in the coach.

In the Alte Rathaus, in the study he had used throughout the Conference, Hitler sat at his desk, and saw in this the final evidence of the hand of fate, that had brought his chosen king to the throne of his former enemy and newest friend. He saw a new future, now that the other great Teutonic power of Europe (for so England was to be classified) had fallen in beside Germany. A future of yet greater triumphs of the will that would carry the banners of National Socialism round the world. And here in Europe, there would be racial and spiritual purity at last. Those who had tried to separate England from Germany, her natural friend and protector, were doomed. He had read that message in the election results. He believed then that he understood the English as he had always understood the Germans. He felt the weight of destiny heavy on his shoulders that morning.

He was concerned that all should be correct when he welcomed the new king. It would be an historic meeting between the two heads of state. It would be right and proper that he, the Führer of Germany, should be the first to hail Edward as king, even before any of his own subjects. A flurry of activity below told him that Edward had arrived. The sentries at the open study door, black uniforms trimmed with white, presented arms with a flourish. Every man there was a Hero of the Reich. Hitler stood up behind the great mahogany-topped desk, clad in the simple brown jacket and black trousers he affected as a man of the people. He looked with approval at the military uniform of the new king, noted he was now attended by only one man. Yes, this was the king he had chosen for England.

Edward stood straight, almost to attention, then bowed, no more than an inclination of his head, allowed a faint smile to play on his lips as he looked at the Führer. Hitler responded with a similar bow, a readier smile as he stepped from behind the desk. He stretched out his hand, ready with the little speech of congratulation which he had learnt in English. He heard the King, still smiling, speak a single sentence to the man beside him, words the Führer did not understand.

"It will be all right, Don, I will not need your help. It has been made easy."

King Edward drew from the holster at his side the ordinary service revolver he carried. He raised the gun, and shot Hitler through the body. Again and again he fired, five shots into the lurching, reeling, spinning body of the man. Five shots that flung spurts of blood out across the brown shirt, marked the contorting face with trails of blood, sprinkled it into the rich pile carpet. Five shots — before the first rifle fired, and the force of the bullet's impact spun the King round, and knocked the pistol from his hand.

A man ran forward, the King's young servant, trying to cover the body of his sovereign with his own. He too writhed as a bullet ripped into his arm. Then a German, a Corporal of the bodyguard, had dragged him down. The two struggled like a drowning man and his rescuer. And finally an automatic weapon cut across the room with its echoing anger, and the King of England fell, mortally wounded, already dying. For a moment he saw the face of the man who had tried to save him. And before they both fell back, the king to his death and his glory, he said,

"Tell mother, I have done my duty."

Epilogue

THE UNFORGIVING MINUTE

Don regained consciousness to a fiery pain in his arm and chest. He had not even felt the second bullet hit him before he was pulled down. The memory was vivid and inescapable across his mind and whole being. He looked up into the face of Adolf Mann, as he had looked down into the face of the King.

"Why did you pull me away from him, Adolf?" he asked, his voice a whisper of pain.

"So that you would not be killed as well, Don. There have been enough killed already," Adolf answered.

"He chose this way. . . . " For a moment Don found the effort to speak too much. Then he asked,

"My King?"

"You could not have save him. Your King is dead."

"What about your. . . . Führer?" His voice was weak now. He wanted to slip back into oblivion, to blot out the death of his King and his friend. But he had to know that one last answer first. Had the sacrifice been merited?

Adolf looked bleakly across the room. He saw the hastily summoned doctor step back. Saw the blood bright on the brown jacket. Through the press of men, for a fleeting moment caught a glimpse of the sallow, wax-like face, set in an utter immobility. The hypnotic eyes closed. A thin trickle of blood between the silent lips.

It was almost a whisper when he spoke.

"My Führer is dead."

No richer crown than a crown of glory
Nor finer robe than a robe of blood

THE HIGH COMMAND OF THE GERMAN ARMED FORCES

Führer and Supreme Commander: *Adolf Hitler*

High Command of the Armed Forces OKW
(Oberkommando der Wehrmacht)

Head of OKW: *Generalfeldmarschall Keitel*
Chiefs of Staff: *General Jodl and Generalmajor Warlimont*

Army High Command OKH (Oberkommando des Heeres)	Navy High Command OKM (Oberkommando der Kriegsmarine)	The Luftwaffe under the direct personal command of: *Reichsmarschall Goering*
Commander-in-Chief: *Generalfeldmarschall von Brauchitsch*	Commander-in-Chief: *Grossadmiral Raeder*	
Chief of Staff: *Generaloberst Halder*	Chief of Staff: *Admiral Schniewind*	Chief of Staff: *General Jeschonnek*

THE BRITISH HIGH COMMAND

Prime Minister and Minister of Defence: *Winston Churchill*

(Churchill was ex officio chairman of both the War Cabinet and the Committee of Home Defence.)

Secretary of State for War: *Anthony Eden*

Chief of Staff to the Prime Minister (and to the Committee of Home Defence): *General Sir Hastings Ismay*

Chief of the Imperial Staff (CIGS):
General Sir John Dill

Commander-in-Chief, Home Forces:
General Sir Alan Brooke

First Sea Lord:
Admiral of the Fleet Sir Dudley Pound

Commander in Chief, Home Fleet:
Admiral Forbes

Chief of the Air Staff:
Air Chief Marshal Sir Cyril Newall
(subsequently: *Sir Charles Portal*)

Commander-in-Chief, Fighter Command and Flight Command:
Air Marshal Sir Hugh Dowding

(For the sake of clarity, only notable participants in the complex structure of committees and sub-committees which characterized the British High Command have been included.)

GERMAN ORDER OF BATTLE – SEPTEMBER 1940

Army Group A (*von Rundstedt*)

	9th Army (*Strauss*)		16th Army (*Busch*)	
First Wave	XXXVIII Corps 26 Div 34 Div	VIII Corps 8 Div 28 Div 6 Mtn	XIII Corps 17 Div 35 Div	VII Corps 7 Div 1 Mtn
Second Wave	XV Corps 4 Pz 7 Pz 20 Mot		V Corps 12 Div 30 Div	XXXXI Corps 8 Pz 10 Pz 29 Mot
Third Wave	XXIV Corps 15 Div 78 Div		IV Corps 24 Div 58 Div	XXXXII Corps 45 Div 164 Div

7th Parachute Division and 22nd Air Landing Division were under direct OKH command. SS Regiments *Grossdeutschland* and *Adolf Hitler Bodyguard* were attached to XXXXI Corps.

GERMAN ORDER OF BATTLE – END OF OCTOBER 1940

Army Group A (*von Rundstedt*)		Army Group P (*Paulus*)	
9th Army (*Strauss*)	**16th Army** (*Model*)	**1st Panzer Army** (*Rommel*)	**2nd Panzer Army** (*Guderian*)
XXXVIII Corps	VII Corps	XV Corps (*from 9th Army*)	XXXXI Corps (*from 16th Army*)
26 Div	7 Div	4 Pz	8 Pz
34 Div	1 Mtn	7 Pz	10 Pz
		20 Mot	29 Mot
VIII Corps	V Corps		Grossdeutschland
			Adolf Hitler Bodyguard
8 Div	12 Div	XIII Corps (*from 16th Army*)	
28 Div	30 Div	17 Div	IV Corps (*from 16th Army*)
6 Mtn		35 Div	24 Div
	XXXXII Corps		58 Div
XIV Corps			
	45 Div		
15 Div	164 Div		
78 Div			

I Air Corps (*9th Army: detached to 2nd Panzer Army*): 7 Para & 22 Air Landing

BRITISH ORDER OF BATTLE – END OF OCTOBER 1940

British First Army (*General Montgomery*)

	V Corps	VII Corps	XII Corps	Army Reserve
Front Line	4 Div	42 Div	45 Div	3 MMG Bde
	1 MMG Bde	36 Ind Bde	1 ATB	2 Arm Div
	43 Div	21 Bde Gp	1 Div	23 ATB
		3 Div		44 Div
				52 Div
Reserve	70 Ind Bde	AIF	20 Gds Bde	
	50 Div	2 Lon Div	24 Gds Bde	
			30 Gds Bde	

General (GHQ) Reserve: 15 Div 55 Div 2 Div 59 Div 24 ATB

In the rest of the country were nine further divisions & three brigades

The following British formations had already been destroyed:

1 Lon Div	NZ Div	29 Bde Gp	1 Can Div
1 Arm Div	21 ATB	22 Arm Bde	

By the same author
writing as Derek Sawde

THE SCEPTRE MORTAL

A classic adventure story of sword and sorcery

★

The story of the quest for the Sceptre Mortal by the prince of fallen Telmirandor and his companions from before time and beyond the stars. The story of the dark secret that haunts their path when other, fearful beings also seek out that talisman of ancient power. . . . This is the stuff that legends are made of, with heroes of mythic proportion, and a breadth of vision encompassing a universe of high adventure. A story as detailed as Tolkien's Middle Earth, and peopled with horrors to match anything in Lovecraft.

★

The Sceptre Mortal is one of the best fantasy novels I have ever read.   David Barrett in **Vector**

A gripping quest story, brimful of action and magic.
        David Cowperthwaite for the **British Fantasy Society**

This is a fine adventure story.
            Don D'Ammassa in **Science Fiction Chronicle**

A complex and interesting story . . . no question of its merits.
                                Lester del Ray

★

Fantasy written as literature:–
Stylish, intricate and baroque,
but full of mystery danger and suspense

★

The SCEPTRE MORTAL by Derek Sawde
304 pages paperback 0 948093 00 5
ORIFLAMME PUBLISHING